D0049203

THE
DARKENING
HOUR

Penny Hancock grew up in south-east London and then travelled extensively as a language teacher. She now lives in Cambridge with her husband and three children. Her first novel, *Tideline*, was published to rave reviews and was a Richard and Judy Book Club pick in Summer 2012.

THE DARKENING HOUR

PENNY HANCOCK

**SIMON &
SCHUSTER**

London · New York · Sydney · Toronto · New Delhi

A CBS COMPANY

First published in Great Britain by Simon & Schuster, 2013
A CBS company

1 3 5 7 9 10 8 6 4 2

Simon & Schuster UK Ltd
1st Floor
222 Gray's Inn Road
London WC1X 8HB

www.simonandschuster.co.uk

Simon & Schuster Australia, Sydney
Simon & Schuster India, New Delhi

A CIP catalogue record for this book is available from the British Library

Hardback ISBN: 978-1-47111-124-2
Trade Paperback ISBN: 978-0-85720-624-4
Ebook ISBN: 978-0-85720-626-8

Typeset by Hewer Text UK Ltd, Edinburgh
Printed and bound in Great Britain by CPI Group (UK) Ltd, Croydon, CR0 4YY

For Aunty Dorothy.

'At every mooring-chain and rope, at every stationary boat or barge that split the current into a broad arrowhead, at the offsets from the piers of Southwark Bridge, at the paddles of the river steamboats as they beat the filthy water, at the floating logs of timber lashed together lying off certain wharves, his shining eyes darted a hungry look. After a darkening hour or so, suddenly the rudder-lines tightened in his hold, and he steered hard towards the Surrey shore'

Our Mutual Friend, Charles Dickens

'But know this; though you set out on a fool's errand, among those who love you, you are beloved indeed.'

Antigone, Sophocles

PROLOGUE

Deptford, south-east London

No one sees the woman push the man in his wheelchair through the market. Amongst the stallholders, shoppers, crack addicts, shaven-haired women, long-haired men, mums with kids heaped onto the backs of buggies, teenagers plugged into iPods, drunks and dealers, amongst the general sense of busy-ness, of chatter, buying, selling, going somewhere – belonging, no matter who you are or where you've come from – this pair do not fit or feature.

They dissolve into the background along with the Somali guy sweeping the road in his Hi Viz jacket, the thin girl with the old woman's face selling the *Big Issue*, the group of Vietnamese huddled around the money-exchange kiosk. They are of even less interest than the young Ukrainians sorting through textiles in the depot under the arches, or the Bengali chef in a doorway left open to ease the heat of a steamy kitchen.

Anyone who did look would notice that the two – the woman and the old man – are not related. The man has pale darting eyes and fragile, crinkled skin, spotted in places with dark patches – the effects of too much sun – while the woman's brown skin is blotchy from the lack of it. She's short with soft contours, her sunken eyes dark. There's another, more striking difference. The man exudes wealth – he's dressed in good quality trousers, polished leather shoes, a thick wool jacket and a cashmere scarf, while the woman wears tracksuit bottoms and a cheap fleece over a blue overall, and ragged trainers that soak up the puddlewater underfoot. More than this, an onlooker might notice the resigned look in her bruised eyes, the indifference to the colourful shops and stalls and the bright chatter. It's as if the woman, pushing the man down the street, his bag of fruit clutched on his lap, does not occupy this city at all, as if her mind is in a place so far away and so long ago she isn't sure it still exists.

But no one is looking, no one is interested. And even the old man in his wheelchair is not sure who it is that propels him along this jostling street at twilight on an early January evening. As long as she gets him home soon, for he can feel hunger rumbling in his belly, and as long as he has his clementines, firm and fresh in his lap, he's content.

The woman steers the wheelchair through the crowds, towards the broad expanse of sludgy river with its smell of oil and of cargo from other worlds. As they move away from the market, and its sweet aroma of roasting chestnuts, the glow of makeshift bulbs dims behind them, giving the impression they are leaving not just light but warmth as well, though the stallholders' breath is white in the cold air.

She pushes the chair all the way to the alley that lies between a wall and the once-majestic Paynes Wharf, only its façade of six grand arches remaining. At the end of the little alley they arrive at the top of some slimy steps that lead straight down into the murky water of the Thames. A hidden place, not easy to spot in the daytime but utterly concealed by shadows at night. Here, she pauses and stares into the water for quite some time. Ten steps are visible – the tide is low.

After a little while she turns. Moves slowly back away from the river and wheels the old man down a narrow street of Georgian terraced houses. Every doorway is flanked by little angels or figureheads frosting as it grows dark. She reaches the house at the end, takes the side entrance to the garden, where she helps him out of his chair, and together they descend the basement steps to the front door of his flat beneath the main house.

Inside, Mona helps Charles into his reclining armchair with its footrest. Charles feels the hand under his elbow but he doesn't know or care at this moment who it belongs to. In his chair he asks for his dinner. Mona brings it on a tray, spoons it into his mouth, wipes the dribbles with a kitchen towel and offers him sips of water.

And when he's finished his sausages and mash she peels a clementine for him. The feel of the segments in their loose membranes is similar to his limp penis which she holds while he wees afterwards in the tiny bathroom.

She takes the peel to the kitchen and drops it into the full pedal bin, takes the liner, knots it and puts it ready to take out, replacing it with a new one. She washes his dishes and tidies up. Then it is time to get him into his night things.

Above, in the main house, footsteps pound down the stairs and a door slams. Mona feels the sounds in her skin; it twitches and her ears ring. Her palms sweat. She longs for the day to end. Longs for the moment she can lie down in the corner of her room on the makeshift bed, because she's weary, and oblivion more than anything is what she craves.

Then it comes. The voice, echoing down the dumbwaiter shaft, floats into the room.

'MONA!'

'Yes.'

'It's seven o'clock.'

'He's going to bed now. Then I'll come.'

'You're late.'

'I'm coming.'

And the old man is demanding her attention at the same time, 'You've hidden it again! Blast and damn you, woman, you've taken my whisky.'

And the shout from upstairs – 'Now!' – and the man's grumbling, and her head beginning to pound.

Early the next morning, when a mist lies over the river and the streetlights continue to glow in their fuzzy orange corona, ripples falter over something larger than the usual rubbish – the plastic bottles and beer cans, the syringes and the burger containers. The water has crept up the stairs in the night, bringing with it a peculiar figure. A torso, arms and legs flailing in the deep, with a head that looks as though it's been mummified, bandaged as it is in a blue overall that the police later find resembles one worn by domestic staff and carers.

And when the body has been hauled out and put in a bag, when the dead person has been identified and has appeared in the local paper, everyone wants to look, everyone wants to know. But it's too late.

Mona's gone.

PART ONE

The Gift

CHAPTER ONE

Three months earlier

The first thing I notice about London is its statues. They people the city, a separate, stone population. Men on horseback, women half-naked, babies with wings, lions and monsters. We're driving through the streets, Mr and Mrs Roberts in front, me in my place at the back, my head resting on the glass.

Everything's lit up. Keeping the night at bay. We turn away from palatial streets onto a wide bridge. The river is broad and dark beneath us, lights reflected in it like swords stabbing the black water. *My* river, the Bouregreg at home in Morocco, is playful, winking bright sparks into the blue air. I want to tell someone that the Thames is darker than I imagined, London bigger than a whole country. But there's no one to tell. If it wasn't for Leila and Ummu, I'd turn round, go back, make do, until Ali returned. Even if he is in London, as Yousseff suggested, I'll never find him in this vast sprawl. The idea was crazy. This city goes on forever.

As the plane took off I saw myself as a kite. My beloved daughter Leila holding the string, letting it unwind as I rose away from her into the sky until somewhere over Spain, she had to let go. Then I felt scared. I was a kite without a string, at the mercy of the winds. The Robertses were huddled behind a thick blue curtain in Business Class. The English couple behind me were busy with their child who'd been running up and down the aisle for the whole flight, unconcerned that his movement might upset the plane. The man in front had his headphones plugged into his ears. Other passengers slept or murmured.

I'd never felt so alone.

Leila wasn't worried. As far as she was concerned, I was going away for a little while to earn some money so she could go to school like the other kids, have new things.

'Don't show her you're upset,' Ummu, my mother, warned me. 'Think of the money. She's going to be fine.'

And she was. Waving one hand, clutching Ummu's with the other, she skipped as they turned away to go to the souk. The furthest I'd been from Leila before, to clean up another woman's mess, was over the Bouregreg.

Ummu was thrilled when I told her I'd got this job.

'*Alhamdulillah*! Praise be to Allah!' she cried, throwing her soapy hands in the air. She'd been scrubbing sheets in the sink, her arms deep in cold water. Now she stood up and clutched my hand in her wet ones. Looked at me through dancing eyes. I could hear the tiny pop of soap bubbles on her arms.

'I can hardly believe it! London!' she shouted. She always speaks too loud; it's something even her friends complain about.

'So we're going to be OK,' I said. 'The bottom wage over there is more than we could dream of here.' I was trying to sound cheerful, though I was filled with trepidation. Working in other women's houses was not my chosen profession for a lot of reasons.

'It's a blessing, Mona, now I'm too blind to work and you've lost your job at Madame's.'

Blind is an exaggeration. My mother's eyesight is poor – the result of too many years weaving carpets in bad light – but she's not blind. She sees what she wants to see.

However, we have no choice if we want to make ends meet. And I have another incentive, one that overrides any reservations I have about leaving Leila. If Ali is in Britain, as I now believe, I can help him if he's got into trouble. We'll be together again, me and Ali and Leila – a family, as we were meant to be.

'I've been thinking. After five years in Britain you get citizenship,' Ummu went on, 'like Rachida. Five years, Mona. By then you'll be reading and writing in English with an excellent job in some top office somewhere. You won't have to clean for other women any more.'

'Ummu, it's not going to be five years,' I said.

But now I'm here, moving through the endless city, more streets, more flats, more traffic lights, more shops, but less grand now and darker and more hostile – I wonder, will I ever see Ummu or Leila again?

The car has turned up a quiet street, we're pulling up outside a house. Even this has statues on the doorframe, two small, naked babies with wings.

'Your new home,' Mrs Roberts says, turning around and smiling at me.

CHAPTER TWO

Mona arrives with the first autumn rains, golden leaves blowing about her feet.

Exactly a year since Mummy died.

'My gift from the south,' Roger jests, brushing his polished shoes on my doormat.

She's not as I pictured her. The word 'widow' had conjured someone elderly, dressed in black. Fierce, but reliable. Instead the woman on the steps is my age. Short, huddled into a cheap blue anorak, strands of dark hair poking from her headscarf. Enormous, earnest brown eyes. I think of those statues of the Madonna in the quaint religious shops up on Deptford High Street, their beatific faces, the epitome of humility.

A little tableau presents itself: this woman, with the *putti* that flank my doorway fluttering above her, the church spire over the road piercing the orange glow of the London sky. My first reaction is relief.

Claudia is getting out of the car behind them. She tiptoes over the cobbles as if there might be some malodorous remnant of Victorian London still lingering in the gutter. This is Deptford in the twenty-first century and not the rough end, but she makes blatant her prejudice.

'Come in,' I say, and they sidle past Mona.

Any regret that remained over our separation is dispelled for me as Roger wipes his shoes on the doormat and walks down my hallway, shoulders clenched, afraid of the walls brushing against him and leaving a mark.

He's dressed in a cream suit and tie, as if he'd stepped out of another century. If it wasn't for the fact that Claudia had something to do with this, his sartorial innocence might have tugged at my heartstrings; Roger has always been out of step with the times, and once, I must have found this endearing.

Mona perches on the edge of a kitchen chair. I pour the others gin and tonic, and she stares ahead, with a blank expression, as Roger and I talk. In spite of the circumstances of our separation, we've managed to stay on speaking terms. Thanks to Leo, our son, I think. Which is odd, given what a worry he is on a daily level.

'So, here she is, Dora. All set and ready to work. I've told her about your father, and she's quite prepared.'

'Thank you, Roger.'

'How's Leo?'

'He's . . . better. Better than he was, anyway.'

'Got himself a job, I take it?'

'He's been trying. There isn't much out there. And he's not in a great position.'

'If he hadn't flunked his exams . . .'

'I know.'

'An internship – that's the way these days. You must be able to find him something, surely, Theodora, with your media connections.'

If Claudia wasn't witnessing our exchange I'd have objected to this. Roger's sentence is loaded with unspoken resentment. I control myself, however.

'Internships are as hard to get as jobs, Roger. And you're missing the point, that his self-esteem's taken a battering . . .'

'All the more reason for him to get out there. He needs a rocket up his arse, that boy.'

I laugh. 'You can try the stick approach if you like. It won't work. You've no idea.'

I kick myself as I hear my voice crack. I don't want to get upset in front of everyone, but I can't bear to hear Leo misunderstood. Any more than I can bear to witness my son, my beautiful boy, so changed. I swallow. Nor do I want to be judged for what's happened to him since he moved in with me.

'He's here,' I say quietly. 'Why don't you talk to him yourself?'

'I'll pop along and have a chat,' says Roger, squeezing Claudia's shoulder. 'Where d'you say he is?'

'In the drawing room.'

I've walked into another trap. Roger will accuse me of letting Leo dominate the TV.

'Be careful, Roger. He's volatile. Easily upset.'

'Volatile. Taking advantage, more like. I'll sort him out.'

I feel all the old self-doubt creep in as Roger straightens up. I should argue, but I haven't the strength. And I'm in his debt at the moment, because of Mona.

'Don't be long, darling,' Claudia simpers. 'The table's booked for eight. It's sticky getting through London at this time.'

'I'll only be a minute,' he says.

When he's gone, I'm left in the kitchen with Claudia and Mona. We make an awkward trio. Mona still hasn't spoken, and Claudia's refused to sit down, is clicking her kitten heels on my quarry tiles, twirling her glass in her hand. I expect she's worried about getting Endymion's hairs on her Aquascutum trenchcoat. I wonder why she doesn't want to talk to Leo. After all, she's the stepmother; he lived with her for several years before coming back to me.

'Mona, I expect Dora would like to show you your living quarters,' she says. 'Wouldn't you, Dora?'

Of course, you don't socialise with staff in Claudia's world, the world I left behind.

'Living quarters' is a slight exaggeration. Mona's to sleep in the room beyond the kitchen that was my study, then Leo's homework den. Through a chink in the door that has been left ajar I'm aware of the bumpy silhouettes of clothes heaped on the floor, a teetering pile of books and magazines on a table. Since Leo dropped out of sixth form, at the end of last year, the room has mostly been used as a dumping ground. It's full of his old school files and books, DVDs he no longer watches, clothes he's outgrown.

I move towards the door ahead of Mona, shielding it from Claudia's prying eyes, I don't want her to spot the mess. I'd meant to tidy it but haven't had a spare moment, with work, and Daddy. Something Claudia with her many domestic staff would never understand.

On closer examination Mona is, I guess, a few years older than me. Crooked teeth. Poorly nourished, pale brown skin. A spattering of dark freckles on one cheek.

A warmth washes over me as I draw the curtains for her, chase Endymion out, smooth the cover on her bed. Everything about her – her cheap clothes, her unmade-up face – is a comfort after Claudia's hard surface. I'd like to hug her.

I show her the small washroom and toilet outside the room.

'I'll let you unpack,' I say.

She takes off her coat.

Now her hood's down I see her black hair is straight, limp and rather greasy. There's a tiny pillow of flesh beneath her chin. The body, though it's well covered in more layers of clothing, is rounded. She wouldn't have access to a gym, will be ignorant about healthy eating, has probably never had dental care – it's expensive where she comes from. I'm helping her, I think. I'll improve her life. A fair exchange – after all, she's here to improve mine.

'I'll show you around tomorrow and introduce you to Daddy. You must be tired. Do you want anything to eat? To drink?'

She stares at me.

'Eat,' I say loudly, miming. 'Drink?'

'Ah. No, thank you.'

She almost bows. I wave a hand in the air, indicating that such subservience isn't necessary and leave her, shutting the door behind me.

In the kitchen Roger's already back from his encounter with Leo.

'I made him switch off the TV. Told him if we were going to talk I wasn't doing it to a soundtrack.'

'And?'

'He's picked up some unattractive habits from somewhere. He's verging on the surly. What's going on, Dora?'

'It's like I said. He's low. The doctor thinks depressed.'

Claudia looks up at Roger. I wonder whether she's had Botox. There's a rigidity in her face, as if it could never give anything away even if she wanted it to.

'Depressed? He's had every advantage, Dora. I've spent more on his education than anything – this house included!'

'It's not the money, is it? It's not the education. He's been affected by us – it hasn't been easy for him.'

That's when Roger comes at me with the punch he knows will hurt.

'Us? Or you, Dora? You're the one who puts your work before everything.'

'Look, Roger, I don't wish to discuss this now. I'm sure Claudia doesn't want to hear it, do you, Claudia? We can meet another time to talk it through.'

Roger sighs. 'I'll take him out for lunch while we're here. He needs some ultimatums.'

'So.' I've had enough of this. 'Thank you for bringing her.' I nod towards the study. 'Does she speak much English? She seemed to know a few words.'

'You'll have to speak slowly. She's picked up what she knows at Madame Sherif's house. I believe they were English-speakers.'

'How old is she?'

'No idea. You can check her passport. But as you may remember, they don't register births the way we do.'

'I don't suppose it matters,' I say. 'As long as she's healthy. Daddy sometimes needs things shifting. He sometimes needs lifting himself.'

'Oh, she's very healthy,' he says.

'Could I use your bathroom, please, Theodora?' Claudia pipes up then, and, knowing she won't want to share with Mona, I direct her upstairs.

When she's gone, Roger leans over to me, speaking into my ear.

'If she pushes the boundaries, let me know,' he mutters. 'You don't want a repeat of Zidana.'

'God, Roger. Don't bring that up, it was years ago.'

'I know, and we managed to sweep it under the carpet. But we were lucky. If anyone had found out . . .'

'But they didn't. And we've moved on.'

'Nevertheless. If things get . . . let me know. Better to nip it in the bud.'

I stare at him. I'd thought the incident with Zidana, a young maid we'd employed in Rabat when Leo was still at school there – had been forgotten. I wish he hadn't mentioned it.

Roger changes the subject as Claudia comes back downstairs.

'Look,' he says, 'these are Mona's papers. You know the ropes – her visa states she's here for domestic purposes only. And she's yours. In effect, she belongs to you. Can't switch employer. If it doesn't work out, it's straight home with her. She owes for the passport and ticket, so you can knock that off her first wages.'

'Thanks, Roger.'

'As I said, we've had her friend Amina for the last year and she's fabulous.'

'I do appreciate this. What with Daddy living downstairs now, and with work and things, I couldn't have coped without help.'

'Make sure you keep her in line,' says Claudia. 'Don't take any nonsense. She may be here to look after your father primarily, but she'll clean, cook, whatever. These girls expect to stay busy.'

'Yes. Thank you, Claudia. I know.' Has she forgotten I was once married to her husband? That I had staff too?

'Darling!' Roger calls over my shoulder.

Claudia drains her gin. 'Coming.'

Watching him hold open the door for Claudia, I know for certain that I did Roger the biggest favour by finally getting out of his life. Claudia slots so beautifully into the role of diplomat's wife, in a way I never could.

But as their expensive hire car disappears back down my street, sending spray up from the puddles, I feel a momentary regret that the lifestyle they inhabit is mine no longer.

CHAPTER THREE

In the dark, I think of Leila.

It'll be her bedtime.

I'd be reading to her from one of the books I bought when I was working at Madame Sherif's, my chin resting on the top of her warm head, my fingers playing through her silky hair. She'd be staring up at the ceiling, her thumb in her mouth. Or doing that thing where she pulls my fingers as if she were milking a cow. Ummu would be clattering about behind the curtain.

Ummu's never learned to read, but she might be telling Leila one of her stories now, the ones she used to tell me, her hands dancing and fluttering, making djinns and princesses.

I reach for my mobile. It takes me a few seconds to work out what the recorded voice is saying. Then the distance between me and Leila expands.

You do not have enough credit to make this call.

I'm alone, in a strange dark country, with not a dirham to my name, and I can't even contact my daughter. Now the worries move in. How long before I can send money home? School commences next summer. Will I have earned enough for Leila's books by then? To pay for Ummu's cataracts? Will I even earn

19

enough to buy the food they need, to pay for the gas supply, the electricity?

I remember Ummu's words, when things had become tough; I'd lost my job at Madame Sherif's and we hadn't heard from Ali.

'It isn't this that hurts.' She swept her fingers down over her eyes. 'Or this.' Her hand moved in an arc, indicating the one room we had turned into two by means of a curtain. It was noisy and we were surrounded by people whom Ummu considered beneath us.

'It's none of this. It's the way people *look* at us since Ali left,' she said. 'As if we've somehow brought it upon ourselves. They see that we live all together here –' once more, she splayed her fingers to indicate our rooms, the thin walls separating us from Hait's place next door, the washing strung out in spare gaps between buildings, the children playing out on the alleys, the piles of rubbish that the council refused to collect '– and they don't see the jobs we once had, or the men who've died. The men who've left.'

She was in her stride now. She lowered her voice. 'They see deviance,' she hissed. 'They think we're inferior. They see people with no morality.'

'Who's "they", Umma? Who are these people you're talking about?'

'The people who look at us with contempt,' she said. 'The wealthy.'

I didn't point out that this was how she looked at our neighbours, that she was as guilty as the rest of them.

When Ali had been gone six weeks I went to talk to Yousseff, his oldest friend, up at the Café des Jeunes where he waited on its clientèle of old men.

'Look,' he said, 'my hunch is Ali's gone to Britain. It was what he always wanted – to get there, finish studying.'

20

'How could he? He doesn't have a passport. He told me he was going off to help his Berber brothers in some territory dispute.'

'Maybe. But I bet that's where he was heading. No doubt, once he's settled, once he can, he'll call you. Ah, *salaam alaikum*!' He turned to a regular customer and I knew I was dismissed.

And now I'm here. My spirits are unpredictable, rising and falling as the floor seems to, after my first ever journey in a plane.

I recall the flight, the distance the plane has carried me, crossing from the warmth of the south to this raw cold of the north, and I realise nothing will ever feel the same again now I have flown. The world is not, after all, as I thought. The air is not empty space; it can hold up even the vast bulk of iron and steel that is an aeroplane full of people. At the same time, I have learned neither is the ground solid; people can disappear into it the way Ali has done. And now I have the most terrifying feeling that, although I'm back on the ground, I, too, could vanish without trace.

I reach out a hand and rest it on the cool of the wall, so that I feel rooted again. And I think about where I am.

This house couldn't be more different from Monsieur and Madame's house in Rabat, with their automated sliding gates, their gardens and hallways the width of streets and sitting rooms as wide as a mosque. This is a tall house squashed up against others, like a poor woman on a crowded bus.

When I arrived, Theodora opened the door herself. She's a few years older than I am. Tall with amber-coloured hair. She smiled, though I know from experience that looks can lie. I think of Madame. How sweet she seemed until I was forced to leave.

Beyond the door, a narrow passage. Paintings on walls, cobwebs on ceilings, bare wood floor, steep stairs rising up to hidden rooms. I could see straight away that 'Dora', as they call her, hadn't looked after her house. It was clear she needed me. This is good. Need creates opportunity. It gives me power.

But the house, though grand, isn't comfortable. It's cold in this room, with a damp that doesn't go, however far I wriggle down under the covers. I've put on a fleece over my T-shirt and tracksuit trousers to keep warm, but still my fingers are numb. There's a lamp by my bed, a vase of old roses, gone brown. The room smells of cat.

The bed sinks beneath me. Fatigue pricks at my eyelids. I tug the quilt tighter around me, shut my eyes to the damp, to the cold, to the strange sounds of the night. To whatever lies ahead of me beyond that door.

I yearn for Leila's warm body, to pull it up against me. The way she slots into the curves in my body the way tiles tessellate on the walls of the mosques at home.

There's always a way, I remind myself, to get what you need if you put your mind to it. Focus. That's what you must do. 'When money is short,' Ali used to say, 'we use our ingenuity.'

I will get Leila into school. I will find Ali. And then, *inshallah*, we will go home together and I'll never have to clean up another woman's mess again.

CHAPTER FOUR

I was the only one of my siblings prepared to bring Daddy to live with them.

Their true natures emerged as we lowered Mummy's coffin into the ground. As if a watchful deity had taken its eye off them. They were like children who believe that as long as they are not caught, they can be as mean and feckless as they want.

The final tossing in of a solitary dahlia – Mummy's favourite flower – the scrunch of earth falling on the oak coffin, all seem now the first steps of a moral descent that the other three were embarking upon as soon as they turned their backs on the blackened graves.

It was the end of October, one year ago.

We hadn't realised that by the time we lowered her into the ground it would be dark. We hadn't predicted either, after the Indian summer, that it would be raining. We stood, a forlorn group, caged beneath the branches of plane trees in the churchyard. The first yellow leaves of autumn span down and stamped themselves on the surface of her coffin like parking tickets.

Simon and Anita assailed me as I leaned on the river wall. I was gazing across the dark water thinking about my name.

Theodora.

Daddy chose it, so I had been told, when I was born. God's Gift. He'd given me a gold chain with the name on it, that I wore always, the metal warm against my throat. I was Daddy's Gift from God. Siblings are always assigned labels in families, roles that define them. I was the the Selfless One. And so it fell naturally upon me to take responsibility when our mother fell ill, to organise her funeral, and to take care of Daddy.

I stared over the river wall, letting my tears fall into the murky depths. It felt like an affront that the world could carry on as normal when we had just buried our mother. Pleasure cruisers ploughed upstream, music blaring, sending waves slapping against the pilings. There was a narrow stairway on the opposite bank. I thought how one could walk down those stairs straight into the shift and swell of the Thames, and how this would be a relief in some ways. A reprieve from the dull ache of grief which was made all the more weighty by the mantle of provider I wore.

Simon's arm was around his latest fling. Simon was the Fun One. The Footloose and Fancy-free One. He taught English to foreign students. I suspected he only did it in order to pick up women. He enjoyed his single life far too much to get attached to them. I wondered whether this one liked my little brother or if she was hoping he would be her ticket to British citizenship. What on earth was she doing at our mother's funeral?

'So,' Anita began, 'Terence has taken Daddy over to the pub. We need to decide where he can stay until we sort something out.'

'He's staying with me, of course. I'm hardly going to evict him the night of Mummy's funeral.'

'I'm not suggesting you would,' said Anita. 'But is he OK in the flat? Can he look after himself?'

'I don't just leave him there. I do keep an eye on him.' Anita's failure to understand just how much I'd been doing for Daddy astounded me.

'Yes,' she said, 'but you were going to let Leo move into the flat, I thought, and—'

'To be honest I wouldn't trust Leo to live on his own, the way he is at the moment,' I said, immediately regretting it.

She raised her eyebrows, exchanged a glance with Simon. Anita was the Pretty One. She skated over life, unaffected by the obstacles and demands that the rest of us had to deal with.

'Look,' she said now, 'all I'm saying is, we're aware you're working, and you've got Leo to worry about, so if needs be Richard and I could have Daddy – well, not for too long, just until we sort something out. But he could stay . . .' she shrugged '. . . a few nights.'

'And you know I'd have him if I had my own place,' said Simon.

'It's fine,' I said. And it was. One of us could and should take Daddy. It was a duty. A privilege, even. Not a sacrifice. If they couldn't see this, it was their loss.

'Good,' said Simon. 'That's great, Dora. He's best off with you.'

'And as long as you make sure he gets out and about,' Anita added. 'He mustn't be allowed to languish now Mummy's gone.'

'What are you saying?'

'Just that he can't sit all day in the flat doing nothing – he needs stimulation.'

'You're suggesting I might neglect him!'

'No, Dor, but you can't meet his every need while you're working.'

'I think I've done a pretty bloody good job so far,' I snapped.

Anita held her hands up, and Simon gave her a look. Luckily Terence, our elder brother, came over then. He was the Successful One, occasionally metamorphosing to Ruthless when he strayed too far from the family fold.

'The sooner we get Dad's house on the market, the better,' he said. 'I've researched the cost of care homes and we're talking a grand a week. Looks as though selling's the only way of funding it.'

'There's no need for a care home,' I said. 'We can talk about the future when we're not all ragged with the funeral. It would upset Daddy to mention it tonight. It would throw him completely. He's staying with me for the time being.'

I was Theodora, the Selfless One, doing the right thing and I could hear the relief in their sighs.

'Has anyone checked that the pub has put out the food?' Anita asked.

'Yes. Terence checked earlier,' said Simon. 'Perhaps it's time we made a move.'

We gathered in the Mayflower in Rotherhithe, Daddy's favourite pub, passing round sandwiches and discussing how Mummy would have enjoyed this reunion – something we had failed to arrange in recent years. We'd all been blinkered by relationship crises, worries about our children. It was only when Mummy fell ill that we noticed how she and Daddy had aged, how it was too late for the family gatherings our mother had spoken of, the holidays she'd planned.

How ironic that it had taken her death to bring us all together at last.

What I didn't appreciate at that moment was how her death would also smash us apart.

We shook the hands of her old friends and some distant relatives who had turned out, thanked them for coming. Leo slouched out to the deck for a cigarette.

Daddy was agitated about the time, as if he had an important appointment to get to.

'Dora,' he said, 'it's high time we were off. We don't want to be late. It's frightfully dark.'

'It's OK.' I put my hand on his arm. 'There's no rush. There's nothing to get back for.'

And he gave me that bewildered look, the one that said, *Are you trying to fool me? Or am I losing my mind?*

Anita was battling with her two young children, arguing with Richard about who was the more exhausted. As soon as the whisky had been downed, they'd strap Jack and Jemima in, plug them into the screens installed in their Audi Estate and be off to their cosy life in Muswell Hill.

By seven o'clock, as I predicted, they were saying their farewells.

'If we go now, we'll make it to Ben's for dinner,' I overheard Richard mutter. Did he lack any shred of sensitivity, or was this his way of 'dealing' with his mother-in-law's death?

Terence and his new partner Ruth were checking they had enough cash for a taxi.

'Dora,' Terence said, placing his hand on my shoulder, 'Daddy needs to get home. He's shattered.'

'I know.' I tried not to sound irritated. 'I'm going as soon as I can prise Leo from the bar.'

He raised his eyebrows, but didn't say anything.

My siblings refused to understand Leo. They thought, as Roger did, that I indulged him, that if I spoke to him firmly he'd go out and get himself a job instead of spending all day every day smoking and gazing at car chases on screens. Right now he was back on the deck with a Red Bull and a Marlboro. It would be a battle to get him away. But I didn't want to leave without him – I never knew where he might end up.

Simon was chatting to his companion. They had snuggled into an alcove and were settled in for the night.

I helped Daddy into his coat, playing for time, avoiding the confrontation with my son.

'I know,' I heard Simon chuckle. 'In your language you say "open" and "closed". Here we say "dark" and "light". Yes, even when we talk about colours. So what is it now, light or dark?'

'It's closed?' she said, and he laughed and I heard the smack of his kiss on her cheek.

Daddy's bereavement, the work that lay ahead of us in caring for him, had passed clean out of Simon's consciousness now the funeral was over.

Yes. It seemed that every one of my siblings began to show their true colours, the day we buried Mummy.

CHAPTER FIVE

I come down on Sunday morning to find Mona in the kitchen, perched on a stool, her hands squeezed between her thighs.

I'm thankful to Roger for organising this, but reel a bit at the enormity of what he's achieved. Transporting a whole person across Europe especially for me. It showed, I suppose, that he still felt guilty that I'd been the one to have to leave, that I was supporting our son.

And it was OK. It was legal-ish. At the border, Roger had had to make out she was *his* live-in help – that she was tied to him. Fortunately, as we were once married, it wasn't difficult to make it all look above-board. If questions were asked, I would simply say Roger had returned and Mona had stayed on with me.

Her visa means she can't change employer, however; she is mine and mine alone.

'You must meet Daddy,' I say.

Mona stands up and follows me out of the front door, along the side of the house to the basement steps. Daddy's main entrance would once have been the back door to the house. I'd sealed off his front door at the bottom of the steps – which led

29

straight up to the road – to prevent Daddy wandering out, or burglars forcing their way in.

The garden is unruly. I haven't time to mow the grass and there are limits to what I can ask of Leo. Golden leaves from the trees at the end of the garden filter through green ones. Pears lie rotting on the grass. The air seems full of falling things – leaves, spiders, seeds, husks, the last languid insects. I can't believe it's October again, a year since Mummy died.

'Daddy has his own flat,' I tell her as we go down the steps to the basement. 'It's a way of keeping an eye on him, while maintaining his independence.'

She looks at me. I wonder again how much English she understands.

I open his door at the bottom and take her inside.

At first, I'd welcomed having Daddy in the house, in spite of the sad circumstances. Mummy dead after her swift illness, Daddy, who had relied on her, uprooted and moved into the granny-flat beneath me. Two lively, successful, even glamorous people diminished within a year, one to dust, the other to a shadow of his former self. Daddy's proximity made me feel whole again, as if two parts of myself that had been separated, adult and child, had been reunited. I would show Daddy I was still the same person, deep down, he'd treasured before I'd grown up.

Work had been going well then. I'd been promoted to mid-morning after my first minor forays into radio and had been given my own show, *Theodora Gentleman, the Voice of South-East England*. Leo had come back to attend a sixth form over here. Roger wanted him integrated into English society in time to go to university, and we'd got him a place at one of the best schools in the area.

Then he got in with a bunch of friends who turned out to be a bad influence. He began to skip lessons. It all came to a head when he was found dealing drugs outside school. He was hauled up to the Principal's office. After that he withdrew, dropped out. Roger still blamed me.

For a while Leo helped look after Daddy. They got along together, though they didn't do a lot. Then, as Daddy's health deteriorated and Leo lost interest in everything, including his grandfather, I could no longer cope with them both. In the end I'd cracked, phoned Roger, listened to him rant about my working too many hours and neglecting our son.

'It's unfair to expect him to care for his grandfather.'

'Maybe. But I have an important job and I can't do everything.'

'We all work, Dora.'

'It's all right for you – you have staff to run your home.'

'I'll get someone for you, if you think that's the answer.'

And here she is. Mona. Roger's 'gift' to me.

'Daddy has a kitchen,' I say, enunciating my words like a nursery school teacher, waving at the small galley area where he has a cooker and sink, 'and shower room.'

'It's OK,' she says, smiling. 'I understand. You don't have to speak slowly.'

'Oh. Good. We're lucky, the previous owners had the basement converted to let out, so it came with the house.'

'Converted?'

I may not have to speak slowly, but it's obvious she is nowhere near fluent.

I don't elucidate, because Mona speaks next.

'He can't live upstairs?'

'Daddy's very proud. He used to live in a big house. Then Mummy fell ill. It was hard moving him at all. He wants to be independent – for his own self-esteem. That's where *you* come in.'

'But it's better he lives with you in the house,' she says.

31

Why does she persist? Does she think I'd neglect Daddy? The man I love more than almost anyone? The man I've brought into my home when no one else was prepared to?

'That's why I'm looking for help.' I turn and speak firmly. 'So Daddy can live here. As he wants to.'

I hold her gaze – a steady look I give my admin staff at work when they're slacking. She looks back for a few seconds and I wonder if she's going to be defiant. Has she, with her soft face and gentle smile, in her headscarf, come to help me? Or is it the opposite? Has she come to ridicule the mess I fear I'm making of life since Mummy died?

Might she be more a hindrance than a help?

Zidana flashes into my mind and away again. I don't want to remember her. But Mona bows her head, clutching her hands together, nods, and smiles sweetly at me. We move on down the steps.

Daddy, bless him, is sitting upright in a suit and tie, a champagne flute in one hand.

'Lovely to see you all,' he says. 'Such a pleasure. So good of you all to come.' He looks up at Mona and me. 'Oh, it's you. I thought you were never coming. You've missed the vol-au-vents.'

'Daddy, this is Mona. Mona's here to help me, to help you.'

'It's a pleasure, I'm sure,' Daddy says. He holds out his hand. Mona takes it, shakes it, smiles.

Daddy's wearing his charming expression – the one in which he holds the eye of the person he's greeting. It's as if nothing has changed at all. He's still the man I adore. When he's like this, I wonder if I've been imagining his Alzheimer's. That he's been putting it on – a little game – and, though I know it's foolish, I allow myself to feel relief that the game is over.

'Dora,' he says, 'get this lady a drink and pass around some cashews, will you?'

32

I glance at Mona. Does she detect anything odd in his request? She carries on smiling at him, unaffected.

Of course, Mona's lost none of him the way I have. What she sees here, now, is all she'll ever know. However batty he appears, he won't rend her heart in two, as he does mine, each time I witness another step of his deterioration.

'Have you eaten this morning, Daddy?' I go to his kitchen.

He's had nothing apart from the imaginary canapés. There are a few unwashed supper things from last night in the sink but not a scrap to indicate he's had breakfast.

'Mona,' I whisper. 'You must make sure he eats. Every morning, noon, night. OK? Then help put his night things on. It's important. He's getting too thin. Look at him. Come.' I beckon her into the kitchenette.

It's sad to see a parent ageing, terrible to see them leave a beloved home.

But it's Daddy's fridge that breaks my heart.

A mini-cabinet, perched on the work surface. How small everything has become, as he's aged! His world has diminished along with his shrinking frame. The fridge contains tiny dishes of jelly, miniature tins of drink, small portions of left-over food. Halves of things; clementines, tomatoes. And his one shelf, bare but for a quarter-bottle of whisky. One solitary glass like an orphan.

I think of our family home with its floor-to-ceiling pantry shelves bulging with packets and jars. Its drinks cabinet of aperitifs and liqueurs. Spirits and vintage port. Rows of glasses: tumblers, champagne flutes, goblets for wine and brandy.

You would never have known how grand he once was. How grand we all were. You would never have believed, in those days, that he would end up like this, a shrivelled old man living in a Deptford basement. Would he have been better off at Anita's? Until we found him a home? Am I guilty of dragging him down with me? Should I have had him in the guest room beside me?

But it would have humiliated him, living with his grown-up daughter in the little room next to her.

I take a lasagne out of the tiny freezer compartment.

How can his life be reduced to this? A Marks & Spencer ready meal for one in a container the size of a box of Cook's matches?

I'd like to run from it as my siblings did.

But someone has to confront it, someone has to care.

I put the lasagne in the microwave and show Mona how to set it. Then I show her how we have to make sure he eats, as you would a child, checking the temperature, making him spoon the food into his mouth without spilling.

Daddy's on his best behaviour.

'It's very good actually, very tasty,' he says, dabbing at his mouth with one of the starched napkins he insists on using. The microwave has slipped under his radar. If he registers me warming his food, he objects that it's not cooked from scratch.

I show Mona Daddy's plastic pill box with the days marked on, that he keeps on the Lazy Susan where Mummy once kept her condiments, feeling that pang again; when did the superior chutneys, mustard and sea salt metamorphose into bottles of flurazepam and Co-codamol? I show her the small en suite bathroom where he wees, washes and does his teeth. I show her where he keeps his clothes and his night things. His whisky bottle – he insists on a measure every night, says it helps him sleep – and how to measure it.

'Aaah!' he says, when we sit back down. 'So nice of you to do all this for me. What did you say your name was again?'

He's looking at me, not at Mona, and my heart plummets. It always shocks me, however I prepare myself. I want to cling to those periods where he's lucid, where he seems not to be unravelling before my eyes.

'Daddy, I'm Dora.'

He frowns, glances from one to the other of us.

'Of course you are. I'm so sorry. Forgive me do. Dora. And who is this?'

'Mona, Daddy.'

'Do I know you?'

'You will,' I say, bending to kiss him goodbye. 'You will.'

And as we mount the steps back to the house, I think with a sudden euphoria, Mona's here now to cope with this.

Mona will make it bearable for me.

CHAPTER SIX

When I've met Charles, the old man who I'm going to be looking after, Dora shows me round her house.

'The drawing room,' she announces, opening a door. The smell hits me in the face – cat, mixed with stale smoke and beer.

Though it's morning, the room's dark. Her son doesn't look up. He's slumped onto the sofa. The cat lies along the back of it, its tail hanging down, its eyes glowing like the lights on the TV. It should be outside hunting mice and rats. I wait for Dora to chase it out. She ignores it.

'It's dark because Leo finds it easier to see his screens like this. This room really needs redecorating – painting, I mean.' Dora makes a motion with her hand.

'I can paint it for you.'

'Oh, no, it's not your job, I'll get a man in sometime. Leo, let me show Mona the room. I'm putting the light on for a second.'

The cat jumps off the sofa. Slinks around our feet into the hall. I watch it, bile rising in my throat.

'Leo, say hello,' Dora hisses.

'Hey,' mumbles the son, without looking at me.

'Don't use street speak,' Dora says. 'Get up, please, and greet Mona properly.'

He stands up, not removing his eyes from the screen, holds out a huge hand and shakes mine, then slumps down again.

'These are Barley Twist banisters,' Dora says as we climb the stairs. 'These houses are the oldest in the area. For some reason, they demolished all the others – thought they were unsuitable for habitation. It brought the area down-market. But this street remains desirable. You can't replace these wonderful old terraces. So, you see, now we arrive at the *piano nobile*.'

She pushes open a door. The room is a pit of ashtrays, dropped clothes, beer cans and magazines.

'Leo sleeps in here,' she says.

I make a noise with my tongue.

'What was that?'

'Nothing.'

'No, you said something,' she says. 'I didn't catch it.'

I shake my head, shrug.

'He's a bloody fright when it comes to tidying his room,' she says. 'And as you can see it could do with a good clean.'

There's a large desk-top computer in here like the ones the kids taught me to use at Madame's house – not the iPads that people were using on the plane. If I can remember the things Madame Sherif's children showed me – how to use Google, for example, how to do a search – I can start to look for Ali. My heart-rate increases. I'll come in here as soon as Dora's at work and Leo's out. If he ever goes out. He looks sealed to that sofa down there.

'Now,' Dora says. 'Up we go.'

The house is tall, one room on top of another. I follow her up the next flight of stairs to the bathroom.

Of all the rooms I've never had, a bathroom is the one I most desire. I've always yearned to lie in a tub of warm water, in a cloud of bubbles like they do in films. Madame Sherif refused to let us use hers, though she had several. Dora's let this one decay. The carpet curls up at the corners, the taps are dull, the windows grimy.

'The laundry room's here, next to the bathroom – there's the washing machine and the airing cupboard.' She holds the door open to a small room, with the scent of washing powder and ironed linen, that takes me back to the garment factory where I worked before I had Leila.

We make our way up again to Dora's bedroom.

This room's as broad as the house with two windows overlooking the street.

I touch her bedspread. 'Very nice,' I say. 'Did you buy it here, in England?'

'I bought it when I was in India with my husband. Many years ago.'

There's a dressing-table with bottles of perfume and pretty glass jars of cotton-wool balls, a jewelry box. I'll find out what it contains when she's out. You can learn a lot about a woman from her jewelry. There's a photo beside her bed – Dora with a man.

'That's about it. There's one more room – the guest room, here, at the back.'

She opens the door onto a smaller room with a white bed and a window overlooking the garden. The bed looks soft and comfortable.

'There,' she says, 'that's about it. Now you know.'

'I'll clean it,' I say. 'Then to keep it nice, I'll do it every day.'

'Thank you,' she says. 'But remember you're here to look after Daddy. You can do the house after you've seen to him. I have to work long hours, and he needs watching.'

'What is your work?'

She straightens up as she replies, 'I present a radio show.'

'Local radio?'

'No,' she says. 'Not at all. It goes out to the whole of south-east England.'

'This is very beautiful, I think, this work?'

She doesn't reply to this, just gives a superior smile as if I can't possibly understand how important her job is.

'My point, Mona, is I am indispensable at work. I want you to look after Daddy as if you were me. As if indeed he were your own father. The house won't suffer if it's left for a while. Daddy will.'

I want to tell her I would not neglect her father, but I can't leave the house like this. I've always been praised for making houses beautiful. It's what I'm good at.

But I remember Ummu's words – the ones she repeated to me before I left to work at Madame's, my first domestic role. '*A wise woman has things to say but remains silent.*'

In the kitchen, Dora picks up her cat, kisses its nose, strokes it.

'The other thing you need to do is to feed Endymion. Every morning, every night. Leo forgets.'

She opens the fridge with one hand and brings out a can of meat.

She puts the cat down and scoops globules into a dish on the floor. The cat purrs and sniffs at the food, and the smell wafts up. I want to put my hand over my mouth and nose.

'It's better he eats outside,' I say.

She looks at me sharply. I step back.

'Endymion eats here,' she says. 'He would eat at the table with me if I ate in the evenings.' She shuts the fridge door. 'You can go to Daddy now. Get to know him, take him for a walk. It can be a trial run. I've got to meet my sister in town, just for a couple of hours. I'm helping her buy shoes for her children.'

'OK,' I say. 'I am here to help now. You don't have to worry. You have a beautiful home,' I add, because I know this is what she will want to hear.

When she's gone, the cat presses its body against my leg, the smell wafts up and makes me gag. I give it a short sharp kick. It yelps, hisses. Then scampers out of the kitchen.

I'm living here too now. There are certain things that will change.

CHAPTER SEVEN

I leave Mona with Daddy and hurry up to Town.

As soon as I arrive in John Lewis's children's department I see why Anita needed help buying her kids shoes. Her au pair, she told me, is having a day off.

The place resembles a riot – a toddler riot. Shoes are scattered at all angles across the floor; wailing children cling to their mothers' necks. Women elbow each other. Harassed-looking sales assistants try to remain polite whilst ignoring the fury on the faces of those kept waiting. Small boys chase up and down the floor brandishing weapons at one another, girls wail that they didn't want *those* shoes, why can't they have the *shiny* ones, babies loot boxes.

Jemima strains at the straps of her buggy, scarlet in the face and screaming, Anita tries to hold Jack down while forcing his feet onto the gauge where they almost skin the face of the young man trying to measure him.

Parents on all sides plead and beg, 'Darling, come here.' Or, 'Please, Tabitha, please put those big girls' shoes down.' Or, 'If you sit for two more minutes, honey pie, we'll go and look at the toys . . . yes, sweetie, you can buy something.'

'Blimey,' I say to Anita as we settle down at last in the café. 'Can't these parents assert themselves? Are they afraid to say no to their children?'

Anita has managed to silence her own two by stuffing the straws from some horrible-looking milkshakes into their mouths.

'You've just forgotten,' she said. 'It's so long since you had Leo. At least you can see why I can't have Daddy living with us.'

'Having a kid of Leo's age isn't that easy either. Demanding money. Smoking in the house, lying around all day.' I look at her, hoping for sympathy.

'Why though? Why's he unemployed? Isn't it time he got a job? It's been months now.'

It's true I've sometimes expressed to Anita how Leo tests my patience. But he is my little boy, I've accepted this is how things are for the time being, only occasionally driven to moments of frustration with him. The fact is, I'd lost him once and didn't want to lose him again. For the years after Roger and I split up, when I was in London and he in Rabat, I missed him terribly, his funny bright-eyed face, his jokes, his physicality. He was still a young boy when I left, pre-pubescent, smooth cheeks and a crude sense of humour, who let me hug or tickle him when no one was looking. By the time he came over to go to sixth form, he was six foot tall with stubble and a deep voice and wouldn't let me near him.

I was determined to make it up to him. To give him every-thing he wanted, if needs be.

I had no idea how giving a person what they want can be so complicated.

'He might look tough, Anita, but he's fragile. It isn't easy find-ing a job in this climate, unless you're brimming with confidence.'

'Hmmm. I suppose I've got it all to come,' she says. 'Anyway, Terence wants to meet up some time. Talk about what we're doing with Daddy's house. He wants it ready to put on the market. We've got to clear the rest of the stuff out. Think there's some idea that since you've taken Daddy on, you should have first shout when it comes to the furniture.'

She bends down to extract the plastic cup from Jemima's mouth that she has decided tastes better than its contents. Most of Daddy and Mummy's furniture's too big for my house, she must know this. It's why I've already taken the things that matter to me, sentimental mementoes none of the others care about.

'How is it with Daddy, anyway?'

'I've left him with his carer. They're having a trial run.'

'I always thought it was a bit ambitious, your taking him on.'

'What do you mean?'

'Well, he was always difficult without Mummy to keep him in order. He needed that matriarchal figure to boss him around. Mummy was so controlling, but it's what he needed.'

'Controlling? I never thought of her as controlling.'

'She was, Dora. All that motherly home-making was her way of manipulating him. Manipulating all of us. But he needed it – he was so wayward without her.'

'That's not how I saw it at all.'

'Don't you feel a relief, being released from Mummy's watchful eye? Not allowing us to be our true selves?' She leans over and picks up Jemima, although the toddler seemed perfectly happy where she was. She holds her like a shield against her chest.

'No, I don't. I miss Mummy.'

'That's not what I'm saying. We all miss her, but there are things I like about not having to live up to her expectations. But you left home before it got really unpleasant to be with her and Dad. You should try being the youngest, living at home when your siblings have all gone.'

'Well, Daddy's been fine with me – until recently. But that's because of the dementia.'

I don't want to tell my sister how hard it has been with Daddy. I don't want her to know that I sometimes feel he is a complete stranger to me. I'm not sure if it's because I have changed – after all, since I last shared a home with him I've been married, moved abroad, divorced, had a successful career – or whether it is him. Daddy is less amiable, less fun than I remember him. I wonder if on one level, Anita's right. Perhaps as a grown-up I perceive things about him I'd overlooked as an adoring child, things that are difficult to accept. Neither of us is quite who we were, and it is hard work getting along together. Can even be painful. What I hadn't predicted when I'd offered to have him live in my basement was just how painful it would become.

As if to illustrate my thoughts, Daddy's in one of his irascible moods when I get home. I go straight down to see how he's got on with Mona. She's washing dishes in his little kitchen, but leaves discreetly when I arrive.

I go and sit with Daddy and he looks up at me.

'You!' he says. 'I was hoping Terence would come. Terence was always so good to me. But he's busy with his work, you know; he has an important conference and couldn't make it. He's a wonderful man.'

'Daddy, Terence will be at his weekend cottage,' I say. He's too bloody selfish to put himself out for you, I think. And what is all this about Terence, who Daddy labelled the Successful, Ruthless One, who put money before people?

'He and Ruth have a beautiful home,' he goes on, 'I loved staying with them. It's so dark here. I can barely see you.'

I grapple for a moment to remember the time Daddy's referring to, when he'd stayed with Terence and Ruth. Sometimes his unreliable memory makes me doubt my own. It takes a moment to register that he's never stayed with them, that this is one of his errant fantasies.

'I don't even know who you are. You could be anybody,' Daddy goes on.

'I'm Theodora, Daddy. You know very well who I am.'

'Theodora . . . Theodora. Which one was she, Maudy? Which one was she?'

Tears rise and lodge behind my eyes. If this is confusion caused by his dementia, it seems cruel. If it is a side of him I've never seen before, it's devastating. Whichever way I look at it, Daddy has the capacity to forget I am – or ever was – his favourite.

As I always do on these occasions, I think of the others, Terence and Anita and Simon, content in their own homes, oblivious to the effort I put in, to the way Daddy speaks to me. As if they have cast him out of their minds since the night of the funeral. It's all very well saying I can have first pick when it comes to the furniture from his home, as if this can make up for the emotional strain I've gone through, having him. They have no idea. Because they never see him.

I leave Daddy pining for Terence and mount the steps to the garden then go round to the front of the house.

'Mona!' I call. 'Daddy needs you again now.'

I watch her hurry down the steps, her face averted, in her headscarf.

I go upstairs and run a deep bath.

CHAPTER EIGHT

At first, I think the distant roar I can hear when I awake is the sea. Then it hits me –it's the traffic that must start up before dawn. I remind myself that though I'm so far from the people I love, Ali could be somewhere this country, this city, even. But this makes me anxious again. I push the fear that he may be in trouble to the back of my mind. They say no news is good news.

I try to recall more of the conversation I'd had with Ali's friend at the Café des Jeunes that day.

'Nah,' Yousseff had said. 'Nothing bad's happened to him.'

'Have *you* heard from him?'

He shrugged. 'Not since he first left. There were a couple of texts.'

I'd had those, too, when he'd first gone away – they said he'd be in touch as soon as he could.

'My advice is, let him do what he needs to do, Mona. It's for the best.'

'Why hasn't he contacted us? Leila at least?'

Yousseff sighed. He was impatient with me, I could see.

'Maybe he lost his phone. Maybe he *can't* contact you?'

If he'd lost his phone he would have written. Perhaps there's a letter waiting for me now, at home. As soon as I have credit on my phone I'll ring and find out. Today then, my goal is to get money from somewhere. Or to ask for an advance on my pay, if I dare.

I look about my room, imagining what Ummu would say if she could see it. There's stuff everywhere – shelves of books, other things wedged onto the book cases: packs of cards and a magnifying glass, badges and a hairbrush, loads of DVDs – and an old TV is shoved into a corner. A lipstick! Cast aside.

What kind of woman throws her make-up aside? I pick it up, open it, try out the colour on the back of my hand. It's pretty. And obvious Dora no longer wants it.

I push it into my tracksuit pocket. I'll try it on later, see if it suits me.

The cat slinks in, puts its two front paws on my bed, claws at the rug.

'Tsssss!'

It looks indignant, as if it has a right to walk over my bedclothes. I push up the window. Pick up the vase of dead roses, take them out and hurl the water at the cat, who leaps up onto the sill and out into the bleak grey world. It's left its hairs over everything. Cats carry fleas and disease. It shouldn't be allowed to creep over my bed.

I'll tell Ummu, if and when I get to speak to her, that my employer, though rich, hasn't time – is too important – for her home, for hygiene.

Even the windows are grimy. Black mildew creeps up the panes like dried blood.

I find a rag in the kitchen just beyond my room, half a lemon in Dora's enormous fridge, and polish – until the pale watery sunshine falls into the room, and I can see outside. My room overlooks the garden at the back of the house. An oasis of green and scarlet, enclosed by grey. Grey sky, grey walls, grey backs of houses beyond. There's even another statue. A grey stone head of a woman on a concrete plinth at the top of the steps that go down to Charles's flat.

There aren't many leaves on the shrubs, but those that remain are gold. The bushes drip with red berries; flame-coloured lanterns. There's a tree whose load of pears has been shed so the fruit lies rotting on the grass. What a waste – lipstick inside, pears out! The pears that have retained their shape will make a lovely clafoutis. I'll bake it later, a welcome offering for my new employer.

It's impossible for me to live in this mess, so I start by arranging the books and files on the shelves and tidying the heaps of DVDs and clothes. What would Ummu think of this? She makes a point of snipping buttons and zips from worn-out clothes to sew back into newer ones, removing laces from shoes beyond repair. Saves tins to use as storage, bottles to refill. All this stuff is worth hundreds of dirham, yet here it's left to gather dust.

When the room's to my liking, I finish taking my things out of my bag. My scrapbook with its photos of Leila and Ummu and, in the background, the chickens that live on the roofs. Some incense, the sandalwood type I love best. Next, Ali's blue handkerchief. A soft packet of black tobacco cigarettes for emergencies. The cosmetics I managed to grab here and there (Nivea face cream, shampoo, a bar of soap in a pink plastic box). A book of English verbs. If I'm going to go home better qualified than when I arrived, I shall have to learn to read and write English. My passport. I open it. My face peers up. I'm hunched up as if I'm afraid they're doing something worse to me than taking my photo. I *was* afraid. That at any moment they would refuse it, say *no passport for you*. I must guard it with my life. I tuck it into the bottom of my bag and place the other things on top.

That's me. Squished into these few belongings.

I put my nose to the bag and breathe. It smells of journeys, airports, strange cars and of diesel oil. I hoped I might smell home. I pick up Ali's handkerchief. Press my nose into it and breathe, drawing in his smell, my eyes screwed tight shut. I want to believe, for a few moments, that I'm on our roof where we were at our happiest.

Before he left.

It's just before dawn. Silver moonlight reflecting off the still water of the estuary. The warmth in the white walls contained since the day before. The scent of roses coming not from a vase where the petals have brown frills, but from Didi's basket on the front of his bicycle as he begins his rounds. And the smell of Ali, coming not from the 20 square centimetres I have left of him, but from the warmth of his body through the cotton of his kaftan as he wraps his arms about me, puts his mouth to my ear.

I'm startled out of this daydream by a knock on the door. I'd forgotten Dora was in the house.

She looks different this morning. Dressed for work in a grey jacket and skirt, her amber-coloured hair that so far she's worn tumbling past her shoulders in corkscrews pinned up into a loose style off her face. I notice now things I didn't on arrival, perhaps because of the lack of natural light – lines fanning outward from her eyes and furrowing her forehead. I guess she's a good ten years older than me, though it's hard to say. She wears a gold chain around her neck with a word on it. It must be her name, Theodora.

I stare at it as it catches the light, wonder how much it is worth. It looks like real gold to me. Solid, precious. I'd like to touch it.

She says, 'Goodness. Hmmm. You've cleaned the windows!'

'Shall I clean the house now? Today?'

'Yes. But you're here to look after Daddy first.'

'And shall I cook?'

'Thank you, no need,' she says. 'Leo likes to eat at seven, but I'll use the microwave. You can put the recycling out. It goes in there.' She waves at some enormous plastic bins beside the garden fence outside the window. 'And you must take the wheelie bins out on a Wednesday night. Daddy needs breakfast, however. You should have done that before the room. He can't wait, the house can. He needs help with his toilet. Then you can take him out to the market, or for a walk by the river. He prefers the wheelchair. He tires easily.'

'I won't forget Charles.'

'And here's some money. You must look after it for him. He gets muddled about what he spends.' She hands me a note, ten pounds. 'When I've more time we'll discuss money: when I'm to pay you, what you'll need for shopping and so on. Now you're here I can cancel the delivery! Thank goodness. They're always out of what I need. And the substitutes! Last week they brought fabric conditioner when I'd ordered a lemon. The only thing they had in common was the scent!' she laughs.

My heart races as she hands me the money. I think of the hours of credit this will buy.

'Get him clementines. Any change, give it to me this evening.'
'Yes.'

'Daddy will have a sleep after lunch and then you can clean. I'll show you how to use the washing machine.'

She goes to the door, turns. 'Oh, one other thing, Mona.'
'Yes?'

'Your headscarf. It's fine to wear it out on the street – I understand it's your religion. But in the house – it might startle Daddy.'

And she leaves.

CHAPTER NINE

'Bye, Daddy.' I bend down and kiss the cool loose flesh of his cheek. I wonder if I'll ever get used to leaving him in someone else's care.

'Be a doll and buy me a paper before you go, will you?' He looks up, takes my hand in his.

'Daddy, Mona's here to do that for you today.'

It's like leaving a child at playgroup for the first time, accepting that another adult must stand in your shoes. Not allowing your child to see it's as hard for you as it is for them. Keeping quiet when you see your status as the centre of their world fade, another taking your place. It's hard but necessary. I can no longer leave Daddy unattended all day. I want him to understand that it's Mona's job now, to get him his meals, to fetch him his paper.

But when I've torn myself away, to hurry along the High Street towards the river, I feel light. Daddy's being looked after! I can switch off, concentrate on work. It's market day. Stallholders, wrapped up against the cold in scarves and fingerless mittens, are setting up. There's the scent of fried breakfasts wafting from cafés, mingling with the constant stench round here of the market debris that's left to rot. It occurs to me that now I've got

Mona, I could leave early, stop for a coffee in Greenwich on my way – I don't frequent the cafés on the High Street, with their dubious hygiene. But not this morning. This morning I'm eager to hear the latest on the chat show that's being discussed – a potential promotion for me.

I get to the corner and turn along the river path to the pier. I think of Max. Check for texts. Wonder when I might next see him. It's going to be so much easier now!

Last time it had all gone horribly wrong. It was over three weeks ago when a text arrived on my way home from work.

Arrived early at St Pancras. Get here soon! I'll book us a room.

My body responded, as it always did when I heard from him, as if Max was right here, now. There wasn't the usual time I'd spend preparing myself to meet my lover. I rued the days when I could have been spontaneous, when throwing on a T-shirt and jeans and washing my face was all it took to look glamorous. Getting older meant paying more attention to the details – make-up, hair, all took that little bit longer to get right, but that night there wasn't time. I dressed in a linen shirt-dress, with rope-soled wedges. I would have to ask Max to start giving me more notice. Our spontaneous rendezvous would have to become a thing of the past. I begged Leo to see to Daddy, and called a cab. My mobile went as I came up the escalator at St Pancras.

It was Daddy. 'I've lost my pills. The white ones I think they were, the ones in the silver poppers.'

'Daddy, I'm out this evening. You're to ask Leo. He's there, he's not doing anything.'

'Leo's not there. I've called. I've banged.'

When he's particularly demanding, Daddy bangs on his ceiling – our drawing-room floor – with a broom handle, something that riles Leo.

'I'll phone him.'

I thumbed Leo's number into my phone – he wouldn't answer if I called the house phone, he'd think it was Daddy from downstairs again – just as I spotted Max waiting under the statue of the embracing couple. There he was, crisp white shirt open at the collar, a linen jacket thrown over the top.

'Leo, didn't you go?'

'I did. I've been.'

I knew this tone. If I pressed Leo in one of his moods I'd end up with two dramas on my hands.

The demands exerted by my son and Daddy tussled with the pull I felt from Max. He was here now. I'd reached him. I could smell him, I could feel the brush of his cuff against my cheek as he put his arm around me.

He bit my ear. It contracted with his breath. Tonight Max made me think of caramels, golden, smooth, sweet. I wanted to sniff him, savour him, lap him up.

'I've booked us a table in the restaurant.'

He put his warm hand on my neck – I wasn't going to be able to resist.

'You're to relax,' he said. 'You look stressed. I'm buying us champagne and you're to choose the most expensive dish on the menu.'

'Have we time to eat?'

'My train's not 'til after midnight.'

I followed him helplessly into the restaurant.

My martini arrived, the glass frosted with ice, but my mobile went again before I'd taken a sip.

'Mum, he's being awkward. He says he's lost his prescription. He's on about Grandma's birthday present. You're going to have to come home.'

'I'll have to go, Max.'

'Theodora! If Leo can't cope, phone one of your three siblings. He's their dad too.'

He was right. They were always offering to help out if I was stuck. I phoned Anita.

'Oh Dora, I'm sorry, I've got a girly evening planned. I was about to go out of the door. It's been a nightmare finding a babysitter. Have you tried Simon?'

I could have argued but didn't want to waste time. I phoned my little brother.

I could hear the titter of young foreign students in the room behind him. 'Sorry, Dor, I'm in the middle of an English class.'

'At this time?'

There was laughter, the clinking of bottles. I jammed the off button down and tried Terence. He was away on some conference.

By the time I'd got home, fetched Daddy's prescription, administered his pills, put him to bed, it was gone midnight. I was disappearing into the depths of my house to care for Daddy, while my siblings did as they pleased. I thought with resentment of Roger and Claudia with their cleaners and gardeners and cooks. I'd been no good at playing the diplomat's wife, it was true, but there were aspects of that life I felt I shouldn't have had to forfeit, just because I'd left it. I wasn't a lesser person for following my career, or for choosing passion over marriage.

But worst of all, I sensed Max drawing away, not just literally on the train that would be snaking under the Channel by now to France, but also in his heart. I wondered how long it would be before he tired of being let down and gave up on me. I've come to know, since Mummy died, that each moment happens only once – there are no second chances. My evening with Max was lost. I couldn't afford to lose another one. After all, he didn't have the same imperative to see me. He had a wife.

I only had him.

Now there's Mona I'll be able to see him without interruption, and the thought lifts my spirits. I'm walking along the river path now. The tide's low, but the river is dark today, turbulent. As I hurry towards Greenwich a crazed voice rises from the shore: 'For whosoever exalteth himself shall be abased, and he that humbleth himself shall be exalted.'

I stop for a moment. On the high, weed-strewn wall across the inlet a thick rope has caught on a steel mooring ring, and has been twisted by the tide in such a way as to mimic a crucifix; the Christ figure's head is swinging to one side, his arms akimbo, his feet, the soggy ends of the rope, dangling in the encroaching tide. The owner of the voice stands beside this accidental rope effigy, preaching his sermon to the waves.

Another of the local lost souls, I think, and hurry on.

By eight I'm on the Clipper from Greenwich Pier. Winter is coming. The cityscape, as the boat lifts and drops on the swell, is all blue and grey: pale October sky, glinting tower blocks, slate-grey riverwater chopped up by the wash from the boat.

I wonder how Daddy and Mona will get on. I mustn't worry. Mustn't think. There was no other choice.

It's a relief to walk into the normality of the offices, to wave at Ben on reception.

'Morning, Theodora!'

'You're looking lovely as ever,' calls Beatie, one of the admin staff.

The voices come at me as I move through the building; people look up from their desks, smile and wave.

I'm a big name. Theodora Gentleman – turning south-east England's worries around. I nearly kicked up a fuss when I got shifted to radio from TV. I could have taken them to a tribunal. Whatever their arguments for shifting you, the fact is you're no longer twenty-something, but a mature woman who doesn't, in the view of the powers-that-be, pull in the viewers the way younger ones do. I wonder when it is one slips from being a presentable face to one that no longer cuts it. I come to the conclusion that it's arbitrary. How can one wrinkle tip the scales from acceptable to unacceptable? But some divinity decrees that one day, you have crossed an imperceptible line, and if you kick up a fuss you're out anyway.

If you're a woman.

However, there are things about radio I've come to prefer. People are open in a way they aren't on TV – I can probe deeper, get stories out of them. It's the psychology of the confessional or the therapist's couch: if they can't see the face of the person they're talking to, they'll reveal more. It's challenging, and I'm good at it. I'm on the way up. My goal is to have a show during prime time and Rachel, my boss, has been working at it. She's asked me to go and see her today. So I grab a coffee from Hayley our intern and go to her office.

'How are you, Dora?' I feel as if Rachel examines me as she speaks. 'You're looking better, I must say.'

'Better than what?'

'Well, you've had a lot on your plate. Ever since your mother died, really. Caring for your father.'

'Maybe it's because I've got a live-in carer for Daddy now, ' I tell her.

I have to emphasise this. The day I told Rachel that Daddy had moved into my granny flat, she'd frowned at me.

'You've taken on the sole care of your father on top of having your son at home? You're a bloody saint, Dora.'

Her expression belied the fact she was wondering whether I'd bitten off more than I could chew. I knew what she was thinking, that my looking after Daddy was going to impinge on my professionalism, the way young children are supposed to on working mothers. I was determined from the beginning to show her this wasn't going to happen. But it was a close call, until now.

She shifts some papers in front of her.

'I'm very pleased to hear it, Dora. We were worried that you'd taken on a little too much. As you know, I'm keen for you to go for the new chat show that's being mooted. You really stand a very good chance with your track record. The main thing is not to let your personal views impinge on the phone-in.'

'Have I ever . . .?'

'Not recently, no. But there has been the odd occasion, when you were under stress. Look, I'm only saying this because I'm gunning for you, Dora. I want to see your name in bright lights!'

I feel my heart swell at the thought that moving on up to a prime-time show is now a reality. It is, of course, what I've always wanted. What I've been working towards. The show she's talking about is a coveted one, involving celebrity interviews, and is more high-profile than anything I've done before. If I get it, I'll be achieving a lifetime goal.

'Dora! You're looking fab.' Gina, my researcher, hands me today's agenda and runs through the callers she's already spoken to. 'We must go for a drink later. How about it?'

I place a hand on her shoulder and squeeze. 'Maybe later in the week. I'm still getting used to leaving Daddy with his carer.'

'OK, one Friday then. Promise?'

I nod. 'All being well.'

'Right. Better get on with the show.'

'Remind me who we've got first?'

'The mother-in-law who feels it's her place to comment on the way this caller runs her home. The caller feels she's doing quite enough having her husband's mother in the first place.'

'Couldn't agree more,' I say, accepting another coffee from Hayley.

'It's a popular one. Feelings are running high,' says Gina.

'I hope the mother-in-law isn't listening!' I say. It never ceases to amaze me what people are prepared to impart on National Radio, as if they were in a private sitting room.

'Her problem, not ours,' says Gina, settling herself at her computer.

The adrenalin kicks in as the jingle goes out: 'Theodora Gentleman, Voice of South-East England, here to turn your worries around.'

I'm at my happiest on air. Engaged in conversation, deep in thought, orchestrating these discussions.

I lean into the mic.

'So, Sue, your mother-in-law has moved in. For the benefit of our listeners, can you explain the circumstances?'

'It's like she moved in the minute her hubby died,' our caller Sue begins. 'I'm all right with it – it's like, what you do, isn't it?'

Her face floats into my mind's eye. Plumpish, attractive, bags under her eyes, and straightened, light brown hair. She'll be wearing something from H&M, fashionable, a little too young for her. Too much flesh on show. I always try to visualise my callers. It's a way of keeping myself engaged, though from experience I know faces rarely match voices. The truth, if and when one ever gets to see it, is always a surprise.

'When was this, Sue?'

'Six months ago now.'

'Does she have her own room? Her own space in your home?'

'Oh yes. She's got my son's old room – he's moved out, is at uni. She's got use of her own bathroom. We've done all we can to make her feel at home. I didn't have any choice. My husband insisted she couldn't live alone after she was widowed.'

'Can she look after herself?' I ask. 'Is she incapacitated in any way?'

'Oh no. She's very young for her age.'

Sue goes on, explaining how she has never got on with the mother-in-law but has worked all her married life to smooth over potential conflicts.

I say nothing. I'm not here to give my views, but I play the psychologist anyway, to myself. It's always so obvious what's going on. This time it's a husband with an Oedipus complex. A son who is unable to detach entirely from his mother and to fully love his wife.

'Which would be fine,' Sue says, and I can hear she's close to tears, 'but now she's determined to find fault with the way I do things.'

Personally, I would have refused to have her move in at all, is what I'm thinking. It's not as if the mother-in-law needs care like my father does. And, though I love him dearly, I don't even have *him* in the house. It's thanks to the flat that I've been willing to have him nearby. But I don't give my opinion – that's not what I'm here for. I'm just a facilitator.

It's something Max loves to hear about. My position at the mic, listening, suggesting, analysing – but keeping my true opinions hidden. He likes me to tell him what I really think of these conundrums – it's one of the things we laugh about when we're together.

The discrepancy between what I say, and what I think.

'Right, Sue,' I say. 'We have Donald on the phone who wants to make a suggestion.'

Donald is, I suspect, one of our regulars. I recognise his voice, though he changes his name each time he phones in. He's one of those who love to offer advice, a psychotherapist manqué who spends his whole time listening for opportunities to offer spurious solutions to problems he hasn't – and wouldn't ever, or so he maintains – have to deal with himself. Or maybe he's moved to phone simply so he can hear his own voice on air. There are plenty of those.

'You've got to write up a contract,' Donald says. 'Make it clear what you're prepared to provide, and what you expect in return. All parties must sign it.'

'Well, there's a thought, Sue. Now we've got Marcia who's had a similar experience. Over to you, Marcia.'

This morning the scenario's genuine, but lots of nutters phone in. Gina filters the more extreme cases, but there are those with problems that make the programme all the more lively, people who enjoy sexual practices that lend the programme a salacious appeal that just slips through censorship. Foot fetishists or people looking for sex with no strings attached, women who've discovered that their sister is really their mother. I'm amazed that people are prepared to reveal their problems over the radio, ignoring the fact that the whole of the south-east might be listening in. I'm astonished that they confide, that they feel I'm their friend, someone they've never met and know nothing about. I wonder why they haven't got friends they can talk to in private about these things. But I know I'm a construct for each of them; they make me what they'd like me to be. A sort of omniscient goddess figure . . . Theodora Gentleman. And to hand it to them, my listeners are appreciative. I get hundreds of emails, texts and tweets thanking me, even some grateful handwritten letters from older listeners.

Rachel comes over as I'm about to leave.

'Well done, Dora,' she says. 'Things are going so well for you. I'm talking to the directors later and hope I'll have some good news.'

I think of Max, his pride at my success. I think of my siblings, how, though they're all better off than me, they've always been in awe of my career.

Even Daddy will surely recognise how well I've done, through the mists of his decaying mind?

It's all falling into place.

And in a way, I think, as I make my way home to see how Daddy got on today, it's all possible now, because Mona's come.

CHAPTER TEN

When the old man's had his breakfast I go back to the main house, hoping to spend a little time in Dora's bathroom, and come face to face with the son. For a few moments we stand and stare at each other, saying nothing. Now he's standing I see he's tall with broad shoulders and a large stomach. Dressed in a T-shirt, tracksuit bottoms and thick socks. His eyes are cold and his face pale. A tide rises up – a fear that grips me though its origins are in the past. I'm alone in the house with a man I know nothing about. My body has a memory of its own. It reacts before I've time to register that I'm afraid. I break out in a fine sweat.

The best thing to do when confronted with someone you fear, Ummu once told me, is to stand your ground, look them in the eye. Disarm them with your confidence. *Make friends with the dog, but don't drop the stick,* she said. And so I don't move, but keep my wits about me.

I follow him to the kitchen, where he fills a mug with water and drinks it down. Fills it again. He takes a plastic bottle of pills, shakes two or three into his hand, swallows them. I wonder if perhaps he is ill. Is this why he was on the sofa all day yesterday, half-asleep?

'Can I get you something?' I ask. 'Some breakfast? An egg? A little coffee?'

'You can make me tea when I get up,' he says.

'You're going back to bed now?'

He shrugs and walks out again, his head low. He does remind me of a dog! The kind with raised shoulderblades that hangs their heads, the sort you don't trust at home for they're sometimes rabid. I listen. Hear his heavy footsteps on the stairs, the click of his bedroom door.

The house falls silent.

I try not to make a sound as I go up to Dora's bathroom. It's a beautiful room, though it's been neglected. There are wooden floors, in need of a polish, the curling carpet, and a huge bath with feet shaped like a large cat's. Along the shelves are cubes of soap, glass bottles of oils and lotions. I turn the enormous brass taps, just to see the water flow. There are two taps, one hot and one cold. I let the water run for some time, discover the hot, enjoy the soothing feel of it upon my skin. Then I lean for a minute on the basin, in a pool of pale yellow sunlight, and gaze out of the window. Next door a woman moves down her garden with a basket of washing. I watch her peg it on a circular washing line, like a small tree. When she's finished, the tree starts to turn circles, the washing swirling around in a kind of dance in the wind. It reminds me of the trees I've seen in the desert, where people tie coloured fabric as fertility offerings, and I feel a pang, and wonder when I'll next stand on home soil.

Later I'll make this room beautiful. Clean the bath and sink, polish the taps. One day when I have more time I'll take a bath. Use a few of Dora's luxury products. For now I just have a wash, dry myself on a thick towel, rub a little cream into my hands from one of the tubes on the shelf. Feeling fresher, I go down to Charles.

He's wearing good clothes – a crisp shirt, wool jacket and trousers. Leather shoes that look as if a shoe-shine boy has just had his hands on them. I think of Ummu in her funny assortment of clothes that she's worn for years and wonder who keeps his so pristine when Dora clearly hasn't the time. I lean over him, catching the scent of his soap, a lemony smell, and a waft of something sweeter, the talc he keeps in his little bathroom.

'I need to get to Billingsgate,' he says. 'Have you ordered my taxi?'

'Dora asked me to take you to the market,' I say. 'To buy your oranges. Have you been to the toilet?'

The minute I've asked, I wish I hadn't. He has pride. He has dignity. I've offended him. I take his arm. Lead him out of his front door and up the steep steps to the back garden.

'I don't understand why you live down there when there's the big house that's so much easier to get in and out of,' I say, and he looks at me. He doesn't ask me to translate.

Charles walks so slowly it takes us over ten minutes to cross the garden with its fallen fruits and go along the path round to the front. He waits while I go into Dora's hallway, tug the wheel-chair from under the stairs, pull it down the steps and help him in.

The woman I saw hanging out the washing next door is sweeping her front steps. 'Morning, Charles,' she calls out.

'Good morning, Desiree,' Charles says, and I nod too and smile, but she doesn't notice.

There's no one else around. The doors along the street are closed, the cars that were parked when we arrived, gone. Only the little stone figures watch as we pass.

The minute we turn the corner at the end of the street, however, everything changes. A market's in full swing. The smell hits me in the face. Foreign odours mingle with those so familiar

– griddled meat, hot leather – that when I screw my eyes tight shut, I could be at the souk.

Drunks lounge openly on upturned buckets or crates, chatting idly, holding cans of lager. Women march past in groups, their hair corn-rowed, or shaved, or dyed bright colours, pink or white or blue. They glance and laugh, reminding me of my friends in the medina when we were young and would have done the same, gossiped and giggled as we walked along, thinking we were the centre of the world.

Music blares out of doorways.

It's like entering a party I have not been invited to.

Snatches of languages I recognise – French, Arabic. Others I've never heard before. Signs on shops in Arabic and Roman script and Chinese. Shops filled with bright fabrics, a window of mannequin heads in different-coloured wigs, purple and yellow and green. Things I didn't expect to see here: halal meat stores, and moolis and a whole stall of eggs. There are beauty parlours, supermarkets. Shops with watches and jewels in the window. Women in African dress, and in burkas, men in turbans and in djellabas, teenagers in denim and leather and shell-suits or Rasta colours. A man with no legs goes past in a wheelchair.

This is not the England I pictured or that Ummu dreamed of.

This is a cross-section of the whole world.

And somehow it lifts my spirits.

If the whole world is here, why not Ali?

We're moving through stalls of mobile phones, pans, cakes and hairpieces, nuts and bolts, bags and scarves. Round piles of rubbish and discarded boxes. Through racks of lovely long dresses and jackets and trousers and out again into the light. That's when I see him. My fingertips fizz, my knees buckle. He's at a toy stall, bent over a doll, its eyes blinking as it moves back and forth on a battery-operated swing. I know that black hair, the white djellaba he wears over baggy trousers, a leather jacket over the top; his hands, the hands I love, holding the toy so tenderly. Only the trainers look different, new. He's thinking of Leila. I stare, feeling a warmth spread all over me.

Charles is saying something to me but I can't hear him; everything has faded, the whole market recedes. All I can see are his strong brown forearms as he straightens up, talks to the stall-holder, holds out his money, the doll in one hand. He is planning to send it to her. He takes his change and then he turns towards us.

As quickly as my body warmed up, it goes cold. Charles is shouting at me to move on. He wants his fruit, he wants his chocolate and a cup of tea.

I curse myself for being so foolish. We're in a tiny corner of one of the biggest cities in the world. I don't even know if he's in the country for sure. I feel the heat of tears in my eyes. A group of men laugh and jeer as we pass, huddled together, smoking, sharing a bottle of whisky. Their eyes swing over me. I flinch, as I did at the sight of Leo, earlier. Everyone drinks here, and the smell that catches in my throat and overpowers everything is the sickening stench of alcohol.

I lower my head.

'Stop here!' Charles raises his hand. He gestures towards a heap of shrivelled-looking clementines. I stare at the pathetic piles of fruit on the stall. Yearn for home, for the mountains of gleaming oranges on the carts in the souks, walls of sunshine.

When we've bought the fruit there's only six pounds left. The chance of buying credit for my phone fades.

'We'll get my chocolate from the 99p shop,' the old man says, waving his stick towards the far end of the street. 'Don't tell Dora. She doesn't believe in bargains. Though it's the same as she buys from her fancy shops.'

The 99p shop is a supermarket, shelves and shelves of food all costing less than one pound. Multipacks of tins of vegetables and beans and crisps. I'm amazed that the bigger the items, the cheaper they are. Bars of chocolate the size of Ali's leather babouches for 99p each! Yet small things cost a lot.

'What are these, Charles?' I point at rows of little jars of powder the size of coffee cups.

'Herbs and spices,' he says. I stare at them. I want to laugh to think that in this country they sell spices in such tiny quantities. I picture the mountains of cumin and paprika and turmeric on the stalls at home, pyramids of bright colours, so tall you can hide behind them, and feel a rush of longing to be there. I yearn for the mountains of mint the boys at the café used to sort through in the mornings, its fresh scent mingling with the salt air from the sea.

We pay for Charles's chocolate and now only have four pounds left.

'Charles.' I squat in front of him. 'Can we buy stamps here?'

'Do I need stamps?' he says. I notice how pale his irises are, clouded like pools of milk. How frail his old skin, like paper. His mind is going, he's easily confused.

'Yes, you do! Remember? Dora said when she left, "Don't forget the stamps, Charles."'

He looks bewildered.

'When she left this morning, she said, "Buy fruit. And don't forget stamps!" You remember?'

The tears that came to my eyelids earlier threaten to spill over. Without stamps, without credit, Leila and even Ummu will believe I've disappeared like Ali. It's so easy to vanish when you've got nothing.

No wonder I haven't heard from him.

'Yes, now you mention it, I think she did,' he says. I'd like to hug him. 'There's a post office here somewhere, but they've hidden it at the back of a newspaper shop. No one seems to use them any more now there's all this e-this and that. Over here, my dear – follow the direction of my stick.'

Back we go, down the street, past dark doorways and strange signs I can't read, past a shop full of stone heads – made for English gravestones. I imagine them watching me, that they have seen my lie.

Charles directs me into a newspaper shop.

'Stamps for North Africa?' The man behind the counter smiles at me incredulously. 'You *writing* to North Africa? If you're sending money, I can do it for you.' He slams the stamps down on the counter. 'Electronically. It's safer and it's instant.'

I look at him. He's handsome, with green eyes in his brown face and closely cropped black hair. His eyes twinkle as if he knows exactly what I'm doing, what he can get out of me.

'How much does it cost?'

'It all depends how much you're sending. Say you send a hundred pounds, it'll cost you a tenner. Two hundred, a bit more. But I can do you a deal. They'll charge you more up at the hairdresser's. You ask them and I'll undercut them.'

'I'll think about it.'

'You won't get it cheaper anywhere else.'

When we've left the shop I ask Charles if I can take him for a walk. I tighten his scarf around his neck. It's cold out here and I don't want him falling ill. I'm hoping if we stay out a little longer, the stamp incident will fade from his mind. He mustn't tell Dora I've used her money for my own needs.

'Yes yes, a little walk. I'll show you the river. A spot of fresh air. It'll give us an appetite.'

I push him across the main road, and under tall trees that shed their golden leaves about our feet as we go. At last the noise drops. The busyness ceases and we're in front of the great brown river. It's even wider than it looked when we crossed it at night from the bridge, the water a massive beast heaving its weight against the walls. On the other side, tall glass buildings tower towards sky that's the colour of stones.

I park the wheelchair and sit on a cold bench. A flight of steps leads straight down into the river, dark green and shiny with water that must have covered them earlier.

'They never used to have those *Danger* signs in the old days,' Charles says, nodding towards a jetty that stands like a many-legged monster out in the river. 'They see danger everywhere now.'

I shiver, feel another wave of homesickness wash over me.

Now the sun's gone in, everything's turned grey, as if the colour has simply drained away.

I feel a keen longing for our estuary. The day I saw Ali in the rocks.

I'm knee-deep in the water, my dress slapping me around the calves.

I look up. Ali is on the natural jetty, staring at me. He catches me looking at him, and instead of smiling and waving as I'd expected, he turns away, lifts his fishing rod, a long bamboo pole, and casts it into the tide. Is he ignoring me? I'm surprised by how much it hurts. Worse than a slap in the face.

I walk up the beach, my heart aching.

I sit with Hait and Amina in the shade of the town wall, and we chat and watch the waves lick the sand. And I try to pretend I don't care.

We're about to leave, to go home to start the evening chores.

A shadow falls over me. He stands above me, his face dark, the sun behind him. The blue of his eyes like kingfishers over the river. He's holding a silver fish in his two hands, cradling it. Gives me the fish, placing it on the rock beside me. It's only just dead; its eyes are bright, the flesh still shiny.

And he walks away. Hait and Amina burst into excited giggles. 'Mona and Ali,' they sing. 'Mona and Ali.'

My heart has stopped hurting and is soaring instead.

We were teenagers by then, still young, but too old to be friends. After that look I caught him giving me, before he turned and walked away – after that was when I swore that once we'd got together, we would never part.

How could you leave me, Ali?

How did I end up here, in London, with an old man, lying for a book of stamps so that I can write home, instead of staying with you by the estuary forever? And an enormous remorse washes over me.

I turn Charles, who is nodding sleepily now, in his wheelchair, and push him slowly back to his underground home. I install him in his sitting room. Then, as he's half-asleep, I look around and find some paper, a pen. I go back up to the house.

I spend the afternoon cleaning, and don't stop until it's beginning to get dark.

I check on Charles again, make him some tea and go back up.

The TV is on in the drawing room, Leo has shut himself back in the dark.

And then, when everyone is settled and the house gleams, I go to my room and write to Leila.

Dear Leila

I am in England now.

We arrived at night and all the lights were on, orange in this street. The city all lit up, lights everywhere, filling the sky with their beams. Beautiful, but you cannot see the stars as we can at home.

Theodora, my new employer, has red hair, the colour of paprika, the colour of amber – you remember the stones I showed you in the medina? Quite beautiful, like a princess from The Arabian Nights.

London is the biggest city I've ever seen. It took us over an hour to drive from the airport to the house! On our journey here we passed some beautiful buildings, like palaces, all lit up too and lots of stone people and horses and lions.

You wouldn't believe the shops – some as long as whole streets with windows full of puppets and mannequins dressed in lovely clothes. When you come, you will see them with your own eyes.

There are trees with leaves the shape of hands that fall onto the soft black road surfaces and form a pattern as if you had done golden handprints all over the ground!

I have a room that is full of books and other piles of things I haven't had time to look through yet. As soon as I can, I will send you something. We are lucky I have found this work. It means things will get better for all of us! Look after your grandmother for me, and keep smiling until we're together again. I think of you all the time and send you all my love.

When I have charged my mobile and put credit on it, I promise I will call.

Your loving

Ummu.

How to explain that while her daddy vanished without trace, I will come home? How can I make her understand that not everyone disappears?

I hear the key in the lock and realise Dora has come home. I see myself through her eyes. The quiet housemaid, having completed her chores, taking a few minutes to herself to write home, because she cannot even afford credit on her phone.

I cover the paper with my arm because I don't want her to know I took it from the old man or that in order to send it, I needed to take her money to buy stamps.

CHAPTER ELEVEN

Daddy's in his chair, a little sleepy, when I get back from work. I'm eager to see how his first full day with Mona went.

'Daddy.' I sit down close to him, speak into his ear. His eyes flash open.

'Hello, Daddy. How are you?'

He stares at me, waiting to surface from his dreams.

'Theodora, God's precious gift,' he says, smiling. My heart warms.

'Yes – hi, Daddy. I just came down to see if you wanted anything.'

'I have everything a man could wish for. I don't want for anything, my dear. Though you might like to be a darling and bring me a whisky.'

'You had a good day with Mona?' I ask as I pour him his 'two fingers' and add a little soda, the way he likes it.

'She's a lovely girl, you know,' he says. 'An excellent cook. Generous too. She bought me clementines. And chocolate. And we bought something else . . . oh, I don't remember now . . .'

I squeeze his hand. Tell myself it's fine that he should believe she bought the fruit with her own money; it'll help them to establish a good relationship. I'll let his mistake pass this time.

I leave Daddy with his whisky and go up to the house.

It smells fresher than it's ever been when I get in. Of lemon and bleach and polish.

Even the air feels cleaner, as if it's been allowed to flow again after being shut in for a long time. I push open the door of the drawing room. There's still the faint smell in here of stale ciga-rette smoke, and Leo's on the sofa, but the debris that surrounds him after a day of TV gazing has been cleared away.

Goodness! I don't know how I stood it before! Mona has done an excellent – an amazing – job. I go over to the mantelpiece and run my finger along it. Yes, she's dusted. I didn't expect, when I employed her to look after Daddy, that I'd have the cleaning thrown in.

I peer into the kitchen. Clean and tidy. Even the quarry-tiled floor – one of the things Roger and I loved about the house when we bought it, but that had got grimy over the years – gleams. It's a beautiful kitchen. It attracted us straight away, with its built-in dresser along one wall, and its window out onto the garden at one end, onto the street and the church opposite, at the other, its Rayburn and the large table I like to sit at in the mornings. But I'd lost interest in its aesthetics recently, since Leo didn't seem to care. Mona's arranged the crockery on the dresser, placed lemons on a dish, even put some of the Chinese lanterns from the garden in a vase. It looks like something out of a magazine.

There's a light shining beneath Mona's door. She must have retreated to her room in time for my arrival, and this discretion is something I approve of too. Something Zidana was very bad at, knowing when to make herself inconspicuous.

I put the kettle on, take a piece of sliced white bread and a cheese triangle, fold the bread over it and bite. This is a secret pleasure. One I would never admit to my friends who are obsessed with the latest organic ingredients, all glued to cookery programmes in the evenings, or on diets. Give me a slice of white bread and some processed cheese, and I'm in heaven.

I go up to the bathroom. It's clear Mona has done more than a superficial clean in here, as well; she's polished the taps so they shine. She has even dealt with the limescale in the toilet bowl. How? The limescale has been defeating me for years, a rough brown scum that looks as if I've given up caring, but that has resisted all my attempts to tackle it.

Full of appreciation, I knock on her door.

She's at my bureau. Writing on a pad of Basildon Bond paper, with a Parker pen I recognise instantly as one of Daddy's.

'What are you writing?'

'A letter home.' Her hand cups the sheets of paper, as if she's afraid I'll try and read it. There's no need, it's in Arabic script, though I have to admit to being a little taken aback that she can write at all. I'd assumed that if she was literate she wouldn't have chosen domestic work.

'Mona, if you want paper, you only have to ask. You don't need to take from Daddy. He doesn't understand.'

She looks up at me through those big brown eyes. 'I must write home.'

This stirs compassion in me for the poor woman.

'You just ask me, OK? I'm not going to bite. I didn't think. You could have phoned.'

'Yes. I no have credit.'

'You should have said! You must tell your family you're OK, that you've arrived safely. You can use the house phone, this once – until you get credit. Have you any change from the ten pounds I gave you?'

She glances at me with an expression that I can't quite interpret. She hands me a few coins. It seems very little but then I remember Daddy mentioning chocolate and something else.

'Thank you,' I say. 'So you got Daddy fruit?'

'And chocolate.'

'Anything else?'

She gazes at me, fixing me with her eyes.

'No,' she says, 'nothing else.'

'Well, look.' I hand her a ten-pound note. 'Take this and get yourself some credit. It was stupid of me not to think of it. Do you know where to buy top-up here?'

She shakes her head.

'I'll get Leo to show you. I'll pay you at the end of the week. You can't go around with no money at all. And I'll give you something for my shopping too, I'll write a list. You're to go to a shop called Waitrose – I don't use the shops on the High Street.'

She smiles but doesn't say anything, and I wonder again how good her English is.

'Come on – Leo can take you to get credit now.'

Leo looks up as I put my head round the door but he doesn't move when I ask him to take Mona to the mini market up the road.

'Can't she go by herself?'

'Leo, I'm asking you to put yourself out for once. It's dark, and she's not safe walking around on her own in a strange area. Now, please. You can buy yourself something while you're there. Here.' I hand him another tenner, angry with myself for breaking my own resolution to stop indulging him. He'll only spend it on cigarettes or beer or Red Bull.

At last he gets up slowly, not taking his eyes off the screen.

I watch them walk out of the door together. I might have had to use bribery, but I've got Leo off his bottom for once.

CHAPTER TWELVE

When I hear Leila's sweet voice a wave of relief and love washes through me.

'When are you coming home, Ummu?' she asks. 'It's been a long time.'

'Darling, it hasn't been long at all. It's Thursday today, so it's only been a few days since I left.'

I know it's not to do with the number of days I've been away but how it feels to her. If I'd said I'd been gone just an hour it might feel like a year.

'You're fine without me,' I say cheerfully. 'I need you to be grown-up and look after Tetta. Are you feeding the chickens?'

'Yes.'

I can feel the pain in her chest in the ensuing silence.

'Dora's got a cat that sleeps in her house,' I say. 'She eats her dinner with the cat sitting at her table.'

More silence.

'How many chickens has she got?' Leila asks at last.

'None.'

'Is she very poor?'

'No, the opposite. Listen, let me speak to Tetta.'

My mother assures me that Leila's been fine; she's only moody with me because she wants to punish me for going away.

'What's it like there? What's the house like? The woman – is she married, has she children? Grandchildren?'

'I've written a letter. It should arrive soon.'

'What's your employer like? What's her name?'

'Theodora. Dora. Her house is a mess. You'd be shocked.'

'Is she married?'

'Not any more.'

'Shame. It's the men you can usually wrap around your little finger.'

'Ummu!'

'It's true.'

'I'm looking after her father – but he's very old.'

'Older than me?'

'Much older. And he's got Alzheimer's, he loses his memory. But Dora's too busy to care for him. She's quite famous. Her job's very important.'

'More important than her father?'

I chuckle at this veiled criticism. My mother loves to judge women who employ staff in their homes. It's pride, but it's also envy. She says they get their priorities all wrong, but for a few minutes, I wonder if what I'm doing – travelling so far from her and from Leila to earn money for them – isn't that different.

At least Dora's kept her father nearby. She's just lucky she can afford to employ me to change his underpants.

'He used to run an expensive restaurant. There are photos on his mantelpiece of him holding awards. He was handsome. It seems sad no one can see the man he once was.'

'No one can see the woman I was. That's why I cover my face.'

'That's rubbish, Ummu. You know very well you're still beautiful.'

'I would be, if I had the kind of luxuries your employers enjoy.'

I'm silent for a while. I don't like to hear my mother resentful, yet she's only voicing things I've thought myself. I'll try to send her something, something she will consider a luxury. She deserves it. She's worked hard all her life until she could work no more. And so little to show for it.

'Charles, though,' I say, to get her mind off her own disappointments, 'I'd like to put a banner on his back showing people he used to be a handsome restaurateur. However important you are, however successful you get, you can still end up invisible. All anyone sees now is an old man losing his memory, living under the ground.'

'What do you mean, under the ground?'

'He lives in an apartment, downstairs.'

She's silent for a moment. 'He has his own apartment?'

'Don't worry. I knew you wouldn't want Dora to know we share a room. She knows nothing.'

'He's lucky to have his own home, Mona.'

'But living down there I worry we won't hear if he needs us. Living all together under one roof has its benefits.'

'All together under one roof in one room, you mean.'

'You think if we had more we could live better, but there are things you lose if you have too much.'

'You lose things if you have too little as well.'

Now her self-pity is beginning to irritate me.

'OK. I know, Ummu. I'm doing what I can. It wasn't easy walking away from Leila to come here. You know that. I wouldn't have done it if there'd been any other choice.' Since Ali left, and our money ran out and there were no jobs at the garment factory where I'd worked before we married, since I'd lost my place at Madame's . . . what choice was there?

You could go further back to see how I'd ended up here; if

my father hadn't died when I was still a child, if I hadn't had to leave school at fourteen, if my mother hadn't damaged her sight providing for me, we might not be in this position now. But we are. I'm doing it for her as much as for myself.

But I know when I've said enough.

When she's said goodbye, I press the off button and put my mobile down on my bed.

I think of home, of the noise and bustle in the tiny room Ummu shares with Leila, with the people all around and the sun beating down outside, and for a few minutes I yearn to be there, however scarce the money, however bleak our futures, because there I was amongst people I love.

I slip back under my covers and hope to get some sleep.

By the end of my first week I've got into a routine. I couldn't say I'd got used to this country, but it no longer feels as strange as the day I arrived. Funny how quickly you can adapt.

On Friday morning, it's tipping down with a slanting rain, the sky barely lighter than it was at night. I go down the steps to Charles. Get him up and dressed, brew some coffee in his little kitchen.

'Is this how you make coffee?' he asks, frowning into his cup. 'So thick and full of grounds.'

'It works with the coffee we use at home,' I say, in Arabic.

I take it from him, find the thing he waves at impatiently, and do as he instructs me: 'Two spoons of coffee in the bottom. Water just off the boil. Leave it to stand for four minutes. That's how to make good coffee.'

While the coffee stands, I lead him to his chair.

'One day, Charles, I'll make you mint tea. Then you'll know what a good hot drink is. Anyway, what are we doing today? We can't go out. It's raining.'

'Oh, I don't mind the rain.'

84

'Charles! You will get wet sitting in the wheelchair. You'll get sick.'

I hand him his pills. One blue and one white. Two orange and one red. Pass him a glass of water and watch him swallow them. Then I pour his coffee.

'One heaped teaspoon of sugar, and stir for one minute. I don't have milk – coffee with milk is a sacrilege! Hmm. That's a little better. We'll soon sort you out, young lady!'

I smile. 'You are a good teacher, Charles.'

'Now you can leave me, there's a concert on the radio I'm listening to. You go and enjoy yourself.'

Enjoy myself! Does he have any idea that I've no money of my own, that I would feel lost in this huge city were I to venture beyond the market? That living alone in a foreign country where you can't read or write the language makes you feel like a small child, vulnerable, uncertain. When you don't know whom to trust, where you feel the officials are suspicious of you so that you keep to the shadows hoping not to be noticed?

I go back to the house and climb the three flights of stairs to Theodora's bedroom. Leo has not got up yet, his bedroom door is closed. I move quietly, so as not to disturb him. I pull back her curtains. The bottoms are frayed and black. The windows need some serious attention. I rest my forehead on the damp glass, look out over the churchyard opposite. Watch for a moment a woman get into a car, open the car window. She waves to a man with a baby in his arms.

It flashes into my head, unbidden. Ali lifting me, placing me down on the banquette while Leila slept in the other room, stripping everything off me in the heat of the afternoon. Pushing my hands up under his long cotton shirt, to find the soft downy skin there, the things we did to each other until we were wrung out like wet cloth. How I loved to feel his hot breath on my hair. I turn from the window, overcome by pure longing. For the house where we lived when we first moved in together, with its tiled floors that I kept swept clean, for its shuttered windows that, when thrown open, let in air that was fresh and had the sharp edge of salt on it from the sea.

I let myself float back – white walls, stark shadows, smell of fresh bread from the bakeries. I think of the black soap I used to shine pans, how they gleamed in the sunlight before I cooked in them. The pride I took in the house we shared.

For a few seconds it's soothing to remember that it existed once. The only sadness being that we didn't know it then. We didn't know how precious our two rooms would come to seem, how sweet the smell of woodsmoke. We thought then we were on the way to something else, we thought there was better to come. I was restless with dissatisfaction, with wanting more – a home in the city, soft furnishings, a bathroom with a bath and hot and cold taps. I watched the tourists carry carpets back to what I imagined to be their opulent, lavishly dressed apartments in grand palazzos lining city streets, in Seville, in Paris. And I yearned to have what they had.

Now in Theodora's house I'm learning how these very things I had once longed for are, in fact, traps for dirt. How to keep them fresh requires constant labour. And I think how the more expensive the item, the more potential for ruin it contains.

I look around the room, at her enormous bed with the embroidered quilt I noticed when I arrived. In the wardrobe, which is of walnut with carvings and a full-length mirror on the door, and whose interior smells of cedar, like the streets where the men carve the latticework, I let my fingers rifle through Theodora's clothes. Satin and velvet dresses, wool coats, soft cashmere sweaters and scarves.

Dora dresses well even if she doesn't look after her house. In her drawers I find silk underwear, stockings, camisoles. The expensive fabrics feel cool upon my palms. On her dressing-table are pots and bottles, pomades and vials. Bottles of perfume with logos I've seen on advertising hoardings. I put my nose to each and smell, drawing in the expensive, delicate fragrances, the waft of privilege.

Dora has more than she knows what to do with. There's a beautiful tortoiseshell fan, a clip holding it tightly bound together, that I long to release, to hold up, like the Spanish women who came to dance in the square, in the good old days.

I lean on the dressing-table. The mirror's in three parts, my face reflected back many times, in profile.

I'm shocked to see how tired I look, how aged. The last few months have told on me, Ali leaving, the trouble at Madame's. The worry about work. The knowing how, without it, we would sink from scraping by to abject poverty. The realisation that my mother and my daughter's welfare rested entirely on my shoulders. Then the travelling and the anxiety about what I was coming to.

I should take more care of myself. If Dora wants me to work hard, then I deserve the odd treat. I dip my finger in Dora's moisturiser; it looks expensive, in a proper glass jar instead of a plastic pot, and I massage it into my cheeks, watch them grow soft, breathe in the fragrance of some kind of flower.

I peer more closely. Somewhere, in the contours of my cheeks, in my eyes, I can see Leila, and this soothes me. In my mouth, I can see my mother.

I think of Ummu, how Ali and I had planned that when he was earning good money, when he had qualified as a doctor, we would bring her into the house on the estuary, to live with us. How everything has happened the wrong way round. How Leila and I had to go back to live with Ummu in her one room, and were worse off than when we first made our lives in the little white house. How far I've travelled from the days when Ali and I first lived together, with all our plans before us. And the full weight of it hits me, that if I *had* appreciated what we had, if I hadn't urged Ali to study hard, to aim high, we might still be where we were at our happiest.

Dora has so much – a whole drawer here of tiny tubes and bottles and vials. And Ummu sounded so down on the phone, talking about being old and having to cover her face. I'd like to send her something to show her she too is a beautiful woman, with a body that deserves a little treat from time to time. I pick up one of the small tubes of cream Dora has put in the dish, one that hasn't been opened, smell it, and put it back.

I'm about to leave when I notice the photo I spotted next to Dora's bed when she first showed me her room. I look at it. The man is white and tall, quite handsome, with a small neat beard, smiling, his arm round Dora. They're standing in front of a building with a statue on the top of it, a naked woman draped only in a headscarf. I cannot read the caption underneath, but I can read the date. This summer.

So Dora *does* have a man!

I'll tell Ummu the gossip next time I speak to her. I can already hear her words: 'I expect he must have offered her something Roger didn't!'

I'm startled then by a rustle outside the door. I put Dora's photo down, my heart thudding, and turn. There's the thump of feet on stairs, the banging of a door. I'd forgotten about Leo. He's up. I hear running water, the clank of the pipes.

I pick up my dusting cloths, pull on the rubber gloves and open the door. I'll slip downstairs before he comes out of the bathroom.

I'm about to leave, when temptation gets the better of me, and I nip back to Dora's dressing-table. She won't miss one tiny tube of hand cream, but for Ummu, it will be like gold dust.

CHAPTER THIRTEEN

By the end of Mona's second week my anxiety about leaving Daddy with her has vanished. Daddy's cared for. Leo's content. My house is clean.

And I no longer have to hurry straight home from the office to check on them all.

On Friday after work Gina and I put on our coats and make for the George and Dragon as we used to do in the days before Mummy fell ill and Daddy came to live with me.

We find a seat by the fire.

'How's it going with this carer?' Gina asks.

'She's a godsend. I don't know how I managed without help for so long.'

'It's done you a lot of good. You look great.'

'Really?'

'Yes. You were looking awful a while ago. There's a marked difference.'

Blimey, I had no idea how haggard I must have appeared.

'But Dora, it isn't surprising. You've been bereaved.'

'Oh come on, Gina, that was a year ago.'

'Yes, but we're so crap at death in this country. We expect

people to get back to normal straight away, which probably means the whole process is far harder in the long run. Mary was telling me that in Nigeria, they give people forty days to get over a death in the family. They expect people to withdraw to grieve. Here we have to go straight back to work.'

I smile, pat Gina's shoulder. 'It has been tough, you're right,' I say. 'Mummy's death was difficult, but caring for Daddy's been hardest.'

'Can't your brothers and sister have him from time to time – give you a break?'

'To be honest, Gina, it's more trouble than it's worth asking them. They don't know him like I do. Anita and Terence are too selfish to put themselves out and Simon's a dead loss. Anyway, now I've got Mona, everything's going to be a lot easier.'

'But where does she sleep, now you've got Leo and Daddy in the house as well?'

'She has the spare bedroom.'

'The one next to you?'

I nod. Later, I'll wonder why I told this small white lie. Right now it comes out so easily, I'm barely aware I'm doing it.

'Lucky her. I forget you've got all that space. I wouldn't have room for a live-in help even if I could afford it. You know, I'm so relieved to see you,' Gina says. 'I need to tell you my problems – if you can bear it. I've been longing to talk to you. The bastard's getting married.'

'Oh, Gina!'

'I wouldn't mind, but the girls are bloody thrilled. They say it means they'll be getting presents from Tiffany's – she's rolling in it, Dora. How can I compete?'

'You can't,' I say. 'Not financially. But for Christ's sake, you're their mother. You don't have to compete. All that bling is worthless next to your love. Look at Leo. He had the life of Riley with Roger, but he came home to me.'

The minute I've said this, I wish I hadn't. Leo may have 'come home to me' but he certainly hasn't come home intact. I can see what she's thinking. Leo's hardly the best example. And I've glossed over the truth. Leo didn't 'come back to me' willingly. Given a choice, he would have stayed in Morocco at his international school, sailing and playing tennis. He came because he had no choice, once Roger insisted on an English sixth form.

And now there he is in front of the TV. Withdrawn and depressed. I almost preferred it when he was getting into trouble dealing drugs. At least he was out there, doing something.

I stare into my glass. It's so bloody hard getting it right. Roger and I both thought that Leo would slot into life in London – a golden boy, returned from abroad, smiling and healthy and glowing with the kind of confidence we'd believed his education had given him. That he would attract friends and admirers. I'd thought we would go out together, mother and son, enjoying London's galleries and concerts.

I never imagined he'd become this depressed recluse. Uninterested in anything that isn't on a screen. Pale and grouchy and monosyllabic.

How differently things turn out to what you plan.

Gina toys with her glass.

'What I'm saying,' I go on, 'is that nothing can replace the mother-daughter bond. This, what's-her-name, she's got novelty appeal at the moment. But will she be there when the girls go through heartbreak? When they need a cup of tea and a shoulder to cry on? Does she love them unconditionally? I think not.'

'I hope you're right,' Gina says. 'Because it feels awful. Him with that woman, the girls all starry-eyed about her too. And me all alone.'

'I'm sure it does. But, honey, it won't last, I promise. *You're* their mother. How's the dating agency going?'

'Oh. Well. There's one possibility. I'm meeting him next week. But to be honest I don't hold out much hope. What are the chances of meeting your soulmate through the bloody internet?'

'You never know!'

I take a slug of martini. It's lukewarm and is missing the requisite sliver of orange zest. It makes me miss Max. He would never stand for lukewarm martini.

I'm doing well though. So far, I've avoided referring to my lover.

Gina disapproves of my affair because Max is married; her sympathies lie with Max's wife. She thinks she knows how Max's wife would feel if she found out about me, because Gina's been through it herself. The difference is Max isn't leaving his wife for me. But Gina remains convinced I'm in the wrong. She thinks I should get out of Max's life, give his marriage some breathing space.

She has no idea how impossible this would be for me. And she doesn't understand that his marriage, I have grown to suspect, survives because of, not in spite of me.

'Don't remind me,' Gina says. 'You met Max at the Albert Memorial waiting for Roger.'

'I wasn't going to—'

'It sounds as if I'm criticising you. But you know, I still find the whole thing with you and the married man problematic.'

'Actually, I've hardly seen Max lately.'

I suddenly feel as if I might cry.

This has happened to me a lot since Mummy died. It washes over me, almost without warning, a need to shed all the pain I didn't even know I was carrying. If I could unpick it, I'd say it was losing Mummy, seeing Daddy change, and missing Max, but it isn't just that. It's something else. Something to do with the strain of keeping it all together. Doing the right thing at work and home sometimes feels too much – I'm afraid one day everything I'm holding up will collapse on top of me. It's only the thought of Mona, the way she's come to take care of things, that affords me a little comfort.

I stare at Gina, blinking back tears.

'Don't take offence,' she pleads.

'Why bring Max up? You know we always fall out when he comes into the conversation.'

'I just thought . . .'

'Perhaps you should try not to think then!' I say, before I can stop myself.

'Dora. I care about you. I don't want to see you hurt. I don't want to see you losing your—'

I pull my coat on, wrap my scarf round twice. It's going to be cold when I get outside.

'Bye. See you tomorrow.'

I leave the pub, distraught. Not just because of Gina's comments, but the reminder that I haven't seen Max for so long. When *will* I see him next? Is Gina right on a certain level? Am I bound to be hurt?

Sometimes his absences seem to balloon, so that I begin to doubt he actually exists, I certainly begin to doubt I'll ever hear from him again.

He's reassured me that when things go quiet it's because he's bogged down with work, or embroiled in his family, but still I find the silences intolerable. Now I've got Mona it's ironic that time I could be spending with him is already slipping by.

I walk home, feeling alone and betrayed.

But five minutes after I've left, the regret sets in that I'd over-reacted. Gina *is* my friend, she's concerned for me.

As I would be for her if she was in love with a married man who is never, ever – however much I carry a secret hope – going to leave his wife and children for me.

CHAPTER FOURTEEN

It's past Daddy's usual bedtime when I get back from my drink with Gina but I go down to see him as soon as I'm home.

It's a beautiful night, cold, cloudless. If it wasn't for the London lights the stars would be visible on a night like this. Strange that they're there, in all their myriad glory, scattered across the universe – but we just can't see them.

I stop. The bust of Mummy I've placed at the top of the basement steps so Daddy can see it when he comes up, or when he looks out of his bedroom window, is silhouetted against the amber light that veils the London night sky.

I knew, and accepted, that Anita and Simon would snaffle the valuables, when we first began to sort the family home. They were the only ones who cared enough about anything's worth. Terence took practical stuff – lawnmowers and power tools and so forth. And, since I knew I wouldn't have room for the large pieces of furniture that Anita had mentioned again recently, I went for things that had sentimental value. Anita had been too young to know the significance of some of these things, so I felt no compunction in taking an old warming pan, a set of silver cutlery with bone-handles in a polished wooden chest. Bales of embroidered linen tablecloths and mats. And things that held special meaning for me. One of these was this stone sculpture, a bust of my mother. It had sat on the rockery in our back garden since I was five or six, and I wanted it now in my own garden, to remind me of how she was when she was at her most beautiful.

I never enquired who the sculptor was, and Daddy's memory was too unreliable now. So it was too late. Whatever, the bust was a work of art. Particular attention had been given to my mother's cheekbones and eyes, and I could see now that the sculptor must certainly have admired her.

Each time I see the sculpture, I'm reminded of how our family was before Mummy died. Mummy held the family together, ringing each of us in turn, communicating any news so we would then pass it on to one another. There was no conflict, no resentment. I often wondered what Mummy would think if she could have seen Anita and Simon and Terence in those weeks after the funeral, squabbling over who had it toughest, at each other's throats about what to do with Daddy.

When our mother was very ill, in her last few days, I assured her Daddy would stay with me until we found something more permanent. I believe sometimes it was what had allowed her to die in peace. I'd done the right thing – for her and for Daddy, and I know she would have expected no less from me. I think again of what Anita said, about Mummy being controlling, and it occurs to me that we're never sure what the truth is in a family.

Things that have been staring at me all my life have, I realise, started to take on a different meaning as I look at them with a new, more mature perspective. The statue had been something that was just there, in the background. Now I wondered what stories it might tell if it could speak.

As Mona emerges from Daddy's back door, and climbs the steps towards me, there's an odd moment where the head of my mother, and that of Mona, are juxtaposed. I feel this is significant.

Perhaps Mona has come to replace, in some symbolic way, the things Mummy stood for. Perhaps she would enable us all to find the goodness within again.

'Is everything all right?' I ask her. 'How did you get on today?'

She nods, smiles. 'Very well, thank you. Did you see I cooked for you? For Leo and Charles.'

'Thank you. I'm just popping down to see Daddy, then we'll have a chat in the kitchen.'

Daddy's sitting in bed in clean pyjamas, listening to *Book at Bedtime* on Radio 4.

He smiles up at me, holds out his hand and squeezes mine.

'You've had a good day, Daddy?'

'Yes, thank you very much. Very good.' His polite tone is disconcerting. Does he know who I am?

'You got on all right with Mona?'

'Oh yes. We bought Mummy a birthday present. I asked Nancy . . .'

'Mona.'

'Yes, the girl.'

'Woman.'

'I asked her to help me choose Mummy some flowers. And a vase to put them in. She says she'll take them to her in the hospital.'

Sometimes it's as if he's losing his memory in tiny steps, incrementally, but this, this believing Mummy is still with us reveals a massive gap in his recall – a catastrophic one. It means he has to go through the grief of losing Mummy all over again. But I can't have him living with delusions. He has to know how things are, or his whole world will disintegrate.

'Daddy,' I say. 'Mummy's dead.'

He looks at me for some time, bewilderment furrowing his brow, before a tear trickles down his cheek.

'Do you know, I completely forgot,' he says.

I squeeze his old hand.

'She died a year ago, Daddy. We had a funeral. Remember?'

'Yes, yes. Of course I remember. Where's Mona, that lovely girl who bought the roses?'

'I'll send her down.'

My chest hurts as I climb the stairs, and I'm not even sure whether it's due to witnessing Daddy's grief, or feeling a different kind of my own.

Mona's at the cooker, stirring.

'Won't you have some yourself?' I ask.

She shakes her head. 'I ate with Charles.'

'He wants you again. He needs settling down for the night. Then you can come and sit with me for a bit.'

'Yes. Very well.'

She comes back in as I'm helping myself to some of the dish she's made. A lamb tagine. I try to remember if I'd asked her to buy lamb.

'Daddy says you bought my mother a birthday present.'

She smiles, moves across to the sink to wash the pans.

'Oh yes. He said it was your mummy's birthday. So we bought flowers for her.'

'But she's dead,' I say.

'I know. But it made him happy. I wanted to make him happy. This is good, I think. To believe for a few hours, that his wife is alive. He enjoyed buying the beautiful roses.'

Mona may well be right, it might be kinder to go along with Daddy's happy memories. Perhaps I'm wrong to jolt him back to reality.

'And Leo was polite?'

'Yes. I told him to go upstairs. I said he cannot stay all day in his pyjamas.'

'You know, Mona, it might seem that I put up with a lot from him. But I want him to feel at home here, that he can do as he likes.'

I pour myself a glass of wine. Mona's being here is softening the terrible things I've been dealing with. Leo's depression, Daddy's Alzheimer's, the loss of Mummy. Here I am, a meal made for me, my disaffected son doing something more useful than his usual indolent TV-watching, and Mona to look after me, to keep an attentive eye on Daddy. I let my remorse about the argument with Gina fade.

'Tell me about your family.'

She shrinks back a little.

'Didn't you tell me you have a daughter?' I ask.

'One daughter,' she says. 'Six years old.'

I see her face plump out with happiness at the thought of her child.

'Where is she?'

'She's at home. In my mother's village.'

'But who is looking after her?'

'My mother.'

'Gosh. Don't you miss her?'

She looks at me blankly, her mouth turned down at the corners. Of course she misses her – stupid of me to ask.

'What happened, Mona? What happened to your husband?'

She turns her head aside. I've trodden on sensitive ground again. How silly of me.

'I'm sorry. That must be painful. Tell me about your daughter?'

She smiles now. She starts to speak, her hands dancing as she does so, emphasising each word in a kind of mime.

'She's six years old. She's funny, she loves the colour pink. She loves to dress as grown-up, and to play at houses. But where I live, there's no money, no work. It costs a lot for her to go to school, for books and clothes. I want to make a future for Leila. And she's OK with my mother.'

I look at Mona, re-jigging the perceptions I have of her. If her daughter is only six, then perhaps she isn't my age at all, but younger – quite a lot younger. I notice now that her skin is indeed quite smooth, that the fatigue that had aged her when she arrived has lifted a little. Like tarnished silver after it's been polished.

'It's hard being away from a child. When my marriage ended and I came back to London, Leo stayed with his father and I was heartbroken. It was like . . . it's like having a bit of your body torn from you. But he was at school out there and was settled and I didn't want to disrupt him. It's so wonderful that he wanted to come back for sixth form.'

The food is delicious. I take another mouthful, another glug of the red wine I've poured.

After I've eaten, I tell Mona to check on Daddy and then to take some time off. When she's gone I fill up my glass – I'm going to take some wine up to drink in the bath – and as I'm about to go up, I glance into Mona's room. She's left the door ajar, the lamp on. On the antique bureau is a vase of roses. They are pink roses, in bud, in my tall glass vase.

The roses Daddy bought for Mummy.

CHAPTER FIFTEEN

I let the rose incident pass. I need Mona too badly to make an issue of minor transgressions.

The following Saturday I take advantage of her. I go to the gym, have my hair done, walk back along the river. It's one of those crisp autumn mornings with a bright, low sun. I feel as if Mummy is very close to me, maybe walking along beside me as I head home.

Feeling her presence, sensing that death has not torn her away from me but that she lies very close on the other side of an imperceptible membrane tensile as the cobwebs that veiled my walls – until Mona arrived – soothes me.

The tide's out. I can hear people with children down on the beach, hunting along the tideline, and pleasure boats pootling about on the water purring gently and sending waves rippling across to lap the shore. I breathe deeply, drawing in the silty smell.

As I walk, my mobile pings and my heart leaps. I barely dare to look. To see if it's Max. It's only 7 a.m. in New York. But maybe he's not in New York – maybe he's here.

Hi gorgeous, I'm coming through London on Wednesday. Meet me under Boudicca, Westminster Bridge, 5 p.m.

I text back immediately, telling him I'm free. Free! I have Mona! I can accept an invitation from my lover with no hesitation for the first time in months.

I feel good. Cleansed inside and out. From the gym, from the hair-do. And from the release of the anxiety that hounds me until I hear from Max.

You could almost be at the seaside here, if you shut your eyes. I enjoy the warmth of the sun on my face, the rattle of the waves on the shore, the mewl of the seagulls. Yet the view itself has its own beauty, the black spikes on the railings echoing the spires of an old church on the other side of the river, which itself reflects in miniature the Gherkin. The towering blocks of the City's Square Mile dwarf old rooftops and chimneys beneath. Layers of London history. The masts of a galleon that has moored a little way downriver are like a marvellous apparition from the past. I feel relaxed and at peace. I walk, rounding bends and taking short cuts between new buildings, following the river walk beneath its cranes and round its creeks and marinas.

At Paynes Wharf, I stand and admire the majestic arches of the old shipbuilders' palace, which frame and contain the sleek skyscrapers on the other side of the river on Canary Wharf. I find the image interesting, the bigger contained within the smaller. Here I am, like the arches, small yet able to contain all this within my vision.

Theodora Gentleman, counsellor to the whole of south-east England.

A woman in mid-life, still able to summon a lover all the way from the States. Daddy's 'gift from god', caring for him when no one else in my family is prepared to.

By the time I get home my face tingles with the cold morning air, and as I open the front door, I'm greeted by a scent that takes me straight back to Daddy's restaurant. The waft of spices, cumin, coriander, paprika.

I stand in the hallway, for once clear of shoes, which Mona has organised onto shelves. Clear of junk mail, and of Leo's discarded clothes that are usually draped over the banisters and across the floor. I remember how when a house is fresh and aired it also feels calmer, and I breathe in the tantalising North African aroma and a warmer, cosier scent of fresh yeast coming from the kitchen. I move down my hallway towards the end, push open the door.

Mona's squatting on the kitchen floor, a floured board in front of her, kneading dough. I stare at her. It's a vision of perfect domesticity and I'm overcome by a sense of appreciation and goodwill – of being looked after. As if my mother had risen from the grave. Not that she had made a loaf of bread in her life, certainly she'd never squatted on the floor like this to bake. But seeing Mona there, lit up by a ray of sun sliding in from the window, gives me a feeling of contentment I haven't experienced for a long time. The scene is like a Dutch painting, a glimpse through the door of a quiet private moment of feminine labour.

'It smells fabulous in here,' I say.

I move into the kitchen, aware that I'm not needed, that Mona is happy here on her own. A fleeting sense that I'm in the way in my own home passes through my mind and away again.

Mona glances at me and smiles before looking back down as if embarrassed.

'I've cooked lunch for you all. Charles and Leo and you. A national dish – I haven't made for a long time. This is our special bread. And I'm making something piquant. Leo likes spicy food.'

'That's lovely, thank you, Mona.' Does she think I don't know that Leo likes spicy food? 'I look forward to it,' I say, taking off my scarf.

'Your hair, it looks nice,' she says.

'Thank you. I've been to the hairdresser's.'

'Very good, very fine,' she says. 'In my country, we don't have this style, we find it very beautiful, like something precious.' She smiles, her fingers dancing in a rippling motion around her head.

'What, curly hair?'

'Yes, like you. And people try to make your colour. With henna. But it's difficult, with our hair.' She pulls a face.

I smile at her. 'Don't be silly, Mona, your hair is beautiful too. Oh, and I bought cupcakes. So we are both thinking of our stomachs today!' I pat mine, and she laughs. 'I got them from Borough Market.'

'Another market?'

'Yes, much nicer. Up the river.'

'I'd like to see.'

'I'll show you.'

We're interrupted by the doorbell. Anita and Simon are on the steps.

'We thought we'd come and see Daddy,' says Anita. 'Wondered if we could scrounge a coffee first. Blimey, it smells fab in here. What are you cooking?'

'It's Mona,' I say. 'Something Moroccan.'

They follow me down to the kitchen.

'We thought we could take Dad out for lunch,' Simon says. He's wearing a beanie, his headphones strung round his neck. Simon's in his thirties but still resembles an errant schoolboy.

'You're a bit late,' I tell him. 'Mona's just made Daddy's lunch, haven't you, Mona?'

Mona nods, lifts the tray she's laid for Daddy and carries it out of the kitchen.

It's typical that my brother and sister's good intentions are mistimed.

'We were going to take him up to the Mayflower. They serve most of the afternoon, I think,' says Simon.

'It's not the pub that's the problem,' I say. 'It's Daddy. He has to eat at twelve so he can sleep after lunch. Anyway, who would drive him? I'm the only one with a car here.'

'We could catch the bus.'

'Have you tried getting Daddy on and off a bus recently?'

'Dora, we just want to help out a bit,' Anita says. 'I've roped Richard in specially. He's taken the kids to his mum's this afternoon. You never let us help. You haven't changed! It's like when we were kids and you always had to be the best, the favourite.'

'You can't spring surprises on Daddy. He's only just got used to Mona. A change of routine would throw him completely.'

'Oh well, it's been a wasted journey then,' says Anita. 'Typical.'

'Mona looks nice,' Simon says. 'Kind of maternal. Reliable.'

'Terence says we should all contribute to her pay,' Anita says. 'He says we could dip into Daddy's savings. It isn't fair that you should shoulder the whole bill.'

'Oh, that's a turn-up – Terence thinking of someone else for once!'

'He wants to help, Dora. We all do. He's our father too. No one would be expected to pay for his care costs as well as having him downstairs. Even if you're getting the benefit of a clean house thrown in!'

'It isn't just the cost that's a drain.' I feel the old resentment course through me – my sister has no idea! 'There's the space Mona takes up in my home. Keeping an eye on her. Live-in carers have to be watched. You can't just trust them and leave them to get on with it.'

'Blimey, Dora, you're impossible to please,' says my sister.

'Oh come on, you two,' says Simon. 'Enough sparring.'

'I'll accept graciously then,' I say.

'So it's all going OK?' Anita asks. 'With her, I mean?'

'It's going fine so far,' I say. 'She reminds me of someone. Someone to do with Daddy's restaurant maybe. One of his waitresses?'

'God, we worked so hard in those days,' Anita says. 'In his restaurant. All that ridiculous stuff he made us do, getting the most slices out of a tomato, the most batons from a carrot!'

We sit silently, remembering Daddy's mood swings when he was at work, how we'd all try our best to stay on the right side of him. I worked twice as hard as anyone else, yearning for Daddy's praise, to show everyone I was his favourite. One or two staff members bullied me behind his back, calling me a sneak, a Daddy's girl.

I should have learned then that being favoured could evoke resentment. I suspected this was behind Anita's snide comments about me as a child.

'Which waitress does she remind you of?' Anita asks.

'I don't know. I keep trying to think . . . it won't come back to me.'

'Right,' says Simon suddenly, jumping up. 'I'm going down to see him. Laters, Dor.'

When he's gone I say, 'I'm sorry, Anita. It's just that having Mona isn't all a breeze. I worry she looks down on me. The house, I mean. She was working for a Saudi in Morocco, and those ex-pat houses were palatial. You remember Roger's? Chequered hallways, marble work surfaces, all those bloody leather sofas. It's different here.'

'Don't be silly,' Anita says. 'Women like her are not in any position to judge. Anyway, you live in one of south-east London's most desirable streets.'

Anita knows I'm sensitive about where I live. I have a theory about London. That the affluent reside on its hills: Highgate Hill, Notting Hill, Primrose Hill. At the base of these salubrious areas are the places where drug abuse, gang culture and prostitution reign: Tottenham, Archway, Wood Green.

Deptford.

She says I'm out of touch, that these are the very areas being snapped up by young professionals. But when you've grown up on one of London's hills, in a large house in Blackheath, moving down is belittling. I'm the only one of us who's ended up in a trough. Terence lives in a detached house on Dartmouth Hill. Anita and her banker husband Richard, in Muswell Hill. Simon is itinerant, but will no doubt wriggle his way into some wealthy woman's home in Hampstead or Highgate eventually.

I've ended up in a house in one of London's dank river basins, where 1970s council blocks dominate and the High Street's a magnet for deviance and vagrancy. Roger and I bought the house, believing our street, with its beautiful terrace of Georgian ship-merchants' houses, would go upmarket.

Which it has, in a way. It's the location that hasn't.

'Anyway, does she know you are "the Voice of the South-East"?' Anita asks. 'She must respect that.'

My sister's right. People don't come across the world to do domestic work for fun. And this house, that Roger and I bought as a bolt-hole when we first went abroad, may not be as big as our Moroccan residencies, or as luxurious, but it's beautiful, and elegant enough in its own way. Mona is desperate, appreciates the work I'm giving her.

I'm about to ask Anita what she thinks of Mona buying the roses, when Mona herself comes back in, closely followed by Simon.

'That was a waste of time,' says Simon. 'He refused to look at me. Only had eyes for Mona. He's certainly taken to you,' he tells her, and Mona inclines her head shyly.

'OK – well, I'm going to see him now,' Anita decides. 'He's finished his lunch now, has he, Mona?'

Mona looks at Anita, her eyes travelling up and down, taking in her fashionable wool skirt, her cashmere cardi and her expensive boots.

'Your daddy needs to sleep now. He'll be ready to see you in one hour.'

Anita glances at me as if to say, 'Blimey, she's feisty!'

And I feel a kind of loyalty towards Mona. My brother and sister can't even get here at the right time to take their father out, while Mona has cooked for him, cleaned up, taken him to the loo and given him his medication.

'I tell you what,' I say. 'You and Simon can spend the afternoon with Daddy when he's had his sleep. Mona hasn't had any time off yet. We'll go for a little walk, Mona, and I'll show you the river.'

'Fine,' says Anita, exchanging a glance with Simon as if it isn't really fine at all, but knowing now that they have no choice.

CHAPTER SIXTEEN

'Do you know, Mona,' I say, as we go past the houses with their figureheads above the doorways, 'this street is very historic. The houses were once owned by shipbuilders.'

She nods but doesn't speak.

'One of them, at the other end, I think, was a girls' club, set up by a local woman to help the "Gut Girls". They were called Gut Girls because they worked with meat. There used to be a cattle market on the High Street, and those poor girls had to slaughter the animals. They slaved away from dawn 'til dusk, hacking beasts to pieces with meat cleavers. Wrenching bones apart. Can you imagine it? It was hellish. Cold, dirty, smelly and gruesome. Imagine how it must have sounded – cows moaning as they died. The crunch of breaking bones. Not a girl's work.'

'No.'

'But of course girls were cheap labour, could be exploited. Anyway, one day, a kind woman, seeing how terrible their lives were, set up a special school in this street to teach these Gut Girls laundry, cooking, and housework. She raised them out of the depths of squalor. Gave them a future.'

I'm aware as I talk of the parallel in what I'm doing now, for

Mona, employing her to do my laundry, the cooking and house-work, to raise her out of whatever depths of squalor she had to tolerate in Morocco.

The city's a closed fan, I want to tell her, its layers of history hidden one behind the other. I often like to imagine the scenes witnessed by the little statues above the doorways – acts of folly and deviance, murders and rapes, dealings and exploitations. I glance at Mona, wondering if she understands the little history lesson I'm giving her, but her face remains impassive.

'We'll take a bus to Rotherhithe and go for a walk along Paradise Street,' I suggest. 'There's a nice view of the river along there.'

The afternoon's already darkening by the time we arrive in Rotherhithe. The tide's up now and the water moves against the wall just a couple of feet beneath us. We find a bench and sit down. I point out Tower Bridge, looming through the dusk as its lights come on, and explain to Mona how it parts in the middle and lifts to allow tall ships to pass.

I unwrap and hand her one of the cupcakes I bought from the market. As we sit and nibble our cakes, two mothers, side by side, I think that everything is getting better again because Mona has come!

Mona and I can help each other out. We're like two towers of the bridge, one essential to the other. Like my mother and I when we used to fold the sheets, when I was a child, something I loved to do with her, holding the corners between us before moving together to fold them. Apart again, and together until we had a compact bundle to put into the airing cupboard.

'You are happy today,' Mona says suddenly.

'Oh?'

'Yes. Today you look a young woman.'

I'm dying to tell someone about my text from Max. I can't

110

mention my lover to my best friend Gina! It's torture to me.

That's when I find myself telling my new maid all about him. One of the sides of my nature, that Daddy used to point out in the old days, is that I'm too trusting.

In retrospect you can see the point at which you should have stopped. But in the fading light of this autumn's afternoon, I feel I've not just employed a carer for my father, and a cleaner and housekeeper for myself, but a confidante too.

And I begin to speak.

CHAPTER SEVENTEEN

'I'm happy because I'm meeting my man next week. I haven't seen him for ages.'

'I didn't know you had a boyfriend.'

I look at her to see if she's acting dumb. Leo said he'd seen her looking at the photo of Max in my room. She must realise there's a man in my life. But she's gazing out over the river, no guile in her face.

'Yes, I do.'

'But I've been here three weeks. I haven't seen this man.'

'No. Well, he lives in the States.'

'Then – when do you see him?'

'When he has time to come here.'

She looks at me, turning her lips down. 'You wait till he has time?'

'I have to, Mona. No choice.'

'You met him in the USA? Or in London?'

'Oh, it was extraordinary how we met. At the Albert Memorial.'

'Albert Memorial?'

'You'll see it, one day. I'll show you. It's in Hyde Park, opposite the Albert Hall. I was waiting for my husband – you know – Roger. We were due to be at a Prom in a few minutes' time.'

'Prom?'

'Promenade concert, classical music, at the Albert Hall. You can stand and listen, or walk around – "promenade" – unless you have seats. You'll see, one day . . .'

'I'd like to.'

'I was looking at the memorial, thinking about the love Queen Victoria felt for Albert. She had it built when he died. She was devastated. Mourned for years . . .'

I stop. Glance at Mona, remember she, too, is a widow and realise with remorse that I have trodden upon sensitive ground again. I move on.

'All along the steps, there were people in love, cuddling, kissing. I wondered whether I'd missed out on something. I had never felt this passion for Roger. It was a shock to me to realise. But you know,' I turn to Mona, to emphasise the feeling behind the words I'm about to say, 'it's almost as painful to realise you don't love someone as it is to learn they don't love you.'

'You were married to him.'

'Yes. But it hit me then. Or maybe not even then. Perhaps . . . my memory is muddled. Perhaps it was after Max appeared that I knew our marriage had been an illusion.'

'Illusion?'

'A lie. Oh, Roger was from the right background. My parents loved him and I wanted to please them. But that evening, on the steps, for the first time I faced the truth. I had married Roger, for Daddy.'

I pause for a moment, letting words I've never said sink in.

'I wanted Daddy – Charles – to approve of the man to whom he gave me away. I was Daddy's gift, you see, Mona – he always called me that, "God's gift" – Theodora.' I pat the chain round my neck. 'It's why I wear this. He bought it for me when I was born. I was always the closest to him.'

'It's very beautiful. Is it real gold?'

'Oh yes. Daddy would never have bought fake. It's eighteen carat.'

'Precious.'

'Yes. Anyway. I owed it to him to marry someone he liked and approved of. That's what I thought.'

'It's important your family are happy with your husband. I think this is good,' Mona says.

'Yes, maybe. But it's not the only reason to marry! Roger was wrong for me. He didn't want a woman with a mind of her own and a career! He wanted the sort of wife who enjoys entertaining and making the house beautiful. I was bored living out there with him, bored and frustrated.'

Mona frowns.

'Sorry. I'm talking too fast. It was as though ... I became invisible when I was with him. After I had Leo, I was content for a while. I felt such intense love for my son it enabled me to tolerate everything else. But once Leo started school I knew it wasn't the life for me.'

There's a silence after this and I wonder what Mona's thinking. I'm hardly concerned. She is an earpiece, nothing more, someone impartial who can't possibly have any real influence or impact on my life. I don't even know how much she understands, I'm simply relieved to talk.

So I go on.

'Admitting I'd never loved him was terrible. It meant either putting up with it, or acting on it. And I didn't want to break up my marriage or tear Leo from the heart of his home. But then we returned to London for a few months. The BBC begged me to come back to work with them. I wanted to desperately, but knew Roger wouldn't have it. It was while we were living back here, the day at the Proms, that I met Max. He had a week off to sightsee. He was looking for the Serpentine Gallery, he said. Was he anywhere near, did I know? Of course I knew! I knew the artist exhibiting there too, someone I loved – Chris Offili. I waved my arm in the right direction across the park, proud to be at home here, that I was a Londoner. "I guess you're local?" he said. He was a doctor – a professor, in fact, over from the States for some conference. He had been to London before, but never alone, never with this time on his hands.'

I've lost Mona now, I can see. She has a glazed look in her eyes, is thinking of something else. She probably doesn't understand half what I'm saying.

'He was handsome, tall with a beard . . .'

'Ali had a beard,' says Mona.

I barely hear her, I'm so engrossed in my tale, in reminiscing. Max's voice was deep and breathy – as if he had just finished making love and was preparing for a cigarette. I found it sexy immediately, wanted to sit and listen to him all afternoon. I almost wished Roger would never come back from wherever he'd gone. The power of the voice! How we underestimate it.

I never thought I'd go for a man with a beard either, but on Max it was another thing that attracted me to him. A neat goatee that sprinkled his chin, greying, flecked, ginger hairs mixed in with black. Like Endymion, my cat, whose three colours are mingled. It was neatly trimmed and, before I could help it, I found myself imagining the texture of it against my skin.

I explained that London had many hearts from which its inhabitants sort of fan out, and from which the energy pulses; that the Albert Memorial was one of those hearts. He looked as if he found me amusing. I recall our conversation.

'You have to be careful,' I said. 'There are impostors. Places you might imagine were crucial to the city that aren't.'

'Fake hearts?'

'Yes. Pacemakers!'

He laughed. 'London's quite a riddle then? I certainly find it hard to navigate. No blocks. It's a maze.'

'Would you like me to show you?' I asked him before I knew what I was doing.

I was overcome by pride in the city I loved. The attraction I felt for Max was instant and so powerful I was practically knocked sideways. My unconscious knew it before I did. I was ensuring we would meet again, before I'd told myself what was happening. I, too, had a week off. Now I knew I was going to spend it with him.

Later, in my fanciful state I imagined that Queen Victoria's feelings for Albert had somehow transmitted themselves to Max and me. That we were caught in its metaphysical force. Before Roger returned, I had arranged to take Max to an exhibition at the Hayward Gallery the next day. And we'd exchanged mobile numbers. I had already, even before Roger and I crossed Kensington Gore to the Prom we were about to attend, fallen in love with him.

Later, when Max had gone back to the States, and I to Morocco, he started to send me photos of the statues he thought we should meet beside whenever we were both in London. We'd met first by Albert's statue, so he wanted it to become our thing.

Max tried to find erotic ones – the naked bronze of Psyche on Chelsea Bridge. Achilles at Hyde Park Corner, wearing nothing but his little fig leaf. Then the stone mermaids on one of the pediments over the eastern entrance to Victoria Station, and the lady wearing nothing but a headscarf draped seductively around her, atop the Palace Theatre in Cambridge Circus – a sexy vision that I would never have noticed were it not for Max, opening my eyes to the secrets of my own city.

When we ran out of erotic statues we moved on. We met at Nelson's Column one night, of course, and on another occasion squished ourselves between Roosevelt and Churchill in Bond Street. We kissed passionately beneath the bronze *Angel of Peace* at Wellington Arch and had a romantic late-summer rendezvous beside the *Goatherd's Daughter* in Regent's Park where Max read out to me the inscription *To all the Protectors of the Defenceless*.

'The only drawback,' I say out loud now to Mona, 'was that Max was married, with three children, and was not about to smash up his family to be with me.'

'But you left Roger for this man,' Mona says.

'It wasn't as simple as that.'

Leo was still a child then. I had no intention of breaking up his home. Neither did I want to let Daddy down. I tried to keep my love for Max secret – I even tried to kill it, to stifle my feelings. Roger and I returned to Morocco and carried on as before. But each time I came back to London – I'd got a little work on the radio with the World Service and had to come for meetings at the BBC – Max and I would meet, returning to our respective families after each liaison. Roger need never find out. I thought that I could lead a double life and get away with it, without hurting anyone.

One day, the inevitable happened. Roger found my phone, the erotic texts.

'You must promise not to see him again, or else you can get out of here and I'll file for divorce,' he told me. He was so used to me doing as he said, I think he believed I'd agree never to see Max again.

I left.

'It broke my heart, of course, leaving Leo. But they'd offered me work if I came back to London. We were in the fortunate position of owning a house here. And it meant I could see Max without guilt.'

'So this Max, you love very much?' says Mona.

'Yes,' I say. 'Yes, I think I do.'

'But he is married. To another woman. He is not your husband. And a husband is good – he makes money, for you, for your child. Lovers don't do this.'

I look at her. Remind myself again that she is widowed and must only feel the absence of a husband. I know how people elevate the dead in their imaginations.

'I fell in love, Mona. You don't behave rationally when you're in love! Anyway, I'm telling you all this because I'm going to see Max on Friday. Now,' I say at last, realising I've gone on far too long. 'Tell me more about yourself. Where did Roger find you?'

A closed look. A look that would begin to frustrate me. A discreet, polite smile.

'There is not so much to tell,' she begins. 'I used to work in a garment factory, before I married. But I gave it up later because Ali was earning money. So when he died, I had nothing. The factory had cut back on their employees. I couldn't find work.'

'Oh, that's terrible.'

'Yes, but then Amina, my friend – she works for your husband and Claudia – found me work near their house with their neighbours. A Saudi family. Very wealthy, with a big house. I thought I was lucky when I got this job, cleaning for Madame Sherif, looking after her children.'

'Where did you learn your English, Mona?'

'From this work. I learned to speak, but I can't write or read English very well. This is something I'd like to learn.'

She looks at me as if she expects me to say something.

When I don't, she continues, 'But then I had to leave.'

'Yes. Roger says the family were going back to Saudi.'

'That's not the truth,' she says. She turns, her eyes are full.

The light's gone, and the bench underneath us is cold. I want to get home now, we've been here long enough. But she goes on.

'She and her husband were not going back to Saudi. But her husband, he touched me, he tried to . . .' She stops.

'That's terrible,' I say.

'Yes,' she says. 'Very terrible for me.'

'What did you do?'

'I didn't know what to do. I was afraid to tell Madame. But one day she saw me in her room, her husband behind me. His hands were on me. She called me bad names. She said I made him do these things.'

'You poor woman.'

'She said I had to go. She said it was all my fault.'

'It's disgraceful that he took advantage of you being in the house, in that vulnerable position where you couldn't object.'

'Yes. If I complained, nobody believed me.'

I gaze at her. She doesn't look like the kind of woman a man would try to take advantage of – although, of course, men are unfathomable. She doesn't look as if she would let him get away with it. She's not a young innocent thing, as Zidana was, though I'm beginning to see that Mona has a certain allure. She's more rested these days, and her hair, now she's washed it, is thicker, glossier. Yes, I can see with a little makeover and the right clothes, she could have her own kind of beauty.

'I said to Madame, "But I am married – why do I want your husband?" And she said, "Your husband is dead. You are trying to get a new one. You see he is rich, and you try to steal him from me. Now you get out of my house." She was a very bad employer.'

Mona begins to cry.

Tears, I think, are useful things. Therapeutic, yes, when one is overwhelmed by emotions, but they can also be turned on easily when someone's desperate to prove something to you. I see it every day on the phone-in.

She wipes her eyes on the back of a wrist. Sniffs loudly.

'You can see it is hard to work for a bad man who is unfaithful to his wife. And for a woman who won't see what's happening under her nose. I wanted to help her. To make her see the man she was with. But Madame, she shouted, she said, "You are

120

wasting my time, my money! I am not paying you to steal my husband." She told me to leave!'

'Awful for you.'

'I told my friend Amina. Amina was working for Roger. She asked Roger to help. So Roger told me about you. And now I'm here.'

'Yes. You're with me now, Mona, and no one will take advantage of you.' I stand up and brush the creases out of my coat. 'Time to go home,' I say. 'It's cold.' And as I start to walk back along the river path, I notice she falls naturally behind, in my shadow as if, in spite of our recent intimacies, she knows her place, after all.

CHAPTER EIGHTEEN

I'm busy tidying my room, after our walk by the river, when my door swings open. Startled, I look up.

Dora's standing there.

For a moment I'm afraid that she's going to accuse me of stealing. Her face is stern. But when she speaks she's as polite as anything.

'Excuse me, Mona, I'm sorry to interrupt you,' she says, 'but I want to pay you. I've taken off the first instalment of the cost of your passport and ticket, for Roger, but here's the month's money that I owe you.'

'Thank you.'

When she's gone, I fold the banknotes, put them into an envelope and write Ummu's address on the front.

In the morning, early, I phone home.

'I'm sending money, Ummu. Look out for it. It's not as much as I'd have liked, but I have to pay off the passport and the ticket first. Tell me some news from home.'

'You missed a spectacle yesterday,' my mother says. 'Fahida found her employer knocked out on the floor. He'd been climbing out of his bath and collapsed. You know him? The old English teacher. There was a gas leak. She got the whole medina up to help her move him. She covered him up with a towel, she said, because he was stark naked – his little thing curled up like a dried date.' She laughs her rough rasping laugh, then starts to cough.

I picture her there, shouting into the phone, her friends in the room behind her, slapping their thighs.

When she's quiet again I speak. 'Did you get my gift?'

'The hand cream?'

'I thought you deserved it. Your hands get so sore, immersed in water every day.'

'It's very nice, thank you, Mona. But you mustn't go spending your money on luxuries. Things aren't any easier here.'

'It didn't cost much, Ummu. Only the postage, in fact.' I don't tell her that I hadn't bought it at all, or how I paid for the postage – out of a little bit of Charles's shopping money he'll never miss.

'Last time we spoke, you sounded as if you needed a little bit of pampering. When you get the money, please do see the doctor about your cough. You can't look after Leila if you're unwell.'

'Stop your fussing, Mona. I'm perfectly well.'

I'd believe her if she didn't break off every two minutes to hack and splutter.

'I know you don't want me to ask, but I need to know if you've heard from Ali. Or if anyone has – Yousseff, maybe.'

'Not a word.'

'I'm afraid he must be trying to get in touch. Something's stopping him.'

'You know what I think.'

'You're wrong.'

'A man who doesn't get in touch doesn't want to.'

'Yes, I know.'

'You must give up on Ali. If people find out you have a husband who's vanished – especially one with his record . . .'

'Don't, Ummu!'

'They won't want you in the house. Careful what you say, Mona, the walls have ears.'

'It's OK. She believes I'm a widow.'

'Good. Let it stay that way. You should be looking about for a proper husband with a nice well-paid job. Surely this Dora can introduce you to an Englishman with a bit of spare cash.'

'Stop this, Ummu.'

'And there's no husband, who might have friends, colleagues?'

'No, but she has a lover.'

'Ooh. Interesting. What's he like?'

'A doctor, she tells me. Max.'

'Rich?'

'What difference would that make?'

'Well, you won't get much out of a man with nothing.'

I laugh. My mother's determination is amazing.

'Since you ask, he's a doctor. A professor. Of course he's rich!'

'Have you met him?'

'Not yet. He's American, she told me.'

'Oooh!'

'I'll let you know all about him if and when I do meet him. But no, as yet, I've only seen a picture.'

'Is he handsome?'

'You are unbelievable!'

'Mona! You are a woman in need. A man with money is useful. If you keep your wits about you, you may find he can help you. Citizenship, for example. He might have connections. That's all I'm saying.'

'OK. I've got the message.'

'You're not in a position to turn down help.'

'OK. Now, hand me to Leila.'

125

Leila seems better, tells me she's been playing out on the alley with Ahmed and some other children, that they've invented a new hiding game. Judging from her happy chattering I guess she's beginning to get used to me not being there. What a mixture of remorse and relief this brings.

But when I'm about to finish the call, she whispers, 'I miss you, Ummu,' and I wonder just how much she's having to put on a brave face for my mother's benefit.

I also think about Ummu's words: *Things aren't any easier here* – and I wonder what she means.

It's time to go to Charles, to get him up.

Dora's in the kitchen already. We greet each other and I go down the hallway to the front door and round to the back steps.

'Mona!' Charles is calling me from the depths of the house. 'Mona! Where are you! I need you! Mona!'

I stand for a few more seconds at the top of the steps, my hand resting on the stone head of the woman, thinking about Leila at home wanting me too, knowing that however loudly she shouts, I won't come.

I wait for my tears to subside.

And then I go down.

CHAPTER NINETEEN

'Your lover, this Max. He comes to the house?'

Mona's twinkling at me, a sponge in her hand, pink rubber gloves enveloping her arms.

'No, Mona,' I say. 'Max is not coming to the house.'

It's Sunday morning – a time I always enjoy having to myself.

When I came down, I could hear Mona's voice behind the study door, talking rapidly on her mobile. I made my tea – Earl Grey – in my favourite bone-china mug – and settled at the table in my dressing-gown with the paper. But her voice was too loud, I couldn't concentrate, and I put the paper down. I couldn't understand a word of what she said, of course, but I heard names, and a wave of paranoia flowed over me as I realised she was talking about me. 'Dora . . . blah de blah . . . Max.' And then a giggle. 'Max' again.

What a massive disadvantage you are at if you cannot understand a language that is being spoken within your own home. She came out after a few minutes and hurried past me, her head down, telling me she was off to check on Daddy.

Now as she bustles about, her eyes are full of laughter, as if she finds something about the thought of me amusing.

That look! It stirs that odd feeling again, the memory of a face from the past that I cannot quite identify. Or is it simply that there is something more behind it than she likes to give away, as if she knows more about life than she appears to?

I assume that Mona is innocent – a woman with little education and whose life experience has been limited by poverty. But could this be some kind of act?

She continues to move about, wiping surfaces, putting dishes away, for all the world as though my kitchen were hers. This is a time I like to sit in my dressing-gown lingering over a cup of tea, buttering my sliced white toast rather more abundantly than is necessary, listening to the radio, or reading the paper. I don't want anyone to observe me in these private moments.

'You told me,' she says, 'that you are going to see Max this week. So I think perhaps you want me to make the house beautiful for him? I'll do it for you. Make it smell good, put some flowers out for you?'

Her tone is conspiratorial, full of intimacy. I think of how I opened up to her yesterday. It is perhaps not surprising that she assumes this is how things are between us now.

I don't like her implying that she knows better than I how to please my own lover, however. If Max were coming here, it would be my job to worry about the house, not hers.

'Mona, I want you to look after Daddy today. You could take him to the park. I'll show you how to get there. Then cook him dinner. Daddy's your job.'

She bows her head, a gesture that has begun to rouse in me a mixture of discomfort and irritation. I realise how rash I've been. I've told her all about my feelings for Max when I know so little about her. The expression comes unbidden into my head: 'You should not cast pearls before swine.'

Is this what I'd done?

* * *

When I was married to Roger and having help in the home was the norm, the staff had their own quarters and knew to keep out of ours until we'd vacated them. It was easy to maintain a polite distance. We could treat them as though they weren't there.

'A drink will be arriving soon,' we would say to guests at a cocktail do, the passive form obviating the need to name the servant – a useful way to prevent familiarity. We were discreet, maintained a quiet authority, and the good staff fell in with this, gliding about with trays of drinks and canapés.

It took me a while to understand the role I played in those days, all so fake, so out of step with the real world. But the rules were clear. When Zidana started to get away with things, Roger chastised me.

'They expect to be treated a certain way. They'll take advantage if you're friendly,' Roger told me.

'I don't think—'

'Dora! Understand that you also do them a disservice. By being pally you're raising their hopes, giving them the impression you are on an equal footing and that you can help improve their lot in life. You can't. Don't mislead people. It's not fair on them or us.'

It's been too long since I had any help at all.

I should never have confided in a person who is my subordinate. There were good reasons for maintaining a distance.

'Mona, please. Go and see to Daddy now. I like to have the kitchen to myself on Sunday mornings.'

There. I've said it.

When she's gone I pour myself more tea and open the paper. But I can't concentrate. Now Mona's mentioned Max, with that twinkle in her eye, her own confession from yesterday begins to taunt me. This woman in Morocco whose husband sexually assaulted her – what if the things Madame said were right, and

Mona *had* been lying? What if Mona had deliberately tried to seduce the husband, then, afraid of being found out, accused him? Or at the very least, what if she'd encouraged him, spotting an opportunity? Who was telling the truth? Mona, or Madame Sherif?

That look in her eye this morning! The way she was taking it into her own hands to prepare the house for Max!

I wish now I hadn't told Mona about my lover. I know nothing about her, not really.

I've let the desire to tell the world about my feelings for Max drive me to indiscretion with an employee!

Mona is a desperate widow; she would consider a wealthy businessman a golden opportunity, not just to escape poverty, but to escape her country. Marriage – an American passport . . . my imagination begins to run away with me.

Max is successful, a consultant, and he is rich.

In Mona's terms.

I finish my breakfast and go upstairs to get dressed. I'll put on some decent clothes and phone Anita, see if she fancies meeting for a coffee. I need to chat to someone who is used to having help in her home, and Anita has always employed au pairs for the kids.

I lean on my dressing-table, putting on my make-up, and reach for the sample bottle of hand cream I've kept.

It isn't where I left it, in the little glass jar of samples.

Who other than Mona might want hand cream in my house?

What could she want it for, other than to make herself more attractive?

I must pull myself together. I put on some lipstick, mascara, and count the days until I'll see Max.

When I see him, everything will be all right.

CHAPTER TWENTY

Next time I speak to Ummu, she tells me she's been to the doctor and that he's worried about her cough. He wants her to have a scan.

'I can't afford it, Mona.'

'How much will it cost?'

When she tells me the price I almost faint. But if she has something serious . . . I redouble my determination to save all my earnings for everything she and Leila need.

I've just finished the call when Dora comes into my room and tells me she's not coming home this evening, that she's meeting her man.

'That's fine,' I say. 'Have a nice evening.'

She smiles. 'I hope I will.'

'If you bring him back here I'd cook a good meal for you,' I say in Arabic.

'What was that?'

'Nothing. Please, enjoy yourself.'

Ummu told me the way to a man's heart is through his stomach and this is also true with Dora's son. Now I've found out what he likes to eat, I can make him do whatever I want. I'm not

131

going to allow him to sit about, like Dora does. I'm going to get him to help me. I can't understand how someone so big and strong, with all the advantages he's had, can laze on the sofa in the drawing room, the TV on, all day long. I go into the room. The curtains are drawn against the small amount of light we get each day here, in early November.

'You think I'm going to pick up all your dirty socks?' I say. 'It's not my job!'

'What do you want me to do with them?'

'Pick them up, and if you're good, I'll wash them,' I say. 'But you – you need to get dressed. Sitting about in your . . .'

'PJs,' he says.

'. . . in your PJs all day long is no good. Get up, get dressed, wash, work,' I tell him, then: 'All the privilege you could ask for and you throw it all away! It's criminal,' I say in Arabic.

'What did you say?'

'Nothing.'

Leo shrugs, bends down, hands me his socks and carries his trainers through to the hall. Then he comes back in.

'I can't work. I don't have a job,' he says.

'And you think you'll get one sitting in front of the TV all day?'

He ignores me. Picks up a packet of cigarettes he's left on the floor, takes one out and changes channels.

'Make me a cup of tea,' he says. 'Tea and two slices of toast with butter while you're at it.'

'I am not your slave!' I say. 'But I'll bring you something if you put on some clothes and get up. I'll bring you tea if you go to the High Street for me. Your mother gave me a list.'

I wait. To my surprise, he grins, shrugs. Stands up.

'Tea and toast first,' he says.

The minute he's left the house, I run up the stairs to his room.

Luckily, since I have never learned how to switch on a compu-ter, the screen is already on, a pattern flickering across it. I move the mouse the way I remember Madame's kids doing. The cursor jumps about. I click, and a page flashes onto the screen. Racing cars. I try to click it off again, but instead another page leaps up – pictures of bodies, close-ups, diagrams of veins and hearts. Some lurid photos of body parts with strange rashes and lesions.

Ugh. I look closer, at yellowing pustules and pictures of the insides of bodies – things I've seen in Ali's medical books at home.

I peer closely, wondering what Leo has been looking at. I can't read these words, they are long and must refer to the pictures – medical terms, maybe – and I haven't got long. I must concentrate on what I'm here for. If I can find the Google page, I'll put Ali's name in, and do a search. Madame's children showed me how to do this. At the time, no results came up for Ali, but things change. He must be somewhere. People don't simply vanish!

I fumble with the mouse and the cursor leaps all over the place.

After several attempts with no success the truth hits me. I'm no nearer finding Ali than I was before I left home. The weeks are sliding by.

I wonder if knowing the worst would be better than knowing nothing. What if he had been hurt – or, God forbid, killed? He has such a temper, it's got him into trouble before. How would I know? I soothe myself, remembering that the last time he went away, before we had Leila, it was to study in Casablanca. I didn't hear from him for a few weeks that time, but he did come back.

Why, though, why did he tell me one story and Youssef another?

I sit on Leo's bed, shut my eyes, listen to the steady patter of a cold rain that's started up yet again against the windowpane. Wish I could get Ali out of my system. Wish his absence didn't accompany me wherever I go.

A waft of rain smell or the quality of the light sends me back to a day on the jetty years ago, before Leila.

*   *   *

It was an ordinary afternoon, but unusually grey overhead. Ummu had finished her morning's work and was having a siesta.

I was alone. I couldn't sleep. I got up and went down to the beach. The tide had withdrawn, leaving the sand scattered with debris. I wasn't supposed to come here alone, but I was feeling something and wanted to work out what it was. It must have been quite soon after the day Ali gave me the fish. I wonder now if he knew somehow I was there, if he felt my thoughts somehow. We were like that, Ali and me, we communicated without speaking.

He came up behind me. Didn't speak, took my hand and led me up onto the jetty where men sat huddled under their djellabas on the rocks, their bamboo rods soaring out into the waves.

I said nothing.

This was a man's place.

But I couldn't resist Ali. We walked out along the jetty to the far end where waves lashed against the rocks, the spray stinging our faces. Here you could imagine you were standing on the sea itself.

Ali held me and turned me round in his arms so we were looking back at the kasbah.

'From here you can see the city as a traveller might who is approaching our country from the sea for the first time,' he said.

Clouds were bringing rain in from the west. The colour of the city walls, white or rose-tinted in the sunlight, today reminded me of the offal in the souks. The imam's call to prayer was rising towards a crescendo above the roar of the waves.

'Out here I feel separate from our country,' Ali said. 'Back there, the souks and hammams are emptying, the mosques filling. Everyone is ruled by routine and ritual. Here, I'm free from those invisible forces. One day, I am going to get away from this country. Travel. Be free. Make my fortune in America or Europe.'

I wondered whether he was aware of me as he spoke. He seemed in his own world, in a kind of trance. And I didn't want to think of him travelling away from me to some strange country.

He pulled me tighter to him. 'You'll come with me, won't you?'

'Yes, Ali.'

His lips when we kissed for the first time tasted of salt.

Now I try to remember his exact words on the day, six months ago, he said he had to go away again.

'I have to help my Berber brothers,' he'd said, like some sort of proud Berber warlord, as if he didn't have me or Leila to support.

I was on the roof of our white house, pegging out washing. Leila had a bowl of water and was washing stones in it, making them glossy, putting them in the sun to dry.

'Why won't they stay shiny?' she said crossly. 'I polish them in the water and they go all dull when I put them in the sun.'

Ali came close to me, a grave look on his face. 'They're taking our Berber territories. I can't just stay here and let it happen.'

'But you are so close to having enough money to finish your studies,' I said. 'You were going to qualify.'

His medical training had taken years. Years of intermittent study and demeaning work as a tour guide to earn the money to pay for it. He couldn't throw it all away.

'That can wait,' he said. 'The struggle can't.'

I knew by his tone that nothing I said would change him. His leaving was as inevitable as the shine vanishing from Leila's stones in the sunshine.

He took hold of my hand, pushed up my chin.

'I'll be back,' he said, gazing into me with his azure eyes.

'You promise?'

'I promise. You don't think I'd leave you and Leila if I didn't have to. You must let me do this.'

I couldn't understand how he could care more for this so-called 'struggle' – for land he'd never lived in – than he cared for us, Leila at least. I sealed my lips. I would not speak these thoughts.

In the end, however, I couldn't stop myself, desperation finding its way into my voice. After all, I'd left my own work to have our daughter.

'How long will you be gone? If it's more than a month, we won't be able to stay here. I'll have to go back to Ummu's.'

'It won't be for long,' he said.

'How will we manage, now I have no work?'

'I'll send money. It'll be OK.'

'But you won't be working, you'll be fighting. I don't understand.'

He lowered his eyelids so his long lashes veiled his eyes as he said, 'It's not your concern, Mona.'

There was an edge in his voice now, one I chose to ignore.

'Ali. I'm afraid. Why do you want to get involved in conflict? You might get yourself killed.'

He laughed at this. 'You worry too much,' he told me. 'Your job is to look after Leila.'

He was leaving already.

With each stone Leila placed on the white roof, I felt him take another step away from us.

I held onto his promise.

But the weeks went by and the rent ran out.

Leila and I went back to live with Ummu.

The door downstairs slams – Leo's back. I must put the pages away before he comes up and finds me. He will tell Dora. I move the mouse, but the cursor does its own thing. I try again, to click the windows shut. Nothing happens.

I can hear Leo in the hall, the flump as he drops his leather jacket on the floor, his keys rattling.

I click again, trying to force the pictures that have come up to vanish.

It's gone silent downstairs. Perhaps he's moved down to the kitchen?

I make several more attempts and at last the images dissolve.

As I slip out of his room, my eye falls on a heap of coins piled onto Leo's bed. I stop in the doorway. Listen again. There's no sound of him on the stairs. I look at the money. He's emptied his pockets and left the contents there as if they were worth nothing. I've heard it said that some people simply throw away small change, finding it a nuisance.

I'm creeping up the next flight of stairs to the bathroom when he starts up the stairs.

'Mona, look, I've got something for you!'

I turn and look over what Dora calls her 'Barley Twist' banisters. He's standing in the hallway, holding something in his hands.

I run down. 'What have you got?'

He holds out a bunch of silver spoons, round, like small ladles, all blackened with tarnish.

'There's a shop on the High Street that buys silver and gold. It's the one next to the halal meat shop with a yellow sign. You might as well make a bit of extra cash. And Mona, if you want to use my computer, you can just ask me. Now, you can give me back those coins you took.'

CHAPTER TWENTY-ONE

Max is waiting for me beneath Boudicca.

I'm so relieved to see his open face, his guileless smile. I want to throw my arms around him, snuggle up close to him, rediscover his smell, his voice. I don't want to waste a second. If I had my way, we'd miss the next couple of hours, move straight on to the bit we're really meeting for, the bar, the hotel room.

But as usual we're awkward to start with, unsure of each other, our conversation strained, polite. It seems so long since we've been together.

Crowds flood past us across Westminster Bridge, butting us, pushing us against each other, bits of us making contact through our winter coats. We apologise. Laugh. We're ridiculously nervous!

'Not the best meeting place,' I tell him.

'It's busy. I hadn't realised.'

'You ought to let me choose! You like the statue?'

'Sure,' he replies, grinning. 'She's alluring, and rather formidable, don't you think?'

'Of course. Boudicca was a warrior. She famously resisted becoming a slave to the Roman invaders.'

Pigeons flap above us. The whole area has that jaded feeling typical of tourist spots that real Londoners steer clear of, but Max is keen to look at this statue and I'm keen to observe his pleasure.

Now we've run out of erotic ones, the statues Max likes to meet beside are often dull renditions of long-dead dignitaries. But I don't say so. He thinks they're an insight into a city's moments of glory, the secrets contained within its folds, its dark past. And I secretly love the way he's made them our special places of rendezvous.

I've never looked at Boudicca properly before.

I can see she is indeed quite splendid, the way her transparent robe drapes her upper body as she stands astride her chariot. She's silhouetted against the evening sky that's turning pink ahead of us, darkening the river behind us. I think Max will consider her legs beautiful, exposed just enough to be tantalising, muscular and taut, and I'm right.

'Aaaah,' he sighs. 'Look at those marvellous thighs. My God, how strong that woman must have been.'

He studies Boudicca for a while, cricking his neck to look up at her.

Traffic rumbles across the bridge; a speedboat roars down the Thames, Big Ben chimes five. I want to get somewhere quiet, somewhere still. At last Max puts his arm around me. Instantly I slide my hand under his camel coat and into his back pocket, and we move up the road towards Villiers Street. The lights come on, pearly strings along the Embankment, twinkly blue over the river, red and green beacons on the boats down below. The sky here never grows dark. It's gone violet now where the sun sinks beyond Westminster. Only the silhouettes of trees along the opposite bank are dark. Those and the river water, which has gone an impenetrable black and is flinging itself hungrily against the wall beneath us.

In the gardens, Max tugs me by the hand.

'I wanted to show you this,' he says. We've arrived at another monument, a bust mounted on a plinth in memory of Arthur Sullivan, the composer. Against his plinth, a woman, her head buried in her arms, is weeping. Her clothes are falling off, her dress draped around her waist; she is the epitome of despair.

'I read that she's an allegorical figure,' Max says. 'Sullivan's Muse, cast in granite and bronze. I had to see it. She's lovely, don't you think?'

'Yes, but rather tragic,' I say. Something about the sight of this woman after the glory of Boudicca has upset me. She's so vulnerable in comparison, stripped of everything, her clothes included. 'Looks as if she's lost everything.'

'A perfect rendition of grief,' agrees Max.

He pulls me down onto a bench. It's icy with a cold that seeps in even through our winter layers. The last leaves on the plane trees float past us, flipping over.

'Look at that,' says Max, only ever looking up, only ever seeing beauty. 'The leaves are luminous! Beautiful.'

A blackbird lets out a solitary melody, ringing through the night air, sweet and high-pitched enough to be heard over the sounds of rush-hour traffic.

'Just listen, he's singing for us,' Max whispers into my ear.

Max has a refreshing naivety about him; he's always surprised, as if he holds the world in awe. Surprised by London's hidden statues, surprised by me, surprised by the sex we have.

His wife, a lawyer, either doesn't have time, or doesn't make time for sex. This is what his marriage lacks – one of the many things Max says I provide for him that she doesn't.

Our arrangement has always suited me. A full-time relationship was not what I'd been after when I met him. I knew its demands and its restrictions all too well from my years with Roger.

But recently, on evenings when I've had no one to see and nowhere to go, and only Leo and Daddy for company in the house, I've resented it. I have given up so much for Max – he, nothing for me. I wonder why we can't see each other more often, and for longer. Then I set eyes on him again and I forgive him. He has a magical effect on me, with his tall, lean form, his surgeon's long, strong fingers, his smell of other continents, bringing to mind cacti and men on horses crossing hot sandy streets, leather holsters banging against their hips. Even though he is in fact a New Yorker.

We grasp at each other until we become aware of tourists peering at us as they pass. Two middle-aged people necking on a park bench attract a kind of prurient curiosity; if we'd been teenagers, I don't suppose anyone would have glanced our way.

This evening we have exactly eight hours before Max has to be off again. We find the restaurant Max read about in an in-flight magazine, just off the Strand, and squeeze into a dark corner, close up together on the red banquettes.

'Get the lady a martini,' he tells the waiter. I love the way he says this, like Humphrey Bogart in *Casablanca*. 'And a cold beer for me. Hey,' putting his arm around me, pulling me to him. 'Good to see you. You've been through a lot as well, honey. Rough times, eh?'

The martini is perfect; the glass properly chilled, plenty of ice, a bright sliver of orange zest. I sip it, feel the slow seep of it in my muscles.

'How's the programme?' Max asks. 'Tell me about the latest freaks you've had to deal with.'

'Don't be cruel.'

'Your words, not mine.'

'It's fine. Good. Listening figures are up. I've heard murmurs – I don't want to tempt fate, but I think they're about to move me to prime time.'

'That's great, baby. You must be thrilled. So what does it mean? You'll be more than the Voice of the South-East?' He pulls my head into his shoulder, kisses my hair.

'I guess so.' I try not to sound too full of myself. 'It'll be much bigger listening figures anyway. I'd be hosting special guests as well, so there would be more kudos – more recognition. The current presenter is in fact pretty much a celebrity this side of the pond, though you've probably never heard of him. And of course there'd be a pay rise.'

'Theodora Gentleman, Voice of the South-East, her voice alone will knock you out.'

I smile. He's said it all before but I still love to hear it.

'What about you?' I ask. 'Where're you off to this time?'

'Conference in Hong Kong. I'm giving a paper. Be there for a couple of days, then a meeting in Paris, and home.'

'How's the family?' The words stick in my throat, but I force myself to ask.

'Not bad.'

I squeeze his hand. Wait. Never sure if Max wants me to ask about his home-life, whether he wants to get his troubles off his chest or forget them when he's with me.

'It's strange,' he says. 'The last kid is about to leave home, and Valerie is away a lot as well. It's not much of a home these days. And I've started to look back, wonder if we could have done things differently. The girls hardly even come home. I think they're relieved to get away from the bad atmosphere.' He smiles a rueful smile.

'Don't be regretful.'

'Ah regret,' he says. 'The curse of mid-life.' He looks at me.

'What bad atmosphere?'

'Oh, you know. Valerie getting at me for this and that. It's so strange. You marry someone when you're twenty-something, for years you're immersed in bringing up kids. You muddle along together, and then you emerge, as if into the light, with time and space to be together. Discover you're face to face with a stranger. Someone twenty years older and quite different to the woman you married. We misunderstand each other constantly. I'm trying to work out who she is. Who I am myself.'

'That's funny. It's what I've been thinking about, having Daddy living with me. That we have both changed in the intervening years and now it's as if we're strangers, getting to know each other all over again. It's really very disconcerting.'

'I can imagine. We all move on as people, and sometimes it's in opposing directions. I seem to have stopped caring about certain things, while Val cares more and can't understand my indifference. I guess once we both wanted the same things.'

'What things, Max?'

'Material things mainly. Owning stuff. And making an impression. Status. Enough of me though. How is your dad anyway? And Leo?'

I don't really want to change the subject. I want to hear more, but Max often does this – closes up the minute he's started to open.

'Daddy's not good, it's upsetting. He loses things, forgets what day it is. He even forgot my mother had died. And Leo, as you've witnessed yourself, can't be counted on. But it's going to be easier now. I've hired a carer,' I say. 'It means I've help with Daddy. As I told you in my text, it's freed me up.'

'Aha. Yes, I do remember.'

He doesn't admit that he never replied to that particular text, but I let it go. He's here now. That's the main thing. 'Well I'm glad you've sorted something. It was a bummer that you had to leave early last time.' His voice drops another note. 'I was all primed for it.'

He's moved on already. I envy him this. He doesn't appear to carry resentment around with him the way I would do if he let me down.

'Is she living in then, this helper?'

'Of course. I wouldn't be here if it wasn't for her.'

Max presses his nose against my ear and I can feel the prickle of his goatee against my cheek, something that, though rough, always arouses me.

'Oddly, finding Mona was thanks to Roger.'

'Oh?'

I'm not sure what passes through Max's mind when I mention my ex-husband. He knows I left Roger after meeting him. What he doesn't know is that he played the key role in our break-up. I don't want to dump that burden of responsibility on him.

'We always had female staff when we lived out there,' I explain. 'He suggested he brought someone over to help with Daddy, since I was coping with Leo as well. A guilt offering! She's a friend of his housemaid.'

I take a swig of my drink. My tongue plays round a piece of ice, toys with it. I want to see how long I can hang onto its chill before it melts.

'Perhaps we could meet in Europe, now you have help,' he says suddenly. 'Just from time to time, to ring the changes? There are lots of galleries I haven't explored yet, and all those sculptures and statues – think of Rome, or Florence!'

I look at him. He's got his twinkle back and I let myself dream for a minute. Max and I strolling arm-in-arm up steep Mediterranean streets, admiring views of vineyards and olive groves. Sitting on rims of fountains, white marble statues writhing above us. The tinkle of water. Me in a sundress, my legs bare, toenails painted crimson, in sandals with thin straps. It's been a long time since I felt that free.

Perhaps I can leave Daddy for a weekend, for longer, now I have Mona.

A warm glow of possibility suffuses me.

His thumb traces the contour of my ear. This is it, I think.

This is the pinnacle. I know it by now, I can pinpoint it. The bit of the evening where we've relaxed, but haven't got to think about leaving yet. The part where everything hangs in perfect balance. This moment, right now. I have to roll it around my mouth the way I'm rolling the ice. Suck every last tang of flavour from it. Assign it to my memory before it melts away. Because I know it will do. It's vanishing even as we speak.

The waitress brings our starters – scallops with a black olive jus and a bottle of Sancerre in an ice bucket. We eat in a daze, chewing the tender white flesh, staring at each other, half-laughing. A candle flickers on the table between us.

Max puts his fork down, wipes his beard.

One arm's around me, his other hand tucked up under my skirt, stroking the top of the stockings I've bought specially. Our half-finished meals are pushed away from us. We've no interest in anything but each other.

'Tell me about her,' he whispers suddenly.

'Who?'

He puts his mouth to my ear. 'Your woman,' he breathes. 'Her thighs.'

Max has never hidden his penchant for women's thighs. It's an innocent enough sexual proclivity, judging by some of the things I hear on the phone-in. And one I'm willing to participate in, even if I don't get the same thrill from it as he does. But the thighs usually belong to imaginary people – the statues or pictures we've looked at – they dissolve the minute we stop talking about them. This request, for me to talk about the thighs of the woman I've employed as carer and home-help, is a new departure. One I don't like.

'Are they firm and strong?'

In spite of myself I find myself whispering back to Max, not wanting to dissipate the charged atmosphere between us as his hand grips my leg.

'Gorgeous. Smooth and firm, the way you prefer,' I say.

'Hmm,' he purrs, moving closer to me. 'Do you look at them? When she's cleaning, I mean? Can you see them when she, say, bends down to sweep up the floor?'

'Yes,' I lie. The trouble is, I like his excitement, I like turning him on.

And Max will never meet Mona. She's a figment of his imagination. So I'm safe – aren't I? – to fan the flames of his fantasy. Me and my live-in maid, a cliché of course, but one which he's embracing so whole-heartedly, so boyishly, I haven't the heart to stop him.

'When else?'

'When she reaches up to clean cobwebs off the ceiling roses,' I tell him.

Mentioning the cobwebs in my house, in order to fuel his fantasy, feels like taking a step across a strict boundary. We don't go to each other's homes. Obviously I can't go to his with his wife and kids, but he's never been to mine either. It's an unspoken rule between us. The snippets I've revealed to Max about it have always been carefully chosen. The view of the church, the way my bedroom spans the whole width of the house, the wooden floors, the capacious kitchen and the drawing room that runs from front to back – they might have conjured any number of images of ideal homes, in his head. I don't want to disappoint him.

'Does she stand on a chair?' Max seems undeterred by the mention of cobwebs. 'As if she were behind a chariot? Like Boudicca?'

'Yes.'

'Oh Theodora, oh God we have to find ourselves a room. Now.'

My moments with Max are as sweet as they are brief, always imbued with the knowledge that they'll end too soon. That Max has to leave in the small hours is nothing new – I'm used to it. Our affair has always consisted of short bursts of passion. I convince myself that this suits me. I have enough to worry about in my everyday life, fitting a lover into it would add to my stress.

But today, as Max kisses me in the hotel lobby, disappears through the turnstile into his taxi, as I make my way through the empty streets, needing time to assimilate our night before I too flag down a taxi, I'm left with the sense that this evening has ended too soon. His words play over in my mind: 'Tell me about her.' Why does he need me to tell him about someone else? Doubts pile into my mind. Why does he only ever text me when he's about to get on a plane or a train and go off again? Why can't he arrange to get here earlier, stay a little longer?

It's true I've been tied up until now, but he could have suggested staying overnight this time.

I rest my head against the taxi's cool interior, watch the sleeping streets of south-east London slip past. There's no traffic on the roads yet. Just me, alone, transported past people sleeping behind curtained windows, in proper couples, snuggled up with one another. I wish I could call Max back, ask for reassurance. *You do love me, don't you?* It looms into focus again, his salacious interest in my housemaid.

The unfinished business between us this evening feels as if we haven't tidied up properly. As if we've uncovered some rotten thing hidden behind the shelves in my drawing room, and then left it there, forgotten to put the shelves back.

Max will go off into the night with his fantasy, while I have the reality to face: a woman, working for me, in my house. It makes me feel exposed and ashamed.

This feeling accompanies me all the way home. I go up the front steps, put the key in the lock, creep in. It's gone four o'clock. I need a drink, something to help me sleep, something to still my mind.

In the kitchen, I put on the kettle, sit at the table, try not to think about Max excited by the idea of the woman behind the door – just there – in the back room beyond the kitchen. I'm letting Mona disturb my peace of mind. She's here to care for Daddy. To clean and to help. Not to add to my worries. She must not be allowed to encroach on the rest of my life.

I drain my mug and, feeling a little soothed, start up the stairs to bed. I've barely reached my bedroom door when my mobile goes.

It's Desiree, from next door.

'He's out again,' she says, without bothering to introduce herself. 'I heard his front door slam. He kicked over the milk bottles. I think he's gone down to the river. He shouldn't be left alone overnight. He's a liability.'

And she puts the phone down.

I drag my coat on and race out of the front door. Sure enough, Daddy's making his way down the street, lit spookily through a swirling mist by orange streetlamps so that he appears pale, ethereal. I catch up with him. He looks pathetically old and frail. I place my hand gently on his shoulder. 'Daddy, please come back to bed.'

He turns and starts. Then he begins to scream.

'You're not Mona! I want Mona! Where's Mona?!'

Mona's on her side, in a foetal position. I shake her, tell her she has to go after Daddy.

She raises her head. Frowns. 'Now? It's dark.'

'Yes, Mona,' I say. 'Go now.' I'm still dressed, too keyed up to sleep.

She gets up, blinks at me, She's wearing a T-shirt over bare legs, revealing firm, caramel-coloured thighs.

She moves so slowly, I grow impatient.

'Wake up! It's an emergency.' I can't bear her slow, laborious gait when I've instructed her to go.

149

When at last I hear the front door close, I go up to bed. I need sleep. I need to be fresh for work in the morning. But sleep is elusive.

I shut my eyes, try to use the relaxation technique they teach you at yoga. But every time I begin to drop off, Mona's thighs float into view, as strong and muscular as Boudicca's.

Accompanying this, Daddy's horrified screech echoes in my ears.

Mona! I want Mona!

CHAPTER TWENTY-TWO

I'm dreaming.

Ali has run into the white house again, covered in sweat, in tears.

'You must hide me!' And each time I try to find a place where he can hide, the walls fall away and he is standing in front of the crowds as they encroach on him down the street, their batons raised, broken glass and sticks and hammers brandished in front of them. I run, to stand in front of him, to protect him, but then I see Leila: she is walking into the crowds and they are turning on her.

I go to grab her and one of the men with a shard of broken glass crosses over to me. The pain is thin and high-pitched. It seeps into my consciousness, expands, blooms, fills my head with unbearable brightness, like flames – red orange yellow. That's when I wake.

A woman stands over me, not a man. Sweet relief. The pain, the fear, was all a dream. Dora's long hair is a copper halo against the soft light falling in through the kitchen door.

For a few seconds I'm afraid. She's discovered I've sold her spoons.

I try to sit up, struggling against the weight of sleep.

'Mona. I need you to get up, go to Daddy.'

I get out of bed, still in that half-dream world.

'Hurry up.'

It's midnight. No, much later. That time of night when the world is dark and the cold so deep it's as if all mankind were at the bottom of a well.

I'm too fuddled, too much in my dream to think straight. Dora's dressed, as if she has just come in.

'Wake up, it's an emergency. Daddy has gone out onto the street.'

She's fully clothed, in her coat. Why hasn't she gone, since she's up and dressed? She looks at me in an odd, cold way.

'Yes. I'm coming.'

And she's gone.

I move down the road, the streetlamps lighting the faces of the cherubs and figureheads so they peer through the mist, half-concealed.

It's so cold my teeth clash together. I'm wide awake now, the mist wet against my skin, my eyes smarting in the chill. The other houses are all in darkness, curtains drawn, softly protected against the harsher side of the city. One of the curtains in the house next door moves as I pass. I'm being watched by more than the effigies tonight.

I see him, emerging from beyond a row of wheelie bins. He shuffles towards the High Street like a ghost, almost as if he too has been sculpted, out of mist rather than stone.

I catch up with him outside the halal meat stores.

'Charles.'

He doesn't look at me but I fall into step beside him.

'Ah Mona. I need to get to Billingsgate before the others,' he says. 'If we go now, we can beat the rush.'

'It's OK, Charles. You must come back to bed. We will go later.

Come, come with me.' I crook my elbow for Charles to take, turn him and walk him slowly back to the house, round the side and across the garden to his steps. I settle him back into bed and return to the house.

There's no point in trying to sleep now.

Though it's still dark, there's a roar in the air, traffic starting up, planes flying overhead. Tubes vibrating through the ground of the city. It must be nearly morning.

Something about Dora's face in the moonlight has upset me. Does she suspect me of lying? Or of stealing?

I can't let her think this. I remember Dora's delight at finding her taps polished, the first day I started work. I take a rag and a bottle of oil and work away at the kitchen taps, rubbing and polishing until they shine.

I'm finishing them off as Dora comes in. I know instantly that the polishing is not to her liking.

'Leave the taps, Mona. There are too many other jobs to be done.' She switches on the kettle without speaking. She's tired. She has attempted to cover the bags under her eyes with some too-white, too-luminous make-up. She must have only just come in when she woke me last night. Now she is suffering, too, from lack of sleep.

'How far did he get?' she asks.

'Charles?'

'Of course.'

'End of the street. He wanted to go to Billingsgate.'

'You must tell him he doesn't need to go to Billingsgate any more. You must tell him, when he thinks he's living in the past, that things have changed.'

'But—'

'This can't go on,' says Dora. 'Daddy needs watching at night too. I've got to go. There's a lot to be done. If you finish the cleaning, washing, shopping and cooking for Leo and Daddy, you can put the rubbish out. Do the ironing. And then you can polish the silver.'

She walks across the kitchen to a wooden box and lifts the lid. Inside are knives and forks and spoons, all arranged in lines slotted into a kind of velvet cushion. I see at once that the spoons I've just sold must have been part of this set. There are two layers; the spoons must have come from the lower one.

My heart almost stops.

'These were my mother's. A family heirloom, though none of my siblings places value on such things, so I felt no compunction in taking them. They're tarnished, you see. They don't look very special to the untrained eye. But once they're polished, with silver dip, they'll shine like new.'

She reaches into a cupboard and brings out a pot of silver polish.

'Can I take Charles perhaps to this Billingsgate one day? To make him happy?' I ask, hoping to distract her, to stop her from lifting the layer of knives and forks and finding the soup spoons missing.

'No! You must stay in this area. Don't do everything Daddy asks, Mona, he doesn't know what he really wants. You're here to do as *I* say. So just keep to the market and the street and you'll be OK. Daddy's confused. You need to help him live in reality, here and now. He needs to know where he is, and who he's with. Do you understand?'

'Yes.'

'He must not go to the fish market.'

'It's a pity, I'd like to make him happy.' I say it in Arabic.

'What did you say?'

'Just that I understand I must do as you say.'

She moves away from the cutlery container.

'And Mona, if he wants to buy my mother flowers, you tell him she's dead.'

I stare at her.

154

She's putting on lipstick in the mirror as she speaks. 'You don't buy things without telling me and then keep them for yourself.'

'Of course.'

'And you don't take things that aren't yours.'

And then she's gone.

CHAPTER TWENTY-THREE

I have supposed for a long time that I am 'in love' with Max. But after occasions like this latest one, when we've been apart for months and then our meeting lasts less than twelve hours, I wonder whether it's worth it. The pain of tearing myself from him seems, in the aftermath, worse than not seeing him at all.

I awake the next morning with a dull headache, nervy and raw-edged from lack of sleep and with that nagging feeling that we've left things unfinished. The vision of Max saying, 'Tell me about her,' as he holds my thigh, still won't leave me.

I consider emailing him, telling him how his curiosity about Mona has left me miserable, but I know I won't do this. He'll reassure me that it was nothing more than a passing fantasy. He'll probably laugh at me – point out that he's never even met this woman; she's just a concept – no more real than the statues he likes to use to embellish his fantasies.

And I'll make myself sound needy – something I'm careful not to do in case it drives him away. I represent freedom from his home-life, his work – he doesn't want another shackle.

Perhaps then I should email and say we have to call the whole thing off?

That I can no longer bear the weeks that lie between one meeting and the next. That being close to him and then detaching myself is like suffering a terrible hangover after only one glass of wine.

Then I remember Daddy in the streetlight, turning his petrified face to me, and crying, 'You're not Mona! I want Mona! Where's Mona?!'

With his words ringing through my ears, I turn the other way at the bottom of my front steps before going to work; take the alley round the back to Daddy's flat. I need to check he is all right, after all. That Mona got him back safely. I want to reassure myself that he was just confused last night. That he meant to call for *me*, not Mona.

'Morning, Daddy.'

'Eh?' He's in his chair, a paper on his lap though he doesn't look as though he's been reading it. His cereal bowl's on the table beside him so he's had breakfast.

I must admit Mona is a conscientious worker.

'How are you this morning?'

'You're not Mona. Bring me Mona.'

'Daddy, I'm your daughter. Theodora. I've come to see if I can get you anything.' I'm fingering the chain round my neck, drawing his attention to it.

'You can get me the lovely Mona,' he says. 'She's a sweet girl and she knows what I like.'

I unhook the necklace, take it off, hand it to him.

'You remember, you bought me this,' I say, feeling tears come to my eyes. 'Don't you remember? You always called me Theodora, your "gift from God".'

I look around to make sure no one can hear this sentimental appeal, though I know there's no one but us present.

'Hold it, Daddy, please. Look after it, and try to remember who I am. I've got to go to work, but I'd be here if I could.'

He looks at the chain at last, takes up the ends in his two hands, stretching it out so he can read the name curling across it. At last he sighs, 'Ah yes, Theodora,' and looks up at me. I feel a flood of relief.

'What are you going to work for on a Sunday?' he asks.

'It's not Sunday, it's Thursday. And Daddy, I'd like you to keep an eye on Mona, while I'm at work.'

'Oh, she doesn't need an eye on her. She's a very hard worker, you know.'

'I'm sure she is, Daddy. But I want you to make sure she doesn't buy things for herself with your money.'

'Oh no, she's very generous. She spends it all on things for me. Now, you and Mona,' he says, examining me, 'I can't quite understand it. You must be the same age, yet she looks so very young, while you . . . Oh dear. You do look tired.'

I mustn't take these comments to heart. Daddy's condition means that he sometimes says hurtful things – it's what's known as 'disinhibition'. I know this. I've read about it. Nevertheless, when he's like this, it seems as if all the things that made Daddy sweet and lovable are crumbling away. As if a shiny veneer has eroded with age, leaving only the crude under-surface on show.

I leave him, my feelings veering from concern to relief that I no longer have to deal with him.

Mona is, after all, here to take some of these tumultuous feelings away.

The Clipper's full, people commuting, using laptops and smartphones, on iPads and on iPods. I buy a coffee – I need a good caffeine fix after last night – and go to stand on deck to get some air. I inhale the sludgy scent of the river. As the engine starts up, churning the murky water below us, the jetty starts to move away, and I stare down into the hurtling tide, racing along with the boat. When I look up, church spires and office blocks that were, a few seconds ago, in front, are vanishing behind us into the distance.

I need this commuting time to think about Max, to unpack what I've felt since last night. I lean on the railings. I can't get Daddy's voice out of my mind, crying out for Mona. It's hurt me more than I like to think. My thoughts are interrupted by a conversation going on beside me.

'I know, darling. I know you want feedback, but it's impossible for me to be objective. I love everything you do. I'm dizzy with pride.'

A man and a woman lean on the railings. He's maybe in his fifties, she twenty or so. They have the same eyes, the same low-slung eyebrows.

Father and daughter.

The girl sighs, says something that's snatched up by the wind and tossed downstream. Maybe it's lack of sleep, or a surfeit of caffeine but time seems to collapse. It's as if I'm looking at my future, not my past. Gaping at the girl I dream I'll become, lanky with adolescence, on the cusp of adulthood, basking in the undiluted approval of a doting father. Then as fast as the image appears, it's gone. I'm catapulted back to now. Just as the spires and landing stages on the banks vanish, Daddy and I as we were, as we might have been, slip into the distance until we're not even dots on the river bend.

A memory comes. One of our early-morning trips to Billingsgate by car through the Blackwall Tunnel to buy fish for the restaurant. Daddy always chose me to go with him, to keep him company, and I treasured these excursions, especially the leaving at dawn to cross a London that was still sleeping.

There was always a salty stench outside Billingsgate, like a mouthful of seawater. I was fascinated by the layers of dead fish in the boxes, the gaping mouths, the milky eyes. I hung onto Daddy as he picked up fish and sniffed them and squeezed them, and their unseeing eyes stared up at him, their mouths turned down as if they said, as they died, *How could you do this to me?*

I wasn't officially allowed on the wet market floor. So Daddy took me into the café in the corner where the fish merchants and porters in their bloodied white aprons ploughed through bacon and eggs and haddock and chips. And Daddy bought me a bacon roll and had his cup of coffee with two sugars. Then he disappeared to barter with the stallholders with their bare arms and tattoos and bloodstained overalls. I hated being left there alone. Tinny music mingled with the intermittent hiss of steam from the urns, and I'd long for Daddy to loom through the door, with his sea food for the restaurant.

I distracted myself trying to finish songs in my head before all the little lights lit up on the front of the fruit machines. If I didn't reach the end of a song in time, Daddy would never come back to me. I would be left here and kidnapped by one of the fish men and taken on a boat to somewhere far away and strange, sold into the white slave trade.

When Daddy did come, the relief was so warm, such a release, I would sing out loud all the way home.

It's that relief, that beautiful warm gush that followed his appearance that I long for today. As the Clipper draws into Bankside Pier, I realise I'm waiting for Daddy now. I feel tears come to my eyes, hot and pressing. I'm waiting for the Daddy I used to love to come back to me.

Knowing that this time, I didn't reach the end of the song in time.

CHAPTER TWENTY-FOUR

'I want you to make those cakes,' Dora says, her back to me. 'The ones you told me about.' She's gathering things – her mobile, her keys – dropping them into her bag. 'Here's some money for today.' She slams a ten pound note on the table, crosses the kitchen to the cooker, and turns suddenly to face me. 'The ones with almond and honey. Leo likes them.'

I nod, aware that her kitchen is an armoury of domestic weapons – its shiny set of knives, the meat hammer, her blender with its blades of steel. Its iron.

'And I'd like you to make up all the beds with fresh sheets. Leo needs cigarettes, he's run out, but don't neglect Daddy.' She bangs the rolling pin down on the work surface, and I watch her back as she stalks down the hallway, leaving me wordless, in her kitchen.

Charles refuses to come out with me today, says he's busy planning menus.

'I'll tidy your room. Then I'm popping out to get Leo's cigarettes. I'll be back soon.'

'Yes, yes – be off with you. I need to get on.'

*   *   *

On my way down the street I phone Ummu.

'I'm much better, thank you, Mona,' she says straight away. 'The medication is helping, alhamdulillah. Thanks to your money I'll soon have enough for the scan. The doctor says he'll arrange one for me – to make sure, you know, that there's nothing nasty going on.'

'Of course there's nothing nasty going on. You mustn't think like that, Ummu.'

'No. OK, Mona, but just to be on the safe side . . .'

I wait.

'I meant to tell you' – another coughing fit – 'Leila's been to see the school. She's so excited, Mona, you should see her face. She's growing up too. Lost a tooth last night, first top one.'

'Is she OK?'

'Of course! She ran around showing it to everyone.'

'She must look funny, with a top tooth missing.'

'She looks cute as ever, Mona.'

'Good. That's good.'

'So we're doing fine.' Cough. 'It's all working out very well. Thanks to you. Your wages.'

'No news?' I barely mention Ali's name for fear of setting her off on another nagging session about finding an Englishman instead.

'No, Mona. Nothing.'

I don't tell her I feel homesick. That hearing about Leila's tooth has brought a lump to my throat. How Theodora, who I thought I would grow fond of, seems to be subtly changing, the way a fruit slowly darkens until it is no longer good to eat.

I imagine my mother and the other women of the neighbourhood, sitting together on someone's steps sharing a cigarette, and long to be there with them so badly it hurts. Where are all the women in this street, with its closed doors and its curtains? Don't they need to laugh and chat together in this city? Don't they ever open the doors of their homes? The doors seem permanently shut, as if they have their backs to the world.

And my hopes of finding Ali are fading. Already the weeks are turning into months. It's mid-November now, and my chances of finding better work, of living a better life seem to be diminishing along with Ummu's health.

'Can I speak to Leila?'

I hear Ummu calling to my daughter. She must be playing out on the street. I wait a minute, two minutes. In the background far off, I can hear children's voices, some Arabic music, and my longing to be home increases.

At last Leila's voice comes down the phone.

'Hi, Ummu.'

'How are you, darling?'

'I'm fine. I've just been out to get Tetta's medicine. She's too ill to go on her own. She's gone back to bed now.'

'Really?'

'It's OK,' Leila's saying. 'I'm looking after her. I'm doing the shopping and the cooking and she says I'm a very good nurse.'

Leila, I want to shout, *you're six years old. You shouldn't have to be a good nurse!* I swallow.

'Good. That's good,' I say. 'And I hear you've lost a tooth?'

'Yes, and I have another wobbly one. When are you coming home, Ummu?'

'As soon as I can, darling.'

'Got to go, Ummu. Ahmed's here.'

'OK. *Salaam alaikum.* Love you.'

I've reached the shops, am paying for my paper in such a daydream I don't hear the voice at first. 'You thought about using Unibank yet? I can do you a deal.'

I look up. 'I don't want Unibank, thank you. I can send money home by post.'

'That's crazy, man. It'll get lost. You wanna send it electronically, much safer.'

'But much more expensive. Just the cigarettes, thank you.'

'How many do you smoke then?' He bangs the Marlboro I'm buying for Leo down on the counter.

'They aren't for me.'

'Who for then? I see you buy twenty every day. You should warn whoever it is they're smoking too much, man.'

'And your job is to sell, not to tell people what to buy! They're for my employer's son.'

'Ah! Now I know who you work for. They live on our street up the other end!'

He grins, and his green eyes light up. With his brown skin and black hair I can't help it, he makes me think of Ali. Those clear eyes like jewels in that dark face. Everyone commented on Ali's eyes. 'It's my Berber blood,' he would say proudly. He knew how gorgeous he was, he knew how to use it.

'You what, a cleaner or something?'

'I do as I'm asked.' Ummu's warning not to say too much rings through my head. *The walls have ears, Mona.* People are suspicious. They'll think you're trying to sneak into the country, to live there illegally. There are ears everywhere,' she said. 'Keep as much to yourself as possible.'

'She's got that old man in the wheelchair.' Another man has joined him at the counter. This one's white, his skin so pale it's almost transparent. He's dressed in a T-shirt as though it were warm outside. A snake is tattooed on his arm. People here don't seem to feel cold the way I do. The damp seeps into my bones so my fingers and toes feel permanently numb, my joints ache dully.

'I've seen you in here before. Buying stamps, buying a newspaper. This is Sayed, by the way. I'm Johnny.'

The tattoo on the white man's arm uncoils as he holds out his hand to shake mine.

166

'You come here for what?' he persists. 'Work? Asylum?'

I've already said too much, and so I purse my lips together. Shake my head.

'Oh come on!' says Sayed. 'Everyone round here – Johnny, me, Costas at the café, Pearl over there in the fabric shop, all the guys at the cab office, they's all from somewhere else. Some is legal, some is illegal.'

'Where are you from?' I ask.

'Afghanistan,' he says. 'Johnny's from Albania.'

Something about Sayed, his green eyes, weakens my resolve. Maybe, amongst this crowd of immigrants, people desperate to get away from desperate situations, to start again or to improve their lives, they might have links? It's possible someone has met Ali. But as I open my mouth, Sayed speaks.

'Listen,' he says. 'You ever need help, like a British passport – you ask me, right? I know where to get documents, and I got people who can help you.'

'It's OK. I don't need documents. I have documents.'

He shrugs. 'Just letting you know I'm here.'

On my way back to the house, the worries start up, along with a dull pain in the pit of my stomach. I've said too much, I should never have told them anything. If I get caught up in illegal practices I'll be putting all of us at risk, Ummu, Leila, me. Even, possibly, Ali. Ali. I'm no nearer to finding him. Ummu. How sick is she really? Should I go home, get her to a hospital? Should I forget Ali, the money I'm earning? That's impossible. The money's essential. Dora. Something's changed, she's working me harder every day. She owes me, for the nightwork I've done. For the weekends I've worked. If I object, she might bring up the things I've had to take for Ummu, the little things that I've taken for myself, or that Leo's given me to sell. Things I'm certain she knows I need, but that so far, she's overlooked out of a mutual understanding.

I'd like to ask Dora for time off to make a short trip home, to see Ummu, to ensure she's not got anything serious, that she's getting the treatment she needs. And to see the gap in Leila's front teeth.

Then the vision of Dora the night she woke me to get Charles from the street comes back to me, unsettles me. And this morning, the way she turned, the rolling pin raised as if she was threatening me. I'll have to bide my time, wait for the right moment.

I'm in the kitchen making the almond pastries Dora has asked for when Leo comes in. He's in his tracksuit and socks, his hair unbrushed.

'Don't you feel guilty, lying about while other people work?' I hand him his cigarettes.

'What are you making?'

'The almond and honey cakes you like.'

'Hmmph.'

'You can mix the almond paste, if you want. Then help me fill the filo tubes with the paste, and you can pour on this syrup.'

'What's in it?'

'Honey and sugar. We made these at home. Before—' I stop myself. 'When we had the ingredients.'

He sits at the table and lights a cigarette. I stare at him.

'Your mother doesn't like you smoking in the house.'

'She can't stop me.'

'Put it out. When I've finished we'll go outside and I'll have one too.'

'You smoke?'

'Occasionally.'

When the cakes are finished, and lying on a tray for Dora's homecoming, I fetch my own packet of cigarettes. The one I brought with me in my bag from home. I haven't had one since

I arrived here, but now the smell of Leo's smoke has given me a craving.

'We'll go outside,' I say, and to my surprise he follows me, out of the front door, round the back to the garden. We sit on a bench, light up, and for the first time in months I draw in the taste of the black tobacco, feel the rush of smoke as it hits my head, and feel for a few moments, as we sit and smoke silently together, that I could, if I shut my eyes and imagine hard enough, be at home.

'You're always on the computer,' I say, 'always playing those games. Car chases and so on. Don't you ever get bored?'

'That's not all I do.'

'What else then?'

'Social networking.'

'Ah yes. Everyone does that these days. I wish I knew how.'

'You don't know?'

'No. I never had a computer before I came here.'

'Fuck me, that's crazy. I can show you, if you like.'

'Really? Can you show me how to search on Google as well?' Things are happening at last.

'Of course. I can give you lessons, Mona, you're fucked if you can't use a computer.'

We sit side by side in Leo's room at his screen. An hour later, he has set up a page just for me.

'You need contacts to put on your page. Otherwise you'll just have to wait for people to contact you.'

I shrug. 'You could perhaps search for a few of my friends.'

I tell him the names, and he punches them in. Hait and Amina and Jasmine. Amina has a Facebook page and Leo presses what he calls a 'friend's request' and sends it to her.

'If she "confirms" your friendship you'll be able to chat to her online,' he says.

'And you could try Ali – Ali Chokran,' I say casually, as if Ali were just another friend.

Photos and names pop up. I peer closely.

There are hundreds of photos, none of them him. I'm swamped all over again with the sense of despair I've felt every time I realise how far I am from finding him, and try to hide the look of pain that must have crossed my face.

As I get up to go and see to Charles, Leo calls me back. He holds out something shiny in his hands.

'Grandad's cufflinks,' he says. 'No one wears them any more. Thought you could sell 'em.'

By the time Dora comes home, Leo has helped me make a Facebook page and I've made a little extra cash and sent it all to Ummu. It's then I realise what the dragging in the pit of my stomach is. My period has come and I have no money to buy tampons.

CHAPTER TWENTY-FIVE

I'm tired when I get in from work. I go straight up to my room, undress, put on my bathrobe which Mona has laundered and is fresh-smelling and fluffed up. It's at times like this I wonder how I managed without her. Hugging it around myself, I walk across the clean landing and down the stairs to the bathroom where I intend to lie in a deep bubble bath, smoothing on exfoliator.

I push open the bathroom door.

Mona, on a stool, her hand in my cabinet.

'What are you doing?'

'Oh!' She turns. 'I'm looking for tampons,' she says, her eyes wide, betraying her guilt.

'Tampons?'

'Yes. I bleed, I wasn't prepared. It's come early.'

'But you have money for tampons.'

'I . . . I have no money, I . . .'

'Mona! I give you money for shopping, I gave you your wages, only on Friday! What do you mean?'

'Sorry. Next time I'll buy them. I forgot. It's an emergency.'

She smiles. I see she's hoping for a kind of conspiratorial warmth from me. I could of course let her take the box, or hand her a fiver, tell her to trot to the shop and buy some tampons for herself, or, if I was the fool I was when she arrived, I would go myself. But I'm not.

And there's something else I can't even quite grasp. Something to do with Mona's periods, using my tampons – such personal intimate things. She isn't a friend. She isn't someone to share things with.

'You may take one, for now. I bought you this.'

Her expression softens as I hand her the package, as if she thinks I might have bought her a present. She takes it from me.

'It's a monitor, you keep one piece by your bed and we'll put the other by Daddy's. Then if he wakes in the night again you will hear and can go to him.'

Her soft expression hardens again. Never have I known such an expressive face.

'I cannot work twenty-four hours a day,' she says.

'You'll work the hours I need you to work,' I reply. 'And you'll buy your own essentials.' She gives me another blank look then begins to walk away.

'And Mona,' I say. She turns. 'You have your own bathroom. You're not to use mine.'

Later, when Mona's down with Daddy, sorting out the monitor, I go into her room.

What *is* happening to the money I pay her? She sends some of it to her mother and daughter, I know, but there's enough, should be enough for her to buy basic necessities as well.

I have a quick look about. The study is unrecognisable, tidier than it's been since I moved back. She's got her little photo album by her bed, a notebook. Her clothes are hanging up on the back of the door. She hasn't got many. Most of them are cheap manmade fabrics, tracksuit bottoms, T-shirts. No wonder she looks so dowdy, so middle-aged most of the time! There's one pretty purple dress, and a skirt, but that's about it.

I go to the bureau. I find Daddy's writing paper. And tucked into it, ten-pound notes.

Mona's accepting my money, stashing it up, instead of spending it on things she needs. So that'll be why she's pilfering other things!

I go up to the dressing-table in my room. I'd taken the precaution, of course, of locking my jewelry up in a box I keep under the bed, and hiding the key. But I'm not worried about this. Mona's too clever to take things of any value and think she could get away with it. It's the little things that have passed across my consciousness without my registering them that are suddenly bothering me.

I open my expensive moisturiser. It's hard to tell, but I'm sure someone – Mona, who else? – has put their finger into the pot and taken some. I'm certain there was more rose-water in the bottle than there is now. I remember then the hand cream that disappeared. I barely paid any heed to this when I saw it had gone; it was, after all, just a free sample I'd been given when buying some other products, but now, in the context of everything else that's happening, I begin to feel a fool.

My heart starts to pound. I feel humiliation heat my skin, almost as if I were blushing to myself. A vision of a scorch-mark on a tablecloth flashes into my head. I push it away.

I'm not concerned about what these things cost me; it's the fact Mona's taking advantage of me.

I notice then that my blusher has been left open; a dusting of powder trails over the lid though I know for certain I haven't used it this week. I go back to the bathroom. Yes, the shampoo, I'm certain has been used.

'Leo!' I push open the drawing-room door and brandish the bottle in front of him.

'Did you use my shampoo?'

'What?'

'I need to know.'

He shrugs. 'Don't remember.'

'Did you help yourself to the dark chocolate I left in the fridge?'

'You know I can't stand dark chocolate, or you should. By now.' He's affronted that my questions imply I don't know him, his tastes. It's an unspoken issue between us. I kick myself for putting my suspicions around Mona before intimacy with Leo. She's even messing up the bond I'm trying to establish with my son!

'I need to know if Mona's been helping herself,' I plead. 'If you haven't, it must be her.'

I want his affection, I need his response.

But he's not listening, has reconnected himself to whatever film or game he's playing. Disconnected himself from me.

I give up on Leo and go to knock on Mona's door. Hold out the things I've shown Leo.

'Just a reminder, Mona. You are an employee, not a guest,' I say. 'You buy these things out of your own money, it's what I'm paying you for.'

She stares at me, with no expression on her face. That mask has come down that's impossible to read.

'I give you money to buy things. You don't have to steal.'

'You don't want me to work for you any more?'

'That's not what I said.'

I look at what she's been doing. It seems she's been studying, in her work hours, from a little book of English phrases, writing into a notebook. I'll tell her later that she isn't here to study, that I've employed her to work. I don't have the strength now. Her expression's unnerved me.

Instead I go down to see Daddy.

*   *   *

He's settled already in his pyjamas, reading the local paper he prefers, the radio on, his whisky by his side. I can't fault Mona on her care for him.

I smile at him. 'Hi Daddy.' I wait to see if he recognises me this evening.

At last he looks up. 'Where's Mona? I want Mona!'

'You can have her later. I've come to see how you are. And to get my necklace,' I tell him. 'The one you gave me when I was born.'

'What necklace? I haven't seen a necklace.'

'My special necklace, the one that says *Theodora* on it. I left it so you would remember that you live with me, your daughter, that I'm the one you always liked best.'

'I don't know where it is.'

'Daddy, you must know. I put it here, on your table, to remind you who I am. Your gift from God. Your eldest. Theodora.'

'I don't remember seeing anything.' A furrow crosses his papery old brow, tears spring up in the corners of his eyes. I've upset him. This is not what I intended.

Mona's made me do this. And I know now that tampons are the least of my worries. Mona is too clever to take things of value from my room, but she's also clever enough to know what an unreliable witness Daddy would be.

Smarting with indignation, I leave him, and return to Mona's room.

'Mona, my necklace is missing, I left it in Daddy's flat. Where have you put it?'

She looks up at me. 'What?'

'My necklace, the one I wear here.' I pat my throat. 'I gave it to Daddy in his flat and now it's not there. You must have it.'

Her face has gone stony blank again.

'Where is it?'

She shrugs. And I know no amount of questioning will make her weaken.

175

There's nothing I can do, because Daddy's started to bang on the ceiling and faintly, through the floorboards, up the dumb waiter shaft, and simultaneously in an echo through the baby monitor that she has set up by her bed, his voice fills the room in a chorus, calling, 'Mona! Mona! I want Mona.'

PART TWO

The Girl with a Dolphin

CHAPTER TWENTY-SIX

It is Saturday, and I am drained and exhausted.

'Today is the English weekend,' I tell Dora. 'I need a day off.'

'I'm sorry, Mona, but Daddy's requirements don't stop just because it's a Saturday. He's very dependent on you. Won't have anyone else.'

'I'm tired. I haven't had any free time since I came.'

'I'll decide when you're to have a day off.'

'Getting up in the night, working from first thing in the morning, I need to rest as well or—'

'I think, Mona, that you have perhaps been paying yourself for more hours than you've worked. We'll talk about it another time. I've got to go now. I'm meeting my sister for coffee.'

'Or,' I call after her, as she gathers her things, 'I could take all my days off at once and you could pay for me to go home for a few days.'

I finish clearing the kitchen, counting the Saturdays and Sundays I've worked, keeping a record of how many days Dora owes me. Then I go down to Charles's – and stop in shock.

The flat has been vandalised! The umbrella-stand has fallen over and the umbrella lies half-open across the floor. Papers from the table are strewn all over the carpet. A photo he keeps on the wall has fallen off and the frame lies snapped on the floor.

Charles is standing on a chair in the middle of his sitting room in bare feet, his walking stick in one hand. The room's in chaos. His broken whisky glass lies upturned on the floor, the liquid forming a dark stain on the carpet. Books have been flung about, and a tin of biscuits has been wrenched open, half of its contents trodden into the carpet.

Charles himself is only half-dressed, in a dirty sagging vest and underpants. He's got little goose bumps on his arms, and his legs look very white in the dim light.

'Rats,' he says. 'A big 'un, just crossed the sideboard. They come in here and eat everything if you don't keep on top of them.'

He thrashes at the cupboard, shattering a crystal glass decanter that he keeps there.

'Charles, I can't see any rats!' I move around the flat, checking. If necessary, I think, I'll drag Endymion down and make him work for once. But I can see no evidence of rodents. Must be one of Charles's hallucinations.

I take the walking stick out of his hand. Help him down off the chair, find a fresh pair of cashmere socks to pull onto his unexpectedly soft white feet, and sit him in the armchair next to the gas fire, out of harm's way.

'Which one are you?' he asks. 'You all keep changing your hairstyles, it's hard for me to keep up.'

'I'm Mona,' I tell him. 'Dora's helper.'

'Mona, of course. My favourite girl, my favourite waitress. Of course Dora's not here. I haven't seen her for months. She's got a very important job. On the radio.'

'Yes.'

'And Terence is all over the world and Anita, the Pretty One, she's got her children. They're all so very busy. Simon doesn't work but he hasn't been to see me in years.' A tear has come to his eye.

'Oh Charles,' I say, taking his hand. He has these times when he's back in the here and now, but it makes him sad. He's happier in his muddled world, where the past and the present tangle and he doesn't know who anyone is, or what he's supposed to be doing. But he's not safe in it. The mess in the flat is a result of his muddled world. I can't leave him down here any more. I was right when I said to Ummu that he should not be left alone under the ground. I help him into a shirt, a waistcoat and jacket, clean pants and trousers and a scarf.

Then when I've gathered the soiled clothes he's left on the floor in a pile, and squashed them into a carrier bag, I fetch some bleach from the kitchen and scrub at his chair where it's wet.

Upstairs, I tell Leo to get up and let his grandfather sit on the sofa.

'I'm playing *Call of Duty*. Leave me alone.'

'It's Saturday,' I say. 'Your weekend. A young boy like you, you need to get exercise. Play football, or go to a gym. Go on. Out!'

He looks at me for a few minutes, then, with a kind of twinkle he stands up.

'Whatever you say, Mona,' and he slouches off.

When he's gone I take Charles's old hand in mine. Funny how, compared to his feet, his hands are so worn, so crumpled, the skin waxen and cold. Blotchy with brown spots. I squeeze it. The human contact feels strange after so long. He looks at me. I can see he's bewildered. Confused about who I am. But wanting to trust me.

And I don't want to let go. Sitting here with this old man in his confusion, for the first time in weeks I feel some affection both from and for someone.

CHAPTER TWENTY-SEVEN

Anita's asked to meet me in a café on Westbourne Grove. I step into its 'shabby chic' interior, a world away from Deptford High Street. Here are the beautiful people, the androgynous, bronzed species whose taut skin seems to give off an inner light. As if it isn't skin at all but some specially designed material, ultra-gorgeous. Even the waiters look super-healthy, flitting between tables, their skirts and trousers slipping just below their narrow hips revealing their tattooed lower backs. There's no question that wealth creates beauty, health, fitness. You want to keep a woman down – you feed her junk food and dress her in things from the pound shop.

Anita's sitting at a corner table, two large cappuccinos and a plate of croissants in front of her. She waggles her nails at me. 'Nice colour, don't you think? It's called Sable. I've just had them done.'

'Lovely,' I say, making a mental note that I could do with a manicure. It's been weeks.

'But I'm a bit down,' my sister says.

'What's up?'

'I found a grey hair.'

I smile. I've never been one to shy away from the changes age brings. I was always, in fact, fascinated by the machinations of my body. How does it know to do the things it is supposed to do at the right time? I observe with detached interest the very slight droop around my mouth, the sharpening of my cheekbones, a more serious look about the eyes. And I like it. I have no problems with it. Max likes it too. I'm more me now than I've ever been.

Our bodies are like planets, obeying laws outside and beyond their control, and there is something rather beautiful about this. I'm impatient with the endless anxieties my sister Anita suffers each time she spots crow's feet about her eyes, the faintest wrinkle in her frankly perfect skin.

'My God, Anita,' I say now. 'Haven't you got better things to worry about?'

'Well, yes, as a matter of fact I have. I'm worried about Daddy. How's it going?'

'Oh, up and down. His old self one minute, the epitome of charm. Terribly confused and forgetful the next, needs reminding to eat. Says inappropriate things. And the other day he wanted to go to Billingsgate in the middle of the night.'

Anita laughs.

'It's not funny, Anita. He could get lost, hurt, anything.'

'It's the thought of him saying inappropriate things.'

'They're sometimes hurtful.'

'I can imagine. But you mustn't take them to heart. It's not him, it's his condition. God, it was hard work taking him out the other day. It took so long! It was exasperating. I can see why you need Mona.'

'She's not a qualified carer.' I pull a corner off a croissant.

'Well no,' says Anita, sucking jam off her beautifully manicured thumb. 'But she's capable of doing the job. That's the main thing. We agreed it would have been impossible to pay for a care home – at least until we've sold the house.'

'Hmm,' I say.

'What?'

'She's furtive. She bought roses for Daddy. He thought they were for Mummy. He thought Mona had taken them to her in hospital. Then I saw she'd put them in her room. And there have been times she's used his paper, pens and things.' I hesitate, unsure whether to tell Anita how foolish I'd been, leaving my necklace in Daddy's flat. I don't want her to think me a complete idiot for trusting that Mona was too clever to steal valuables.

'For goodness' sake, Theodora. Mona's poor! She'll be desperate. You leave things lying around, she'll think you're not bothered about them. She's bound to pilfer the odd item.'

'I don't want to mistrust her. I don't want to accuse her of things she might not have done.'

'I'd be careful.'

'What do I do?'

'Sack her? Find someone else?'

'I can't! Daddy's devoted to her. No one else will do any more. As far as he's concerned, the sun shines out of her—'

'Daddy's always liked a pretty young girl.'

'She's not a young girl, Anita. You've seen her – she's my age. But Daddy's got to know her. He needs consistency, and she's always there for him. When she isn't, he gets upset. What I need to know is, how can I make sure she doesn't take things into her own hands? I'm out during the day. She's there. I can't keep an eye on her all the time.'

I don't want to say I can't cope or admit I'm afraid of things getting out of control, the way they did with Zidana. Anita doesn't even know about Zidana. I don't want to tell her that I'm afraid that Daddy is becoming so attached to Mona he is forgetting it's me whose house he's living in. Or that she has won Leo's respect in a way I've never achieved.

'Lock up your valuables, of course, Dora – tell her you're watching her. That you know what she's doing. That she's here to look after Daddy and is earning money for the things she wants to buy. She must have a contract?'

'Of course.' I hadn't thought about a contract. It hadn't occurred to me.

'Show it to her and remind her. Of her timetable. Of what she's allowed and not allowed. If she's pilfering already, who knows what she might do. A tight rein is what you need.'

'Thanks, Anita. You're right. I've perhaps been too lenient. Too keen to trust her.'

'Think what she's eating and drinking; what that's costing you. She has a wage if she wants to buy extras.'

'I sometimes wonder if she's got another agenda other than being here to work.'

'They all do, Dora! Like I said, you just have to keep a tight rein. It's good you've got someone though. To be honest we all thought you were being a bit of a martyr, insisting Daddy move in with you.'

'A martyr, Anita?'

'The way you took him on when you had Leo to worry about. It seemed beyond the call of duty. But you insisted.'

I drain my cappuccino. This conversation is suddenly veering off into something else. Unsaid things are bubbling to the surface.

'Someone had to. I thought you'd all be glad. In fact, it would seem you're all thrilled to be let off the hook. You've shown a total lack of interest in him.'

'You see? "Lack of interest"! It's not *our* lack of interest. It's *your* refusal to let us help. Like when Si and I came to take him out.'

'Ha! Exactly. You came too late! If you visited more often you'd *know* he has his lunch at twelve. Neither of you had been for months. I've given up on Terence completely – he's vanished as far as I'm concerned. Who else was going to be there for Daddy?'

'You sure it wasn't just your way of ensuring you got his—'

'What are you saying, Anita?'

'Oh, I don't know. He's living with you, yes, but suddenly, hey, you've got a live-in helper and the blue china's in your house, Mummy's statue is in your garden. It's like you feel justified in helping yourself to everything, including the last remnants of Daddy's affections. Yes. You always *seem* to do the right thing, but Simon wonders and so do I, whether sometimes this philanthropy has a hidden advantage. Daddy living with you means you can bask in his approval.'

'What?' I stare at her. 'You've no idea, have you? Daddy isn't the man he was, he doesn't know how to approve of me any more. If there was at least that consolation, it wouldn't be so hard!'

'Well then. It means you have all the control over his house, his stuff. How come Mummy's head is suddenly in your garden, for example?'

'You didn't want Mummy's head. You used to hate it.'

'Yes, but it was the assumption that somehow, because you're the big sister, you could just take it. There's some vested interest in your being so marvellous all the time, not letting the rest of us get a look-in.'

So this is it. The real reason she wanted to meet. Why didn't she get to the point straight away? Save time on the niceties.

'It just seems sometimes, Dora, that you've got it all . . .' Her voice has started to wobble, with that pent-up tension that is obvious in someone who's been keeping their true thoughts to themselves for some time. 'The perfect job. The vindication of dealing with Daddy – and half the family heirlooms.'

'I thought you wanted to have a civil conversation,' I say. I stand up. Make as if to leave.

'Sorry, Dora.' She capitulates. 'Don't go. I shouldn't have said those things. But I'm so tired. Absolutely knackered. Jemima's been up three times a night for the last fortnight and my nerves are frayed. I suppose I'm upset about Daddy, too. As is Simon.' She goes on: 'Look, he's sent some halva from his last trip to Greece for him. Here. He remembers Daddy used to like it.'

'He can't eat it,' I say. 'He can barely chew now, with his teeth. Another example of what I was saying . . .'

'Bloody hell, Dora! What you don't get is we do care. You just won't let us.'

'Oh please, come over, see him, be my guest.'

'What you need to understand is that the boys do love Daddy. They do things their own way. Terence is sorting out his finances, it's his way of contributing. I've talked to Ruth about it and she says he's all cut up inside.'

I soften a bit.

'OK. Well, for your information I don't actually care about the stuff. If you want Mummy's head, take it. All I ask is that you and Simon and Terence come and see Daddy sometimes.'

'Actually, I was going to suggest you, Leo and Daddy come to us for Christmas,' Anita says.

'Oh?'

'So, would you like to? You could bring Mona, too, of course, to help, then you'd get a bit of a break. But Daddy might enjoy being with the kids.'

'Leo's going to Morocco for Christmas, to Roger. But yes, thank you, that sounds nice, Anita.'

I feel the usual depression move in, knowing that while everyone else is in festive mode, I will only be aware of absences. Leo, of course, this year. And Max, as always. But at least Anita is contributing something.

'Thanks, Anita,' I say, and we peck each other warily on the cheek as I leave.

*   *   *

I don't feel like going straight home when I leave Anita. I might as well make the most of Daddy's sudden devotion to Mona.

I pop to Selfridges, where a make-up saleswoman offers to do my face, and I have my own manicure. I check my mobile several times. How long now since I last heard from Max? I have a rule that I won't contact him until he's contacted me. It's a pride thing but I'm also afraid of my text arriving when he's with Valerie. That I'll blow our cover. After the manicure I treat myself to a new dress, some gloves. Then I go to the gold counter and look at the necklaces.

Nothing will replace the one that's gone missing. The frustration I felt at Mona's rigid expression when I asked her where it was assails me again.

I'm completely impotent. If I accuse her of stealing, she'll deny it. If I sack her, I'll be tied down caring for Daddy alone again. As I leave the shops I feel the absence of the gold chain round my neck, a chilly imprint on my skin.

It's dark by the time I arrive home. The light's on in the drawing room. Odd – Leo usually sits in the dark.

I push open the door.

Daddy's there, on the sofa, watching TV, his feet up on the pouffe.

'Daddy! What are you doing up here?'

'Mona brought me up. It makes a jolly good change.'

'But where's Leo?'

'Leo's out at work,' Daddy says in his happy stupor.

I leave Daddy and go to find Mona, Anita's words running through my head. *A tight rein is what you need.* She's walking all over me now, ignoring my rules, taking things into her own hands.

She isn't in her room or in the kitchen and there's no sign of Leo.

I mix a much-needed martini, wondering how Mona's managed to get Leo out of the drawing room again. Then I take a slice of white bread from the bread bin and am about to squish a cheese triangle into it when Mona appears. For some inexplicable reason I hold the bread out of sight behind my back.

'Mona, Daddy needs to go downstairs.'

'I was just going to—'

'Take him! Leo needs the drawing room and Daddy doesn't like car chases. You're not to bring him upstairs without asking me.'

I don't say that I'm afraid of Leo's reaction when he sees he's been banished from his lair.

It's then I notice the bag she's carrying.

She's been off shopping again, buying things with my money while she should have been watching Daddy!

'Give me that.'

'What . . .?'

'The bag. Give it to me. I want to see what you've bought.'

She stares at me, blinking, that inscrutable expression on her face, then hands me the bag.

Inside are some crumpled garments, and the stench of stale wine.

'What . . .?'

'Your father's clothes – I'm going to wash them. He . . . he soiled them. That's why I brought him upstairs. His chair was damp. His flat was in a mess when I went down this morning. I thought there were burglars! I've cleaned the chair and left it to dry but Charles is warmer and more comfortable up here.'

And without looking at me again she goes off up to the laundry room to put the clothes in the washing machine.

CHAPTER TWENTY-EIGHT

It's Monday, and in the studios, Gina is poring over her computer, reading today's cases.

'Here's a woman who thinks her sister's unreasonably taken their father's swimming medals. He had two, and the sister took them both when he died, arguing that as she'd cared for him, she was entitled to them. The caller thinks it's only fair she should give her one. The thing is, they're not worth anything but they have sentimental value.'

Gina and I haven't mentioned our conversation in the pub, or my churlish leave-taking – and I hope it's forgotten. I've done my best to gloss over it, and we seem to be getting on all right again.

'The usual load of loonies.' I laugh. Gina hands me the list of callers she's found.

'There don't seem to be many,' I say, looking at it.

'It's all I could get.'

'Well, perhaps you could try a bit harder. Put a few more tweets out. There must be a way.'

I take a sip of my coffee.

'God, this is hideous. It tastes like dishwater. Where's Hayley?

Hayley – look, we've got a cafetière for coffee. Make it again. Three spoonfuls.'

I look back at my computer, start to read through the emails.

'You OK?' Gina asks me.

'I'm fine.'

'You were a bit abrupt with Hayley. She's only a young thing. Go easy on her.'

'She's here to get work experience,' I say, 'not to droop about making weak coffee. She needs to do what she's asked quickly. I've a programme to run. I need efficient people about me.'

If I'm to be fronting the biggest programme, I feel like reminding Gina, people need to understand I mean business!

'She's not being paid, you know. It's just work experience. You could speak nicely to her.'

'I think you should get on with your job and I'll do mine,' I say, without looking at her.

We're on air at eleven.

The first conundrum, the sister who thinks she's entitled to one of her father's swimming medals, creates quite a furore. One after another, people phone in saying it's only right that since there were two, the sisters should share them. I work through the calls, enjoying the power I have that allows me to cut off the more bigoted opinions.

At the end of the call I sum up.

'So let me recap. One of these women has sacrificed her life to look after her father. All she asks in return is to have her father's swimming medals. Her sister has done nothing, yet she expects to have one of them. Is that fair? Surely the sister who's put in all the time should have first shout?'

I wonder if Anita's listening to this. She probably isn't. She makes a point of ignoring my show. But maybe one of her friends will report back to her.

Gina's gesticulating at me across the studio. What's wrong with her?

As I pull on my coat, Rachel puts her head round the door. She's had her grey hair cropped.

'Your hair – it looks fantastic,' I say.

'You OK, Dora?'

'Yes, I'm fine. Why?'

'You got prickly with the callers.'

'None of them could see the issue. I don't know why Gina let them all through.'

'You're not supposed to give your opinion, Dora. You know that. You've always been impartial, but today you were pontificating. Are you tired?'

I don't say that I felt for the poor bloody sister who had done all the work. That there was a point to be made here.

'No, I'm not tired.'

Rachel frowns. 'Is your dad stressing you out still?'

'Well, of course he's a concern,' I say. 'No, Rachel, I felt, on this occasion, there was no argument. It needed saying.'

Doesn't she recognise that I am, after all, the expert here? It's my show. I'm the one they're head-hunting for the prime slot.

'Would you come into my office? I need to have a quick chat with you.'

I've been waiting for this. I picture Max's face when I tell him it's happened.

I've even secretly started to imagine the posters, my face, on billboards across London.

I've been working for Rachel for over two years – we're friends. We've had dinner at each other's houses. We've discussed clothes and hair endlessly over coffee. But sitting here in her office, on the chair strategically placed opposite and lower down than hers,

I remember that I am in fact her employee, someone she can pick up and drop at a second's notice. I'm at her mercy.

I sit up. Shift a little in my chair, link my fingers in my lap.

'I need to tell you that we're having to do some reshuffling,' she says. 'This economic downturn is affecting us like everyone else. The listening figures for your programme have dropped recently.'

'Have you any idea why?' I ask. I try not to sound alarmed.

'Who's to say?'

'You'd think people had more need of a programme like mine in these times, not less.' This could be a good thing though, I think; if my programme is losing listeners, all the more reason to move me to the celebrity chat show.

'Yes, it's odd,' she agrees. 'People seem to want to unburden their problems when other things are going well. When they're fighting to put meals on the table, minor emotional issues perhaps seem less urgent.'

'They're not minor to the listeners or they wouldn't be phoning in.'

'Whatever, the directors are asking everyone – not just you, Dora – to apply for a limited number of positions. I'm sorry. You know I've always championed you, your programme, but things change.'

I can't speak for a few seconds. It's as if the horizon has suddenly swung away and I'm looking at a different one entirely.

'Rachel.' I hear a strange, urgent plea in my voice that startles even me. 'I assume you still want me to apply for the prime-time show you mentioned to me only a couple of weeks ago?'

She moves a few things about on her desk, uncomfortably. Swings back in her chair to face me.

'Things have changed, Dora. They seem to have re-thought the whole thing . . . I'm sorry. I feel rather responsible for having misled you.'

'You certainly have.' Max's delighted face looms into my mind, the way he looked when I told him I was to move to the prime-time slot.

'But I'm afraid I have to tell you: there have been some concerns too about your attitude on air.'

'*What?*'

'Just, you know, be aware that you're veering towards a bit of bias. We've had a few tweets.'

'What do you mean?'

'That you have to keep your feelings out of this. You know that, Dora. Just lately, you've been letting a few things slip. Last month it was the university fees issue. Then there was the time you said it always falls on the shoulders of the oldest daughter to look after their parents. Listeners are like vultures. They swoop on anything they can. Stay neutral! It's always been one of your strengths. Don't let me down now.'

'Now?'

'When everything in radio is so precarious.'

'Is it?'

'Dora! We're up against smartphones, people downloading what they want when they want. Stay on your toes.'

'I'm trying to, Rachel. I've perhaps not been up to scratch lately, with my mother dying and everything, but I can get the figures back up. Give me a couple of months. I can apply myself fully now I've got this carer for Daddy.'

'Dora, believe me, I've argued your corner. And they're willing to consider your application. But please do be aware that things are not looking good. You'll be receiving notification about the application processes and so on. And if there's anything I can do to keep Theodora Gentleman on air, please believe me that I'll be there.'

'*Keep me on air*? You mean there's a chance I won't have a programme at all?'

'It's not up to me, Dora,' she says.

'Right.' I stand up. 'I'm sorry, but I can't hang about. I need to get back to my father. I need to check he got on all right with Mona today. For some reason,' I can't resist this, 'it seems to have fallen upon my shoulders as the oldest daughter to take him on.'

I take the river walk home. It's late November and has turned colder.

I need to do something to secure my place at the radio station, not just my present place but the promotion I have begun to think myself into. To rely on.

I pass a window glowing in the lamplight and see a group of people laughing around a table. There's a woman waiting on them. She's wearing a blue overall, and it suddenly occurs to me that this is the way to denote a person's position. Mona has been overstepping the boundary because she forgets she is an employee in my house. The women who worked for us in Morocco never forgot because we made them wear overalls.

Filled with a sense of renewed optimism, I begin to plan. I haven't had a dinner party for ages. Rachel's my friend. A dinner party wouldn't go amiss. My house is looking good these days with Mona there to clean and she's a pretty amazing cook as well. I could do some gentle socialising, a little schmoozing.

I'll get Mona to make the whole thing look beautiful. She can serve drinks and canapés the way the women did when I was married to Roger.

I turn off the main embankment into the alley. The street-lamps throw off a murky light along the river path ahead of me. I have to squint to see through the dark and a mist that has rolled in off the Thames. The mist catches in my throat; it's cold, with the harsh taste of London fumes. My feet make barely any sound as I walk. I reach the creek where the path turns inland a little way to circumnavigate what is now a small marina. It's lonely here.

I begin to hurry. The path immediately ahead is narrow, lined on either side by converted warehouses, now in darkness. I've forgotten how remote parts of this walk can seem by night, as if, however many new buildings are constructed, the hinterland of the river remains stubbornly forlorn and hostile, just as it must have been in Dickens's day.

There's someone behind me. I increase my pace. I can hear the blood bang in my ears. I've been foolish deciding to walk when I could have got on a bus amongst the crush of commuters.

I take the next bend, into more shadows, fear propelling me so that I'm almost running. There's no one else around. Down below, the river rolls against the wall, the slosh of the water the only sound, apart from the distant rumble of traffic and the occasional plane overhead. I see myself as if from above, a lone figure, insignificant, hurrying along this dark ribbon of riverside path, the water below waiting to swallow me. My vanishing without trace.

So different from the image I had of myself the other day, able to contain and orchestrate the whole of the south-east. One day the whole country, even.

Surely it can't be true, what Rachel's just implied – that instead of moving up, I may end up with no show at all? My heart's racing and I'm no longer sure if it's due to this news, or the darkness that seems to be full of grey shadows.

At last I see the welcoming sight of the pub, its sign lit up, a crowd of people with cigarettes standing about outside, blue coils of smoke rising and mingling with the misty night air.

I ease my pace. A hand clamps down on my shoulder and I swing round.

CHAPTER TWENTY-NINE

Leo!

'Hello, darling. Where have you been?'

'The gym.'

'The *gym*?'

'Yes. What's wrong with that?'

'Nothing. I'm surprised, that's all.'

Exercise is anathema to him. I haven't mentioned that I was worried he was putting on weight. I tiptoe around him so as not to cause conflict.

'What, Mum? What's that look supposed to mean?'

'It's just . . . What's brought this on?'

'Just decided I'd like to do weights.'

'You know it costs a bit?'

'Not that much. I thought you'd be pleased.'

'I am, darling. I didn't think it was your sort of thing, that's all.' I nod at the cigarette he's lighting to emphasise my point, hoping he'll see the irony and laugh.

Instead, he ignores me and says, 'Mona suggested it.'

'Mona? What does *she* know about the gym, what it costs? She's in no position to tell you to go to the gym when you don't earn anything and she doesn't have to pay for it.'

'Fuck that then. I won't bother. You go on and on about me getting out. When I decide to do something, you manage to spoil it.'

We walk on a few steps.

'Look! Go to the gym. I'll pay. It'll be good for you. But you know . . .'

'What?'

'Maybe one day you could also think about getting a job.'

'Maybe one day you could think about cooking a decent dinner for once, like Mona does, instead of filling me up on junk food. Then maybe I wouldn't need to go to the gym.'

I wonder if he's doing this deliberately, knowing how his words sting.

We walk the rest of the way home in silence, and once back, Leo stomps up to his room.

In a little while Mona appears in the kitchen door.

'Dora?'

Her eyes are wide as if she's frightened of what she's about to say.

'I haven't had any time off since I came. I need to go home, just for a few days. Can I go? Take maybe four days, in a row. Then no more.'

'When?'

'Soon. Next weekend?'

'No. I'm having a dinner party next weekend, and I need you to cook. You've still got to pay off the fifty pounds a month you owe for the air fare, and you know very well you're supposed to pay for your own food and toiletries. You can't afford another flight.'

'I wonder if maybe you can lend . . .'

I could do without this. I need Mona here. She's part of my plan. If she's such a wonderful cook in Leo's eyes, then *I* should be benefiting from it as well.

200

I think of Anita again, reminding me I must stay in control, that I'm paying Mona to do what I want her to do.

'I'm having six people for dinner next Friday. You're to make the dining table look beautiful. You're to serve drinks and canapés and your lamb tagine.'

'So I can't take some days . . .'

'You must buy the meat from Waitrose. I don't want you getting that stuff from the butcher's.'

She blinks. Speaks quietly.

'It's cheaper at the butcher's on the High Street. It's very good there – I know good meat. And the butcher can do the bones for me.'

'I don't want you buying things for me from the High Street. I can't risk my guests getting food poisoning. You go to Waitrose, I'll draw you a map. And you can make some of the bread you made that Saturday, as well,' I say. 'Organic flour. You might as well get some of the stuff today, I'll write you a list.'

After dinner, I go on the internet and Google maids' uniforms. I should have guessed that the first images to pop up would be of women in sexy French maid outfits. Demeaning and ridiculous. Max's clichéd fantasy comes to mind. These outfits are exactly the opposite image to the one I want to create for Mona. I scroll down until I reach some plain uniforms. I buy three of the least appealing I can find, and will offer them as a gift to Mona to wear while she's in my house. I want her to understand that she's at work, that she dresses appropriately when she's cleaning for me and caring for Daddy.

My status on the radio may be in question but I am, after all, Mona's employer – and I intend her to remember it.

CHAPTER THIRTY

'Ummu,' I whisper into the phone, 'I can't come home. There is some important work Dora needs me to do.'

'Oh well. I thought it might be difficult. Don't worry, Mona, we're coping. As long as you keep sending the money.'

'Have you had your scan?'

'It's tomorrow. The doctor says I may need treatment afterwards, depending on the results. I'm sorry, Mona, this is all costing more than I imagined.'

'If I could find Ali,' I blurt out before I can stop myself, 'he could provide for us. We wouldn't be in this situation! If he's got citizenship, you could come over too – hospitals are free here. And we could all be together!'

'Ali Ali Ali!' she says. 'I told you to forget Ali. A man who leaves his wife and child and doesn't get in touch . . .'

'Ali is my oldest friend as well as my husband,' I say. 'He would never just leave us. I will find him. I'm making enquiries.'

'Yousseff had some news,' Ummu says then.

'*What?!*'

'Yousseff. Says he had some news of Ali. Says he's living in London for sure. He doesn't know exactly where.'

'Why didn't you tell me this?'

'Because Ali hasn't told you himself. It makes me wonder if he wants you to find him.'

'But perhaps he can't. Perhaps he's in some kind of trouble and can't contact me. Perhaps he's waiting for me to help him.'

'If he's in trouble, Mona, you should stay away.'

'I don't mean in trouble with the law. I mean perhaps he's not been able to get work, has no money, is living rough somewhere. Perhaps he lost his phone or had to sell it – I don't know, Ummu. There are lots of things that happen to people when they come to find work – tragic things, you know that. He may be being exploited somewhere: you remember the things Rachida told us, about immigrants getting picked up. I'm afraid for him.' My heart's racing. 'Please ask Yousseff to give you all the information he's got.'

Ali in London! Closer than I dared to imagine! He could be round the corner. My imagination starts to work. You never know in a city like this, you can go for years without knowing who is living right next door to you.

Sayed's words come back to me: *Everyone round here . . . all the guys at the cab office, they's all from somewhere else. Some is legal, some is illegal.*

I'll ask him to make enquiries for me. The thought that I can do something definite to find Ali at last fills me with the kind of hope I haven't felt for weeks.

The street's bright and cold this late-November morning, and it smells of something sweet and smoky, masking the usual toxic odours of cooking fat, diesel fumes and stale alcohol.

'Ah, look, roasting chestnuts,' says Charles. 'Let's buy a bagful and take them home to eat by the fire. Follow my stick.'

The market swirls about me. The bales of purple and orange and gold fabric seem brighter, the saris, the sparkling piles of watches and mobile phones. Everything looks pretty in the light – even the nuts and bolts and rolls of tape in their gleaming blue baskets. I look longingly at the stalls of sweets and toys. Oh, to have the money to buy something for Leila! But there's no need to fret. Soon I'll be back with Ali, and Ummu and Leila can come and join us!

A picture of Ali comes to mind, swinging Leila into the air when she was tiny. And I can feel Leila now with my whole body, the weight of her tied onto my back as I go about my chores, or in my arms as I feed her. Her body sprawled wetly against mine as we bathe together at the hammam, the warm dense doughiness of it.

How her eyes would have shone, if she could have seen these stalls of toys, as if the world did after all possess some magic dust that could bring to life everything she'd ever wished for. I pick up a toy London bus, turn it over in the palm of my hand, picture Leila pushing it over the floor on her tummy, humming to herself gently. She deserves to have these things. I never wanted my child cast into an adult role so soon.

I remind myself, however, that Leila finds it easy to be over-joyed. She might not have many toys, but she can be mesmerised by a pregnant spider spinning its web, by the jewel-like seeds set in the flesh inside a pomegranate. She finds the magic around us, in the everyday, in stones made shiny under the water.

Sayed's at the counter in the newsagent's, scanning an old woman's shopping at the cash register. I wait for her to pay up and leave. Charles sits and looks at the papers, allowing me a moment to myself.

'Sayed,' I say in a low voice, 'I need your help.'

'Sure. What is it? You need documents? I can get passports, at a cost. Or you want me to send money?'

'No, it's nothing like that. I need you to keep this secret.'

'Don't worry, man. I know the score. Tell me.'

'I'm looking for this man.'

I pull Ali's photo from my tracksuit pocket and hold it up for him to see. Ali with Leila, his arms around her, their eyes squinting into the sun.

'He's in London, and I need to find him. He's a medical student. He believed he could get work here.'

'Does he speak English?'

'Yes, well. He always talked of coming to London. I've been told he's here but I'm afraid something's happened to him because he hasn't been in touch.'

Sayed examines the photo. 'What's his name? He's a medic, you say? I'll ask around. See what I can do.' He grins and looks at me, waiting for something. Then I see what he wants.

'Here.' I hand him five pounds, five pounds out of the money Dora's given me to spend on the food from her favourite shop, Waitrose.

He rubs his thumb and finger together. 'You expect me to help you for a fiver?'

I look at the money in my purse. Hand him another five pound note.

'I'll do what I can,' he says.

We leave the newsagent's and I push Charles up the street to the 99p shop where he bought his chocolate that first day I was here. I can get exactly the same stuff Dora wants from Waitrose for less than half the price here.

If this leads to something it will be worth a thousand pounds – and anyway, then I won't need Dora or her money any more.

Later, I ask Leo if I can check my Facebook page on his computer. My hopes soar as I see that there's a message from Amina, my friend who works for Dora's ex-husband. Has she heard news of Ali? I click on the message and it pops up. But what I read, instead of throwing any light on my situation, casts a shadow over everything.

Mona, my lovely friend, I've been talking with the gardener, Idriss. He's been here for years. He told me how much better it is now Claudia's in charge. I asked him what he meant but he wouldn't say any more. I just wanted to check you're OK. That Theodora is treating you well. I don't know what happened. What I do know is that he said if he had to work for Theodora again, after what happened to Zidana, he'd rather go and beg on the streets.

CHAPTER THIRTY-ONE

'Gosh,' says Sally, standing in the hallway, looking around. 'I can see you have help. Blimey, Dora, it's made quite a difference – the house looks pristine!' Sally's an old friend from my Blackheath days. We've known each other years, and kept in touch, as she still lives locally.

'Are you saying it didn't before?' I ask, smiling, taking her coat.

Mona's cleaned the house from top to bottom, and everything gleams. I'm feeling positive. My applications for the new presenter posts are in, one a move up, one a replacement of my current position, and though I've heard nothing, I feel certain they'll be well received. I've more experience than most of the likely applicants, and Rachel has always held me in high regard.

Sally's partner Bob is behind her holding two bottles of wine, one white, one red. As they stand there, Gina arrives brandishing more wine. Then Rachel, with her partner Martha. It's going to be a drunken evening – for them. I'm going to stay sober, keep my wits about me. Ensure I'm seen in my best light.

My only regret is that Max can't be here to share the evening with us. One of the many drawbacks of my affair is that I cannot share special occasions with the man I love. Christmas,

New Year, Easter and holidays, he has to be with his own family. It's at these times my yearning for him threatens to subdue any enjoyment I take in the occasion. Oh, I can smile, and talk and laugh with the others, but Max's absence leaves me melancholy underneath. My senses become heightened to other couples' intimacy, the protective shell afforded by a relationship. I yearn for that lovely post mortem where you can reveal your true thoughts about the people you've had to be polite to through-out the evening.

Without him, I feel raw and vulnerable.

It's one of the reasons I've included Gina. Two single women provide solidarity for one another.

Mona's laid the table we use at the far end of the drawing room with the white linen cloth, the antique embroidered table mats, and monogrammed white starched napkins that were my mother's. She's polished the silver bone-handled cutlery and put long tapered candles in glass holders. The only things missing are the soup spoons.

'Mona, we use the round spoons for soup.'

She's in the kitchen, wearing the overall that's arrived, blue polyester with a white collar, her head bent over the large pan that's giving off that mouth-watering smell only Mona's capable of producing.

'What?'

'Soup spoons.' I open what my mother used to call the 'canteen of cutlery'; an antique walnut box where she kept the bone-handled knives, forks and spoons.

I lift the top layer. The soup spoons live in the bottom layer, cupping each other in their little velvet slots.

'Where are they?'

She doesn't reply, continuing to stir the soup. It's happening again – the expressionless mask that descends when I question her.

'Mona, I want to use my mother's spoons for the soup. They're not here. They're not on the table. Where are they?'

She's pouring the soup into a tureen as if she hasn't heard me.

'Mona! Have you seen them? The spoons.'

No reaction.

'Dora!' Gina is calling from the drawing room.

I give Mona a hard stare before I rejoin my friends, but she doesn't look back.

My friends gasp and exclaim at the table.

'You're so lucky having Mona to help you!' Gina says. 'It all looks so beautiful.'

'She's an absolute star,' I say.

'Not meaning to be indelicate,' Sally says, slumping down on the sofa in the bay window, 'but doesn't it cost a fortune having a live-in . . . what do we call her? She isn't a nanny, and I suppose she does help with your dad, but she isn't a carer as such.'

'A live-in help?' says Gina.

'A maid?' offers Bob.

'We don't have maids in England these days!' says Sally.

'It's coming back into fashion,' I say, filling their wine glasses. 'Those of us with jobs and families are overworked, but there are plenty of people like Mona desperate for domestic placements. It works all round.'

'Has she got a PhD?' asks Sally. 'Like the Eastern Europeans who come over to do our menial work?'

I wonder if she's making some kind of point here.

'In Mona's case, no, she hasn't,' I say. 'I know a lot of workers over here, doing stuff no one else is prepared to do, are highly educated. But Mona's not had that benefit. She's delighted to have a job at all.'

I'm thinking about the spoons. What would Mona want with soup spoons? Yet they've gone! We'll have to use the stainless-steel ones I don't like. I think of her stony expression when I asked her where they were, and wonder suddenly whether they were ever there.

Have I insulted her by suggesting she might have taken them? Her pride is formidable, and I don't want to cross her. I haven't used the cutlery since bringing it from Mummy and Daddy's house – it's possible the spoons were already missing. There's also my necklace – which Daddy quite possibly put somewhere 'safe' and then forgot about. I need Mona too much to lose her by making any more accusations that might offend her, yet I can't let her humiliate me.

When Mona appears with trays of briouates, the little Moroccan pastries I've told her to make, everyone gasps and exclaims again.

'Did you make these?' Sally asks, and Mona nods. 'Well, Dora's very lucky.'

'Won't you stay and have a drink with us?' Bob asks.

I give him a look which he misses.

Mona smiles, and says thank you but no, and backs away. At least she knows the etiquette.

'She might not be educated, but my God she knows how to cook,' says Bob. 'You could put her on *MasterChef*.'

'*We* could do with someone like her,' says Sally. 'It's a bloody juggling act working, with the kids at two different schools, and Bob away most weekends.'

'Where the hell would we put a live-in maid?' asks Bob. 'We talked about having an au pair and agreed we don't have the space any more. Or the money. You have to have room. Dora's lucky. She's only got herself and Leo here and it's a nice big house.'

Sally gives him an accusing look, which says something like: *If it wasn't for you, we wouldn't be in this situation.* Sally's a teacher but she married Bob when he was earning a massive salary in some boom company that was hit by the recession. They had to downsize and now live in a cramped house in Brockley. Sally resents him for 'deceiving' her, even though she knows the economic crisis is not solely Bob's fault.

'You have to give them a decent space of their own,' I agree. 'Mona has her own room, where she can do what she likes in her free time. She goes in there to read, write, watch TV, or what-have-you.'

'Quite a nice life really,' says Gina. She's moving around the room with her gin and tonic, as she always does when she comes to mine, picking up books and turning them over as if she's checking I haven't acquired anything I haven't told her about. She's a very competitive best friend.

'She's got that lovely spare room up at the top of the house to retreat to, hasn't she? Spends the day doing a bit of mopping and polishing, then a couple of hours in her room to read. Then – what – a couple of hours preparing dinner, popping in to see your father.'

I wish Gina would sit down, stop examining my things.

'The best thing is that you know you're helping them out,' I say.

I'm feeling stupidly ashamed that I've misled Gina about Mona's room; worried my tiny lie might be spotted. That one of my guests might put their head round the study door and see where Mona's really sleeping.

Mona comes into the room with the steaming tagine.

Everyone's voice drops as she moves around the table, and Bob thanks Mona as she serves the lamb which is savoury with the zing of fresh coriander and a spicy undertone – saffron maybe, and cinnamon.

'Has she got family?' Rachel asks when she's gone again.

'She won't talk about it. It upsets her.'

'Bloody hell,' says Bob. 'That's dreadful. I wonder what she's been through?'

'So I suppose she had nothing to lose,' says Rachel. 'In coming over here, I mean. It must have been a lifeline.'

'But can you imagine it? Working for another woman, having to be subservient in *her* house. I'd hate that,' Sally says.

You can divide the world, I realise now, into those who feel it's OK to hire help and those who don't. It's a flashback to the times when the classes in England were more divided. It was easier then, when the employer and the servant had clearly defined roles and the rules about socialising were strictly adhered to. Now everyone's so conflicted about it, feeling guilty on the one hand for affording help, on the other pleased to be able to offer employment to someone who otherwise wouldn't have it.

'She's used to domestic work,' I say. 'She's not got a problem with status, it's her job. Things have always been like this. Once upon a time every house in Deptford had a domestic servant, even the working families with no money. It's nothing new. Some people are born to serve. It's what they do.'

'And others to be served upon,' says Gina, who's knocking back the wine and sounds tipsy.

'Anyway, going back to what we were saying, I think it must be bloody tough, leaving her own home in order to work so far away,' Sally goes on.

'Don't be too soft, Sally,' says Gina. 'These migrant workers know which side their bread's buttered. She's got a contract, hasn't she, Dora? Stipulating her hours, days off and all that. Holiday pay and so on.'

This is the second time I've heard talk of a contract recently; it was Anita who assumed we had one last time. But Roger made no mention of a contract and for the time being I'm happy to muddle along without. It's a learning process for me, and I wouldn't know what the contract should consist of anyway. I need to keep our arrangement informal until I've ascertained exactly how much I'm going to need Mona to do.

'But what courage,' Sally persists, and I begin to wonder whether she does indeed have a hidden agenda – that she wants to make me feel guilty for some reason. 'When we travel, it's for amusement, even those who claim they're contributing. You know – gap-year students, gap-year oldies.'

'Oldies?' I ask.

'Yeah! Semi-retired people who bugger off thinking they'll help build schools in Burundi because their kids have left home. Frances did it – that woman I used to work with. But that's temporary, a lifestyle choice. Imagine not having a choice, your only hope being to work for some complete stranger in her house. It must be horrid.'

'Horrid? I hope not,' I say. 'I hope she appreciates living here with me. She's earning a better living than anything she would achieve in her home country. What you have to understand, Sally, is that Mona was desperate. She was terribly poor. It's hard to imagine what that means, sitting here in middle-class London. Literally, she was living hand-to-mouth, one step from begging.'

I pause. I don't really have any idea about the circumstances Mona's left behind, she's so closed. So proud.

I go on.

'Here, she's getting huge advantages, apart from the wage – a comfortable bed, regular, wholesome meals, she's learning English, and it's taking her mind off whatever happened to her husband. So I don't think there's any need for middle-class guilt.'

'I wouldn't call it middle-class guilt,' says Sally. 'If you put yourself in her shoes, you can see that it must be lonely some-times, and you know – demoralising.'

'Oh come on, Sally,' says Gina. 'We don't know what's true and what isn't! Could be she just fancies a British passport. You'll have to watch she doesn't bring her whole family over. You might have taken on more than you bargained for, Dora!'

'Does she get the chance to meet up with other women from her country? People in a similar situation? Does she get to ESL classes or anything like that? Does she get time off?'

I open my mouth to say that I'm not a charity, that Sally's concern is all very well, but when you find yourself caring for an elderly father, whilst supporting an unemployed son, when you're in charge of a programme which goes out to a whole swathe of the country – you make use of the resources available. Which includes domestic workers eager to improve their lives. But I'm getting a little tired of the conversation.

Rachel senses this, and steps in.

'I think we need to recognise that Dora's situation is problematic at the moment,' she says. 'Employing Mona has been the best thing she could have done for everyone. For her father, for Leo and for Mona herself.'

I smile across at her. I know what she's saying: it's also the best thing I could have done for my career.

Mona brings in the dessert.

'And,' I say, 'she likes it here. You like the river, don't you, Mona? We had a lovely day walking up to Tower Bridge, didn't we? We had cupcakes.'

Mona smiles, her eyes darting round the room from one to the other of us.

'And you like taking Daddy to the market, don't you? Choosing fruit and vegetables. Mona's an excellent cook.'

'I can see that,' says Bob. 'This is all bloody delicious.' He smiles and winks at Mona. Is he flirting?

I wonder if Mona's the kind of woman men find alluring because she looks naive, vulnerable. And the thought flashes into my mind that perhaps she knows just how to exploit it.

'Do you get out much?' Sally asks her. 'Have you seen any of London's tourist attractions?'

I give Mona a look. She glances at me, understands what she's meant to say.

'I hope to, soon. I've seen Tower Bridge,' she says, 'and I'd like to go to Harrods.'

Everybody laughs.

'Selfridges is better than Harrods these days,' says Rachel, 'isn't it, Martha?'

'Oh yes. Selfridges is fab. You mustn't miss it.'

Sally says, 'Or Harvey Nics.'

It's lucky that at this point, Mona backs out of the room. My friends have talked to her quite enough.

CHAPTER THIRTY-TWO

I carry the steaming tagine into the sitting room.

If I were at home, as I should have been this weekend, we would never eat in such a lavish way on a Friday night. We would be content with a simple couscous. Or the cheap cuts of meat the butcher sells off at the end of the day. And this thought causes a torrent of resentment towards Dora for refusing to let me go home just for a short while.

Here she is, laughing with her friends, charming them, as she did me when I first arrived.

I now wonder whether this is all an act. Amina's message has unsettled me. But Zidana was a young girl who probably didn't know how to look after herself.

Ali once whispered to me that when people took advantage of him, as they sometimes did when he worked as a guide, he found ways of retrieving what they had taken from him in terms of his dignity. He might take something small from them, or he might give them a piece of false information that led them to a rough neighbourhood rather than a tourist attraction. Just some little practical joke that gave him a sense of redressing the balance.

At the time I was shocked, and told him he was wrong, but

now I'm understanding more and more that when you're a subordinate, you have to do little things to preserve your sense of self.

As I carry the dish to the table, I pass two women who sit close together – a couple, I'm guessing – one with grey hair shorn like a boy's, the other tall and black, her long legs sprawling across the other's. She stares at me as I move and I wish I was invisible, that the tagine could carry itself across the room so I was not the subject of their curiosity.

A short fat man opens his tight little mouth as I pass.

'Did you make these . . . whatever they are?' he asks.

'Briouates,' I say, and nod.

I feel his eyes on me, the way men's eyes are drawn to a woman's body.

The others smile politely, and wait for me to leave. They all have glasses in their hands; they've already drained one bottle of wine, and Dora's going about filling their glasses.

Outside the room I pause, put my ear to the door. They're discussing me. It seems one of the women is concerned for me.

'Is she attending ESOL classes?' she asks.

I could burst in, shout, 'No, I'm not – but I'd like to. Even better, I'd like to attend IT classes. Please, have a word with Dora. Suggest she lend me the money to visit Ummu.'

Of course I don't do this. I know my place.

I return to the kitchen.

I take a knife from Dora's block and slice oranges. The blade's so sharp it slips straight through the flesh, sending juice spurting up into my eyes where it catches and stings. I place the glossy slices on a decorative ceramic dish she must have bought when she lived with Roger in Morocco, lift it, weighing it in my hands, imagining the crunch it might make were I to drop it from a height . . . sprinkle the orange slices with sugar, add cinnamon from a tiny glass jar.

As I move across the kitchen there's the ping of a text coming into a mobile. I look around. My phone is tucked in the bottom of my bag, and the sound was closer than that. Then I spot it – Dora's phone that she left lying on the kitchen table when she was having her large martini before her guests arrived.

I click 'inbox'.

I can just about work out that the text is from Dora's man. Max.

I peer at it.

I wonder if I'll ever meet him, this wealthy doctor. I think of Ummu, her insinuation that it's the men who one can make use of when one is in need. Perhaps she has a point. After all, he's from the States, that legendary land all my friends used to dream of getting to – including Ali.

There's a photo of a statue with the text. A naked girl with a dolphin. What an odd fascination Dora and Max have with these monuments! The girl in the photo by Dora's bed, then the day she went off to meet him beside the famous Boudicca statue. Ummu will find this amusing.

I can't read the text which is, of course, in English, but I pick up my phone and put Max's number into my contacts box. Just in case. Just because you never know who might come in useful. It's something Ummu taught me, to look out for those who might help you get out, move on.

I put my mobile back in my bag, take another look at the text and smile.

'What are you doing?'

I look up.

Dora is standing in the kitchen doorway watching me, and I freeze.

CHAPTER THIRTY-THREE

'Nothing,' Mona says. 'I'm doing nothing. I heard a text. I think it's yours.' She hands me my phone.

I take it from her, see at once there's a text from Max. My heart lifts.

'I'm going upstairs,' I say. 'Mona, kindly take in the next course.'

If it wasn't for the fact Mona can't read a word of English, I might have felt disturbed by the fact she had my phone in her hand, but I'm far too eager to read Max's message to worry about anything else now.

In London on 12 December, he writes. *Be under the Girl with a Dolphin. By Tower Hotel St Katherine's Dock. 7 p.m. Can hardly wait. Miss you badly.*

I smile. Tower Hotel! I know what this means. He only books hotels if he doesn't have to leave before morning. I'm filled with warmth and goodwill. I sit down on my bed and compose a text to send back to him. It's as if he has a sixth sense, knows how much I have been yearning for him all evening.

When I get back downstairs, Mona's sitting on a stool amongst my guests, a book open in front of her.

Sally is pointing out pictures of London monuments, and giving Mona a potted history lesson.

'You must try and go to St Paul's while you're here,' she's saying, 'and, of course, the Houses of Parliament.'

I grow hot. If I say anything to Mona in front of my friends they'll think me unreasonable. Mona's not stupid, that's becoming more apparent each day – she knows I won't want to appear harsh in front of them. But if I say nothing, I'm letting her step over a boundary – mixing socially with my friends. She must know this is not allowed. So why is she flouting an unspoken rule? Is she trying to inveigle her way into the affections of my friends as well as my father and son?

'That's an interesting book,' I say.

Mona looks up, startled, realising I've come into the room. Seeing my expression, she relaxes and smiles back.

'Sally, she offered to teach me about London.'

'I did indeed,' says Sally. 'I was telling Mona she should go to the Tower, Madame Tussauds, and both Tates while she's here.'

'Mona, it's Daddy's bedtime,' I say.

She put Daddy to bed some time ago, but I raise my eyebrows at her, hold her gaze.

She blinks up at me. Gets the hint.

She picks up the book. Turns as she gets to the door, looks at Sally, or is it Bob – I wonder again if she's flirting – and says, 'There is just one problem. I haven't time to go to see these beautiful places. Or the money.'

It's gone 2 a.m. when Sally and Bob – the last of my guests – leave. I go into the kitchen. Mona's gone to bed. She retreated into her room hours ago, but the dinner-plates are piled unwashed on the side, the sink is full of pans.

I push open her door, switch on the light. She's asleep. I shake her awake.

'The kitchen,' I say. 'You haven't cleared up. You're to finish your chores before you sleep!'

I march upstairs feeling her eyes on me as I go, refusing to look back. How dare she insinuate to my friends that I'm not paying her enough? How dare she suggest I've not given her time off?

I lie in bed, listening to her crashing about with the dishes until sleep finally comes.

CHAPTER THIRTY-FOUR

I work in the kitchen while the rest of the world sleeps. The hums and clicks from the fridge and the pipes keep me company; the light from a streetlamp outside lends everything a soft orange glow. The constant vibrations beneath the city cease for a while. The cat creeps in and jumps onto the work surface. I push it off, shoo it down the hall and out of the front door.

Sayed has Ali's photo! I can tolerate any amount of scrubbing and washing pans and scouring to be with Ali again.

The first time Ali left our small village to study in the city, I thought that once there, he would meet new clever educated women and forget me. But he came back, brought me to the white house, where I lived as his wife while he studied and worked. That was my happiest time – when I fell pregnant with Leila, and then when she was a baby, Ali working by day, studying by night. We were the perfect, happy family. I learned to love cooking, and cleaning, and caring for Leila. I didn't miss my work at the garment factory. At first I missed the talking with my women friends there, but then I started to meet with a group of mothers in the Andalusian Gardens where we'd sit with the children and exchange gossip and recipes.

It was the first time I'd had equipment with which to make the dishes I liked. A tagine, a couscous steamer, pans and earthenware bowls. People came to our house for dinner and congratulated me on my bread, my *sfouf*, my *harira* and clafoutis. I dreamed one day of working as a cook, not a garment worker. Sewing was dry and methodical, but cooking was sensual and comforting. At the same time I was learning some English phrases from Ali, who came back each day more convinced he would be fluent enough to find work in Britain or in the States once he'd qualified.

When he came home each day, he'd grab Leila, throwing her into the air so she laughed with such intensity I was sometimes afraid she would explode. Then he'd put her down on one of the couches that ran along the walls and kiss her. I'd never seen him so lit up. We were both happy. His silence now can only mean one thing, that he's become stuck somehow, lost his phone, his papers, unable to go home to Morocco or to contact me.

I go to my bed at last at about three, locking the door behind me, welcoming the privacy.

I wake up to a harsh banging. It's already morning.

I drag myself up. Look at my mobile. It's 6 a.m. – I've only been asleep for three hours. The thumping comes again.

'Why did you lock the door?' Dora's scowling, her face rumpled after her drinking last night.

'I need to sleep. I didn't want to be disturbed.'

'I hope you had the monitor on, for Daddy.'

'Of course.'

'Today you're to buy a Christmas tree from the market. I want it placed in the front window. Leo will help you. He needs to get out and about and he's always enjoyed getting the Christmas tree.'

'A tree? In the house?'

'Yes, Mona. Christmas is coming, I want to make it nice for Leo and Daddy. The decorations are in the loft. Hoover up first. The room must be clean for the tree. I've left a list of shopping for you to do. Then the washing needs sorting. I'm popping into work to do a bit of research.'

As soon as she's left for work, I phone home. Leila answers, which is unusual.

'How's Tetta?' I ask, alarm surging through me. Why hasn't Ummu picked up? Did the scan find something serious that needed operating on immediately?

'The doctor says she must stay on the pills. We buy them with your money. But it's never quite enough. Hait's coming in every day to help me. When are you coming home, Ummu?'

'Soon, sweetie. I'll come soon.'

'Before Eid?'

'Of course.'

I think she knows I'm lying. That I have no idea when I'll be home.

'Are you being a good girl?'

'Yes, I am. Ahmed has lent me his scooter. We've been playing out on the alley. But I've been watching Tetta. I make her mint tea – Hait showed me how.'

'Good girl. Let me speak to Tetta.'

My mother's voice is even rougher than it was before. She has to break off the call to cough.

'How was the scan, Ummu? Have they told you anything?'

'No results yet. I have to go back and ask next week. But I don't feel any better, Mona, if you must know.'

'Ummu, I'm worried about you. Is there anything else I can do?'

'You can just carry on with what you've been doing. The money's what we need. Badly. Mona, once we've bought medication, there's barely enough for food. Can you send more?'

Perhaps it's the bad night's sleep I've had, or the lack of sunlight, or hearing Ummu wheeze into the phone, but everything feels hopeless, and home, and Ali, and everything I've been working towards further away than ever.

I give Charles his breakfast, get him into his coat, help him up the steps and round to the front door. I fetch his wheelchair from the cupboard under Dora's stairs and push open the drawing-room door.

'Your mother wants a Christmas tree,' I tell Leo. 'I can't carry a tree with the wheelchair by myself. You'll have to get up, get dressed, and come with me.'

I leave Leo and his grandfather choosing a Christmas tree from a stall on the High Street and pop into Sayed's shop. If he's heard anything, anything at all, it will give me the strength to carry on.

He tells me he's on the case, but so far there's been no news.

'I've got a mate who says he can check out the immigration holding centres,' he says, looking at me askance, 'but he'd want skrilla for more info.'

'Skrilla?'

He rubs his thumb and fingers together. 'Money, mate.'

'I already gave you money, Sayed. How much more does he want?'

'Ooh I dunno. I'll ask him. But he won't do it for nothing.'

If I could, I'd check these centres myself, but it's impossible with my inability to read English. I think of the city, sprawling for miles in every direction. The thought of venturing into its endless crowded streets, finding my way through the traffic, and the buildings, the subways, the shops and tower blocks and across its great river, is so intimidating I shiver.

Yet I can't afford to pay anyone else to search, with Ummu so badly in need of every dirham I earn.

I give up, tell Sayed I'll think about it and, feeling worse than ever, go out to find Leo and Charles.

Charles is pleading with Leo to take him home so we rest the tree on the handles of the wheelchair and push him back down the street, the spiny branches scraping against my arms as we go.

Leo sets the little green fir tree in a pot in the window of the drawing room, where it gives off a fresh piny smell like the trees in the forest where the basket-weavers work at home. Then he says I'll have to help him get the decorations down from the loft.

We leave Charles in the drawing room, and I follow Leo upstairs to the spare room beside Dora's bedroom. I haven't noticed the trap door in the ceiling before. He unhooks it with a pole, pulls it open, letting down a ladder which he then climbs up, his head disappearing into the black hole.

'You'll have to come up,' he calls.

I climb the ladder and follow him up into the roof.

There's a massive space above the house, a secret cavern overhead, full of suitcases and trunks, boxes and crates. Through the darkness, for there is no window here, I can make out the shape of a child's cradle, a cot, a train set. Remnants of Leo's childhood stashed away and forgotten.

Leo has disappeared into the shadows on the far side of the attic. The sounds from outside, from downstairs, fade. We are alone in this strange dark space. I remember the way I was afraid of Leo when I first saw him and I stay near the ladder so I can move quickly if I have to.

'I'll show you something,' Leo says. 'I don't think even Mum knows about this. Watch.'

He's in the shadows by the far wall, pushing against a tiny door, barely big enough to crawl through. The door gives and he goes forward on his hands and knees.

'Come and look!'

From behind him I can see that the door opens onto another greater, lighter space.

'Next-door's attic. Desiree's. I wonder if she's got anything worth nicking?'

'It's not your house!' I say, feeling a little thrill at his nerve. It reminds me briefly of Ali, when he said it was OK to take from those who stole your dignity. I don't think I really knew what he meant until I came to work for Dora.

'You're not to steal,' I tell Leo, thinking of the woman on the street who greets Charles but always ignores me. 'You're not to take things from next-door's house.'

He's backing out towards me again. 'I'm worried I might not squeeze back through if I go in there,' he says. 'I used to fit – before I put on weight. I used to go right to the other end. Meet up with Sayed and Johnny from the shop. The attics interconnect. I guess the original builders couldn't be bothered to put partitions up.'

I remember now, Sayed saying he lived in the same street as Dora. You never know who lives nearby, with the doors all permanently closed. For a wild second I imagine that Ali could live in one of these houses, that we might just have missed each other, coming and going at the wrong time of day and night. Then the thought strikes me as foolish, one that only serves to make the reality harsher.

I leave Leo hanging the decorations on the tree and go to complete the chores Dora asked me to do. It's almost dark again by the time I return. The tree is now covered in little animals and baubles and figurines, and a string of white lights.

'When you've finished your fussing with the tree, you can take me to Billingsgate,' Charles says, watching from his chair.

'OK, we'll do it, won't we, Mona? Take Grandpa to Billingsgate,' Leo says. 'We'll leave really early one morning. Before five. It can be your Christmas present, Grandpa.'

It's the happiest I've ever seen Leo, showing his grandfather the coloured balls, the little things in the shape of birds and stars and reindeers that he says he remembers from when he was a child.

After lunch, when Charles has fallen asleep, I go up to find Leo who has retreated to his room. I want to check my Facebook page.

We sit side by side at his desk.

'What do you do at the computer?' I ask him. 'Apart from all this social networking?'

'I look up stuff,' he says.

'What do you look up?'

He glances at me and away again, pulls up his hood, wraps his scarf tight around his neck.

'Illnesses,' he says.

'Illnesses?'

'To see if I've got one.'

I remember the first time I tried to use the computer, the body parts and cross-sections that popped up.

'Why? Do you have pain?'

'I don't know. Sometimes I do.'

'What pain?'

'Not pain, feelings. Do you understand the word "tingle"?'

'Tingle?'

'Your skin feels as if it's fizzing. Pins and needles.'

I know what he means, the feeling you get when you have pure fear.

'Or I think perhaps it's something deep, slow, that might take a long time before I know I'm going to die.'

I know that feeling too. A long, slow journey towards something inevitable. I shiver.

I run my eyes up and down his big strong body.

'But if you don't have a pain, a sign, then you don't need to be looking for some illness you might or might not have. You can be happy that you are well, without symptoms.'

'But what if I'm not well?' he says. 'If I don't spot it?'

'You don't have to look for it. Your body tells you. Is this why you have this in your room?'

I hold up a zip-up bag of medicine and pills and monitors.

He nods slowly.

I want to laugh. I'd even like to give him a hug.

I stare at this big, tough boy, with his massive shoulders and his head like a dog's, and remember the first day I saw him.

How afraid I was of him.

And I realise that the reason he cannot find work, and doesn't like leaving the house unless he's drunk or on some kind of drugs is not because he's lazy and good-for-nothing, but because he's paralysed with fear. His fear isn't like mine and Leila's back in our country after Ali disappeared. His fear is not of poverty or people who can exploit or harm him, but of demons inside his head that tell him he's sick when he isn't.

I wonder if Dora knows this. If anyone does but me.

'You should never be afraid of what Allah gives you,' I tell him. 'The thing to be afraid of is what human beings are prepared to do to you.'

He gazes at me for a few seconds.

'And Allah's given you good health and you don't even believe it? Shame on you!'

He shrugs, looks away. If he wasn't such a big tough man, I might have thought he was about to cry.

'Can I look at my Facebook page?' I ask him.

'Of course.' Then: 'There's a message from someone,' he says. 'It's in Arabic, I can't read it.'

I peer at the screen. Another message from Amina. I won't let myself hope she might have heard something about Ali. I'm expecting something funny and light-hearted so I have to look twice at what she's written. It's been there for some days.

Been trying to find out more about Zidana. She worked here until before Dora returned to England, just over five years ago. She was pregnant. While she was working here, something happened that meant she lost her baby. It was something to do with Theodora. I'm afraid there's worse. I tried to find out where she was living now, to see what actually happened. Just to give you the picture, Mona. But no one knows where she is. She's dead.

When I am able to tear myself away at last, exhausted, to take a kind of refuge in my room, I find the lock on the door has been chiselled off. That's when I get the feeling Leo spoke of, the tingle of pure fear.

CHAPTER THIRTY-FIVE

'Dora.' Rachel's opened her door. 'I'll wait for you to finish what you're doing, then I'll speak to you in my office.'

Work's picked up again lately. I've been presenting some excellent shows, received some good feedback. I was pleased with the application I made for my own job. So I go eagerly, fully expecting good news – that they've found me a position presenting a new programme.

In Rachel's office a bevy of grave faces greets me. My stomach collapsing, I sit down opposite the formidable group, across the large desk.

'It's been brought to our attention that the listening figures . . .' Rachel begins, as if we hadn't already discussed this. She's in role, my boss, no longer the friend who shared Mona's tagine with me the other evening.

A new cleaner is busy polishing the interior window. I watch her for a while. Rachel's mouth opens and closes, but I don't hear her words, just the squeak of the cloth. But I must hear her on a certain level, because I can feel the shudder in my body as her words sink in, the collapse inside a child feels at being blamed for something it hasn't done.

'So,' she says at last, placing her hands on her desk, as if she is preparing herself for a less than acquiescent response from me. 'It's unavoidable, I'm afraid. Your application, Theodora, though of course excellent as we would have expected, has not been successful. Your programme's being cut.'

'You're firing me,' I say.

'What we've decided, is to offer you the opportunity to work . . . we would like to think you still had a job here if . . .'

'But—' I say.

'I'm sorry, Dora. As you know, we simply can't afford to . . .' and so on. Her words blur. 'The figures have plummeted. The programme will no longer be broadcast. We're having to make a lot of cuts, and there'll be far more changes to come.'

I lose my cool. Words tumble out. I am some-one for whom responsibility, a sense of duty matters. I apply this to all areas of my life, my family and my job. The squeaking of the cloth on the window grows louder. The words keep coming. How I love my job. How my listeners will be lost without me. How I am the Voice of the South-East.

I think of that vision I had, my name emblazoned across bill-boards, my face, my voice, my fame when I took over the prime-time show.

Rachel and her colleagues stare back at me, their faces impas-sive. I think of Mona, her expressionless face. I feel as if everyone around me is turning to stone, that I make no impact on them, however loud I shout.

'Theodora, we're not getting rid of you. We're asking you if you'd like one of the jobs we do have – if you'd consider a differ-ent role with us. You're not the only one. At least we're offering you something. We haven't been able to do this for everyone. It'll be a different workload, of course – the hours may be longer, the salary adjusted to reflect the job – but that's the best we can do at the moment. We thought perhaps you would be interested in presenting the consumer programme. Charlotte is taking maternity leave so there's going to be a vacancy in the New Year.'

Rachel lowers her head. She knows what this means. She is offering me a position on the graveyard slot.

She probably thinks I won't take it, but she has to do something to compensate for her guilt.

I give up arguing, stand, fighting to hold back silly humiliating tears that threaten to roll down my cheeks.

My knees buckle as I walk out of the room. I catch the eye of the cleaner who is polishing the glass inner windows, clutching a spray bottle, a slight smile on her lips. It's OK for you, I think, your job can't get any worse. What does Rachel think she's doing, anyway, imparting this kind of information in front of the office cleaner?

The cleaner turns her blue eyes upon me. She stops her polishing for a split second and I know her eyes are on my back as I cross the corridor. I turn. She holds the bottle of disinfectant spray in her rubber-gloved hands, poised, directed at the glass, as if she were aiming it at the very place I have just been sitting. Then I notice that under her headscarf, she has wedged her mobile against her ear. She's chatting, holding a conversation with someone while she is supposed to be working!

I retrace my footsteps, put my head back round the door. The other directors have gone.

'That woman,' I say to Rachel.

'What woman?' She's already engrossed at her screen. I have walked out of her conscience the minute I've left.

'That one there, the cleaner – you should watch her. She isn't pulling her weight. She's talking on her mobile when she's supposed to be working. Take a good look.'

'Dora,' Rachel soothes. 'Don't take this so badly. I didn't want to say this in front of everyone, but there have been more tweets about your attitude on air. And in the office. Hayley, the intern, has made a complaint. Try and take some time off, eh? I think you're a little stressed.'

I can't reply to this. I collect my coat from my office and leave the building, my eyes smarting as I confront the cold breeze.

I take the tube to Bond Street. It's the week before Christmas, and lights are strung along Oxford Street. The crowds are intense, their eyes fixed on the windows searching for ideas, hell-bent on spending. The road's being dug up and vast sewage pipes are on view – the squalid underside of the commercial heart of London we don't normally see. Beneath all this glitz, beneath the pretty façades, the window displays, the Christmas trees and the designer fashions, is a steady flow of shit.

Rachel said there had been complaints. That they could not afford to upset listeners. What had I done to upset my listeners? I pride myself on my tact and diplomacy. It must have been that woman who wanted the swimming medal when she'd done nothing to deserve it. Or one of those perverts who attempted to get a bit fresh with me over the air and who I had to switch off.

Retail therapy is what I need. I'll buy a dress, shoes, and a new bag. And I'll buy stockings. I'm due to see Max at the Tower Hotel in a few days. I'll take my mind off this news by treating myself.

I turn to go into Fenwick's in a dream. A woman stands in the doorway and I push past her.

'Look out!' she growls.

'You're blocking the entrance!' I'm not in the mood to apologise to people.

Rachel's news rebounds in my ears. I can't believe it – it can't be true! I'd been about to be promoted. Now I'm being sacked! Where is this going to leave me? What am I going to tell Max?

I'll splash out. I won't be cast down by this.

I rummage through the packets of stockings in the lingerie department, ignoring the sales girl who wants to help. I don't need help, I need to concentrate on getting this right. I want something with a sheen, something silky and sexy. On the way out I decide to buy a little more. Hell! If I'm about to have a salary reduction then I deserve to spend a bit on myself before it happens. I'll look better than I've ever looked to Max. He'll never guess what's going on underneath.

I turn back, return to the lingerie department and spend a small fortune on a sea-green silk bra and knickers.

After this, feeling the relief buying good new clothes affords me, I take a walk along New Bond Street to Burlington Arcade. Roger used to buy me Armani or Gucci or Versace or whatever I wanted, when I lived with him and money was no object. At the time I began to see it as another way of his controlling me, of keeping me in place. If he spent money on me, I was under an even greater obligation, or so he led me to believe, to dress beautifully for his business dinners, to play the role, to keep the silence.

Now I wonder whether I don't miss it at all.

When my head was turned by Max, everything else faded, as if precious metal had turned to pewter before my eyes. Nothing else held any interest for me. Only Max shone, only Max mattered.

I gaze in at the watches and rings and necklaces, and feel a pang for the life I'd have had if Roger and I had stayed together. For that sense of ease, the lack of worry. I was a successful man's wife. It was straightforward and it was secure. I didn't have to prove myself in a job that was under constant scrutiny. I only had to prove I was the perfect wife. Which was easy, of course, until Zidana messed it up for me.

Now my job defines me. Without it I'm nobody.

When I'm assailed by self-doubt, I usually soothe myself by thinking of Max. Picturing his doting gaze, remembering his fingers stroking my collar-bone, playing with my hair. I'm seeing him this week! But even this doesn't comfort me. What will Max see in me when he knows I am not, after all, the Voice of the South-East but the presenter of a tiresome consumer show that goes out when the whole of London's in bed?

I feel my surface eroding, that a dark underside is about to be exposed to Max like the sewage pipes on Oxford Street.

I tell myself not to be so stupid, that I am Theodora, Daddy's Gift from God, erstwhile wife of Roger and mother of Leo.

Leo has come back to live with me. But even this isn't any consolation since the truth is that it wasn't Leo's choice. Now he's a layabout who doesn't get up in the morning for me but who will do so for Mona.

I am Theodora, with the red hair, wild and passionate lover of a doctor from New York. Theodora Gentleman, Voice of the South-East.

I finger the gap where the gold chain should be around my neck. The full significance of its loss hits me.

It defined me!

Now it's gone.

Suspicions flare up. Was it Mona who took it? Mona who is taking *me* apart, piece by piece?

The facts are these. I am no longer Daddy's Gift from God.

No longer an elegant ex-pat wife.

No longer certain that my lover will stay with me – a doctor who needs me to talk about my migrant domestic worker's thighs in order to keep his interest.

An horrific vision comes to my mind, of me and Daddy, our smooth exteriors crumbling. Like statues whose gold leaf is peeled away to reveal the black stone beneath.

Outside my house, with its angels guarding my entrance, the windows shiny now that Mona's come, with its little bay trees in pots, I pause at the bottom of the steps. The brass door knocker and letterbox gleam, speaking of someone with good taste. I've been foolish to imagine that Mona can threaten my sense of self. But it's employing her, after all, that proves to the world that I am still somebody of note.

CHAPTER THIRTY-SIX

In the hot water, I shut my eyes and think about the hammam. I think of the water slopping over me in the dark, Leila leaning against me, the masseuse with her rough glove scrubbing at my skin, and the way we all sat and talked and told our secrets in the steamy heat.

When we've got a house of our own, Leila and I will be able to share bathtimes every day!

I climb out, feeling warm and relaxed, and pull one of Dora's lovely big white bathtowels around me.

Dora had never offered me a bath, but she wouldn't be back for hours and I knew Leo and Charles wouldn't notice.

It was dark already by half past three, the streetlights flicking on outside. Charles was asleep, Leo engrossed in a computer game. I yearned for hot water, for the soothing feel of heat on my aching bones. But I also needed solace. To replace the physical comfort that had been missing since leaving my child, my mother, since losing my lover. The thought of hot water was irresistible, especially with the cold outside, the cold that grips me all the time here.

I lit the candles around the bathroom. It was looking lovely now I'd cleaned it. Got the grime off the light-pull, repaired the carpet where it was curling up. All it needed was a nail, found in a kitchen drawer, banged in with a hammer, found in the garden shed, to hold it down. I'd polished the mirrors, shined the taps.

I filled the bath with hot water, turning the big brass taps on, pouring in a capful of bubble bath from one of the bottles Dora keeps on her shelf. When it was full to the brim and the bubbles looked like banks of clouds, I took off my clothes and stepped in.

The hot water was like a hug, soothing the pains in my arms and legs and back. I didn't know how much they hurt until the aches retreated in surrender to the heat. I closed my eyes. For a little while I floated, listening to the clank in the pipes as they eased up again, the wind in the trees sighing in the back garden. I didn't know how the anxiety about my mother, about Ali and Leila and now that odd message from Amina had been weighing on me.

In the water my worries floated away. Nothing seemed that bad, everything was going to get better. I'd keep sending the money for Ummu's medicine, and for Leila's education.

Sayed would help me find Ali.

I would watch Dora's movements with a wary eye; she might have upset this young Zidana, but she would not intimidate me.

I'd done it! Taken our futures into my own hands. And then, buoyed by these thoughts, I felt an even greater conviction of my own strength.

Even should I never find Ali, I *could* hold it all together for Ummu and Leila – on my own. I was earning a good wage for them. My English was improving. I was learning to use the computer with more confidence. I could deal with Theodora.

I wondered how long it was since I had allowed myself to throw my head back and really sing? I sang 'Inchaallah' with my heart and soul. I felt an exuberance I hadn't experienced for weeks as the words flowed out, as my voice rebounded off the bathroom walls, as my lungs filled, then released the sound.

This warmth was what I'd been missing. But one day, if I continued to work hard, it would be ours too, mine and Ummu's and Leila's. A house of our own, with a bathroom, where we could lie and sing as loudly as we liked whenever we wanted to. *Inchaallah*.

Now, with the soft towel wrapped around me, I rub a hole in the steam that's clouded the mirror. I lean forward and look at my face. It's bright and clean and healthier-looking than when I arrived and examined it in the mirror in Dora's room. Something else good is coming of this work!

Then I'm no longer the only face in the mirror – Dora's is there too.

CHAPTER THIRTY-SEVEN

I look up at the drawing-room window. The tree's in place, tiny lights glowing against the darkening afternoon. Mona's done as I've asked.

I climb the steps, put my key in the lock and push open the door.

In the drawing room, Leo's lounging on the sofa, playing some kind of game on his DS. Daddy's next to him, snoozing quietly.

It isn't Daddy's presence in the drawing room that upsets me today, but Mona's deliberate flouting of my requests.

'Where's Mona?'

Leo glances up. 'She's taking a bath.'

And from upstairs I can hear a voice, singing, singing so powerfully I'm taken aback, singing as if its owner is completely at home.

For a few seconds, our two faces are reflected back side by side.

I see Mona glance at my reflection and back again at hers. Comparing!

I can't speak. I remember for the first time since Zidana what it is to feel white-hot with rage. I try not to register that her skin is firm where mine is loosening – it isn't relevant. But a thought worms its way into my head. Has she only been looking so old and dowdy because she's been fatigued, first from her journey here, then from the long hours of work I've been giving her? Was Daddy in fact making more sense than I wanted to believe when he said how young Mona looked next to me? I remember the day on the river when I noticed that she might have a certain beauty, were she to have access to decent clothes and make-up. But she will never have access to the kind of products and therapies my friends and I are able to make use of.

I've never been someone to worry about ageing, so why do these thoughts assail me now?

At last I find my voice and it comes out low, tremulous.

'I'll wait for you to get dressed. Then I'll speak to you in the kitchen.' I'm aware that my words echo those of Rachel's earlier this afternoon. Mona doesn't turn, but stares at my reflection in the mirror. I stare back, my lips tight, the muscle in my leg shaking, my breath panting in and out. I'm fighting to control the urge to move towards her, a vision of Zidana flashing into my head, stopping me in my tracks. This must be done with dignity, with control, not in blind fury the way I dealt with Zidana, when my passion got the better of me.

I go down and wait for Mona at the kitchen table, allowing the truth to sink in. My maid's been helping herself – and now the certainty hits me that of course it is Mona who's taken my chain, who's taken Daddy's cufflinks, who's stolen the silver soup spoons that were my mother's! How foolish I've been to overlook these things.

She's been cultivating Leo and Daddy's affections and now they cannot see what she's up to under their own noses. Impressing them with her cooking and cleaning and that singing voice. What more is she going to take from me?

And it's all been happening while I've been out working,

250

earning the money for everyone so they can enjoy my home without me.

Mona comes down five minutes later, in her shabby skirt and fleece, her hair wet, her face glowing from the heat of the water – from my bath.

'Where's your overall?' I ask her. 'You know you're to wear your overall while you're working.'

'It's in my room. I'll get it.'

'Yes. Now.'

She walks past me and I feel for the first time the ridiculous inconvenience of having put her in my study so she has to pass through the kitchen each time she goes in or out.

Then she stops and speaks.

'Oh yes. I found this,' she says, holding out my necklace. 'It was under the cushion on Charles's chair.'

CHAPTER THIRTY-EIGHT

Dora's at the kitchen table, clinging onto her martini glass as if it's there to save her. She stares at the necklace for several minutes.

And then, without thanking me, she says, 'What's your least favourite job here, Mona?' Her voice is soft. She must be grateful to me for finding her necklace. And perhaps that moment when our eyes met in the bathroom mirror, when it was clear we weren't very different as women even if she is older than me, made her change her mind about me. I'd thought she was going to be angry that I'd taken a bath without permission, but perhaps it was a second's intimacy.

'I don't like cleaning the toilets, of course,' I say. 'But I had a nice day today, in the end. Buying the tree with Leo and—'

She stands up, marches past me, goes into the little washroom I'm supposed to use instead of her bathroom and returns with bleach and a toilet brush.

'You can do that first.'

After this she begins to pour forth orders.

'This is *my* house.' As if I didn't know it! 'My house. I've asked you to look after Daddy in his flat, not in the drawing room. And you are *not* to use my bathroom or my products. It isn't a holiday resort, it isn't a talent contest.'

'A talent contest?'

'I heard you singing. You're not here to bathe in my bubbles and sing in the bath. You're here to work!'

'I know.'

'But you weren't working when I came in, you were in the bath. Daddy was upstairs. Your job is to care for him in the basement.'

I want to retort that I wouldn't want this house, that if I had her wealth I would choose somewhere light and modern, not this dank place with its dusty corners and its clanking pipes.

But I can't afford to let this go wrong.

I think of Ali, how much he had to tolerate before he snapped that terrible day. The day I took him into my arms and promised no matter what he was accused of, no matter who came after him, I'd protect him.

I think of Ummu's cough, how urgently she needs the money for her operation, then afterwards for medication. I think of Leila's education.

It's easy when you have enough motivation. To keep quiet and get on with it.

In my room I tie my hair up in my headscarf, put the blue overall back on. For now I am back as Theodora needs me to be.

Mona. Domestic worker.

CHAPTER THIRTY-NINE

I awaken to a room bathed in brownish light. It's the day I'm due to see Max. The sweet anticipation I usually experience is tinged with anxiety.

I pull back my curtains to reveal a sky that is pregnant with snow. As I get dressed, pulling on a cashmere dress and suede boots, running my fingers through my hair in the mirror, the creeping unease I felt when I awoke intensifies. Is the anxiety about what Max will think when he hears I'm not being promoted, after all, but shifted to the graveyard slot?

Or is it something else, something slippery, indefinable, to do with that vision of Mona that won't leave me?

The soft white towel wrapped around her, her big brown eyes. No housemaid would be allowed in an employer's bathroom in Roger's house, or those of his ex-pat friends! She must know this. I had good reason to object.

But what bothers me now, in the leaden light of morning, is the *level* of rage I experienced at the sight of her. And the fact that even now, the vision of her in the bathroom will not leave me. The thick black hair hanging over one side of her face. The slender fingers that should by rights have become calloused given the work she does unreasonably smooth, holding my fluffy white towel to her chest. The slow defiance in her movements. Her strong thighs. That voice! I still can't believe it can have been her singing. Daddy in the drawing room against my instructions, and Leo, too, knowing she was there, in the bath, letting her sing, letting her make choices in a house that doesn't belong to her, as if *I* no longer existed.

And I remember the sensation I had when I saw her for the first time, the sense that she might be more than she appeared. That she might have another agenda for coming into my life. Where *did* Roger find her? A new thought enters my head, filling me with a brief shiver of horror – that perhaps Mona knew Zidana, had inveigled her way into my life to *avenge* her? Impossible! Yet she was friends with Amina, the maid who moved in after Zidana left. I'm plagued by dreadful suspicion.

So many similarities! The way Zidana won Leo over, the things she took. The way she went blank when I tried to get her to confess. The way she flirted with every man that came to the house. Then I remember that Mona had not, after all, taken my necklace; she had found it and given it straight back, and I'm overcome by confusion and self-doubt.

But again and again, as I go about my day through the dismal short winter hours, I'm haunted by the sight of the smooth skin on Mona's arms, the shiny hair like liquorice now she's used my shampoo, the slow gaze of her enormous eyes. How can I stop her from invading my thoughts? Taking over my home, my father, my son?

Yet I can't do without her.

I've got to work. I need help with Daddy.

Most of all, I have to see Max. I'm seeing him tonight! My anxiety is spoiling the one thing I most treasure in my life.

* * *

When I get home from work, however, things are back as they should be. Daddy's in his flat, Leo's out, and Mona's got her hands in the sink.

I go upstairs, and spend longer than usual preparing. I pull from my drawer the silk underwear I bought from Fenwick's, the frail stockings. I pull on a pencil skirt and a satin blouse. My favourite Rupert Sanderson shoes.

I'm dressed, made-up, perfumed and about to go out of the front door to my taxi when Mona comes along the passage. She's in the overall with her hair tied back, her face tired and drawn-looking after all. As it should be, in her place.

'Dora,' she says quietly. 'You forgot this.' And she hands me my mobile.

The snow begins to fall gently as we move through the south London streets – confetti dancing around the streetlights.

'There's more on its way,' the driver says, and I barely listen, aware only of the bald back of his head and my tumbling thoughts. 'You won't want to leave it too late to get back tonight, love. Most of us'll be knocking off early. Wonder if it'll be a white Christmas, eh? With only a week to go, you never know.'

We're crossing Tower Bridge, enmeshed in a silver shower of snow. The water beneath us is glossy and black and dimpled, and then I spot the *Girl with a Dolphin* lit up by white lights, and my heart-rate increases for I'm about to meet my lover, that soon I can abandon myself to Max's caresses, and forget all my troubles.

Max likes the *Girl with a Dolphin* even better than the *Muse of Music* in Embankment Gardens. We look at her soaring naked through the veil of snow. Her supple skin shines dark against the silver spray.

Like Mona's, in the steam of the bathroom.

'Gorgeous,' says Max, without even looking at me when I arrive, but putting his arm round me and his hand straight up under my faux fur. 'What a feat! To create a sculpture where neither figure appears supported, as if they really had taken flight.'

His touch thaws every bit of my frozen body. Eases the stiffness from my tense limbs.

'I've booked us a room.' He turns and looks at me. 'Happy Christmas,' he adds, kissing me briefly on the lips.

Thank goodness, I think. Thank goodness for you, Max. I lean against his shoulder, turn my face so I can draw in the smell of his good wool coat, the melting snow that has settled upon it numbing the tip of my nose. He's wearing some new kind of aftershave, an expensive fragrance with notes of old leather and spice.

He walks ahead of me into the dimly lit hotel bar. A huge Christmas tree twinkles in the centre of the room. There's the smell of pine, and of mulled wine.

Max gestures towards a luxurious sofa in a corner and goes off to order my martini, his Scotch. He brings them over to the window beside me to stare out at the snow over the river.

'Beautiful,' he says. 'It's good to be here.'

'Really?'

'Yes. Jeez it's been tough at home lately, it's great to get away.'

'Tough?'

'Work, kids, stuff. You don't wanna know.'

'No. I do.' I'm desperate, I feel like saying, to hear about someone else's tangled family problems for once.

'It's the usual Christmas show-down,' he says. 'Two out of our three kids decided to spend it with their boyfriends and the third doesn't want to be alone at home with his mom and me. Can't blame him.'

His face is solemn. There are lines I haven't noticed before, running between his nose and upper lip. He looks tired. 'But where else can he go? We don't have grandparents on tap. His sisters find him annoying.'

'So he'll have to put up with it and stay at home,' I say, thinking of Leo's trip away. I must help him pack or he'll end up flying off with no clean underwear. I must buy Christmas presents for him to give Roger and Claudia too. He'll never think of these things for himself. My heart sinks again at the thought that I'll be spending Christmas at Anita's without either my son or Max, the two men I'd rather be with than anyone in the world.

'Do you ever wonder if it's worth it though?' he asks, slumping down next to me on the sofa. He puts his arm round me.

This is the moment, I think. Snow tumbling down outside, my martini yet to drink. Mona, Daddy, my family and my job, a million miles away across the river. I wish I never had to move away, could stay here, on this sofa, with Max's scent and the Christmas tree. We would be figures caught for eternity in an intimate embrace like the *Girl with a Dolphin* – a perfect moment preserved forever.

'When I first met you,' he says, 'what was it, God, can it be four–five years ago now? It seemed so important. My career. Being recognised. Earning a sackload of money. But lately, I don't know, it must be middle age. I wonder what it's all about?'

I look up at him and he squeezes me into him.

'Max, I thought your career was what kept you going. What you get up for in the morning.'

'It was. But you know, with the kids growing up I'm aware of the way Valerie and I fight over whose job is more important and I wonder, perhaps neither is. Perhaps it's the simple things that matter. A game of soccer in the park. Pancakes for breakfast. Home-made, I mean, not some junk from the mall. We screwed up, Dora, we should have made more effort. Now the kids are almost gone, I'm afraid. We could have, should have done it differently. Better.'

'You must stop this, Max. Come on. You know as well as I do there's no ideal family model.'

I think of my messy family, Roger and Claudia in Rabat, me and Leo here, Leo unemployed, Daddy down in a dark basement while his other children swan about doing as they please. 'We all muddle along as best we can,' I offer lamely.

'Hmm.'

I know what he's feeling. It's that devil that assails us all as we get older – I've heard it time and again on the phone-in. Anxiety that we messed up. Regret that we didn't do things differently.

'Anyway, what's in all these bags? Have you bought up the West End?' I tease him. I want to lighten the atmosphere, fend off the compulsion to unburden my worries, to tell him too much.

He lets out a long, weary sigh.

'It's just money though, isn't it, Dora? I spend money on my children to compensate for not being there. I never saw it before. Being in those shops today – people were frantic! I had a kind of epiphany. What the hell am I doing on the other side of the Atlantic, buying gifts when I should be with them?'

He swirls the ice around in his glass, gazing into the amber liquid.

I'm afraid. He's about to say he's leaving. Going home to be with his kids. He can no longer see me. It's all been a mistake, I'm a component of the regret that's assailing him.

A void opens before me: no job, no family, no Max.

But then he goes on, 'I'm on the wrong track, but I don't know how to get off. I've been so hell-bent on the pursuit of success. I'm thinking of giving up my job before it's too late.'

This *is* his way of telling me he's decided to spend more time at home. With his youngest son, with Valerie! I feel panic course through me.

'If you gave up your job you'd have no excuse to meet up with me,' I blurt out before I can stop myself.

'Oh, I don't know. I'd get away to see you from time to time. That would be a priority. Of course.' He bites my earlobe gently.

'From time to time?'

'As often as I could.'

'Well, I'm glad to hear it,' I say, the panic receding a little. 'But how would Valerie feel if you left work?'

'She'd love it. It would mean she could put herself first, make sure she gets all the promotions she's been angling for.'

I wince at the word 'promotion'. But he goes on. 'If I left my job, she could move on up the ladder. It would mean our down-shifting, of course, but hey. You only live once. I want some quality time. I've had enough of the rat run. And in fact . . .' he pulls me in closer to him, 'it would mean I could see *more* of you, rather than less. I wouldn't be constantly jumping on the next plane to go to some conference on the other side of the world. I could actually stay over, listen to you on your show . . .'

Oh Max, please, don't ask about the show.

I say, 'Are you sure about all this? Your career has always been part of you. You might miss it.'

'It's different for me than you,' he goes on sweetly. 'I am just an invisible cog in a very big wheel. I'm doing work that frankly I'm getting a bit old for. *You're* about to become a household name. My sexy-voiced goddess!'

'Oh come on, Max . . .'

'No, really. It was the best thing you could do for yourself, getting that woman to help you out, so you can focus. How's it going, by the way? How are those marvellous thighs? Is she still climbing the furniture to brush your ceiling roses?'

'Max! Honestly! Her main role is caring for Daddy. But she's freeing me up. I wouldn't be here with you otherwise.'

'That's good. I've rather come to depend on her as much as you.'

I force myself to laugh. I must not let this get to me, Max's determination to bring Mona into the conversation.

I think suddenly of the way she handed me my phone with his message on it as I left the house, and a burning anxiety creeps through my belly. She couldn't have somehow taken his number, with the intention of contacting him? I think of her flirting with Bob that night. Of what she said about Madame's husband. No. I'm being irrational. She can't write – she can't text. My thoughts are encroaching on what could be a perfect evening.

'It's not been easy, training her. She's not all that bright, not educated.'

'Sure. You don't clean other people's houses if you're a professional with a string of letters after your name.'

Another unpleasant thought I've been trying to keep at bay creeps in.

Now I've been demoted at the radio station, Mona's and my positions aren't that different. Mona might not have had a formal education but she isn't stupid. She's probably as clever as I am. Maybe more so. She can, after all, speak our language while I'm monolingual. Her lack of qualifications are due to poverty, not a dearth of brain cells. And I think again about that sighting of her next to me in the mirror, how much more beautiful she could be, with my help; how her dowdy look, when she arrived, was, like her education, all down to lack of money. What am I afraid of? That somehow she is going to take away from me the last vestiges of what makes me Theodora Gentleman? That she might even steal my lover?

When we're eating, and halfway through the second bottle of wine, Max says, out of the blue, 'I want you to ask me home one day soon, Dora.'

This is so unexpected, so abrupt, I can hardly take it in.

'You know we don't do that, Max. It's what we agreed.'

'We've been together so long now, I want more of you. If you do too, that is.'

'I don't know. I . . .'

He goes on, 'Look, Theodora, another reason I want to leave work is so I can see more of you. I'm fed up with meeting in hotels. Yes, I know it's a little unequal. I can't ask you back to mine. There's Valerie and the kid – and it's too bad, because I'd like to sleep the night in a bed with you. Not an anonymous bed in a hotel, but in a proper bed, that shapes itself to you. To us. The only way we can ever do this is if I come to you. And I wondered whether, now you have help, I could come?'

I examine his face. He's looking at me earnestly. And I suddenly see myself through his eyes. This loving daughter who has taken her old father in while juggling her job as a successful radio presenter with a beautiful London home and a housekeeper, her long red hair, her carefully picked out clothes.

I picture the day he comes back – putting any suspicions about Mona aside. I can show him a side of myself he hasn't seen before. My house *is* looking gorgeous these days, restored to its original elegance, now I have Mona.

The ceiling roses and picture-rails, the cornices and the intricate tiling around the fireplaces are now features to be proud of instead of the encumbrances I had previously found them, gathering dust so I was ashamed to expose them to him.

I know Max will adore the charming cherubs on my porch, their chubby legs and their shipbuilders' instruments, he'll love the sculpture of my mother that adorns the steps down to Daddy's basement. I have things to be proud of. My home is a true reflection of me as a person, I think wildly. It's sophisticated with an olde worlde charm; it's furnished tastefully and is artistic without being overstated.

With quarry tiles in the kitchen that sparkle now Mona has polished them, the freshly laundered Egyptian cotton sheets I've told her to ensure are always on the beds, with gleaming mirrors and windows, and its polished wooden floors, it is a house of which to be proud.

I *could* allow Max to come home, see a little more of me, see in a sense inside me a little. Perhaps he would heal the hurt I've been feeling about losing my job. Sharing more of my life with the man I love might be exactly what I need.

'OK,' I say at last. 'I suppose we could consider it.'

'I'm back here on the twenty-third,' he tells me. 'I was thinking, if I stayed overnight with you, then we could spend Christmas Eve together before I fly home. I can give you your Christmas present.'

I think of Anita's invitation to spend Christmas with her. My mind quickly adjusts the plans. I can send Mona and Daddy over to Anita's and have the house to myself on Christmas Eve with Max! The whole world suddenly feels warm and bright.

Max is looking at me with that guileless smile – so sweet, so trusting, I feel overwhelmed with love and appreciation for him.

We sit for a while longer, silently watching the snow fall outside, getting faster and thicker, and I feel that, despite everything, things are going to start to get better.

CHAPTER FORTY

The snow doesn't settle. When I go to work over the next few days, the sky is grey again, the river restless. Leo has gone off to Roger's in Rabat and the house feels empty. My show was dismantled last week. I'm asked to shadow Charlotte on the consumer programme so I'll be ready to front it in the New Year.

Ben, the receptionist, doesn't look up when I arrive.

'Morning,' I say, waiting for his usual greeting. He glances up.

'Oh yes. You're to go down to Charlotte – she's waiting for you in the IT suite.'

The administrative staff's eyes glaze over as I pass them. Even the longer-standing cleaners who usually smile and wave look away. People who would have gone out of their way to shake my hand, to sit next to me in the canteen, don't even glance at me.

I move on towards the windowless office at the back of the building, where people's heads are bowed over their work. No one looks up.

'Oh, Theodora.' It's Charlotte. 'I've been asked to show you the ropes.'

Charlotte came to the station only a year ago, a new fresh-faced presenter whom I'd had to mentor. How come the wheels have suddenly turned, that *she's* mentoring *me*?

'What we have to do,' Charlotte says, focused on her computer screen, clicking on various emails, 'is chase up two main complaints. We've got one here about a games console that the vendor refused to exchange though it was faulty when the purchaser bought it. We need to track down the manufacturer and the retailer. You could perhaps take the retailer. Get them to give you a comment.'

It's only nine thirty. I wonder how I'm going to get through the day, how I'm going to force myself to focus. I've never had to do anything so dull.

I spend the next two hours talking to gormless salespeople on the end of the line, trying to find a manager who's prepared to talk to me. Half the time I'm put on hold listening to tinny renditions of Vivaldi as the minutes tick by.

By eleven I'm wondering whether Gina might come down to see me, as she's researching upstairs, but the day drags on and she doesn't appear.

I'm about to go out for my lunch, when Charlotte comes across and leans over me, her heavily pregnant belly almost in my face.

'How did you get on?' she asks.

'I've got a couple of contacts to phone back this afternoon,' I say. My stomach's rumbling, I want to get out, buy a sandwich. I need fresh air. The office is stuffy, and the work so tedious I can barely keep my eyes open.

But: 'This afternoon's no good,' Charlotte says. 'We have to have something now – it's going out tonight. Phone them again, hassle them. Let's get something in the bag.'

'I really need a break,' I say, standing up. 'It's lunchtime.'

'I'm sorry, Dora, we've got to get a story. Have another go. I'll ask Hayley to bring some sandwiches in. What else would you like. Coffee?'

I can't believe this is happening, that I'm working for my inferior. Charlotte's tight-lipped tone is beginning to irritate me. I wonder why she's left it so late to go on maternity leave? She looks as if she's about to drop any minute.

'When you've finished on this, we need to speak to other consumers, get quotes on their similar experiences.'

I'm supposed to grovel to these sad consumers, beg them to speak live. It's like the work Gina used to do for me. Her work, however, required skill and sensitivity, an eye for a good story and a nose for what was genuine and what wasn't. The pinnacle of excitement in this one involves vacuum cleaners that don't suck and package tours that were disappointing.

'It's all got to be researched and the facts verified by the end of today,' Charlotte goes on.

'I'm surprised you haven't already died of boredom,' I mutter.

'What was that?' she asks, frowning.

'Nothing.'

I put my head down and make a show of being fascinated by the small print on a gas supplier's contract.

At the end of the day, I leave work feeling drained, but unsatisfied. How has it come to this? I used to leave work on a high – with that wonderful glow a job well done gives you, a buzz from the sense of achievement, and the knowledge that my voice had been heard, sorting out the issues of my confused and troubled listeners. Today I feel as if the energy has been sucked right out of me. I catch the bus and sit amongst other exhausted commuters, women who look as if life has passed them by, men whose eyes reflect despair, a freight of souls who have lost everything.

I get off the bus on Creek Road and walk along the High Street, avoiding the rubbish that's collected on the pavement, recoiling at the ripe smells that always linger at the end of a market day. I wish again that I lived in a more salubrious area. The possibility is vanishing fast, now my career's taken a nose-dive.

By now I'm craving a piece of my white sliced bread and a cheese triangle – the only thing along with a martini that might afford some comfort when I get in.

I don't like to ask Mona to buy the bread for me – it's a pride thing – so I pop into the minimarket, grab some Kingsmill and a packet of The Laughing Cow cheeses and move towards the counter where the lottery tickets and game things I never buy and don't understand are on sale. At the end of the aisle I stop. There, talking to the person behind the counter, is Mona, gesticulating, for all the world as though she belonged here.

CHAPTER FORTY-ONE

I wait for Sayed to finish serving someone, then call him over.

'Have you had any luck? Have you got any news of Ali?'

'Been asking around,' he tells me. 'There's a man who says he has contacts at an immigration detention centre up north. Says he can give you the details, but it's all a bit hush-hush. Don't know why. He wants to meet you.'

My heart leaps.

'Tell me more! Who is this man? What contacts? When—'

'Hey, calm down, man. He *thinks* someone might have seen your Ali, he isn't sure. A guy who sounds a bit like the way you describe. Dark skin, blue eyes. Moroccan Berber. Seeking asylum over here. Ended up in detention – he'll be waiting for the authorities to check over his application. But the guy who found him, Hamid, he's cagey. I don't know what his business is. All I know is, he says if you want the info you need to meet him. You must take all your documents, passport and so on. He says he can't do anything without those. And he'll need money.'

My heart sinks.

Ummu phoned only this morning to tell me the result of her scan.

'They found something in my lung, Mona. It means I need an operation and some treatment. More cost, I'm afraid to say. They can do it soon, if you can just send as much money as possible.'

'How much?' I ask Sayed.

'He'll tell you. He lives on the creek.'

'Can you find out more?'

'I can ring him if you like.'

'Please.'

When he's finished the call, Sayed looks at me. 'He says he can meet by the statue of Peter the Great. I know where it is, can do you a map. One o'clock, tomorrow.'

I stare at Sayed. He looks so nice with his green eyes and his smiley face, I want to trust him. But has this Hamid really seen Ali, or is there some other thing going on? Do they want to use me in some way? And why does he want my documents?

I've heard about women coming to Europe thinking they've found work, and then being forced to sell themselves. I've heard of others who have simply disappeared, their families left distraught at the lack of contact. I've heard stories that make me grateful for everything Dora asks me to do, cleaning the toilets included.

I don't want to put myself in a situation that might be far more dangerous. But if this man *has* seen Ali, if Ali is locked up unable to contact me, then . . . this might be our only chance to find each other. One I can't afford to lose. Thoughts race through my head as Sayed sketches a map on a piece of paper, showing me where the statue is on the river.

'Meet there at one tomorrow,' he says. 'Bring all your stuff. Hamid was very clear about it: without your papers, he can't help you. And, if you find your husband, you won't want to go back to that woman to work, will you? So you'll need them. Or, if you're found wandering undocumented, Immigration will have you out. Just like that.'

'OK,' I say, pushing the loaf into my bag, the cheese Dora will also want when she gets in. My heart speeds up. I know that even with my passport, it is illegal for me to look for other work here. I came as Theodora's domestic worker, and my visa forbids me to seek other employment. If I take this step, I'll risk losing my right to stay here. But if Ali's in a detention centre he'll be desperate. Lonely, waking every day longing for me to find him, to help get him out. He would do it for me! So I must do it for him.

'What, so I need to be at the statue at one o'clock tomorrow? But who is this guy? How do I know he's trustworthy? Is he your friend, Sayed?'

Sayed looks at me through his laughing green eyes and winks.

'Not exactly a friend,' he says. 'I must admit. But he's got contacts. And he might be your only hope.'

CHAPTER FORTY-TWO

I take a step back and hover behind the Bombay Mix and the poppadoms as the man behind the counter passes a piece of paper to Mona.

He seems familiar with her – intimate, almost, the way he leans on the counter as if he wants to be closer to her. He points out of the door as if he is giving her directions, too. I move around to the front of the aisle and approach them.

'Tomorrow, then?' the man is saying. 'The statue is of Peter the Great.'

They're arranging to meet, like me and Max, beside a statue! The statue of Peter the Great that I pass whenever I walk down-river to Greenwich.

Mona looks up. She gasps audibly and takes a step away as if I were about to bite her.

'I came to get a magazine,' I say, not wanting to admit to my bread compulsion.

The man at the counter has slicked-back black hair and oddly lit-up green eyes. I've never had a conversation with him. Now I see that he's handsome with those lucent eyes and lips that turn up at the corners as if he can't help smiling.

I don't make conversation with the shopkeepers in the High Street. A lot of them are crooks, running fronts for other businesses. There are dealers who hang around at night in their Audis and BMWs, and the arches behind the High Street house dodgy enterprises run by heavy-looking gangsters whose paths you wouldn't want to cross. I'm cautious about who I mix with around here, and I've warned Mona to be circumspect too. I'm concerned for her that she's mixing with someone who's clearly not to be trusted.

'I got your bread,' Mona says. 'Look – I have it here in my bag.'

She opens the big pink floral shopper she uses and shows me: she's got Daddy's fruit and some chocolate Christmas novelties, but she's even remembered my bread, and the little processed cheeses I'm ashamed to like so much. Stupidly, I find myself blushing.

'Oh. That's good,' I say awkwardly. 'So I can put these back.'

She shrugs. 'As you like,' she says.

I imagine she and the man exchange a look as I retreat, to put my purchases back on the shelves.

'It's gone six o'clock,' I say into her ear. 'You need to come on home or you'll be late getting Daddy ready for bed.'

'Yes,' she says. 'I know. Thank you, Sayed, for your help. I'll see you tomorrow.'

'Sure,' he says.

As soon as we're alone, walking towards my house, I speak.

'You were arranging to meet that man?'

She lowers her head. 'Sayed,' she says. 'Yes.'

'Mona, you're here to work. For me.'

'But I'll be meeting him at lunchtime,' she says. 'While Charles is having his sleep.'

I stop. Place a hand on her shoulder and turn her to face

me. We're under a tree whose roots have pushed up the paving stones, so that I, on the elevated part of the pavement, gain the advantage by appearing quite a bit taller than her.

'You can't leave Daddy to sleep,' I say. 'What if he wakes up and wanders out? You have to stay in the house with him, now that Leo has gone.'

'It would only be for an hour.'

'Who makes the rules around here?' I ask.

She hesitates, cowers a little.

'You do,' she says eventually.

'Yes, I do. You're not to chat with the local shopkeepers or to meet with them. It's not what you're here for. You're here to work for me. Apart from anything else, you know nothing about them. They could be dangerous. I've already told you.'

She stares at me, but she doesn't object.

We arrive at my front door. The *putti* look on as I turn the key in the lock and Mona stands on the threshold as if hesitating about going in. I give her a little push, just a gentle one to urge her to go ahead of me, but she stumbles on the step and falls forwards, putting out her hands to catch herself.

'Oooh!' she says.

To avoid tripping over myself, I step over her, my foot catching her thigh as I do so.

She stands up, gathering the shopping that's tumbled out of the bag, and follows me.

In the kitchen I notice that she's left the floor grimy. It looks as it used to before I employed her. She's been slacking, just when I need the house to look its best for Max.

I get out a bowl, bleach, and a small, worn washing-up brush that I no longer use for the dishes. I hold out the brush and point at the tiles.

'But your supper . . . Your father . . .' she begins.

'You are my *maid*,' I remind her. '*You* don't decide what you do and when. *I* do. You will clean this floor once you have put Daddy to bed.'

She stares at me.

'This is my house, Mona. I make the rules. It's not your house. Not your street. Not your home. Mine.'

I hear her scrubbing the kitchen tiles until well into the evening. I consider saying she can stop now, but the thought of her in the shop laughing and making plans with Sayed stops me.

When Mona's finished, when the kitchen floor is to my liking, I tell her, 'Tomorrow I want the drawing room tidied, and the ironing done. Oh, and by the way, you must press the creases in the sheets when they're folded. I want the house looking its best. Max is coming to stay.'

When she's gone to bed, I take the bottle from the fridge, mix myself a martini and make myself a pile of my special cheese sandwiches.

Satisfied that I've dealt with Mona effectively, asserted my authority and put her back in her place, I take my drink through to the drawing room. The moment I sit down, however, I recall a conversation I had with Leo shortly before he went to his father's for Christmas. A conversation I'd dismissed.

He'd been sitting on the sofa eating a pizza out of the box and swigging at a can of Red Bull when I came in to help him wrap some gifts.

He didn't look up when I entered, but simply grunted, 'You know she's leaving.'

CHAPTER FORTY-THREE

'What do you mean leaving?' I demanded. 'Where would she go?'

'She wants to look for her husband.'

'Leo, Mona is a widow.'

My son shook his head. 'One of her stories,' he said. 'He's alive somewhere, she just doesn't know where.'

Are they all the same, these so-called maids? I thought. Wriggling their way into our houses to work under false pretences?

Mona's face came back to me, the day she arrived. How she hadn't looked as I had pictured her. What else had she told me that wasn't true?

'How do you know she's leaving?' I still didn't believe it.

'She told me she's going to find her husband.'

'Whatever Mona thinks, leaving's impossible without my permission. She's illegal here without me. Her visa precludes changing employer. Anyway, she can't leave. I can't manage without her.' I was taken aback by the desperation in my voice.

'Find someone else?' Leo shrugged.

It was all right for him. He had no responsibilities whatsoever.

'It isn't that easy!' I snapped.

Leo was a mystery to me. Most of the time he didn't speak to me, unless it was to ask for more beer or food or money. I assumed he didn't notice what went on around him, that he was oblivious to everything except his computer games and his violent films. But every now and again, he would make a comment that surprised me, something acerbic or astute, as if he'd woken temporarily from a sort of coma with heightened perceptions.

'What? Not easy to find someone Grandpa will put up with?' he asked.

'Yes, I suppose that is what I mean.'

'It's not surprising there aren't people queuing up to clean big houses and change grumpy incontinent old people, is it?' Leo said. 'You're right. You were lucky to find Mona. It won't be easy to find anyone else. Anyone better.'

But Mona's lucky too, to have the job in the first place, I thought. I'd given her cupcakes, for goodness' sake. I'd given her a comfy room with a garden view. And I was paying her!

It occurred to me then that I did, in effect, own her. After all, Roger brought her here for me. She couldn't have got into the country without him and couldn't stay here without me. She wouldn't last a minute away from my house. If she tried to get away, all I had to do was tell the police – and she'd be straight back. She belonged to me!

'She has to stay.' I tried to sound calm. 'As you point out, Daddy's become very attached to her. No one else will do, it'll confuse him.'

Max was coming soon: I needed Mona to take Daddy to Anita's. As Leo took another swig of Red Bull, I said, 'And it's not as if you lift a finger to help. I can't cope all on my own, not with Daddy the way he is. And not unless you, Leo, either get a job or you start to help a bit more.'

'I've got a job,' he said then, knocking me sideways. 'Starting when I get back from Dad's. In a bar. And I'm thinking of moving out.'

'Well, that's good,' I say slowly, shocked. 'Which bar? How did you . . .?' but he'd gone.

Now I go through to the kitchen, mix another martini, sit down and put my head in my hands. Why does Mona *want* to leave? Leo said she was looking for her husband. Then why did she tell me she was a widow?

Doesn't she realise that without me, she'll be sent straight back where she came from? And I suspect – though I scarcely know what's true and what isn't about her any more – that she would have no work if she did so. Whatever the story is, she should be grateful for all I've done for her, not shoving it back in my face!

She's even planning to meet that shop man – and beside a statue! I don't know why this detail bothers me so much, but it's a fact that seems to mock me. She has stolen something intimate from me, even if it is just a silly romantic notion – meeting beside a statue. Where did she get the idea? I remember Max's text again, the one she had looked at. Has she deliberately taken the idea and twisted it for her own amusement? It occurs to me she must have information on her mobile. I've taken her charger, so she can no longer use it. But I know where she keeps it. Within seconds I'm scanning down through all her contacts, looking for clues, ideas, Ali's number maybe. It's hopeless, all in Arabic script. But then I spot something and rage flares up in me. Max's number! I look twice. Sure enough, she has Max's mobile number on her phone. I think of the day of the dinner party when I found her in the kitchen, looking at his message. So this is what she was up to!

This is worse – more personal and more insidious – than anything else she's slipped from under my nose.

She wants to snatch my very identity.

Thoughts tumble about my head. Max is coming.

Without her, Daddy'll be shouting for me. I won't have time to make the house look presentable, to cook.

As I refill my glass for the third time, the truth hits me.

Without Mona, Max will see me for the person I really am. A nobody.

You're the desperate one, whispers a voice in my head.

CHAPTER FORTY-FOUR

I'm not sure, as I pick myself up off the floor, whether Dora deliberately kicked me while I was down. Everything happened so fast and she was stepping over me, perhaps trying not to fall on top of me as she came through. But then Amina's message on my Facebook page flashes back into my head, warning me that she treated Zidana badly. This incident, her foot knocking me while I had fallen down, on top of what I've heard, alarms me.

By the time I've regained my breath, gathered the shopping that's tumbled across the floor back into the bag, and stood up, I've resolved not to let Dora get to me. Whatever happened to Zidana is not going to happen again.

I *will* take Sayed up on his offer, at least go and meet his mysterious Hamid at the statue. Find out if he has indeed seen Ali. Dora will be at work and won't be able to stop me. If Leo were here, he'd cover for me. He'd do anything for me these days, for the promise of a little bit of good cooking, a bit of maternal affection. It's a shame he's gone away for Christmas.

In another mood, at another time or place, I might have shouted at Dora, objected. But I clamp my lips shut, screw up my eyes, and get to my feet. If what Sayed has told me is true,

I could be about to find Ali. I can't afford to lose everything now.

I scrub the kitchen tiles as Dora tells me to, with the brush that is meant for dishes. If she wants it clean she can have it clean. I get down on my hands and knees, working away at the grime, scrubbing until my elbows ache. Tomorrow, I will be closer to Ali. Dora can't imprison me! When I've found Ali, we will be able to stay together. I don't know how I'm going to get him out if he's being held as an illegal immigrant somewhere. I don't think about the details. Instead, I let myself dream. Focus on what I want.

We'll bring Ummu and Leila over, get Ummu the treatment she needs, and we'll be a family again. Everything will be OK.

At one point Dora comes in. I can see that she feels uneasy, that she's gone a little too far. I stand up and rub my back.

'I don't know what you were telling the man in the shop,' she says, going to the kettle, plugging it in, 'but you're not here to chat to strangers.'

'I'm not supposed to work in the evenings,' I say. 'I need time off like everyone.'

She shrugs, refuses to look at me.

At last, once she's gone up to bed, I go to my room. I pick up Leila's photo, the scrapbook of home and put them back in my bag. I'm on the move again; my bag is coming with me. Containing me. I fold up the few clothes hanging on the back of the door – my T-shirts, my other tracksuit bottoms, the one nice dress. I put the overall Dora bought for me on the bed, folded up.

Then I check that I still have some money, the notes I haven't yet sent to Ummu, and tuck them inside my purse. Finally I push my hand down to the bottom of my bag, where I keep my phone charger and where I've hidden my passport, and feel about.

There's nothing there. I search frantically through the bag, around the room, lifting books and papers and the few things I've left on my bed.

Then the truth hits me fully. My passport and my visa and my phone charger. My access to the world. They've gone.

CHAPTER FORTY-FIVE

I stand up, leave my room – that anyway no longer feels like a haven now Dora has taken off the lock – and make my way down the hall, past the drawing room. I take the stairs. All the way up. Three flights. Past Leo's room and beyond the bathroom to Dora's bedroom.

She's in there. I can hear her moving about. I step forward, put my eye to the crack in the door.

Dora is framed, her hands caressing her sides, in front of the mirror. Dressed only in green and cream lace underwear, a bra and knickers, she twirls this way, and then that way. As I watch, she puts her hands up above her head, lifts her hair high up off her face, tilts her head to one side, examines herself.

This woman, the one I see framed in the tiny gap in the door, is quite different from the Dora I know. Here in front of me is an anxious woman, frowning at her image in the mirror. As if a mask has been taken off and a softer, more vulnerable – even frightened – person revealed beneath.

That's when Dora turns, startled by some tiny sound or movement I've made without realising. The mask snaps back on.

I back away. Tiptoe down a flight of stairs to the bathroom. I wait a few minutes, to check she doesn't come out and chastise me for spying on her. When I'm certain she hasn't heard me, I creep back, knock.

She opens her door a chink. She's in her nightgown now, more satin and lace. It's clear to me she has no idea I've seen her.

'My papers are missing,' I say.

'Yes.'

'You know?'

'Of course.'

'Where are they?'

'I have them,' she says. 'They belong to me now.'

'I cannot live in this country without them.'

'You can live here with me. You are fine as long as you stay here with me.'

'I need my passport, my visa. Without them, they can send me to a detention centre, or out of this country.'

'Don't worry so, Mona,' she says, smiling. 'No one can send you to a centre as long as you are my employee. No one can take you away from me.'

'You took them from my room?'

'Yes, I did.'

'That's stealing!'

She looks at me, a smile still playing on her lips. 'I think we know who the thief is in this house. No, Mona, I didn't steal. It's the rules. I should have taken them straight away, when you moved into my house. It's normal. Your papers are quite safe with me, you really don't have to be afraid. When it's time for you to leave, I'll give them back to you. Right now, they are mine, because you belong to me.'

I pray that my tears will not fall. She must not see me weaken.

She stares back, and I see her waver. Is she going to take pity on me? She has a good side – I've seen it when I first arrived and she offered me money to buy credit. When she told me her secrets and I told her some of mine.

'Mona,' she says, 'if you try and leave without your passport, I'll give your photo to the police and I'll tell them about the things you've taken from me.'

Police. She knows if there is one word that frightens me more than any other, it is 'police'.

'Have you finished the ironing?'

I bow my head, walk down the stairs feeling her watch me as I go. And as I walk I feel my future, the one I had so brightly drawn in my head, with me and Ali and Leila together, recede behind me.

Rage and fury, and a horrible sense of impotence, take hold of me. There's nothing I can do.

Later, I lie in bed, and from somewhere an image comes, blossoming out until it's a memory and then a story, a story with a message that has come to me when I need it most.

I'm very small. Running up the narrow alley to the bakery with Ali. We both have unbaked loaves shrouded in white muslin cloth, balanced on trays on our heads. After delivering the bread to the bakery, Ali doesn't take the usual route home but leads me on a detour up steps along streets between whitewashed walls, bright in the sunshine, then through blue shadows, places I've never ventured into before, round corners and along tiny hidden passages until we come to a small patch of orchard at the top of a little cliff-edge. The trees both above and beneath are laden with white almond blossom. We crawl to the edge, encased in this cloud of white petals. I imagine I'm dressed in swathes of intricately embroidered lace. A bride maybe. A princess.

At the edge we gaze down through branches.

Two things happen to me that day. The first is a dizzying sense of wonder at the beauty of the white blossoms, whose petals I can now see are etched with fine veins. The vision does something to my mind, lifts it up as if to new realms of awareness. The structure of nature is made plain to me, a coordination that has struck me time and again since then, in the movement of waves on the shore, in the patterns in the sand, in the melodies of birdsong, in the symmetry of butterflies' wings.

The second is an awareness of the absurdity of human sexual desire. What I see that day stays in my mind forever afterwards and has been aroused again by the sight of Dora swirling in her silk underwear in her room. The texts from her lover with those photos of statues!

Between the lacy boughs I see a man's bottom, rising up and down. Two pairs of legs intertwined. This vision stirs something within me, something disturbing and faintly alluring. I know from the henna patterns that the uppermost soles belong to a woman.

Ali turns, looks at me, his bright blue eyes set in his smooth, dark-skinned face. He scrapes together a handful of almond husks from the ground and tosses one over the edge onto the couple below. The shell catches for a second in the branches of one of the almond trees, then falls onto the man beneath.

'Bull's-eye!' Ali whispers. All the impact seems to do, however, is accelerate the man's humping. Ali urges me to throw an almond husk. Mine misses the man's bottom, catching instead in the folds of his djellaba that is rucked up around his neck. Emboldened by our success, we rain almond husks down upon the couple until suddenly the man shudders, growls, and throws himself aside, revealing the woman beneath him who looks straight up at us.

Madame Le Bon! Our terrible schoolteacher. I shrink back. Too late.

Ali and I run screaming back down the alley to our street.

Afterwards when we're back at school, Ali and I behave as if the incident never happened. But I have seen my teacher's true self. And every time our eyes meet, a knowledge passes between us that gives me a little shudder of triumph. My teacher might threaten or humiliate me. But I know, and the teacher knows I know, that she is just another woman, who likes to make love in an almond orchard with a fat man who isn't her husband.

CHAPTER FORTY-SIX

The next day, I get the Clipper to the South Bank. Terence has decreed that we all need to meet, in order to talk about Daddy.

I've got Mona's passport with me. I remind her that if she disobeys me, or attempts to run away, she'll be picked up immediately by the immigration police. I'll phone them, say she's absconded undocumented.

The sun's almost white, sinking directly in front of us as we plough westwards, casting its glow onto the water, which throws it back up so it dazzles me. The tide's out, rubbish rolling about in the shallows. The plane trees along the Embankment throw mottled shadows onto the path. It seems to me that the sky is thinning out. Like ageing skin, I think. Like being tired of life.

Simon and Anita are in the foyer, sitting with glasses of white wine, leaning towards each other talking avidly. They stop the minute I arrive.

'We were just saying,' it's Anita who speaks, 'that it would be good to bring Daddy here one day. He'd love the music, the life.'

'You could try,' I say. 'But he may object. He's so taken with Mona that no one else will do these days.'

'That's a blessed relief,' Simon comments. 'It's worked out well then.'

At that moment Terence sweeps in, in his dark suit; he's clearly come straight from the City. He asks if anyone would like a drink and I ask for a martini.

'How do you have it again?'

He's known me all these years, but still hasn't got it. Then I remember that Max is coming tomorrow, and my spirits rise. He would never forget how I have my drink.

'Terence. It's a double Tanqueray with 10 mils of Cointreau, shaken with ice and a twist of orange zest.'

'We were just discussing whether a home is the best place for Daddy, if he gets worse,' Anita says, when Terence returns. 'The problem is, obviously, if he needs twenty-four-hour care, Mona won't be able to look after him. He'll need nurses. Which means a care home.'

'Well,' says Terence, 'if it comes to it, a care home is going to be problematic. I've been going through his accounts, and it's all a bit disappointing. Unfortunately, Dad couldn't have fore-seen that the recession would decrease the value of most of his savings. I'm not certain we could afford the kind of home we were thinking of. It might be a question of looking into local authority care, though I suspect we wouldn't be eligible for that either. It's a bugger – financially, we seem to fall between two stalls.'

'What about the house?' asks Simon. 'What's happening to the money from the sale of the house?'

There's a tense pause. We've often, in recent years, agreed with one another that at least we have the security of the family home – if everything else goes pear-shaped. I remember Anita hinting – and I cherish the notion – that since I was the one to have given up my time and part of my home to care for Daddy, I might even be treated favourably when it came to dividing up the proceeds of his estate. It only seems fair. Whatever, we'd all agreed that when Daddy died we'd sell it for a killing – large detached houses in Blackheath are worth millions these days – and share out the profit. None of us had bargained for the fact that we might have to use the proceeds to pay for his dementia care – but if it comes to that, we are all realising glumly, it will have to be done.

But then Terence drops the real bombshell.

'It seems Dad has left a portion of the money from the sale of the house to someone called Nancy Partridge.'

'What the fuck . . .?' says Simon, looking round at me and then Anita and back to Terence. 'You're joking. Tell me you're joking, Terry.'

Terence wipes a drop of beer from his upper lip, looks down at the paper in his hands and says, 'Apparently, Dad was seeing someone else while we were growing up.'

'You're saying he left the house to someone we haven't even heard of and has left nothing for us?' says Simon.

'Who's Nancy Partridge?' I ask. The name is familiar, but I can't put a face to it.

'Oh – my – God,' Anita says. 'I don't believe he's done this.'

She looks from one to the other of us, an infuriating gleam in her eyes, the gleam of someone who has access to the gossip before anyone else and is in the powerful position of choosing to impart it when it best suits her, when it will make the most impact. She's chosen her moment, all right.

'Nancy Partridge!' she exclaims. 'The cook at the restaurant.'

'What do you mean?' My mouth's dry. I feel as if something that's been lying submerged, that I have only half-sensed, is about to rise up and wreak its damage at last. A face floats into my mind, the cook, a shadowy figure always in the background in an overall, her dark eyes, her glossy hair: is this the person Mona reminded me of when she arrived?

'They had an affair – one of Daddy's many,' Anita tells us. 'She worked in the restaurant, was a cook. But when Mum found out, he sacked her. Nice work, Daddy! But it was typical of him – he's always picked up and dropped people when it suited him; he's always been a selfish old bugger.'

'You knew?' asks Simon.

'Mum told me,' says Anita coolly. 'Mum thought you'd be upset. You in particular, Dora.'

'When? When did Mum tell you?' Had she been in Mummy's confidence in a way I never had?

'Recently. It was after Daddy started getting symptoms. He started to talk about this Nancy person and I asked Mummy who she was.'

'Bloody hell,' says Terence, for once showing some reaction, some emotion. 'Have you met her?'

'Not recently. But I remembered her, once Mum mentioned her,' says Anita. 'I'd never have thought he'd do this though. Mum said Nancy accused him of treating her badly, not paying her properly or something. Unfairly dismissing her. She wouldn't let it drop for quite a while after he sacked her. Mum said it was horrid – they both felt they were being stalked.'

'How on earth did he fit having an affair in with the restaurant?' I manage at last.

I wonder how reliable Anita's information is. I knew Daddy better than anyone in those years, the years he used to run the restaurant and we'd make our early-morning forays to London's markets and hidden stalls and wholesalers.

'You know those mornings he used to take you to the markets with him?' Anita said. 'You were a decoy, to distract Mother from suspecting anything.'

'That's rubbish,' I said. 'Why would she suspect anything? He had to get his produce for the restaurant, that's all. There was no reason on earth for Mother to be suspicious.'

'Ah, but she was. Because she had caught him once, at the restaurant. And she remembered that Nancy had often gone with him on those trips. Mother forbade him to see her again. But when he continued to go off early in the mornings, she accused him of carrying on. He said, "If you don't believe me, I'll take Theodora along." He knew you'd never complain about being left in the cafés, or in the car. Do you remember, Dora? You used to tell me how he left you for hours some-times. But Daddy knew you'd never blab to Mum. Because you were always so desperate to prove how good you were. He made you feel you were his favourite – when it suited him, of course. He did it to each of us.'

I *was* his favourite. He took me because I was the one he liked to spend time with. The special one. I was always helpful. Never any trouble. His gift from God. The one who's been prepared to take him in, in his old age.

'Anyway,' says Terence briskly. 'I'm afraid this is something we all have to confront. There is no spare cash for any of us at the moment. What there is, we have to put aside in case Dad does ever need full-time care.'

'If there's anything left,' says Simon. 'At this rate we'll be bankrupt before he kicks the bucket.'

'Look, this is getting rather nasty,' I say. 'That was in bad taste, Simon.'

'I think we need to talk to this woman. Here we are, paying for Dad's care, and there she is, about to inherit the family wealth, doing fuck all. Or perhaps someone ought to have a word with Daddy, persuade him he's made a mistake. It's typi-cal of the mean old sod to cheat us all out of what was our due.'

'So it's bad news, I'm afraid,' Terence goes on, ignoring him. 'If Dad does need care, it might mean one or the other of us remortgaging . . .'

'Then the best thing is, we keep him out of it for as long as possible,' says Anita. 'Anyway, he would hate to be in a home with a lot of old people all going gaga.'

I can't speak. *I'm* not thinking about the money. The money is the last thing on my mind. I'm thinking about the fact that if I'd ever been Daddy's 'gift from God', I was a gift only because I provided cover for the fact he was with his lover.

'So I think we're all agreed,' Terence is saying. 'For the time being, if you're OK with it, Dora, I think we'll leave things as they are. All seems to be going well with your . . .'

'Mona,' Simon fills in.

'Yes, her, and we'll review the situation in say . . . six months? Is that OK with you, Dora? We'll all continue to contribute financially.'

'At least we've all got decent homes and jobs,' Anita says. She doesn't seem to have been affected at all by this startling news.

'I'm sorry it wasn't a more cheerful meeting,' says Terence.

When the boys have gone, Anita and I walk together along the river.

The tide has come up in the time we have been inside, and is now gobbling up the steps that lead down to the beach. The water is dark and a murky green and bits are floating in it that I don't want to look at too closely. I walk with Anita towards Waterloo tube station with the sense that nothing is as it seems, that the past and the way we see it shifts and alters and flickers like the river. I think of how, when Daddy moved in, I realised he was different from the person I remembered, and now I wonder whether I ever really knew him at all.

PART THREE

The Silence of Statues

CHAPTER FORTY-SEVEN

'So, Mona,' I say, as she comes into the kitchen. Max is due tonight, he's coming to my home. He wants to see the real me, to sleep in my bed. The thought of his being here heals somewhat the hurt I felt after learning about Daddy, his past, the way he's used each of us to his own ends. Me more than anyone. Max, at least, wants me.

Mona has brown shadows around her eyes today, and is looking, I notice with a certain satisfaction, worn and unattractive in one of the dowdy blue overalls.

'Just a reminder. The house is to gleam! What I thought was, it would be nice if you could make more of your traditional bread.'

She stares at me, wide-eyed. Is she still resentful that I took her passport?

'If you can do this for me, we can talk about your having a few days off in January to pop home.'

She moves her head imperceptibly. She's acquiescing.

'I'll be arriving home at about six and I'd like you to make the bread then. Also, I thought it would be rather nice if you could cook one of your warming soups, the one with chickpeas . . .'

'*Harira.*'

'Yes. And then I've arranged for a taxi to take you and Daddy to Anita's.'

Her face is still hard, expressionless.

'Mona,' I say softly. 'We can help one another. Let's work together like we did when you first arrived.'

'I have to go to Charles now,' she says. 'He needs his medication.'

I've arranged with Charlotte to leave work a little early today. The show's not going out again now till after Christmas and everything's winding down. Half the staff have disappeared for Christmas drinks at 3 p.m. so I pull on my coat, my heart pounding, in anticipation of the evening ahead.

My mobile goes as I hurry towards the South Bank again. It's Anita.

'So sorry, Dora. We're going to have to cancel the Christmas thing. Jack's come down with chicken pox. Jemima's whingeing too, so I think she's probably sickening.'

It takes a few moments for it to sink in. Max is coming! Mona and Daddy will have to stay in the house after all. But there's nothing I can do. I'll just have to keep Mona out of our way. Hell, she can sleep downstairs in Daddy's flat with him. It won't do her any harm, and it means she'll be there if he wakes.

Max is walking around the *London Pride* sculpture outside the National Theatre on the South Bank, admiring the women's rather oversized legs, their bronze breasts. The two nudes are almost identical, stylised, larger than life, sitting on the plinth.

'Like you and your housemaid,' jokes Max.

It's begun to rain, a fine steady downpour, and we find seats under Waterloo Bridge outside the BFI. It's cold, but we're both wrapped up in thick coats, my faux fur one, Max's camel, and scarves. There's something delicious about sheltering from the rain here; the way its pattering mutes the other sounds of the city, the smell of the wet pavements, the way people's umbrellas go up. Rays from the sinking sun light up the rain from the west, forming a golden veil over the dark river, and over the black bridges, and over the slate-grey buildings on the opposite bank. The book stalls are closed today; the Embankment is quiet, the winter and the rain have thinned out the tourists. I sit huddled into my coat, under the bridge watching the little blue lights glow in the dark branches of the trees along the Embankment.

Buses and taxis, rumbling invisibly overhead, cast shadows that slide across the plane trees and vanish.

A rainbow appears, arching over and touching the buildings at Aldwych. A woman with a bright umbrella, matching the orange stripe of the rainbow, leans on the railings, a vibrant image against the muted greys and greens of the river. I think how much I love London, how to me it is my heart, that this is something that maybe Max will never really quite understand, however much of it I show him.

When we've finished our drinks we make our way to the pier to wait for the Clipper.

'Have you made any decisions about downsizing?' I ask him.

'My New Year resolution,' he says, 'is going to be to have cut down my hours by June. I'm going to spend more time away from work.' He looks at me, a gentle smile on his face as if he's waiting for me to say something. For the first time I wonder whether the allure of his status as a professor will fade for me when he resigns. It's something I've always found sexy, the thought of the sway he holds over his juniors, his expertise and the kudos this carries.

'It's the beginning of a new era. Mattie will have left for college by then.'

'You'll be a new man.'

'I hope so.'

We arrive at Festival Pier.

'So we take the boat from here?' he asks, his arm around me, the twinkle back in his eyes.

'Yes, if you're not sea-sick. It's the nicest way to the pub I want to show you.'

He takes hold of my hand, pulls off the glove. Weaves his fingers through mine. 'Love it. Theodora Gentleman goes home by boat,' he says. 'Why did you never invite me before?'

I know the answer: I didn't have Mona before. The house was a mess. Daddy was constantly crying out for me. Leo was a drain on my space and time. It's thanks to Mona I'm bringing my lover home! I say nothing, but shudder, whether with the cold or the anticipation I can't be sure.

Then the boat arrives. The tide's up tonight, the river swelling and heaving as we climb on board. The boat rises and falls, throwing Max and me together, and I cling to him, a strange terror taking hold of me. The river tosses us about carelessly as if we were playthings riding on its back, and I have a vision of us as we must look from above. Two pathetic human beings at the mercy of this great waterway. I glance at Max to see if he, too, is struck by this, but he's gazing out at the lights on the far banks, his arm about me and his fingers gently stroking the collar of my faux fur coat, as if he's in the most comfortable place in the world.

The boat draws up at Hilton Docklands Pier, with a clanking of chains, and it rolls and groans as we clamber off onto solid ground.

'What a quaint old place,' he says, as I lead him into the pub. 'Almost Dickensian,' sitting back on one of the benches by the fire that the proprietors are always careful to light. There are mince pies on the bar, and the tree in the corner is tastefully decked in white lights.

Later, warmed by the two drinks I've had on our way east, I take him out onto the platform where Leo sat during my mother's funeral wake, and we stand and gaze at the view over the river, so different here from the view from the National Theatre. Instead of the grand façade of Somerset House with its green domes on the north side, here are dark crevices and pilings. I spot the steps down which I imagined descending, the day of the funeral. Remember how I'd thought that to walk into the river's depths might be a relief from the strain I felt swamping me at the time. And I remind myself how I have pulled things around since then, taken Daddy in, got my house looking presentable and am at last bringing Max right into the heart of my life.

I feel a wave of love for Max. A keen need for him that unsettles me.

Unsettles me, because underneath I realise that everything I've achieved has been thanks to Mona, and I wonder, will Max love me when he knows that I've lost my job? Will he see that I cannot properly supervise Mona, that I've failed with Leo? What if he judges me for having Daddy live in the basement? Should I have agreed with Mona about moving Daddy upstairs?

'Come on,' he says as if on cue. 'Show me your home.'

A bus ride through the increasingly squalid streets of south-east London. I wonder what Max thinks as the streets turn rougher, the warehouses give way to KFCs and betting shops, cheap barbers and pound shops nestled beneath cheaply constructed 1970s apartment blocks.

'Look, Max, I want to show you the hidden treasure inside this church. Follow me.'

I take him into St Nicholas, past its gaping skulls on the gateposts, and show him the lists of ships' names on the wall, where I'd got the name Endymion for my cat. Then I show him the Grinling Gibbons carving, an illustration of the psalm 'O Ye Dry Bones'.

As we stand and look at it, however, I suddenly wish I hadn't. Why am I showing him a depiction of skeletons and skulls, of heaps of weeping bodies? Max likes sensual statues, depictions of life; he doesn't want to see this harrowing carving of bodies writhing and rotting underground.

I hurry him out again. 'Let's go home,' I say.

We walk down the High Street, and I'm acutely aware of all the nail bars and the Thai massage parlours, of the guys hanging around with cans of Special Brew outside the cab office. I don't want Max to look, I want him only to see the things I'm proud of.

Max is silent, and the anxiety surfaces again that he might change his mind about me when he sees my home.

We turn into my narrow street of terraced houses.

'This is better than I imagined,' he says into my ear. 'An old London street with cute houses. I thought you might live in some converted warehouse. I hoped it might be something like this.'

'This is the one street round here that escaped demolition in the '70s,' I say. 'It's a gentrified oasis in a working-class wilderness.'

He laughs. 'Hey, look at these little statues by the doors! They are something else.'

I smile. 'The houses originally belonged to shipbuilders and merchants,' I say. 'Some of them have figureheads, see? But mine's got two little cherubs guarding the door. Angel babies.'

I put my key in the lock, push open the front door. The warm yeasty smell of bread greets us. The house throws off a gentle light; it's spotless, calm, welcoming.

Mona has obeyed my instructions to the letter.

The kitchen door at the end of the hallway is ajar so we can see her framed in it from the passage as we approach.

She squats on the floor, in her overall, which is pulled up around her knees, kneading dough in a big shallow earthenware bowl I've given her for the purpose. Her hair is pulled back into her black and orange headscarf, strands falling through and over her cheeks; her feet are in the little soft leather slippers she wears indoors.

Her face is drawn, her eyes tired.

Endymion has settled himself on the kitchen table, seems to be gazing down at Mona, blinking sleepily.

Max stands in the shadows, watching through the gap in the door, remaining out of sight.

As I walk into the kitchen, Mona stands up, and says quietly into my ear, 'There was a message on the telephone. She tried your mobile but there was no answer. From the radio station. About a new job for you.'

'What?'

'She said to ring tomorrow morning. It is a cooking programme. She has good news.' My heart lifts. I'm about to ask more, when I remember neither Mona nor Max know I've lost my previous job.

'Thank you, Mona,' I say. 'When you've done that, you must go to Daddy. It's quite late.'

'I'm doing what you told me to do.' She says this loudly, squatting down again, not looking at me any more, refusing to show Max that we get on. I feel nervous. She looks resentful. This isn't how I want Max to view our relationship.

I want him to see that Mona and I have roles, yes, that she does as she's asked. But that I'm a well-liked employer.

'You told me to make bread when you came in. That's what I'm doing. I need to leave it one hour, then I must knead it again. Then I must leave it to rise before I bake it.'

'Yes,' I say. 'But you must go to Daddy while the bread's rising.'

She doesn't answer but continues to knead. I grow hot and cross at her insolence on this one occasion when I most want her to cooperate.

'Mona,' I say.

She doesn't look up. It's as if she hasn't heard me.

'Hi,' says Max, stepping forward out of the shadows. 'I'm Max. Lovely to meet you at last.'

Mona looks straight at him through her wide brown eyes.

I have the strong urge to slap her. Is she flirting with my lover?

'Mona, isn't it?' Max asks, holding out his hand to shake hers. 'How are you?'

I look at Max, try to discern what he thinks is going on. I've given him his glimpse, isn't this enough?

'Dora and I will finish the bread, Mona,' he says next. 'Dora's Daddy needs his supper. It's a priority. You may go now.'

Does he think I've let her get out of control?

Mona continues to stare, wide-eyed, and turns to look at me, for affirmation that she may go. The way she looks is ironic, an act for Max's benefit.

She *is* trying to communicate something to him.

'Max is right. Go now, Mona. Forget the bread. Go on.'

She struggles up, rubbing her back, letting the overall fall around her knees. Bends over and picks up the bowl and places it on the sideboard so it is near the warmth emanating from the Raeburn, which is giving off a gentle heat.

'Mona,' I hiss, following her into the hall, 'you will sleep in Daddy's flat tonight. Do you understand? Anita's son is ill so you're not going there after all.'

'But where? There is no bed in Charles's flat.'

'Yes, there is.' I lower my voice. 'You can use the cushions from the sofa. Make a bed on the floor, don't complain. I don't want you in the house tonight.'

'But the floor is cold.'

'Mona! You do as I say, not as you wish.'

How dare she challenge me, the one night I need to show my authority over her?

Finally she acquiesces, goes back through the kitchen, pushes open the door to her room, disappears for a second and comes out with her bag and her anorak.

I watch her as she goes out of the front door, listening for her footsteps round to the back of the house. Then I go to Max who is sitting at the kitchen table, nursing a glass of red wine. I steel myself for some kind of prurient comment from him, something about Mona's lovely thighs. But Max puts out his hand and pulls me onto his lap.

'It's like coming home,' he breathes. 'Really. The house, the cat, Mona, the breadmaking – it's all amazing. When are you going to show me upstairs?'

Mona has done me proud in the bedroom. The sheets have been laundered and ironed as I asked – starched even, by the feel of it. She's lit the lamps around the room and they cast a dim light and soft shadows. She's placed some kind of incense on the dressing-table, something she must have brought from Morocco, I guess. It gives the room an exotic, sensual feel.

Max sits on the side of the bed and undoes his watch-strap. I wonder if this is how he goes to bed with Valerie, unbuttoning his cuffs, loosening his collar, using one foot to prise the shoe off the other.

And this worries me. We spend no time at all undressing, when we're in the throes of our usual fast and furious passion. Several times we haven't even got as far as undressing, too eager to be inside each other's garments to bother to remove them properly. Sometimes I've come home, my underclothes torn to shreds, treasuring the sensual dissolute feeling this lends to my journey amongst early-morning commuters who, I like to imagine, have never experienced passion like ours. I cherish the secret knowledge that we are unique in our carnal desire for each other.

Max's slow, formal undressing this evening alarms me. I reach across the bed, put my arms around him, feel the usual thrill of pleasure I get from the toned body beneath the white shirt, move my hands up over his chest, something that usually makes him groan with pleasure. He doesn't respond, but continues to remove his trousers, his socks, as if I were his wife!

I give up and swing my legs into bed, pulling the covers up over me, and wait for him to join me. Perhaps it's being here, in my home, that threatens our passion. I should never have asked him to come. But he wanted to! He was the one to suggest it.

His words come back, sweet and reassuring. 'I'd like to sleep the night in a bed with you . . . that shapes itself to you . . .'

'Max,' I breathe. 'Is this a mistake?'

'What?' he asks.

Am I imagining it, or is he refusing to look at me?

I do not want to trap Max. I have never demanded that he leave his wife. I have never tried to own him in any shape or form.

But I cannot lose him. I love him. I gave up everything for him. Roger. Money. A luxury lifestyle. I've given up my home to him now – I've even offered him a sighting of my maid.

'You coming here, was it a mistake?' I persist. 'Perhaps we only work when we're out in the world – and we're not meant to see inside each other's homes?'

He sighs, looks at me, tucks his feet under the covers too and puts an arm around me, pulling me to him. I rest my head in the dip between his shoulder and his chest.

'Don't, Dora,' he says. 'Don't start to nag. I need to sleep. I'm jet-lagged.'

I stay where I am. He has never ever complained of jet-lag before, not with me.

'Is it to do with Mona?' I ask, and this feels brave of me since it is the last thing I want to know the answer to.

'Mona? Oh yes, I was going to suggest . . .'

I wonder what he's going to say. Can hardly bear to hear. But he goes on, 'I don't have to get up for an early flight for once. Could we ask her to make us breakfast – and bring it up? Is that within her remit?'

Why does he want Mona to bring up breakfast? Why can't I do it for him?

'Did she disappoint you though, to look at? Did I bring you here on false pretences?' I test him.

He shrugs, leans back over to his side of the bed, switches the lamp off. There's just the one light now, over on the dressing-table, the small one, giving a soft glow, so he is in shadow as he speaks, I can't see his face, but as he talks I feel with relief his hand on my thigh, the warmth of it, the way it does something to me instantly.

'It's nothing, Dora. I realise it was foolish, our little fantasy. She's just doing her job. I felt bad, seeing her in reality, that I'd objectified her. That night after Boudicca, I was on a roll, seeing those bronze thighs!' He's laughing, pulling me to him whispering, 'Let's forget it and enjoy now. We have all night, and all morning.'

And I'm so relieved I take special care over Max tonight, giving him all he wants without his even asking, and he doesn't even need me to mention thighs or statues or domestic servants.

Afterwards, I go downstairs and fetch the newly baked bread Mona has left on the side, and bowls of the *harira* she has made, and we eat it in bed, side by side, and share a bottle of wine. And soon, with the alcohol and the fatigue and the deep feeling of contentment, I am fast asleep.

I wake an hour or two later. The small lamp is still throwing its soft light across one corner of the room, a beam falling upon Max's goatee. I lean across and stroke it gently. I run my lips across it, enjoying the abrasive, masculine feel of it, wanting to wake him and start all over again. But I remember his jet-lag, and so I reach across and switch off the lamp, turn over, pull his arm around me, place his hand on my belly. At peace. At last.

When I awake again, it's still dark.

Something has startled me. Something abrupt – a door slamming, or a window smashing – and I lie, rigid, trying to work out whether it was a dream. I feel for Max's hand, but he's moved. I put my arm out behind me. Grasp at an expanse of sheet.

His side of the bed's empty.

I sit up, my ears straining. Listen for sounds that tell me he's gone to the bathroom. All I can hear is a low purr – Endymion has slunk into the room and curled himself up at the foot of the bed.

I can't stop trembling. Whatever startled me awake has taken hold of my body and won't let go.

For once I should feel safe, not rigid with fear. For the first time since I left Roger, I have a man – other than Leo or Daddy – in my house. But I'm unable to move. Pinned down by the kind of dread I've only ever experienced when alone, convinced that someone has broken in. Broken in and is about to make their way through the dark house, up the stairs to my room. No one can do this. Max is here to protect me. He's downstairs somewhere – he'd tackle any intruder.

Even these thoughts don't comfort me.

It feels as though it should be morning, given how long I've been sleeping, yet the darkness is dead, silent.

As my eyes adjust I see that Max's watch is still on the table at his side of the bed, his trousers draped across the back of my chair, his polished shoes placed neatly beneath it. What time did he say he had to leave? Maybe he's gone down to make a cup of tea before getting dressed, before he has to be off? No! He said it wasn't an early flight for once. He wanted Mona to bring us breakfast.

The numerals on the digital clock move on. The hands on Max's watch tick around.

I'm here with Max at last. I've let him in. We'll enter a new phase, one where he'll come home with me, cook Sunday lunch sometimes, we'll drink white wine together while the shoulder of lamb sweetens in the oven. I'll get Mona to make her pear clafoutis for pudding. We'll all sit together. Leo, Mona, Max and I. Endymion. Almost a family.

It's OK. I'll be back in my position at the radio. Mona said they phoned this evening with good news. A cookery programme! They never wanted to lose me. They'll produce a recipe book, with a photo of me on the cover.

Max can't have gone for long, he'll be back soon. We have another couple of hours before dawn – we can start all over again; we can linger over each other until it grows light, tease every last drop from each other's bodies. For once not in a rush. Then I'll get up and do as Max suggested – ask Mona to make breakfast and she can bring it to us in bed. Max will be impressed by the way we work together, a mistress and her maid. Max and I will linger over the croissants. We can even eat bits of them off each other . . .

It's no good. I can no longer bear the silence. There is no tell-tale sound of water gushing through the pipes. Max is not, after all, in the bathroom.

I lie alert.

I can hear nothing.

The same dread I used to feel at Billingsgate, when Daddy left me alone, assails me. Images flit in and out of my head: Nancy Partridge. Mona. Stony faces. Abandonment. Rejection.

No one has broken into my house – that's not it. They have, rather, broken into my soul. In this otherworldly dark of night, I no longer know who I am. The precious gift I was, that made me Theodora, has been violated; parts of my persona have been stolen.

My foundations are subsiding and soon the whole edifice that is me will follow.

At last I unleash the fear that was there all along, a vague presence to which I haven't dared give shape. A flash of panic rips through me, so violent I think I'm going to be sick.

He has not, after all, been able to resist.

Max has gone to Mona.

CHAPTER FORTY-EIGHT

The cushions are lumpy and narrow. I push them aside. Spread a blanket on the floor instead, and stretch out on this. Pull the quilt over my body. I could put it underneath, but that would leave me with only one thin blanket on top to keep warm. I put a cushion under my head. It's easier to stretch out with the hard surface beneath me. I desperately need to sleep.

I started early this morning, before dawn. If Dora wanted the house to look good for Max then she would have it. I shut out all other thoughts. I took care of Charles. Washed, starched and ironed Dora's sheets. Made her bedroom seductive as I knew she would want it for her lover's visit. In the back of my mind a new plan was hatching: if I could somehow impress this doctor, if he had an influence on Dora, then he might, as Ummu suggested when I first arrived, help me to look for Ali. He might also persuade Dora to pay me more and to return my passport – or at the very least, give me some time off.

Charles was irritable this evening.

'You haven't heated the plate. Now it's cold. I can't eat cold food!'

'OK. Then I'll heat it for you.'

'It's soup on a Thursday – I thought you knew the menu.'

'But it's Friday today, Charles.'

'It's Thursday!'

Sometimes he is so insistent I begin to doubt the reliability of my own memory. *Have* I got the day wrong?

'OK, Charles, let's say it's Thursday. I'll do you some soup.'

Finally I got him into his pyjamas, and he wet himself, and I had to begin all over again. And throughout all this, I thought of Ummu, sick in bed, Leila her little nurse, their waiting each week for the money that would buy Ummu the operation she needed so that she would live.

And this kept me going, though my back ached, my knees complained, and I knew that even when I finally lay down it would be on Charles's sitting-room floor to make way for Dora and her lover upstairs.

Now, however, though I pray for it, sleep slips in and out like a thief at night, never giving me any peace. I flip over, stretch, curl up. And finally, just as I drift into a shallow slumber, something awakens me.

Charles is calling, 'Mona, Mona!' And then an echo in the baby monitor next to me: *Mona, Mona*!

I sit up. An intense pain shoots down one leg as I straighten slowly. I place my feet on the floor. Pull my fleece over my T-shirt.

Charles is sitting up in bed, his eyes wide, his breath coming in short gasps, his puny chest beneath the loose pyjama top rising and falling. I put a hand on his forehead. He's clammy.

'Charles, are you all right? What's wrong?'

His eyes look up at me, unseeing. His breath rasps in and out. He doesn't speak.

I'm frightened for the old man, but I'm frightened, too, for myself. I must do the right thing, if I'm not to enrage Dora. My mind is cloudy with fatigue. I go to Charles's phone that Dora has warned me not to use. 'It costs money, Mona. It's not for you. Only for emergencies.'

But this *is* an emergency. I search through a pile of pamphlets and discarded letters for the doctor's number Dora showed me when I first arrived.

I finally find it and dial, my fingers clumsy. I have to wait for a list of options. I'm not sure I've understood. I dial again. Listen, my ears straining. *In an emergency, press one.* An automated voice gives me another number to ring. The emergency late-night number.

At last, after a long wait, a live voice tells me I will have to bring the patient in.

'But,' I begin, 'I can't – I have no car. Can the doctor come here?'

'If it's a real emergency you don't need us, you'll have to call the ambulance.'

'But he's very ill, he's not breathing properly.'

'Do you have a neighbour who could drive you to Accident and Emergency?'

And then I remember. Of course! There is a doctor here already. Dora's boyfriend Max is a doctor!

I pull on my trainers, leaving the basement door open, and hurry up the frozen steps to the garden and round to the front door. I unlock it, and step inside.

I'm wary of going up to Dora's room. I only ever go there now when she is out, to clean, to change the sheets, to prepare it for her.

But tonight is an exception.

I put my ear to the door. Silence. I push it open gently. It rustles over the soft carpet. The room is dark. Smells faintly of the incense I lit earlier, and of sleep, and of intimacy – a smell that I don't want to inhale for it feels like intrusion. For a second I'm a small girl, awake in the night, walking through to the alcove where I believed Papa slept alone. I see them, my mother and father together on the banquette, smelling something like this, something like sweat, and body heat and secrets. And I know I am not meant to be here.

Tonight there's no choice.

Dora and Max's two heads rest on my starched pillowcases, Max the doctor's nearest to me. I shake his shoulder. He moves a couple of centimetres, looks up, his eyes blinking open, confused. I put my mouth to his ear, whisper that Charles is ill, needs a doctor.

Max doesn't hesitate. He's up and coming through the door grabbing a dressing-gown but without even bothering to pull his trousers on over his boxer shorts.

Down in the basement I stand in Charles's bedroom doorway while Max listens to the old man's chest, feels his forehead, checks his pulse.

He turns to me.

'Upstairs, does Dora have a medical kit? A first-aid box, something like that?'

I run back up the steps to fetch Leo's zip-up case, the one he showed me in his room, the one he often raids when he thinks he's got something that needs treatment.

I find the case. Pause, wonder if there's time to check my Facebook page. But the computer's switched off. I take the medical case down, and stand at the end of the bed while Max asks Charles questions.

'Can you tell me your name, your date of birth?' He looks into Charles's eyes. Takes his pulse. He puts his ear to the man's pale concave chest and listens.

I stand, shivering. It's that pit of night long before dawn. A dreadful silent time, when even the traffic in London is still, when no bird sings – the time, they say, when people are most likely to die.

'Oh please, Allah, let him be OK,' I pray. 'Do not take him from us yet.'

And I realise that I want Charles to live not only because I'm afraid of what Dora will do to me if he dies, but also because he is my friend and I have grown, in a certain way, to love him.

'It's nothing serious,' Max says at last, straightening up, coming over to me. 'I think he's woken suddenly with a panic attack – most probably. And he may have caught a cold. I'm giving him something to soothe him. But you must go back to bed, Mona.'

I move over to my heap of cushions and quilt on the floor.

'Hey,' says Max. 'You have a room to go to, don't you? It's cold. You can't sleep there.'

He nods at the rough bed I've made.

'But Dora. She says—'

'I'll tell Dora. I'll look after her, you need to sleep. In fact, go to the room next to ours. There's a nice bed made up there.'

'But Charles, what if he's sick again . . .'

'You use this, don't you?' he says, picking up the monitor.

I nod.

'I'll take it tonight, up to our room so I will hear if he wakens again.'

I look at this man. He is kind and gentle, I can see that in his eyes. And what's more, he's a doctor – like Ali! I remember the text I saw on Dora's phone from him, from America, and I see my one last chance flit before me.

I fish in my tracksuit pocket, bring out my photo of Ali and I say, 'Please, Doctor Max, I'm looking for this man. Ali. Ali Chokran. It's possible he's working in a hospital, or has been looking for work. It's possible he's in an immigration centre. But I know he's in this country.'

317

I hand him a slip of paper. 'If you find him, you tell me?'

Doctor Max takes the photo, looks at it, nods and gives it back to me.

'Doctor,' I say, and I open my eyes wide. I know how to make a plea to a good man like this. 'I told Dora he's dead. It was to get work. I thought, They'll employ me if they think I'm a widow. I couldn't change my story.'

He smiles. 'Don't worry. I'll see what I can do. Now you go back to bed.'

I start to go. And he calls me back.

'Mona. Listen, you told me a secret. Can you keep one for me? Just until the morning?'

I nod. 'Of course.'

He pulls something out of his pocket. A small box – the kind they sell expensive jewelry in. I've seen them in Madame's house, and on Dora's dressing-table before she locked everything away.

He opens it. Whatever it is gleams in Charles's lamplight. It's something precious. More precious, I can see, than the chain she wears. Worth hundreds, if he were to sell it on the High Street . . .

'It's a locket – for Dora,' he says. 'Tomorrow, I want to ask her if she'll let me come and try living over here. With her. If she'll have me. And Leo, of course, and you too, I suppose! So, in the morning, I want you to make a good breakfast of coffee and can you get croissants?'

I nod.

'Croissants and maybe some flowers. Here.' He gives me a twenty-pound note. 'Keep the change for yourself.'

'Thank you,' I say.

I smile at him, happy for him, happy that he will make Dora happy.

As I go back up the steps to the front door, I feel a lightness of heart, the kind that comes after you've been lost in the labyrinth of a strange medina and suddenly you see a landmark and know you'll get home again. The American doctor is going to help me.

CHAPTER FORTY-NINE

It comes to me like an eruption of all the fears and doubts I have felt since Mona came breezing into my home.

She's taken my daddy's affections from me, and Leo's, and now she's taking Max.

Things I've suspected come back to me. What she told me about Madame Sherif and her husband. All the time, Mona has been building up to this. I've let her off, when my instincts told me otherwise, when she deceived me over the roses and the soup spoons, duping me with her 'goodness' and with her concern for Daddy and Leo.

Stories from my ex-pat friends echo in my ears. That you have to keep domestic workers from your husband. That they lack moral awareness and see anything of yours as theirs as well. That they're uneducated and lack sophistication. Why else would they choose this sort of work?

I think of the way Mona flaunted her golden thighs at me – was that a deliberate attempt to undermine the confidence I've always had in my own body? Her lies about being widowed – were they to gain my sympathy, and make me believe she's still mowning her husband so is no threat?

Mona's strange defiance earlier, in the kitchen when she was making the bread, gave away what she was really thinking. It was a way of communicating to Max that she was not happy with me.

That she wanted him?

I'm out of bed and down the first flight of stairs, nausea rising with each piece of evidence. The bathroom light is off, it's empty. The house is silent.

Down the next flight, hoping that maybe, just maybe, I'll find Max making a cup of tea in the kitchen, that he'll simply say he couldn't sleep, his body clock is all skewed after his flight.

But he is neither in the bathroom nor in the kitchen. In a panic, half-hoping to find him in there, perhaps reading, perhaps needing somewhere to deal with his insomnia, I push open the door to the back room, my study, where Mona usually sleeps.

Empty.

He's not here at all. He's gone to Mona down in the basement!

The irony hits me – that I told her to stay down there tonight, expressly to ensure she was out of our way!

I turn to face the hallway. And then I know.

The front door is on the latch, someone has gone out.

Max.

I try to stop the images marching into my head. Max biting her thighs, telling her how much he desires her, for she is softly rounded and bronzed. For the skin on her thighs is still smooth and not uneven as mine has become. For she is hard-working and clever while I am ageing, and no longer visible, and unable to command power over anything, or anyone.

A ghastly image comes to me, the stone faces outside my door jeering, as they witness Max passing beneath them on his way to her.

Your lover and your maid, they whisper.

I brought him here! I led him to her! Of all the people he

might choose to be unfaithful with, he has chosen Mona. My housemaid. My subordinate.

I pull my faux fur coat over my satin nightie, chosen for my lover's first visit to my home. A pair of boots over bare feet. Through the front door, round to the back of the house. Over the frosted grass to the top of the stairs.

The door is open at the bottom, a pale lozenge of yellow light thrown onto the first two steps. My heart pounds at the realisation of my worst fears. Max has gone in, left the door ajar in his haste. I stand at the top and listen.

Sure enough, I can hear voices, soft voices – Max's breathy lovemaker's voice, the voice that makes me think of Tom Waits and smoky late-night blues bars. He's using it on her! In Daddy's flat while he sleeps!

The rage, the hurt makes me tremble so much I'm afraid I'm going to collapse.

Between them, Max and Mona have made the ultimate fool of me.

The shadow of a figure in a skirt looms out of the basement doorway. I move to the side, into the dark.

My hand strokes the top of Mummy's stone head. If only she had never died! If only you'd never left me, Mummy. If only it wasn't for Anita and Simon and Terence's selfish behaviour. If only Daddy hadn't duped me into believing I was his favourite!

I wouldn't have needed a maid again. I should have learned the first time round that they are nothing but trouble.

I was right that night of the funeral, when I predicted that my siblings were all changing for the worse now Mummy was dead. I have a sudden overwhelming desire to hear our mother's calm, rational voice. Compromising. Helping us all to see right from wrong. None of them knows what's good and right since she died. They've all lost their moral compasses.

If only I hadn't had to be the Selfless One, taking care of

everything, sorting everything out. You do your best and everyone takes advantage; they take and take and belittle you until you are invisible to your own lover.

The shadow creeps up the steps ahead of its owner.

My body acts as if it is quite separate from me, gripping Mummy's stone head, giving it an almighty shove, putting all my rage and hurt into the motion. The bust rocks for a second, then crashes down.

It lands hard on the head that is appearing at my feet.

I don't know if there was much noise while this was happening, whether there was a cry, whether the body made a scrunching sound as it collapsed at the bottom of the steps, where its head is now bent up against the doorjamb at an odd angle. Where, I can't help noticing, a bare thigh lies uppermost, a slice of light falling across it highlighting the hamstring, just there, the sinewy area of flesh Max was so obsessed with, that it drove him to cheat on me with my domestic worker.

But suddenly the world falls silent, with the kind of silence one only notices once an incessant background noise stops.

And whittling through this silence comes the thin, sweet sound of a blackbird's song.

CHAPTER FIFTY

I stare at the body. It's so still. Why doesn't it move?

I run down the steps. This is all wrong. It was Mona coming out of the flat. I saw the shadow of her overall. Impossible! To my horror I realise the shadow must have been made by the dressing-gown that Max is wearing.

'Max!' I cry. I kneel down next to him. Kiss his neck, his chest, his thigh.

'Max!'

I sit down on the icy ground next to him and cradle his head in my lap.

But where is Mona?

There's no sound from the flat. She must be hiding in there, afraid I'm about to discover her. As well she might be. I will let her cower, let her suffer, knowing what's to come. For now I need to give my full attention to Max.

He's gone a funny colour in the yellow lamplight spilling from Daddy's flat. Is it just the cold? I take off my coat and lay it over him, to warm him.

And I stay there with him for I don't know how long.

*   *   *

It's still dark, but a less weighty dark when a voice stirs me out of my stupor.

'What happened?'

I turn, confused. Above me, at the top of the steps, silhouetted against the moon, is Mona, her headscarf lit by the streetlamp in the alley, turning both it and her face an amber colour, the way the angels along the street turn orange at night. For a second I feel as if I'm looking at one of the statues Max and I met beneath early on – the beautiful girl who stands demurely on the top of the Palace Theatre wearing only a headscarf. Benign, innocent. But alluring.

I stare at her for a few minutes, hardly believing she's real. The real Mona is hiding somewhere in Daddy's flat where she's just had sex on Daddy's sitting-room carpet with my lover.

'What is it? What happened?' she asks again.

'What are you doing there? You were meant to be in with Daddy.'

Her face is crumpled, she is frightened. She moves down the steps, one at a time, holding the wall at the side, her eyes deep, dark sockets. As she gets to the bottom she begins to whimper.

'Stop that – that's not going to help!' I tell her. 'Where were you? Why was Max down here?'

'He went to Charles,' she says. 'Charles was ill. Not breathing. Coughing. I came up to find Doctor Max. He told me to go to bed. He said he would stay with Charles, check he was OK.'

In spite of the cold night, I have broken out in an unpleasant sweat. It veils my forehead and is dribbling down behind my ears. My thighs, too, feel sticky and unpleasant.

'You were upstairs, in the house?'

'Yes. Max came down to help Charles. He told me to go to bed in the house.'

I look back down at the man whose head lies in my lap.

Max, you fool. You bloody fool, I think. Mona was sleeping in Daddy's flat so she could take care of him. It was her job to look after him. So that she wouldn't interfere with our night together. It was so we could be alone.

And you tell her to go upstairs!

You think you're the one who has to look after Daddy? It's what I've employed the woman for. You should have left her to it. You shouldn't spoil these people, Max.

It doesn't do to be too kind. Too trusting. They'll take advantage if you're friendly.

'Max must have fallen,' I tell Mona. 'He must have come up the steps, they are slippery – look, you see? There's a frost. He obviously lost his balance. He was near the top, put out his hand, grabbed the statue, but the statue came with him as he fell. Backwards . . .'

'So we must call a doctor? Or an ambulance?'

Yes, I think. This is what we should do. Call a doctor, call an ambulance. Let them take him. There may still be something they can do.

I'm trembling. It's with the cold, I think. My arms and legs twitch as I try to make sense of the situation. I must instruct my body in what to do. I tell it to move, up the steps, back to the house, to the kitchen, to the phone, where I must pick up and dial. Dial who? The ambulance? The police? A doctor?

Then what?

Max isn't moving. I shake him gently, but he doesn't respond. I press my thumb against his wrist. I can't feel a pulse. Does this mean he's dead? Can't they resuscitate people these days? Can't they do something with their chests, bring them back to life?

I need to ask Max.

But this *is* Max.

And that's when I begin to wail.

'I'll call an ambulance,' Mona says. 'What's the number? The doctor's number I called for Charles is too slow.'

She steps over Max. She steps over Mummy's head, lying on its side, staring sadly into Daddy's flat.

Mona makes for the phone. She is thinking more clearly than I am, though she is still whimpering, crying, as if this were her problem, not mine.

Then I do begin to think – with a terrible clarity.

As if a light has gone on in my brain.

'Wait, Mona!'

She turns.

When they find he's unconscious, in a coma, or God forbid, if he's dead – they will want to inform his wife, his kids that he's here, in a basement in south-east London. That he was spending the night with me, a woman they've never heard of. And if he is dead . . . I look again at him, feel his wrist, try to find a pulse, try and try again. *Come back to life, Max. Come on, pulse, let me feel you.* I put my ear to his chest . . . he can't be. It isn't possible.

'Max!' I cry. 'Max!'

No response. If he's dead they'll do a post-mortem to check how he died, and they will ask why, if he fell, is there this blow to the skull, just here, where this terrible dark stain is spreading down from Max's hairline to his eye. It cannot have been caused by a fall, it is too acute; it's obviously the result of assault.

This thought is so vibrant in my head, I am startled to find another equally bright one move in.

If I am found guilty of assault, manslaughter, whatever charge this kind of accident brings with it – what will become of the new programme Mona said they'd phoned about earlier? I was to be reinstated, after all, as Theodora Gentleman, running a new cookery programme. On air again, with the following I've always enjoyed, maybe more so.

Max never told his wife about me. No one will know where he's gone.

He will be an unsolved disappearance.

No one knows he came here.

Except Mona.

CHAPTER FIFTY-ONE

'Mona,' Dora says.

She holds out her hand, she tugs me down. We sit side by side on the bottom step. She turns my face towards hers.

'Max never came. Do you understand? No one must know.'

I nod, and she lets go of my chin. 'I understand,' I say. There's something wrong here. Something I should object to. But Dora can do what she likes. She has my passport. My lifeline. I'm not in a position to argue.

'And so, Mona, I need you to help me move him. You are my maid, and you must do as I tell you. And I'm telling you to help me. We need to take Max away in my car somewhere. We need to get rid of him.'

I know not to ask questions. I must do exactly as she says. I shut off all thought. Do as I am told.

I know where they put the bodies when they are in too much of a hurry to bury them. I know from stories about the conflicts Ali was always so interested in. Conflicts in our neighbouring countries, during what they now call the Arab Spring. Ali told me how his Berber cousins had fled violence and conflict between rebels and government forces, how many had attempted to escape on

329

boats to Europe. Those who didn't survive, he told me, his blue eyes flashing in anger, were simply tossed overboard into the sea. But where else is there to put a body that would otherwise begin to rot and smell and attract disease?

And so, because I have no choice, because I can guess what she will do to me if I don't help her, I tell Dora, 'We must put him in the river.'

'I can't bear to look at him,' Dora says, and I follow her gaze and see that Max's head, which I thought had simply bled a little, has in fact caved in at the top. There is stuff leaking from the gash – not just blood, other matter. I flinch with horror at the thought that it must be his brains.

I wretch, fighting back the urge to be sick, but I can't look away. I stare at the material oozing from the open wound, the black parting in his fine hair filling with froth. I visualise the thoughts that this very matter must have contained, until he slipped so violently on the steps and his poor head shattered under the weight of the statue. Intelligent, kind thoughts. Thoughts that were going to help me. Where are they going? Are they leaking out with the offal that is bubbling up like the sputum at the edge of the sea, vanishing as they meet the air?

Dora must have moved in these few seconds, for she emerges now from Charles's flat, holding a bundle of fabric in her hands. She squats and dabs at the blood with a towel and, when the towel is saturated, she lifts Max's messy head and slips some more fabric – one of the overalls she bought me, the one I left on the floor when I got into bed last night – beneath his head and then draws it tightly around and around his face, until his whole head is wrapped up. She fastens the overall by tying the sleeve in a tight knot, so that the fabric is bundled around his face, shrouding it.

'At least now I won't have to look at this ghastly mess,' she mutters. 'We'll cover his body with a blanket. Fetch the one from your bed. Mona. Quickly! And while you're there' – she tosses me the bloodied towel – 'stuff this in Daddy's bin. We'll sort it out later.'

In the silent flat, I glance into Charles's room. He is sleeping soundly on his side. Whatever Max gave him earlier to calm him must have had a sedative effect. I push the towel into the bin and pull the blanket from my makeshift bed.

Dora is shivering as she takes her coat off Max and slips her own arms back into it. Together, Dora and I wrap Max in the blanket, until he resembles no more than a heap of bedding or dirty laundry that we are bringing out of the flat.

'Now, you take his feet, Mona, and I'll take his shoulders.' She puts her hands under his arms and hoists him up, his bound head against her chest, and I lift his feet. It's impossible to get a grip on the blanket, so I push it out of the way and pull his bare legs up on either side of me, the way I sometimes carry Leila.

As we begin to climb the steps, trying not to slip on the ice, Max's white feet dangling out of the bundle to either side of me, my throat fills with an acrid scent that I mistake first for a mixture of frost and diesel fumes. It is the smell of blood. It's dripping on the steps as we go, leaving a dark trail in the frost.

At the top of the steps, the weight grows too much for me. My arms are going to give way.

'Please, Dora. Can we rest for a moment?' I gasp, and she, in relief, lowers his blue head to the ground. We stand for a moment in the icy night, panting. Already one side of the overall tied around his head is saturated, dark with the blood that has seeped out on our way up.

'We can't be long,' Dora pants. 'We've left Daddy all alone in his flat.'

'He was sleeping soundly. Max . . .' My voice falters. 'Max gave him something to relax him.'

'I need my car keys,' Dora gasps, and she darts across the garden, leaving me alone with the body. The only light comes from the streetlamp in the alley, which just misses Max's shrouded form. It occurs to me in that moment that I could just run. Run as fast as I could away from all of this. Disappear.

I look about me. I have nothing: no money, no papers. And where would I go? And how soon before Dora alerted the police that her undocumented maid had disappeared just as her lover had died violently in the night? My heart begins to hammer against my chest.

'Mona, we need to move.' Dora's back. 'Lift him. Come on, we haven't time to lose.'

Can this really be happening? Is she really determined to take Max's body to the river without seeking help from the police or a doctor?

Why? Can it be due to her fear of what his wife will say when she learns of his affair? There must be something else, something that Dora wants to hide. But if I ask, Dora has the power to make it look as though I had something to do with the death of the doctor. And so I say nothing.

After this we don't speak again. We work silently together. And, because I am thinking more clearly than Dora is, she lets me take charge.

She does exactly as I tell her.

'Wait!'

I point up at Desiree's windows next door. Dora hasn't thought of this. *Alhamdulillah*, the woman's house is dark, her curtains drawn. In fact, the curtains are drawn at the backs of all the houses along the terrace. No one is looking.

Dora goes ahead, carrying Max's top half, across the garden where the frost is beginning to harden. Along the little alley by the side of the house.

'Stop,' I whisper as we come to the street. 'First we must check there is no one.'

We rest the dead weight of Max on the ground for a moment, out of sight of the road in the entrance to the alley.

The street is empty but for Endymion who sits on the wall by the steps blinking slowly, like a lion, half-asleep.

'You can open the car,' I tell Dora.

Dora gets the keys out of her coat pocket, presses them and the locks clack open noisily.

She lifts the boot.

We heave Max up again, and try to get him in, head first. He's almost there, when the head slips from Dora's grasp and Max tumbles back onto the road.

'We must bend him over,' she says, heaving him from around the waist this time, so his head flops forward onto his knees. She then struggles to drag him upwards into the boot again. At last, with me clasping his thighs and Dora his waist, we manage between us to manoeuvre him, until he is half in, his legs and head lolling out. Then we have to exert ourselves and find the energy to push and shove until, at last, he is in.

He lies crooked, his head awkwardly rammed against the back seat. The blanket falls open, and the towelling dressing-gown, so hastily thrown on, gapes to reveal a white chest, greying hairs coiling over it. His bare feet hang out of the boot, large and white and grotesque in the moonlight. I yearn momentarily for Ali's smooth brown ones, but now is not the time to pine.

Dora heaves his legs, shifting them around, bending them, before she can press the boot door shut.

She gets into the driving seat.

I glance behind me before I get in on the other side. A light has come on in the house two doors down, where the big family live, with the kids who throw stones out on the street. When I look up, the light goes off.

I get in the passenger seat, closing the door quietly, and Dora waits a few minutes before she starts the engine. It splutters and dies.

She turns the key again.

'Oh God,' she says. 'I'm shaking so much I'm not sure if I can drive.'

'You want me to?'

'Can you?'

'I know how to. But I don't have a licence.'

'We don't have to worry about that now!' she whispers. She tells me to get out and go round to the driver's door. Then she shifts across into my seat and slithers down, her head bowed, so she is out of sight of the road though there's no one about to see us.

I glance up at the next-door window. Is that a face I can see, pressed to the glass? Impossible to say, in the dark. It could be a reflection, a trick of the light. The shadow of trees opposite, their bare branches frantic, batting this way and that in the wind.

The engine, at last, starts up. We leave the headlights off.

I press the pedals and we lurch forward, bumping over the cobbles down the street that I have walked along so many times with Charles. Strange to sit on this side of the car, holding the steering wheel on the wrong side. I turn right along the High Street. It's empty. The shops are shut up, many with metal grilles over their windows and doors. At the end, the lights are on red. The main road silent.

'Go!' Dora says from her position low down in the passenger seat. 'Just go, ignore the lights!'

And so I drive across the red lights, over the road that is so busy by day, and down the back streets past the apartment blocks towards the river. I glance in the mirror. There's one other car, some distance behind us, moving slowly in the same direction. I shudder.

'Stop over here,' Dora says, 'where the road curves to the

right. There's a gap in between the buildings on the corner. Turn the car, we'll park, and then we can get him out and carry him straight down through the gap into the water.'

It's hard for me to turn; several times the engine splutters and dies. The car that was some distance behind us stops, its lights on, about 100 metres up the street, I see it in the mirror.

Dora grows impatient.

'I'll do it,' she says, and we swap places again. She turns the car round and then reverses it again into the gap between a building site and a high wall, a dark passageway that leads to the steps down into the river.

I've seen how hidden this place is by day, on my walks with Charles, but it's utterly concealed at this time of night. You would never know the steps were here unless someone had shown you.

'What is it, Mona?' Dora asks. 'You are trembling terribly. You must be strong and help me.'

We get out, and I feel the cold water seep into my shoes from puddles encrusted with a thin layer of ice. The wall is graffitied with white lettering glowing against the brick.

We slide the body that is stiffening already – is it to do with the cold? – out of the boot.

I, being smaller than Dora, take his legs, and she takes his shoulders. The ground is slippery and I drop him; his feet fall to the floor with a flump.

'Hurry.'

I struggle to get a better grasp on him, holding him under the knees.

The steps are slick with ice and river water. We cling to the algae-covered walls, and I pray we won't lose our footing and slip too far, towards the place where the water swirls below us. I am numb, my mind as well as my body.

The river flings itself against the steps. It sucks and snarls.

'Wait.'

A light slides across the road behind us, the sound of a car in a low gear.

'Move back,' Dora hisses. I step into the shadows, press my spine against the wall, against the white graffiti-ed lettering. We squeeze Max to us, me his legs, Dora his shoulders, his weight distributed in a heavy sausage, like one of the rolled-up rugs Ummu used to weave in the Tapis Cooperative that weigh so much more than you imagine.

The car stops. A door slams. Footsteps come hurrying along the road. There are voices, a squeal. I hold my breath. I daren't breathe. Seconds go by. Minutes. I'm sealed to the spot, too petrified to move. As I stand frozen against the wall, I think of my first sighting of this river, how I saw it as deep and broad and serious and forbidding. But never did I imagine, when I was full of desperate hope, determined to build a future for Leila and my mother and, in my wildest dreams, Ali, too, that my journey would lead me so close to its dark heart.

CHAPTER FIFTY-TWO

My arms ache with holding Max, my fingers feel like dead things. When we reach the third slippery step, the water just beneath us, I tell Mona to let go of her end. I want to be the last person to hold him.

She lays his feet down, and I lower his head. He lies, the water lapping at the sleeve of the blue overall, moving it this way and that in the current. His feet are uppermost on the steps, as if he's resting, ready to slide backwards into the river.

I have to walk down the steps in order to get a purchase on him. I let the water slop over my boots as I descend, trying to ignore the way the cold bites into my legs, clamps its jaws around my muscles so they contract. A shocking pain sears through my calf. I'm unable to move. I clutch the wall with one hand.

'Mona – my leg, it's so painful. I've got cramp.'

A light sweeps across the street at the top of the step.

Voices approaching.

I look at Mona, pleading with her to help me. They will see us, two women holding a dead man between us, unable to move either forward or back.

Frozen forever on these hidden steps.

I scrabble at the wall, trying to get a grip on it with my finger-nails, to prevent myself from continuing helplessly to the bottom of the steps, to be concealed under the water's surface.

Just as I imagined doing the night of Mother's funeral.

The voices are coming closer.

I stare at Mona, wanting her to speak, to tell me what to do, but she just looks ahead, her mouth set, the way it was when I accused her of taking things from my home. Impassive, impossible to read.

Then there's another sound, the gentle purr of a boat's engine, and the water begins to slop more violently against the steps, splashing up and wetting my clothes and enveloping me in cold waves that fill me with horror at the reality of what we're doing.

We stand for a little longer as the boat passes, lighting up the water around us; the beam reaches into this inlet, but just misses us as we draw back again into the shadows.

The voices from the street fade. The engine starts up again and the car draws away.

The cramp in my leg eases. Now urgency makes me strong. I grasp Max under the arms and pull.

'Mona, you're going to have to get around the other side and help me.'

Max is dressed only in boxer shorts and the towelling robe he always travels with. I have a foolish desire to wrap him up warm in the blanket again before he goes into the water but there isn't time. I gaze at his legs, his naked thighs, and feel a shudder of thwarted desire. I want to give him a last hug, a last kiss. *I still desire you, Max. You are, after all, my lover. I still need you. Still want you. I misjudged you. Your fantasy about my maid was just that. You let it go no further. In fact, when you saw her, the person, you felt only concern for her. But look where this led you!*

It doesn't do to be too kind, too full of compassion. It's a curse. Look what's happened to me.

I heave again and his body gathers momentum, slithering at last into the water.

He's in, and bobbing out of reach. I find a brick lying on the side of the path, and throw it, so it plummets onto his head, knocking him off-kilter so his head is submerged. I have to make it look as if this was a random attack, a mugging maybe. Some burglars must have broken into the place where he was staying, stolen his things, beaten him up, driven him here and deposited him.

I shut myself off to all feeling. I must not weaken. I remind myself that Max as I knew him, his shining eyes, his lovely American smell, is gone. This is just a figure in the water, like one of the stone or bronze statues we have always met beneath, unseeing, unfeeling.

Then I look at Mona. And strangely, as he flops and turns in an eddy, one toe elegantly pointing out of the water, I feel as if this is the biggest job I've asked her to do when it comes to sorting out my life. His sinking will leave everything clearer, cleaner. I loved Max, but he caused me so much pain! Because he would never leave Valerie. Because I could only have him in brief, desperate bursts. Because tearing myself from him afterwards made me wonder if it was worth it at all. And the terror that has accompanied me to these steps all of a sudden vanishes and I rise up on a high, with a feeling of possibility and opportunity opening up before me. Once he's gone and forgotten, I will return to the radio, run a cookery programme and receive adulation again from listeners across the nation.

I basked in Max's admiration for me, it's true, but I will never miss the hollow feeling I'm left with each time he leaves. The abject fear that when he saw the real Theodora underneath the one he had placed on a pedestal, he would abandon me for a better woman.

CHAPTER FIFTY-THREE

It's colder than ever in Charles's flat when I wake. There's an eerie silence. The light that comes through the curtain has an unearthly, silver quality to it.

I reach over and light the gas fire, pull the thin blanket over me, try to create a warm cocoon. I lie listening to Charles grunt and cough in the next room. The events of last night were so bizarre, I struggle to believe they were real. But the ache in my arms tells me yes, we did lift a dead man, shift him to the car.

The dark ends of my tracksuit trousers, lying on the chair, damp from the water, tell me that yes, we did slide him into the river.

I shiver. Hug myself. Why, if he slipped, did Dora not call an ambulance?

It comes back to me, the recurring nightmare of Ali, running in, covered in sweat and tears. How he lay in my arms, shaking, twitching. Related to me bit by little bit what had happened. How he swore me to secrecy. How good I am at remaining silent when I have to.

I promised that of course I would never utter a word of what he told me, that I would do anything for him, to keep him safe.

'He went one step too far,' Ali sobbed. I knew straight away he was talking of Driss, his rival. Ali was working as a guide to finance his medical studies, to support me and Leila. Time and again he would talk of the way Driss would undercut him. How he enjoyed watching Ali grow enraged.

And now, back in a similar situation, I let myself remember the whole story, to confront the full extent of what Ali did. He had taken his group of tourists up to the top of the kasbah, when Driss appeared and accused him of stealing business from him. To Ali's chagrin, the tourists dropped him then and there, said they were going with Driss.

Angered that he was losing his day's earnings, and humiliated by the way the visitors had rejected him, Ali left, then returned to the kasbah in a stolen car. Spotting Driss in his wing mirror, emerging with his posse of tourists from one of the alleys, he reversed towards him. He didn't mean to hurt anyone, Ali told me, just to scare the other guide, to give him a shock. One of the tourists must have stepped out at the last minute. He heard the thump, Ali said. It had been such a violent blow the car shook.

People had come out of their doors, shouting, chasing the car as he accelerated down the street. He could do nothing but drive away, keeping his head down.

He knew the tourist was probably dead. He also knew that no one had seen him. He argued that, in the end, the fault lay not with him but with Driss.

And he begged me to hide him. To keep quiet. 'Or I'll lose my place at medical school!' he wept. And so I kept quiet and have kept quiet ever since. For him.

I wonder now what really happened to Max. If it was an accident, why was Theodora so afraid?

I should have ignored her, called the emergency number again when I slipped into Charles's flat, before we moved Max. Taken the situation into my own hands and done what I knew was right.

I did what she told me to do out of fear.

I am overcome by shame at my own cowardice.

I think of Ali. It was different with him. With Ali, I *wanted* to protect him. I couldn't face life without him.

The thoughts swirl about my head, flashing in and out, on and off until I feel I'll go mad. I knew what we did was wrong, but where would it have left Leila and Ummu if I'd crossed Dora? What extremes would she go to if she knew I was betraying her?

I am not free to weigh up moral pros and cons while I am tied to her.

A ray of sun pokes into the room, making a patch of yellow light dance and flicker on my thin covers. I think of how the morning might have been. Of Max's plea, that I should buy croissants and flowers for Dora and bring them to her in bed. She would have been happy, and a nicer woman to work for.

The way things have gone, she will never know this. Instead of the romantic morning that awaited her, she has lost her lover forever.

I reach in my tracksuit pocket for the money Max gave me to buy breakfast and the extra to send home. It's gone. Not surprising, with the contortions and efforts we had to make to get his body into the water. I imagine it working its way out of my pocket as we held him against the wall. Somehow it is this tiny loss that finally fills me with despair, for when will I ever have enough for Ummu's operation?

All I can do is get up, carry on, pretend – as Dora has forced me to do – that nothing happened, and hope that Dora will continue to pay me.

Max never came here. He never died. We never put him in the river.

I get off the floor and throw on as many layers of clothing as I can find. I even borrow a cardigan from Charles and wrap that around me. The tracksuit bottoms are damp but I have nothing else except a flimsy skirt that gives no warmth.

I pull them on, look about automatically for the overall Dora insists I wear, and realise with shock that it's gone; that it's wrapped around Max's bleeding head in the murky River Thames. I'll have to fetch the spare one from the laundry room upstairs.

I go to the window, pull back the curtains. Look out. Everything is covered in a layer of white, the steps, the small part of the garden I can see from down below. Snow.

The light spills in. I stand, my eyes screwed tight shut against the bright sun dazzling off the white. When I open them again, my breath has formed a white veil against the glass. I rub a circle in it. The birdbath in the garden is caked in a thick tier of snow. The bird with the red breast pecks hopelessly at it. There's a gap at the top of the steps where the statue was.

I go to Charles, find he has wet his bedding again.

'Come on, Charles. Let me make you comfortable.'

He's become more irascible lately, more confused.

I get him up, lead him to the bathroom, wash him and dress him in clean clothes. He's unwell. I'm certain he needs a doctor. I go to his tiny kitchen to make him some breakfast while he sits in his chair, but when I take it to him he turns his mouth away. Refuses to eat.

What will become of me if he dies?

I see my future narrowing, as if I'm descending the flight of stone stairs into the dark river, my freedom swallowed up. I remind myself that Leila's future is growing in direct opposition, broadening, her opportunities becoming clearer and brighter until she has the world at her fingertips. And this is enough to keep me strong.

*   *   *

I clear up Charles's dishes ready to take back to the kitchen, and that's when my eye falls on the little jewelry box Max showed me in the night. It's lying on the floor near the doorway. He must have dropped it when he slipped and fell on the steps.

I pick it up, press the tiny button so its lid flips open and there it is, with its diamond encrusting the little locket and its beautiful gold chain.

I know I should give it to Dora straight away, but something – some sense that this thing with Max has not quite ended, is simmering and will at some point erupt – makes me slip it into my tracksuit pocket. We put a body in the river. The river will return its dead. The crime will revisit us. And then what will I do?

I tug off Charles's sheets and gather up all the soiled laundry. Then I open the door to a blast of cold and move up the steps. The snow makes a strange creaking sound beneath my feet. At the top, I stand for a minute. The garden, the railings, the houses beyond are all beautiful, white, like the houses in the Kasbah des Oudaias, as if coated in a thick layer of icing. Several centimetres of snow lie on the top of every branch, soft like the almond blossoms on the trees that day Ali and I threw husks down on our teacher.

I move round to the front of the house. Even the wheelie bins look pretty with their white layer. The good and the bad all evened out by the snow, all made as one. All the blood and mess from Max's fall, gone.

CHAPTER FIFTY-FOUR

Christmas Eve is a calm day in our street, made more so by the snow that lies on the ground. It is as if nature has taken it into her own hands to cover up any wrongdoing, a soft hand of forgiveness.

I go to my bedroom window and look down upon the silent street. The angels wear thick white halos.

Mona and I seem more harmonious together than we've ever been.

I have Max's things to remember him by. I open the case he left in my room with care. My fingers caress his shirts, his underwear, all such good quality, all smelling of him. I put my nose to them and breathe.

'Mona,' I say, 'I don't want you to talk to anyone outside this house. No one must know Max came here – Leo especially, when he comes home. You may of course talk to Daddy, but that is all. When you go to the shops, you will keep quiet. If you don't do as I say, you'll be in serious trouble. I can call the police any time and tell them what happened to Max and have you removed. But I won't, not if you do everything I tell you.'

Mona looks at me with awe, and I realise she respects me now in the way she always should have done, the way the women respect their employers in Roger's world.

When Christmas Day comes, Mona cooks and we sit and eat together, me and Daddy, and Mona brings us each course, but Daddy soon tires and asks to be taken back to his flat to sleep.

Over the following days I work Mona hard.

She is to sleep every night down with Daddy, on the floor, using the cushions from the sofa if she so wishes. But she must not make herself too comfortable, for then she won't want to get up in the night if he needs her, or for her morning's work. I do not want her in my study any longer. This is to be my space again, where I can relax. I have made too many sacrifices over the last few months, allowing Mona to take over that room and Leo the drawing room. This is my house.

It's right to have Mona downstairs; she must understand that her place is beneath me.

When she complains that she has backache, I lose patience with her. I don't want her going to the doctor's, discussing her ailments.

'Registering for the doctors here takes forever. You may buy painkillers with your wages,' and I scribble down the names of some common ones on a piece of paper. 'You can buy them at the chemist when you go for Daddy's medicine.'

She stands up and makes an ostentatious show of rubbing her back.

'The best thing for your back is to keep moving, keep work-ing,' I say.

And so Mona works silently for me doing as I say without objecting. It's how it's meant to be.

'Dora,' she tries. 'I'm worried Charles is getting very weak. I think we need the doctor.'

If this is a ploy, another desperate attempt on her part to reveal secrets to the outside world, she isn't going to get away with it.

'We don't need the doctor,' I tell her. 'Max told you, didn't he? That Daddy is OK.'

Once or twice I feel a jolt. It's usually when my mobile pings and a text comes in and I wonder for an instant, with a flicker of excitement, whether it is from Max.

Then instead of disappointment I feel a strange kind of relief. I no longer need to go through the agony of separation each time we meet. I no longer need to worry about how short-lived our meetings will be, or whether I will be able to get away in time to meet him. I no longer need to worry that he would rather be with Valerie, or worse, with Mona.

I don't feel lonely either, for I know Mona's there, a silent presence in the basement. When I wake up afraid, haunted by the sight of Max, his head against the doorframe at that odd angle, his face gazing up at me with his empty eyes, I go to the dumbwaiter shaft and call Mona to me. And I ask her to sit with me until I fall asleep.

I'm in the kitchen one evening before New Year, drinking my martini at the table while Mona scrubs the tiles around the sink, when the phone rings. It's Rachel. She tells me they do indeed want me to run a new cookery programme. It is due to go out in late spring.

'We had a major rethink. Cooking's the one thing that's escaping the recession,' she laughs down the phone. 'Everyone's desperate to learn about it, though no one actually does it. The faster cookery books sell out, the more restaurants open up so people can eat out. It's a strange phenomenon but one we're going to cash in on. And you're going to be at the forefront. We all feel you can be relaunched, Dora: you've got the voice, and we can develop the domestic image, do a little bit of chat about your favourite kitchen implements and so on.'

When I put the phone down, I'm overcome by a mixture of relief and remorse.

'Good news?' Mona asks, looking at me.

I can't answer. The conversation has released a barrage of emotion I must have been keeping at bay. Max will never see me in my new role!

And this regret precipitates others, not just grief over Max's death, but the strain of keeping our affair secret from his wife. Most of all, that it has seemed easier to have him out of my life completely, than live with the constant insecurity that I wouldn't see him again.

I wait, as the tears come down.

I don't want Mona to see me crying.

I turn my face from her.

'Go, Mona,' I gasp. 'Go away for a minute.'

She doesn't move.

'I'll get you a tissue,' she says, keeping her face still, unemotional.

'No need.' I'm sobbing now, my chest heaving.

She won't go away.

Then she speaks.

'I understand how you feel.'

'You have no idea how I feel.'

'I do. That you lost your lover. It's a terrible thing.'

I look up at her. Her words belie the rigid expression on her face. What is she really thinking?

'You don't understand, Mona.' I wipe my eyes, take a deep breath. 'It's not just grief over Max, the terrible accident that killed him. It's the strain of all these years of secrecy. Uncertainty. Playing second fiddle to his wife.'

'Second fiddle?'

'Of course! Never being the most important person in his life. However hard I tried.'

Now I've started, I can't stop.

'You've no idea the sorrow I have carried around. That I could never have Max completely. How hard I've worked, to be the person for whom I thought he would leave his wife. How much I yearned that one day, we would live together in one house, sleeping together every night. And now, he'll never know that I'm to present a cookery programme during one of the prime morning slots.'

I want to tell her it's also sorrow that I could never be the person Daddy loved the best, that I've never lived up to the person he or Mummy wanted me to be.

But I stop myself.

'And now he's dead.'

Enormous sobs wrack my body. For quite some time I let emotion take over, give in to the almost luxurious release of tears.

At last I arrive at a kind of empty, silent place, void of all feeling.

'Go now,' I say to her. 'Make the beds, do the laundry. Leave me.'

Instead, she speaks.

'You are wrong about Max,' she says. Her words come out quietly. I'm not sure I want to hear what she's going to tell me. Did Max try, after all, to seduce her, that night down in the basement? Did he confide in her about his other lovers, in other cities, scattered across the globe? Did she steal Max's affection from me as well as Daddy's, and my son's? She's going to tell me that I am nothing.

But she goes on before I can stop her.

'Max asked me to bring you a special breakfast in bed. He said he wanted to come and live with you, if you would let him. He

351

loved you very much. He was leaving his wife for you. It is so very sad that then he had this terrible accident.'

Before I know it, I've lifted my hand – and the slap I'd wanted to give her the day Max came back resounds loudly on her face.

CHAPTER FIFTY-FIVE

The snow lies on the ground for three or four days, then one morning I awake and it's gone, leaving the garden exposed, all the ugly bits returned. The grotesque wheelie bins, the stone bust with its nose broken off now, the black twigs and branches overhead.

My face smarts after the slap Dora gave me last night. I look in the mirror. It's left a red mark across my cheekbone.

I don't want to see her this morning, so I spend longer than usual giving Charles his breakfast and wait until I hear the front door slam to go upstairs to an empty house.

I hear the postman arrive, and a letter drops on the doormat with a Moroccan stamp on it.

I recognise Hait's writing.

Dear Mona,

I'm dictating this to Hait as it's hard to speak on the phone when Leila's little ears are flapping. We nearly have enough for the operation now. It's not looking good. The doctors say there's a chance it will be effective, but only a chance. I haven't told Leila, but I have had to convince her that the treats have to stop. The cost of this treatment is phenomenal! And she's been very grown up about it.

She does ask for you. But I explain that you have to work in England so I can get better and so she can one day have a good education, earn money so she will not have to go away from her own children to work. She accepts this.

And remember, after five years, you may apply for citizenship. It seems a long time, but it will go quickly now you have a good placement with Theodora. Leila sends a drawing she has done with some new pens I have been able to buy for her. Don't worry that all the animals she draws have sad faces – she's going through a phase where she always draws down-turned mouths!

Ring me soon.

I send you love and blessings, my dear daughter.

Ummu xx

I put her letter down. Fold it in half.

I then go through to the study, the room that used to be my bedroom, and look out of the window.

The bust of the woman's head is back at the top of the steps. The one that killed Max. For a while, I sit down and stare at a small bird with a red breast that has landed on top of it.

Endymion, the cat, sits beneath, batting at it with its paw. I watch, astonished, as the bird continues to sit, oblivious to its predator. Endymion squats, ready to pounce, and as he leaps, the bird flies off into the winter sky.

I think how, if Leila were drawing the cat and the bird, they would both have down-turned mouths, the predator and its prey as sad as each other.

When I've finished cleaning I go back to Charles.

He is a little better, insisting he needs to go out, to buy fruit, buy his paper.

I have to wait until it's growing dark. Dora's instructed me not to speak to anyone. This was unnecessary. I never do speak to anyone, except Sayed, and I haven't been back to his shop since I failed to turn up to the meeting he arranged, too ashamed to admit my papers had gone, that I had no money.

I wear my blue anorak, hood up over my headscarf, pulling the collar of my fleece up as far as I can so it conceals my face. And I keep my head down, as I wheel Charles to the High Street. The street is a little subdued now the Christmas festival is over, its usual noise and movement reduced, though the stalls are still open and women gather to fill their bags with produce.

I pay for Charles's clementines without making eye-contact with the stallholder. I buy him a paper. Sayed isn't in his shop today; it's someone I haven't seen before who doesn't speak, just gives me my change without looking.

The snow is now a grey slush along the pavements; the air is raw and cold.

We pass people I know so well by sight, but with whom I've never exchanged a word. The guy in the luminous jacket who sweeps the road, the skinny girl with the old woman's face selling magazines, the group of youths in hoods huddled around the money-exchange kiosk. We pass the chef who often stands outside a door left open to ease the heat of a steamy kitchen beneath street-level.

I see them, but they don't see me. We're of no interest, an old man in a wheelchair, and his carer in a fleece, tracksuit bottoms and a blue overall, an anorak over the top, walking slowly, her face turned to the ground.

I don't know what makes me return to the river today. It's so cold out there. In the market, the lights and smells and music thumping from doorways give the impression, at least, of warmth. I push Charles through the back streets to the path, to the steps down to the water.

Here, the sound drops; it's silent but for the slosh of water against the wall and the occasional drone of an aircraft overhead. I don't look into the depths. I'm afraid of what might stare back up at me. Yet, at the same time I want to see, I want to know. I imagine it, and shudder. Max's long surgeon's fingers reaching out, reaching for me. But there's nothing, just dark water lapping at the bottom of the steps. Ten steps are exposed, along with a layer of rubbish – beer cans and cigarette packets, burger containers and plastic bags, all swirling in a brown scum on the surface of the Thames.

I stare across at the posts stained green and the landing stages with the signs that I know say *Danger Keep Off!* and I think how it is good that the river is dangerous, the structures precarious. Because then if someone does find Max's body and Dora does tell the police that I am responsible – I will come here and walk slowly down these steps, into the river, and disappear completely and forever. Better this, than that Ummu and Leila believe I have killed a man and am in prison. I will end my life in the same country as Ali, but beneath the water, and somewhere, some day, our souls will meet and mingle. And this gives me a kind of bleak comfort.

It's dark now. My shoes have soaked up puddlewater. I don't care, but Charles, whose hands look blue with cold where they clutch the paper bag of clementines on his lap, must get home before the January night sets in.

Every day now it's the same. After our walk I take him back, prepare his meal, fetch his pyjamas, warm them for him in front of the gas fire. I keep going. It's OK. It's not hard to work silently. To keep quiet for Leila and Ummu. Ummu will have her operation. Leila will go to school.

Every day we turn the corner at the pub, as we're doing now, and I push the wheelchair down the street under the shadow of the dark church. Past the angels and figureheads with their eyes shut tight. I reach the house and take the side entrance to the back garden. Help Charles out of his chair and down the steps to the basement, disappearing into London's bowels, its underground.

Back inside, I assist Charles into his reclining armchair with its foot-rest. It's more of a struggle than it was, getting him in and settled. He no longer seems to remember how to make himself comfortable and I have to do this for him, adjusting his feet, placing his hands on the arms of the chair. He demands his dinner and I take it to him on a tray; I sit and spoon it into his mouth, and wipe his mouth and offer him sips of water.

And when he's finished his supper I peel a clementine for him. I feed him the pieces of orange, and the juice runs down his chin, and I dab it away.

I spoon Charles's medicine into his loose pink mouth, and help him into clean night things. Pour him his two fingers of whisky. I kiss him on his papery old cheek. He moans, says he needs the toilet. I lift him, let him hang on to me as he totters into his little bathroom. Hold his penis while he wees before I wash him and lead him back to his bed. Then I take the peel into the kitchen and drop it into the over-flowing pedal-bin. I take the liner and knot it. I put it ready to take out. I replace it with a new one. I wash his dishes and tidy up.

Above, in the main house, comes the thud of someone pounding down the stairs, the rumble of a chair scraped across the floor. I feel the sound in my skin; it twitches and my ears ring. My palms begin to sweat. I long for the day to end, for the moment I can lie down in the corner of this room on the makeshift bed with its one flat pillow, because I'm so terribly weary, and oblivion more than anything is what I yearn for now.

But that sound, the scraping of the chair in the kitchen above me, means only one thing: it is time for me to start on the next shift.

Dora's voice echoing down the shaft into Charles's sitting room.

'MONA!'

'Yes.'

'It's seven o'clock. I'm hungry.'

'Charles is going to bed now. Then I'll come.'

'You're late.'

And the old man demanding my attention at the same time. 'You've hidden it again! Blast and damn you, woman, you've taken my whisky.'

And the shout from upstairs – 'Now!' – and Charles grumbling, and my head beginning to pound.

As I hand him his whisky, he picks up his paper and we spot it together. There, in the bottom corner of the front cover, staring out, is a picture of Doctor Max.

And Charles speaks.

'That's the doctor who examined me – American chap. I saw it happen through my bedroom window. Dora pushed the statue of Maudy at him, and he fell down the steps.'

CHAPTER FIFTY-SIX

Max wanted to come back and live with me. He loved me, he wanted to leave Valerie for me.

And now he's dead!

I spend the whole of the night rearranging history in my head. Placing things where they are meant to be.

It is a relief to go to work, to focus on something outside my house, to throw myself into creating the new show they have chosen me to present, 'A World of Flavour'.

And now, as I arrive home, almost falling over his enormous trainers lying haphazardly on the floor, my heart lifts to realise that Leo must be home. His return, I believe wildly for a moment, will erase everything that has happened since he left. Things will go back to normal. Max never happened. I drop my bag in the hall and rush through to the kitchen, where I fling my arms around my son. I stand back to look at him.

He's tanned, thinner, healthier-looking than I've ever seen him. And he's smiling.

'You look so well!' I exclaim.

'I bought you Argan Oil, Mum. Claudia says it's the next big thing for hair.'

'Thanks, Leo.'

I feel like crying. It's seeing someone I love again. It's realising how much this means to me. It's knowing he must never, ever, learn the truth about the terrible things I have done.

'I've got some figs for Grandpa, too, and some new slippers for Mona – *babouches*, the kind she likes but says she could never afford. Where is she?'

'She's with Grandpa.' I'm wondering, though I'm trying not to, whether slippers are a more generous present than Argan Oil, and why Leo feels my hair needs help while he doesn't feel Mona's does. But I'm not going to let these thoughts take over. I'm going to relish Leo's return.

He left a hole in my life I couldn't see until now it's been filled again. If he hadn't gone away, things might have been so different.

'I've made loads of New Year's resolutions,' he says, going over to the kettle. 'Do you want a cup of tea, Mum? I've got so much to tell you. But it's my first shift at the bar tonight.'

I sit opposite him at the table. This is what I've needed, time with my son. Time in which I believe he actually wants to be with me, rather than in front of a screen or with Mona.

'And I think, Mum, once I'm earning a decent wage, I'll move in with Barnie and George.'

'Good,' I hear myself say. 'That's great, Leo.'

But I want to tell him not to, to stay with me, that I'll pay for whatever he wants, that he doesn't need a job.

You spend half your life resenting your dependants for sucking dry your time and energy, then, when they inch away, you want nothing more than to gather them back to you, beg them to need you again.

Later, when he's finished telling me about his travels, he says he's going off to the bar.

It's OK, I tell myself. Leo can leave, he can live his life. I do, after all, have the thrill of a new career in front of me again, and Mona to meet my every need.

I go to the dumbwaiter now, and shout down for her.

When she comes up, she hands me a pile of catalogues offering summer bulbs, and those lovely Toast clothes I've decided I'll wear all the time from now on. I give her back the envelopes for the recycling.

'Have you done the rooms today?' I ask.

'All done,' she says. 'The bed's ready for your massage. I was going to make a tagine.'

'Good. The recording of my new show starts next week – and you're to help me with the recipes. You'll need to explain the techniques you use for spicing dishes. You must tell me about the ingredients my listeners may never have heard of before, to give them the feeling they're discovering something unique. I'll need two recipes for each programme. It's going out once a week to start with and I'll need six weeks' worth, so that's twelve recipes. I want you to tell me how you make your clafoutis, your *harira*, your meatballs, and those lovely almond pastries you made with Leo.'

I sit in the kitchen Mona has made pristine and watch her, the way she chops the vegetables as if she were a trained chef, with those hands that gesticulate and wave and work so hard. Mona nods her head each time I ask her to do anything. She doesn't look at me. She keeps her eyes down.

A vision comes into my head, of Boudicca, of the night Max and I met beneath her and the way he gazed up at her – her strong legs, her valiant expression.

I feel that I have conquered everything – everyone. No one can humiliate me again. I am indeed a Boudicca figure, strong, powerful, in command.

And I thank Roger silently for bringing me Mona.

'Mona,' I say. 'Full body massage today.'

This is something new I've discovered about her, her skill when it comes to massage.

'Where did you learn such good techniques?' I ask her, my voice muffled as she kneads my back, erasing all the tension, all the anxiety and fret, and yes, the sour taste left in my mouth by recent events. 'It is really extraordinary, the way you are able to reach deep into my muscles with your fingers. Your hands were one of the first things I noticed about you. They are so expressive, so strong.'

She has lit candles as I instructed her to do, and some more of the incense she placed around my room the night I brought Max home. I tell her to put Nina Simone on the CD player and I lie down on the massage table and let all my troubles float away. I've dealt with each problem as it's come. The fear that I would be made redundant. The fear of rejection. The fear of fading the way I've seen other women fade when their lives become dominated by the needs of others and they are shunted off to the sidings.

It is safe to relax, to let go. I've taken control and it's paying off. I don't let myself think about Max in the river. He's gone. It's as if he's just returned to America again, is going through one of his silences.

I remind myself, however, that he loved me. And this soothes away some of the pain.

Mona's fingers find a particularly tight knot in my neck and ease it out.

She bends a little closer. 'I saw it,' she whispers.

'What?'

'In Charles's paper.'

I can't turn my head as her hands are on my neck, my face pressed into the mattress of the divan.

'A picture of Doctor Max. And the steps – the steps where we took him. Oh Dora,' she says right into my ear, 'they've found his body.'

CHAPTER FIFTY-SEVEN

I rear up, shoving Mona's hands off me.

'Bring me the paper!' My hands shake as I snatch the pages from her. 'Where? I can't see it. You must have made a mistake!'

Mona points at the page, where I spot the item, my heart leaping into my throat.

It's a tiny report in the bottom corner, as if this death was really very insignificant.

> *A man's body has been found washed up at the Upper Watergate steps at Deptford. Police believe it might be the body of a New York doctor who disappeared a week ago whilst on a stop-over trip to London. The death is being treated as suspicious. Police are carrying out enquiries in the local area. At the moment questions are centring around items found on the man's person, including a blue overall of the kind worn by domestic staff.*

'It was wrong to put him in the river,' Mona says.

'No, Mona. We did the right thing. We didn't hurt him – we just got rid of his body after his accident. It was to protect his family, his wife, his kids. They don't need to know he was seeing me. We must keep quiet. Say nothing, do you understand? Nobody knows that Max came here except for you and me. The police won't find us. Oh, it says here, they found a baby monitor on him – the alarm thing we had for Daddy. What on earth was he doing with that?'

'I gave it to him,' she says. 'He said he would bring it up to your room.'

'Your fingerprints will be on it,' I say, 'unless the water has washed them off. That, in addition to your overalls, will implicate you, I'm afraid.' I smile. I don't want to frighten her, but it's important she understands that if she speaks, she will be the prime suspect.

She takes a step back, like Endymion when he feels cornered. Her eyes widen.

'Don't be afraid,' I say. 'You just have to keep doing exactly as I say. And then you will be all right.'

Does she realise how important it is not to speak about this?

'Do you see, Mona, if the police find out that Max died here, in my house, I will have to tell them it must have had something to do with you. I found Max at the bottom of the steps. He fell. But perhaps you pushed him?'

'But why don't you say he fell. It's better always to tell the truth.'

I think this is rather rich, coming from someone who has openly thieved.

'I told you, Mona.' My voice is hard, I can hear it myself, but I feel she's being a little slow and I'm growing impatient. 'They don't need to know he came here at all. He has a wife in America. She doesn't know about me! She need never know. If you speak . . .' I make a slashing motion across my throat and Mona blinks.

Good God, there are a thousand reasons why it's better not to tell 'the truth'!

If the police discover this man died in my house, that we hid his body, what will become of my new radio programme?

'You mention this to a single person, I'll tell the police that *you* must have killed Max. Accidentally maybe. Or even deliberately. I'll tell them you flirted with Max, the way you did with Monsieur Sherif—'

'I didn't.'

'I'll tell them you must have wanted money from him: you wanted him to help you. That you'd already told lies to get work, said you were a widow. After all, you'd even saved his number on your phone!'

I stare triumphantly at her.

'Then you grew afraid of him, and you pushed him and he fell and cracked his head, and you wrapped it in your overall to stem the blood flow.'

She gives me her blank look, the one that's impossible to read.

'I wonder who they will believe,' I go on. 'Theodora Gentleman, The Voice of South-East England, or a domestic worker, desperate for money, for a passport. For British citizenship.'

She remains speechless.

'Another thing. CCTV. When we drove him to the river, I made sure I wouldn't be seen, do you remember? I kept my head down. But you were driving, Mona. I imagine there is plenty of evidence if I choose to use it against you, so I hope you won't make me have to. The point is, Mona, Max is dead, but we had nothing to do with it There are no other witnesses.'

Still not a flicker of emotion crosses her face.

'There *is* another witness.' She speaks at last.

I look up. I want her to continue with the massage – I've had enough of this.

'There is Charles,' she goes on. 'Your daddy. He saw you push the statue. He saw Max fall.'

CHAPTER FIFTY-EIGHT

I leave Dora on the massage table.

I can hear her shouting after me, 'It's all your fault! If you'd never come, this would never have happened!'

My heart's racing, I don't know what Dora is capable of doing now I've revealed what I know.

I hurry up to Leo's room. He's out.

I need to check my Facebook page for messages. See if there's any news. It's many days since I last checked.

Charles's words as I left his flat earlier this evening come back to me.

That's the doctor who examined me – American chap. I saw it happen through my bedroom window. Dora pushed the statue of Maudy at him, and he fell down the steps.

Images flood into my head. Dora forcing me to work on my hands and knees; the day she kicked me. Amina's message, that Dora hurt Zidana. That she disappeared, never to be seen again.

What if Dora killed Zidana! Like she killed her lover.

I go cold then as the full realisation hits me.

The moment she turned and saw me at the top of the steps,

she stared as if she thought she'd seen a djinn. She'd thought *I* had been in the flat with Charles.

She thought Max was me!

Dora pushed the statue over because she thought Max was me!

She tried to kill me.

I feel all the strength drain from me. I whisk round, terrified suddenly that Dora has come up, that her intention is to finish me off after all. I must tell someone. The police? But the police have found a dead body in the river. I helped to deposit it there. The baby monitor and my overalls are clues that will prove, if Dora wishes to claim it, that I was involved.

I'm clicking on the screen as these thoughts tumble through my head.

Who will believe my word against Dora's? Who will believe the words of an old man with senile dementia?

Yet if I run, I have no passport, no documents. I'm here as Dora's domestic, tied to her, and she knows it.

One message.

From Sayed. It's in Arabic.

We have news! An address for Ali in London. It's a residential address, not a holding centre, and it's not far from here. This is nothing to do with that crook Hamid. I found it for you. Come to the shop and I'll give you directions. I won't charge you much!

My heart is a heavy drumbeat against my chest. The date on the message shows it's been here for two days! Two days when I could have gone to him, got away! But there's no point in thinking of what might have been.

I look about me. I have nothing. I've sent the last of my money to Ummu, saving just twenty pounds for the week, which is in my bag in Charles's flat.

I remember I still have the locket that Max was going to give to Dora; it's in my pocket, my only safe hiding-place. I may not have documents, but with money, with enough money, you can get most things.

Perhaps I should forget my bag. Just walk down the stairs now, go straight to Sayed's shop. Hand him the locket, demand to have Ali's address – even ask him to take me there.

Yes, that's what I must do.

I start down the stairs.

As I reach the landing outside Leo's room – what Dora fondly calls the *piano nobile* – I stop. Dora's downstairs. I daren't face her again. The door – the front door onto the world – is not an option for me anymore. I'm not free to walk through it without her permission while Dora is there.

CHAPTER FIFTY-NINE

Mona's words play through my head. Daddy's too unreliable, surely, to be used as any kind of witness? But I can't tolerate the smug way Mona thinks she's won something over me.

I'm startled out of my reverie by a thump on the floor. Daddy's banging with the broom handle on his ceiling, and I can hear his voice floating up through the dumbwaiter shaft.

'Mona! Come on, Mona! I want you.'

I go to the foot of the stairs and shout up, 'Mona, it's time to go back down to Daddy! You can finish the rooms later when you've done the dishes.'

As long as I have Mona, if this thing erupts, I have the perfect story. That my maid, in her desperation to get a better life, made a pass at my rich American lover. She's done it before at Madame's. And, when my lover refused her, in her panic that he would tell, she killed him then drove his body to the river . . . The baby monitor may still have her fingerprints on it. The overall will have her DNA on it – after all, she had been wearing it all day. Yes, that version of events sounds credible.

Then other thoughts start up.

That Max did love me, after all, that he was preparing to come and live with me. I stand up, run my hands through my hair, go to the mirror and look at myself. Put my hand on my necklace, telling the world who I am. It's all right. I am Theodora Gentleman. No one will ever suspect me.

It's several minutes before I realise Daddy is banging on the ceiling again.

I go to the bottom of the stairs again, shout up. Still no response. I grow impatient.

I take the stairs, calling Mona to me. She doesn't respond.

I feel that tingle suddenly, the one I felt when I realised she was using my bathroom without my permission.

Is she snooping about my room? Silently rifling through my documents? Is she looking for her passport, planning to run away again? The tingle intensifies. Is she about to side-step me again, just when I need her most, for my programme and, if the worst comes to the worst, for the police if they come?

Panic mounts as I reach the top of the first flight.

I check Leo's room. His computer's on, its screensaver dancing across the screen, but nothing else moves.

I climb the next flight. She is, perhaps, in the bathroom preparing it for me the way I like. Candles, incense.

No one there.

Up the third flight, blood banging in my ears now.

At last I push open my bedroom door.

It's empty.

CHAPTER SIXTY

I take the pole, the one Leo used the day we got the decorations down. Unhook the trapdoor. Thankfully, from all the physical labour I do every day, my arms are strong. The ladder slides down easily.

Dora will lie to save her reputation. I've seen her do it, she is capable of saying and doing anything to save herself. She *will* weave a story and the police *will* come after me.

Then I'll never see Leila or Ummu or Ali again.

I climb up the steps and into the warm quiet dark of the attic.

It's more complicated shutting the attic door than it is opening it. And Dora's calling, 'Mona, Mona, I need you. Come now!'

I pull at the ladder, but it's heavy, and awkward to move it from this angle. If she finds me up here, I daren't imagine what she'll do to me.

At last I manage to drag the weight of the ladder up, until it clanks down onto the floor and the trapdoor bangs shut, enclosing me in darkness. I sit and wait for my eyes to adjust to the lack of light.

I feel for a moment as if the darkness is soft, a protective layer that holds me safe for a while, and I breathe deeply.

Then there's the thump of footsteps on the stairs, and I know I must keep moving.

'Mona. Mona – come at once!'

I move across the rough wood beams on the floor, groping, splintering my hands and grazing my shin. At last I reach the far wall where I can feel the tiny doorway into the next-door attic, the one Leo showed me the day we found the Christmas decorations.

I push it. It seemed to open with ease for Leo, but for me it won't budge.

I feel in my pocket. Check I still have it. Max's gift to Theodora tucked up against me. I was going to give it to her, but it's too late now. It's all I have.

Then I hear more footsteps – Dora making her way upstairs. How long before she works out where I've gone?

I push at the little door again but still it won't open.

I take a deep breath. Lean back, press my feet against it and give an almighty push.

The next bit is easy.

There is no partition between Desiree's attic and the one belonging to the children who play with stones out on the street, and the next door swings back.

I must now have entered the large house with the women's heads on the porticoes. This is the biggest attic so far, with a window in the roof looking out onto the sky.

Moonlight spills in and falls upon broken piano keys, an old round table turned on its side, a rocking horse and a doll's house. The toys make me think of Leila and my head begins to spin at the danger I'm in. How if I mess this up, I'll lose her forever.

There doesn't seem to be a door in the next wall. I feel for a crack, a gap in the panelling. Nothing. My heart begins to race. Am I going to have to give up, after all?

I can see the trapdoor down to the house below, go over to it, put my ear to the floor. There's music playing, the faint murmur of voices. Then another sound startles me – the harsh whoop of a police siren. Has Dora decided to tell them? Have they come for me already?

I go back to the wall, press my hands on it, and eventually find one panel that is more loosely fitted than the others. With a few shakes I manage to get it out and I crawl through into a space as dark and stifling as the previous one was light and airy. I replace the loose panel. Feel again for the locket, my passport to freedom if there is to be one.

I think how for the months I've lived here, I have been invisible to people outside. But now there's a body, a crime, it won't be long until everyone is interested. I hug myself. Now they are looking, now they care, it's too late. If things go to plan, by the time they come I will have melted away completely.

CHAPTER SIXTY-ONE

I check my study, the wash room. Mona's not there. Daddy's thumping now and shouting. He's not going to give up until someone goes.

'Mona!' I run up the stairs again.

I can't cope with Daddy without her.

Daddy thumps hard again. There's no choice, I'll have to go down and quieten him.

I go out into the cold night and round the back.

I shudder as I pass Mummy's head, feel her watching me as I descend the steps.

Daddy's in his sitting room in his pyjamas. The broom in one hand, banging on the ceiling.

'It's OK, Daddy, you can stop that now. I'm here.'

'I want Mona.'

'Daddy, you're going to have to come up to the house. I can't stay down here with you and I'm not sure where Mona is.'

I fetch a dressing-gown for him, and his slippers, and help him put them on.

He hangs onto my arm and slowly we make our way up the steps. He stops after a few steps.

'I need my handkerchief.' He starts to turn. He wants to go back to the flat to fetch it. If it takes him as long to go back as it's taken to get here, we'll be here all night.

'I've got tissues in the house, Daddy. Keep moving.'

'I need the handkerchief. I'm not using paper things. I'll have the embroidered one Maudy did for me.'

'Then you'll have to let me get it. It'll take you forever.'

I leave him hanging onto the railing on the steps. It takes me ages to find the hankie he wants.

When I get back to him, he takes it, starts to slowly wipe his nose. He's shaking from the icy-cold night air. I grow impatient, want to shout at him, 'Move faster, Daddy, I haven't got all day!' I want to pick him up and carry him if it means we'll get there quicker. Instead we have to move laboriously, stopping every other step for him to gather his wits or regain his balance. I had no idea what hard work it was, these days, taking Daddy out. Imagine if I had tried to get him to concerts and the things Anita and Simon are constantly advising but failing to help with themselves.

It takes forever to struggle with him round to the front, along the pavement, up the steps.

At last I manage to get him into the house and install him in the drawing room in front of the TV.

I realise with repulsion that he's wet himself. His pyjama bottoms are sodden. I need Mona! Do I dry him first? Bathe him? Pull off his soiled trousers, or find him some dry ones before I do anything? I run back down to his flat, fetch a towel and some thermal underwear. By the time I've sorted him out, I feel exhausted.

I look at him half-asleep, oblivious to the world and everything that's happening to me.

Daddy then opens his eyes and demands to see Mona.

'I'm trying to find her, Daddy! I'm doing all I can.'

At last Leo comes in. 'Mum, I think Grandpa's really unwell. I reckon he needs a doctor. His colour, it's not good. He looks jaundiced.'

I'm wondering where Leo has heard the word *jaundiced* before. He's never revealed any medical expertise in the past. He's right though. Daddy's skin is an odd dark yellow colour and he's barely able to open his eyes; his breath coming in short gasps.

How can he do this to me now? With the picture in the newspaper taunting me. Now that they've found Max's body! And with Mona goodness knows where.

'You'll have to shift off the sofa,' I say to Leo. 'Help me make up a bed for Daddy. He isn't well enough to move again.'

Together we fetch pillows, a duvet, a hot-water bottle and his medication and try to make Daddy comfortable.

'Where is Mona?' Leo asks. 'Has she gone?'

I look up sharply.

'What do you mean? Why would she be gone?'

He shrugs. 'She just seemed a bit edgy, a bit homesick, since I brought her the *babouches*.'

'She can't be gone,' I say without thinking. 'I've got her passport and documents in my bag. She wouldn't dare leave without them.'

Leo stares at me.

'You what? You took her passport?'

'It's normal,' I say. 'Anyway, there's no time to discuss Mona now. We need to sort out your grandfather.'

'Look, Mum,' says Leo with uncharacteristic grace, 'Grandpa needs you. I'll look for Mona. You stay in the drawing room with him in case he gets worse.'

'Where will you look?'

'She must have gone to the High Street. I must have missed her. Perhaps she got chatting with someone. Something must have delayed her.'

379

I say nothing, but am quietly appreciative as he goes upstairs for his hoodie and some duty-free cigarettes, and then yells, 'See you later!' as he slams out of the front door.

He's doing something to help, at last.

CHAPTER SIXTY-TWO

I don't know which attic is the last. They seem to be eternal, one opening after another. I see these attics as representations of my life, how each stage has felt dark, then revealed a way out to me, led me into a new space, from which I've then had to escape. How I have to keep on moving: one more and I'll be a step closer to Ali.

The one I find myself in now is cramped and dark and smells of rotting things. The trapdoor in the ceiling hangs half-open; the ladder down.

I crawl across to it. Lights are on in the house below. I put my ear to the opening.

I can hear voices.

Relief washes over me.

Sayed, Johnny.

Hearing the voices of people who have tried to help me, even if it was at a cost, is such a relief I almost weep.

I climb down the rickety ladder into the house. The carpets here are damp. There's a fetid stench of stale smoke, and mould. There doesn't seem to be anybody about, but I slip quietly down the stairs, the pulse in my throat banging.

I'm in a narrow hallway, mirroring Dora's own, but even less well-kept than hers was when I arrived. It's badly painted and the carpet underfoot is in shreds, scattered with debris – as if it's never been cleaned. Along the passage, through a chink in the doorway, I see Sayed, sitting at a kitchen table rolling a cigarette or a joint.

He looks up, alarmed, as I walk in.

'Sayed, I need your help.'

'You! How did you get in here?'

'Through the attics.'

The two men laugh, looking at each other in surprise.

'Why didn't you come down the street like a normal person?'

'It's not funny. I had to get away – I am in danger. I had to leave the house without being seen. I don't know how long I've got.'

'We've been waiting for you to come to the shop, haven't we, Johnny? You never met Hamid, but it's probably for the best. He was into something dodgy.'

'You said you had an address, for Ali?'

'Yes. We've got an address. But you never came by, so we couldn't tell you. We know where he's living, but there's a bit of a problem.'

'Tell me!' They glance at each other. 'If it's money, if that's what you need to give me the information, look, you can have this.' I hold out the locket reluctantly – once I've let it go, I have nothing left but hope.

They exchange another glance. Johnny takes the locket. Examines it.

'Oh Jesus!' he says. 'This is worth mad skrilla, man.'

'Can you get me to his address – please – without anyone seeing?'

'Calm down. Yes, we've got the address, but . . .'

'You can have the locket, Sayed, but only if you take me to him.'

I feel a surge of excitement tighten my stomach muscles. Once I've found Ali, I won't need documents or passports. I am his wife.

I can take his name, share his documents.

My goal is within reach. I close my eyes and pray.

Sayed drives his scooter through the night like a djinn.

I cling to him, my head clamped against the leather of his jacket. We zip between cars and buses. We dip beneath railway bridges and zoom over tube tracks. We veer left and right, tipping this way and that so at times I feel we're going to turn right over and I'll fly across the road under the great tyres of a truck. But I'm not afraid, I'm not afraid of anything, because I'm about to see Ali.

Sooner than I imagined, Sayed pulls up in front of the gateway to an estate of flats. He looks round at me, speaks through his helmet.

'Paradise Street. You sure you want to go alone?'

I nod, climb off. 'You go, Sayed, but thank you. *Barak Allah feek*. May God bless you.'

He shrugs, revs his engine. And then he's off, and I'm alone. I wonder how I look. I must be dishevelled, windswept, and my clothes are the ones I work in – tracksuit bottoms, a fleece, old trainers. The hideous spare overall.

But Ali has seen me looking exhausted after Leila's birth, he's seen me with my hands in dishwater, he knew me as a child, he loves me for who I am. I do not need to paint myself for him.

I walk through the gate.

The estate is a square of reddish-brick blocks around a central yard. Here, behind wire-mesh fences, teenagers rollerblade under spotlights, over black tarmac and up steel ramps covered in graffiti. A group of little kids squat in a group on the only scrubby patch of green outside, staring at a mini-beast of some sort, a worm or a snail. Unused to wildlife, amazed by the movement of such a tiny thing, they are poking it with sticks, seeing if they can make it move, make something come out of it, or make it go back inside.

There are several entrances with the flat numbers displayed. I find numbers 150-250 and climb the concrete stairwell. It smells of stale urine and things cooking. Number 204 is on the second floor, along a shadowy walkway past front doors. Each door is different. Some have windchimes or fancy door numbers screwed on. Others are unadorned, tatty, the paint peeling. Tricycles lie on their sides, next to airers for washing, empty bottles and piles of newspapers. Muted voices float out from the open windows: a child crying, a man shouting, a radio blaring out an Adele song. More cooking smells – spices, curries, chips. Down below, the whoop of a car alarm, the screech of a siren. And further off, other sounds of the city – the rumble of traffic up on the main road, the rattle of trains, the drone of aeroplanes.

I remember my first sighting of this city, how massive it looked from above, how vast as we drove through it when I arrived. I've only occupied a tiny section of it. Beyond, lie endless hubs and centres and seething crowds, the palaces and shops and parks and monuments I imagined, and have told Leila about, hoping to show her one day, but in all my time here have never yet seen.

I look over the balcony. From here, all I can see are endless buildings and cranes lit up, their necks like stalks stretched out to peer at the bright London sky. The dark ribbon of river, with its spears of light piercing its depths.

No one passes. No one sees me.

My heart batters against my chest. I'm so near to him.

Soon, when we're together again, who knows, I might phone Ummu and Leila and get them to come straight over. I'm not sure what the visa rules are for dependants, but if we show we're a family, that Ali has been working here for months now, earning good money, paying taxes, then the authorities must allow us to be together. Ali will know what to do. Ali will sort it out. Ali with his good English and his cleverness, his doctor's charm. And even, perhaps, when he is fully qualified and able to get work, we will go home, back to the little white house on the estuary, live as a family where we belong and want to be.

Whatever the outcome, all that matters is that I have found him!

I will not have to subordinate myself to another woman ever again. I will be in my own home, with my own family, my own work. I feel, in anticipation, the sweetness of relief, not to be holding it all together alone any more.

Number 204 is nicely painted, unlike some of the others. It is blue, the colour of the better-kept doorways back home in the medina. Ali was always tidy, always paid attention to detail. The flat has a familiar air about it; maybe it's the box of flowers on the windowsill, holding light within them so the colours sing out even in the dark, as if a tiny piece of Morocco had found its way into this hidden fold of London. A gold-framed arch-shaped mirror swings on the doorway. Another echo of Morocco.

Ali has been dreaming of home.

I feel warm, as if I, too, am close to home. Ali has kept his links with Morocco alive because I am part of them, a piece of home.

I imagine his face when he sees I'm here, that I have come for him, found him, when he must have felt it impossible for us to be together after his time in detention, his struggle to get a visa.

Now that I too have been treated like an underdog, I understand why he lashed out at Driss.

I understand his longing to escape to a better life where he believed he'd be respected. For him it meant coming to a country where he could be the person he always planned to be – a doctor, helping others. Where his crime would not be known.

I raise my hand to ring the doorbell, a proper electric doorbell. There's a light on inside, but it's dim, the kind Dora leaves on at night or when she goes out to tell burglars we are at home. If he's not in, I'll sit on the step here and wait.

Funny how, having waited to hear from him for so long, these few minutes feel like an eternity.

I can hardly tolerate the silence as I ring the doorbell again, wait some more.

Please come, I whisper to myself. *Please find me before Dora works out where I've gone. Comes for me, or sends the police after me.*

At last a shadow falls across the misted pane in the door, and there's the rattle of a lock. The door swings open.

'Hello?'

I jerk my head up.

There's no one there.

CHAPTER SIXTY-THREE

I don't know how many hours go by as I sit and wait for Leo to come back with Mona. Daddy's breath is coming in shallow gasps. He's staring up at me, frowning slightly. I'm afraid that he's going to die. I don't want to leave him. Eventually, overcome by fatigue, I take some cushions from the chairs around the room and make myself a bed on the floor next to him. I can't get comfortable. Each time I relax, I become aware of a draught, or the itchy fabric against my skin, or the discomfort of the uneven surface beneath me.

After a while, however, I must have fallen asleep for I awake later in a terrible sweat, my clothes soaked. I'm shaking. A vision of Max has come to me in my sleep and remains before my eyes, his face with its mouth open, his sightless eyes gazing up at me.

An incessant wind has been blowing all evening, a crane's claw knocking against its side, like the toll of a bell. I don't want to be alone with Daddy, his frail breath, his waxen face. I wish Mona was with me. I need her here to soothe Daddy, to lie with him so I can go to my bed, get a decent night's sleep.

How long before Leo finds her? Filled with a sense of

foreboding, I look at the time on my mobile. If she'd gone to the shop, they would have been back hours ago.

The newspaper article, the picture of Max in the corner, has brought it all back to me, slamming into me like a wall of cold river water. Another newspaper report swims before my eyes, one I've tried to forget. *Zidana, a young maid, eighteen, takes her own life after falling down stairs and losing her baby.* I didn't intend it. I didn't mean to hurt anyone. She had humiliated me, just when I was being accepted into the ex-pat life. A burn mark from the iron on the tablecloth. Roger shouting at me. Me trying to explain it was her fault. And a gentle shove as she smirked at me, carrying the sheets at the top of the stairs. That was all it was.

I lie on the hard floor and stare at the ceiling, wishing I could do what I have done every night since Max's death. Call down the shaft to Daddy's flat and ask Mona to come and sit with me.

After all, it's what Mona came for, to make everything bearable for me. And to make *me* bearable to *myself*.

CHAPTER SIXTY-FOUR

I look down.

There *is* someone there. A child of about seven or eight is gazing up at me. A girl in a pink dressing-gown and slippers.

I take a step back.

The child stares at me, the way children do when caught off-guard. Unsure what to say or what to do in a new situation.

'I may have the wrong address,' I say, holding out my piece of crumpled paper. 'I'm looking for Ali. Ali Chokran, he's—'

'Daddy?'

I stare down at the child. Her dark hair is scrunched back into a ponytail with a little turquoise band and she wears tiny gold earrings in her ears. Her skin's a shade darker than mine, but she has the most amazing blue eyes set in her beautiful dark face. A Berber face. Unmistakable. Familiar.

I remember Leo using the word 'tingle'. It's how I feel now; I tingle all over with a kind of anaesthetised layer, an instinctive need for protection from what I know is to come.

My feet go numb. Things are sinking in even before the child's mother arrives, even before she apologises for being in the bathroom when I rang the bell, then invites me into the flat, gives me sweet mint tea, the way I would have been treated by women back at home. She asks if I am a relative over from Morocco, tells me that Ali will be back from work later. He works shifts, will of course want to see me. Am I a cousin? A niece? Not a sister, they have met Ali's sisters.

They are lovely, both of them, the mother and the child, bringing a plate of almond pastries, concerned for me. And the mother – petite and pretty with long black wavy hair. Smartly dressed in Western clothes, a pencil skirt, high heels, a tailored jacket over a white shirt – tells me she works here as a doctor, specialising in the elderly – 'geriatrics' she calls it – and I think of Charles and my own mother, and how she is who they need – but the biggest barrier that can exist sits between them and this woman.

'My husband only recently joined us – ooh, six months ago – once we finalised his documents. He's working here now, in a bakery.'

'Not a doctor too?'

'A doctor? Ali?' She laughs.

How can I hate this lovely woman and her daughter? They are in the dark just as much as I am.

I don't want to shatter their bliss.

So I stand up. 'Thank you,' I say. 'But I have to go. Tell Ali that Mona called.'

I bump into him at the bottom of the stairwell, his physical presence, even with the filter of the information I've just gleaned, impacting straight upon me as if no time has passed.

Immediately, stupidly, as if I had no brain, my body wants him again. I want to press myself against him, feel his hands in my hair.

I look up at his face and know straight away that he is not mine after all.

A lifetime's fantasies shattered in seconds.

'What are *you* doing here?'

'I came looking for you.'

'You can't come here. This is my home, my life, my family.'

'I thought *I* was your life. I thought Leila and I were your family.'

He lets out a hissing sound. 'You were in Morocco,' he says grimly. 'How did you get out?'

'I was brought here by an English couple, on a domestic worker visa.'

He looks disgusted. 'Domestic work? That's degrading, Mona.'

These words hurt me more than I would ever have imagined.

'I did it because I had to. For Leila and Ummu, because you had gone.'

I'm gulping in air, hardly able to breathe, like a child who has been winded after a fall.

I helped him when he was in trouble, when he was afraid the police would come after him.

Surely he must help me . . .

He turns his face from me.

'When did you meet her?' I nod towards the flat. I can't express rage. All I feel is a dull ache in my chest, a need for answers.

'Leave it, Mona. I'm tired. Just back from a late shift at work.'

'But when? That child, she's older than Leila! Is she yours?'

His fist hits the wall beside him.

I've done it now. Enraged him. I've chosen over the years to make allowances for his rage because I thought he loved me. It was not his fault, I told myself. He was a man of violent passions, good and bad. I was in love with him. But I don't want to witness his dark side now.

'Of course she's mine. As is Slimane – my son, my boy. Hafiza and I were together way before Leila. We married before you and I.'

'How can it be before you and I? We were together ever since we were small . . . we were meant to be.'

'No, Mona. I met Hafiza the time I went to Casablanca.'

391

'What? But you came back to live with me in the white house. You were working as a guide so you could continue your studies. You were about to become a doctor.'

Anger darkens his face. 'I had to tell you something.'

'It was a lie?'

'You went and had Leila. How could I tell you then? I was waiting for my visa to come through. Hafiza was living here, waiting patiently for me to come.'

'But you never told me. About her.'

'I couldn't care for two families at once. Hafiza's is my first family.'

'You were never a medical student?'

'No! Hafiza was. Is. She is working here now. She's a registrar. You made the assumption and I didn't want to disillusion you.'

'But when you left this time, you told me you were going to help your Berber brothers. That wasn't true either? You came straight to England?'

He holds up his hands as if to say, *It's not my fault you fabricated a story about me.*

Nothing he has told me was true!

Was Ali *never* the man I thought he was?

'This woman got you out of the country, to a better life. Is that why you chose her?'

Somehow this explanation makes it less painful. If he's used her as well. If he doesn't love her.

If I am still his true love.

He sighs, stamps his foot as though it were me who was in the wrong. As if I'm a nuisance he'd rather not have to deal with.

'We met at university but I was never studying. I got a job as a janitor there. Then she came over here. We agreed I would follow when I could. This is where I live now, Mona, this is my marriage. I have two children here. You met Jasmine. Slimane will be in bed. But you, you should not be here. Go now.'

'You never even sent money to Leila or to me.'

'How could I, when I have mouths to feed already?'

'And do you love them?'

My question feels pathetic in the yellow lighting of the concrete walkway. Too weak, too insubstantial. What does it matter what his answer is?

Everything's too broken already.

'Of course I love them.'

The truth seems to expand and deepen and is worse than anything else I've heard tonight.

He loves them.

He doesn't love me.

'And you won't help me?' My voice comes out small, barely audible. 'I need help, Ali, you've no idea, the situation I'm in here. My employer is cruel but I can't leave her. I'm afraid she wants to kill me!' I stop, worried this sounds too dramatic. 'I'm tied to her, with the domestic visa. She has my passport. I need something. A little money perhaps, some documents that say we're married, so I can get another job. Ummu's very ill and I need to work, I—'

He thrusts his hand into his pocket. Drags out a battered leather wallet, the wallet my father gave him years ago when he was maybe fourteen. A waft of home follows it – hot leather, the tannery where my father worked. He hands me some money, a fifty-pound note.

And then he walks away.

I leave Paradise Street. Paradise for Ali maybe, Hell Street for me. And Hell for Hafiza, Ali's real 'wife', if she ever finds out about me.

I cannot hate her.

If I can only get to Leila and Ummu first, show them I did my best. Tell Ummu she was right after all about Ali. I've let her down. I believed all my dreams were to come true and instead they're shattered.

393

I have nowhere to go. No papers, only this fifty pounds.

I return to the road. There's no sign of Sayed or his scooter. He's vanished into the night.

Do I return to Dora's, beg her to let me stay, to hide me if the police come? But why would she, when if she doesn't place the blame on me, she will be next in line as suspect? And now I know she's killed . . . intended to knock me down with the statue. I shudder again.

At best, I will end up in jail unable to provide for my child, my mother.

Back on the street, propelled by terror but not knowing where to go, I start to walk. I make my way along the side of the river. It's silent, cold. The water seems to breathe heavily below me. I remember the way we pulled Max's body into the tide: what choice did I have but to do as Dora told me?

The water heaves and sighs.

Frightened suddenly by its presence, I begin to walk faster. I don't know where I'm going. Perhaps I can make my way back to Sayed's home, beg him to give me a little of the proceeds from the sale of the locket. Ask him to get me a fake passport to get me out of the country?

Suddenly, I am aware that I'm not alone: someone is following me. The path veers to the left, between tall buildings that are in darkness. I begin to hurry.

The figure behind me hurries too. I pass under a lamp and the footsteps behind me accelerate.

At last I feel a hand clamp down on my shoulder and I turn and see a dark, hooded figure in the shadows.

One I recognise.

One who gave me an instinctive shiver of panic, the first time I'd set eyes on him. One whom I had wanted to flee and hide from.

One who had raised the hairs along my spine, and turned my blood cold.

CHAPTER SIXTY-FIVE

There's a sudden rattling sound that makes me sit up. It's Daddy. His breath is laboured, bubbles coming out of his mouth.

'Daddy, are you all right? Speak to me, Daddy.'

He opens his eyes, stares blindly at me.

I move without thinking, lifting the phone, dialling the doctor's out-of-hours number.

'Can you bring him into the emergency clinic?' the cool voice on the end asks, as if she had better things to concern her and finds my call nothing but a nuisance.

'Look,' I say, 'I am Theodora Gentleman.'

I wait for her reaction, to see if my name makes her jump to it, as it should do. 'My father may be dying. I need a doctor here urgently. Get someone round immediately or I'll sue you for neglect.'

'We're extremely busy. You'll either have to bring him in, or if it's a matter of life or death, you'll have to call an ambulance and go straight to Accident and Emergency.'

I slam the phone down.

I take Daddy's hand in mine. It's frozen, the skin waxy.

I pick up the phone again. Dial 999.

'I think my father may be dying. Please, can you get an ambulance here as quickly as possible.'

Then their ridiculous questions, all taking up crucial time: what are his symptoms, does he recognise me, can he speak? At last they concede that I'm not dramatising this, that Daddy *is* genuinely in need of urgent medical attention.

'We'll be with you as quickly as we can.'

I put the phone down with a small shudder of relief.

I strain my ears for sounds of Leo and Mona returning. The house feels deathly quiet upstairs. Only Endymion moves, nudging open the door, slinking into the room. I pick him up and hold him, and feel the soothing vibration of his purr against my chest. I'll sit here and wait for the ambulance, and Endymion will comfort me.

Then, all of a sudden, Daddy sits up.

'I feel poorly,' he says. 'Bring me Mona.'

'Daddy, Mona's not here at the moment. But I'm here.' I put my hand to his brow. It's clammy, there's a sheen of sweat on it.

'I think I need a doctor.'

'Yes. It's OK, Daddy. The doctor's coming.'

'Poor nice Doctor Max!' he says. 'The one in the paper. The one they found in the river. The man you pushed down the steps. They found poor Doctor Max in the river and he's dead.'

My hands are damp, there's a choking feeling in my throat – I can't get enough air. Daddy's so ill, so muddled, why does he suddenly sound as if he's making perfect sense?

And he won't stop his ranting!

I can hear it now, the sound of the ambulance coming down the street, a low purr – what other vehicle would be arriving at this time of night; and yes, I can see the blue lights now reflecting off the church opposite.

'I want Doctor Max,' Daddy says weakly. 'He was a good doctor, but you pushed him down the steps.'

'Don't be silly, Daddy. I didn't push him.'

'I saw you. He came to help make me better. Then you pushed Maudy's statue. I saw you through my bedroom window – you pushed it and he fell. Now he's in the paper.'

I can hear the ambulance doors outside slamming shut.

'Please, Daddy. Stop this. You mustn't speak any more. Be quiet.'

If he tells the ambulance people, I'll be finished.

The blue lights are flashing outside the window, filling the room with a strange lurid light, and Daddy's voice grates on: 'You pushed him down the steps. And now he's in the paper.'

He's the only person who knows, he and Mona, and no one will ever believe Mona.

I'm Theodora Gentleman, about to become a household name. Daddy mustn't tell them, I have to stop him.

I stand, staring at my daddy, the cushion in my hand as they come up the steps.

CHAPTER SIXTY-SIX

'She sent me to find you,' Leo says.

I nod. 'I knew she would look for me.' I'm too exhausted to fight.

'And then I saw Sayed on his scooter. He told me about your husband – Ali, who you've been looking for on my computer. Asking questions in the High Street. Sayed told me he was afraid for you because he knew this Ali was already married. That you would be in deep shit once you found out, because you were counting on finding him so you could go home. Or get a proper job and a British passport. Or whatever.'

I turn my eyes down. 'I was counting on him to provide for his child,' I say.

'And you don't want to come back to us either – which I understand. It's not a great job, though my mother does need you. And Grandpa loves you.'

'Yes.'

'But I understand you want to go home to Morocco. It's a lot warmer there.'

I smile.

'It's hard to make a living out there, though. I know from the people who used to work for Dad.' Leo sighs. 'I never wanted to come back here either. They made me – Mum and Dad. Thought I should go to an English sixth form. Look what good that's done me!'

He has a brown envelope in his hand, and holds it out to me. I take it. Inside is my passport, my visa. Ten twenty-pound notes.

'It's all I had,' Leo tells me. 'I can't take you any further. I can't ride a scooter like Sayed. It's all I can do. I hope it's enough. Gotta get back. Grandpa's not well.'

I take the river-walk west, knowing there must be a tube station eventually. The water reflects the lights on either bank and a moon that ducks behind the clouds.

The water is smooth and silent below me, as if it could never hurt anyone.

I walk quickly, but keep to the narrow paths, avoiding the roads, hoping not to be spotted. Once at the tube station I will be able to travel swiftly under the city. I go into an all-night Tesco and ask for directions to the nearest tube station. An Indian man stacking shelves tells me I want Bermondsey and directs me past more flats, down more dark roads to the station.

I sit in the bright lights of the tube, my bag clutched on my lap, Leo's envelope stashed inside it, melding once again into the throng. No one notices me. I'm aware of how shabby I look, of my smell of sweat, of the twitch in my eye, but they draw no interest.

I am just another body moving through London's bowels, moving to what I now simply have to pray will be a passage home.

The tube is packed even at this time of night. I have that feeling again that everyone except me belongs. They belong whether they are tourists or Londoners, workers or leisure seekers, students or parents, or even if they are homeless, coming down the carriage asking for money. People are reading or talking or swaying about under the influence of an evening's drinking or thumping their feet, wires coming out of their ears. Everyone belongs. That is how it seems to me.

I think of Charles, how I did feel I belonged for a short time, when I became close to him, and I wonder how he's got through the evening without me.

By the time I arrive at St Pancras I am missing the old man.

I think about how he liked to dress in his best suit and imagine he was back in the restaurant that he ran when he was a younger man, and how no one could see the man he once was, with his Michelin stars and his chef's outfit. Why is it, I wonder, in this city of stone figures, that some people are immortalised and others allowed to sink without trace?

I get off the tube and am carried along by the crowds up the escalators, and down miles of tunnel.

I go over and stand beneath a statue of an embracing couple, called *The Meeting Place*. I gaze up at the statue of the lovers and let myself wish for one minute that this is how it had turned out with Ali. And when the minute is up, I tell myself that my longing must now be – will have to be – over forever.

I think of my months at Theodora's. I wonder how she and Charles and Leo will manage without me?

But it doesn't matter now. I have become strong. Stronger than the statue Dora and Max met beneath – the queen called Boudicca. I've read about her. She said, 'Let the men live as slaves, I will never do that.' And nor will Leila ever have to do what I had to do.

I think of the things I know, the things I've seen. Madame's husband with his wandering eye, and his grasping hands.

Ali stumbling in weeping and bleeding, after mowing down the tourist.

And Theodora heaving the body of her lover into the river.

I have seen all this – looked on and said nothing.

401

I have kept the silence of statues.

So far.

I have enough money for a ticket, with what Ali and Leo gave me. It is time for me to leave this cold country.

I shall get on board, keep my face down, let the train carry me along another tunnel, through another underground world, beneath the English Channel – at last I will emerge into some kind of light.

ACKNOWLEDGEMENTS

I am hugely indebted to the women from Justice for Domestic Workers (J4DW) who generously shared their stories with me, especially **Marissa Begonia** and **Khadija Najloui**, and to Steve Rowlatt for answering endless questions about domestic workers rights.

Huge thanks also go to:

Emma Lowth and Maxine Hitchcock for all their ideas and patience! Florence Partridge and the team at Simon and Schuster, Stephanie Glencross for inspirational early in-put, my fabulous agent Jane Gregory for all her work and her great initial reaction, Claire Morris, Linden Sheriff and everyone at Gregory and Company. Joan Deitch for the title, Beatrice Pemberton for encouragement, Anna D'Andrea for reading, Victoria Rance with whom research always turns into its own story, John Davy, Kate Rhodes for suggestions, Jethro Pemberton, Tanya Pemberton, and the amazing Cressida Downing for feedback, coffee and reassurance at just the right moment.

Special thanks to Andrew Taylor and Polly, Emma and Jem who always come up trumps when I'm stuck.

AUTHOR'S NOTE

From 6 April, 2012 domestic workers who apply to accompany their employers to the UK are tied to one employer. If they experience abuse and exploitation they will face the choice of continuing to suffer or fleeing and becoming illegal.

You can read more about this at:

www.j4dw.org

www.kalayaan.org.uk